'In some ways this story is about the plight of women in 19th century China but, more importantly, it's about their spirit. Jane Yang is a hugely talented writer whose elegant prose, eye for historical detail and storytelling prowess fully immerse the reader in her exceptional novel'
Natasha Lester, author of *The Paris Secret*

'I love novels that take me away from my everyday life into different cultures, societies and times, and I enjoyed every single page of *The Lotus Shoes*. It is a wonderful novel, embroidered with colour and skill'
Elizabeth Chadwick, author of *The Scarlet Lion*

'Stunning, transporting, unforgettable. *The Lotus Shoes* caught me hook, line and sinker from the first pages. Jane Yang is going to be a star'
Amanda Geard, author of *The Midnight House*

'Jane Yang gives us a fascinating insight into the lives of Chinese women in the 19th century, and a sweeping story wrapped around their pain, joy and tenacity. You'll love it!'
Mandy Robotham, author of *A Woman of War*

'I very much enjoyed *The Lotus Shoes*, an enthralling tale of a bygone era'
Judy Nunn, author of *Black Sheep*

'A remarkable, transportive debut novel. Jane Yang has created multi-dimensional, rich characters in Little Flower and Linjing, young women who must make morally fraught choices in a world that gives them little option. *The Lotus Shoes* will sweep you up in a tangle of emotion'
E.M. Tran, author of *Daughters of the New Year*

'Stitched intricately together with vivid characters, fascinating historical insight, and a gripping story'
Rachel Louise Driscoll, author of *Nephthys*

'Lush and sumptuous, *The Lotus Shoes* is a stunning exploration of female friendships, societal pressures, and identity in 1800s China. An epic piece of historical fiction with characters who will take up root in your heart, Yang weaves together shock, tragedy and hope in a story you won't soon forget'
Alli Parker, author of *At the Foot of the Cherry Tree*

Jane Yang was born in the Chinese enclave of Saigon and raised in Australia where she grew up on a diet of superstition and family stories from Old China. Despite establishing a scientific career, she is still sometimes torn between modern, rational thinking and the pull of old beliefs in tales passed down through the family. She lives in Australia.

JANE
YANG

THE
LOTUS
SHOES

SPHERE

SPHERE

First published in Great Britain in 2025 by Sphere

1 3 5 7 9 10 8 6 4 2

Copyright © Jane Yang 2025

The moral right of the author has been asserted.

A CIP catalogue record for this book is available from the British Library.

Hardback ISBN 978-1-4087-3030-0
Trade paperback ISBN 978-1-4087-3031-7

Typeset in Garamond by M Rules
Printed and bound in Great Britain by Clays Ltd, Elcograf S.p.A.

Papers used by Sphere are from well-managed forests and other responsible sources.

Sphere
An imprint of
Little, Brown Book Group
Carmelite House
50 Victoria Embankment
London EC4Y 0DZ

The authorised representative
in the EEA is
Hachette Ireland
8 Castlecourt Centre
Dublin 15, D15 XTP3, Ireland
(email: info@hbgi.ie)

An Hachette UK Company
www.hachette.co.uk

www.littlebrown.co.uk

For my husband, the anchor in my life, and for Mum and Dad – your sacrifices gave me a life in Australia with opportunities that wouldn't have been possible if we had stayed in my birth country.

PART 1

1

Little Flower

I sat shivering on a low stool in our farmhouse kitchen. The frosty air stung my cheeks and chilled my hands and feet until they hurt. To warm up, I rubbed my arms and legs. Though it never snowed in southern China, this winter in the sixth year of Emperor Guangxu's reign felt brutally cold. Normally, I would still be curled beneath our patched quilt, but my *aa noeng* had woken me at first light.

'We are going on an adventure today,' she announced, turning to me with a basin of boiling water. For the first time in months, her thin, pale face broke into a smile. But it wasn't a proper sparkling smile, like the ones she used to shower on me before my *aa de* died. This smile looked stiff, and her eyes remained dull.

'I'm taking you to Canton City,' she continued. 'Farmer Tang will give us a ride on his cart.' She poured cold water into the basin.

I squealed, clapping with delight. I had never been to Canton City, but I had heard all about it from travelling storytellers. Pedlars prowled the streets, selling sugared plums, sweet buns and roasted chestnuts. My belly grumbled at the thought of them, reminding me that I had not eaten since yesterday's bowl of watery congee. The storytellers also boasted of travelling acrobats, men who swallowed live snakes, and puppet shows.

'Is Little Brother coming too?' I asked.

'He is too young,' she said. 'I've sent him to our neighbour for the day. This is a mother-and-daughter trip.'

'Why are we going?'

'Little girls should not ask questions,' she chided. 'Good girls keep quiet, follow rules and obey grown-ups.' Her tone was mild, but her face sagged with misery, frightening me into silence.

She knelt in front of me, cradling my golden lilies in her palms.

'Do you remember why I started binding your feet when you were only four?' she asked.

'Because ... because ...' I shook my head.

With a heavy sigh she explained, 'Other six-year-old girls in our village wouldn't start foot-binding until now. Some farming families might even wait until their daughter is seven or eight, if they're desperate for an extra worker around the house. But that is risky. Do you know why?'

I shook my head again.

'The bones might already be too stiff to be shaped. I love you *so* much that I bound your feet two years ago, as though you're a little lady, to make sure you get perfect golden lilies so you can be like Consort Yao Niang. Do you remember her story?'

'I do!' Eager to impress her, I merrily recited the bedtime tale she had often told me. 'Once upon a time, before the Manchu invaded and when China was cut up into lots of little kingdoms, like a patchwork quilt, there lived an emperor called Li

Yu. He loved to see new things. One day he asked his many, many wives to surprise him with a new dance. Everyone tried but no one was good enough except Yao Niang. She wrapped her feet into crescents and danced on her toes!'

'What else?' she quizzed.

I frowned.

She prompted, 'The emperor was so impressed that he promoted her to Royal Imperial Consort—'

'Oh!' With a bounce I finished her sentence, 'So no other wife could boss Yao Niang around except the Empress. All the ladies of the court copied her and soon rich girls across the country started to do the same. Now all re-respectable girls have bound feet. And the most loving mothers make sure their daughters have perfect four-inch golden lilies.'

I expected the rest of my speedy answer would earn praise, especially since I had only stumbled on two characters, but Aa Noeng's lips trembled. I reached out to hug her, but she shook her head as she straightened her back and smoothed her faded-tunic-blouse, *ou*.

'Even the poorest boy might hope to pass the imperial exams and become a mandarin if he is clever and studious,' she said, 'but a girl's only chance for a better life is through her golden lilies. This is my priceless gift to you. No matter what happens, I want you always to remember how much I love you. You're my precious pearl. Do you understand?'

'I love you this much too!' I swung my arms behind my back until my palms touched. But she didn't return my smile.

'Why is it important to have perfect four-inch golden lilies?' she asked.

'To get a good marriage,' I chirped. 'Matchmakers and mothers-in-law like tiny feet. Golden lilies are proof of a girl's goodness.'

5

'Yes,' she agreed. 'Only girls with immense endurance and discipline can get perfect golden lilies. This is what mothers-in-law from nice families want for their sons.' She squeezed my hands and asked, 'Do you want to marry into a nice family when you grow up?'

'Yes.'

'How do you get four-inch golden lilies?' she asked.

'I must sit very still when you clean my feet and change my bandages.'

'What else?'

'I mustn't complain when you tighten the bindings.'

'That's true,' she replied slowly. 'But . . .' After a long pause she said, 'You are a big girl now. It's time you learnt to take care of your golden lilies yourself.'

'I'm still little!' I protested, alarmed by her grave tone.

'Watch carefully,' she instructed. She unravelled the binding and eased my left foot into the basin of warm water. She massaged away the dead skin on the sole and between my toes. Next she trimmed my toenails and wrapped my foot in a towel before sprinkling alum onto it.

'Be sure to use a generous amount of alum,' she said. 'It wards off sweat and itch.'

She wound a length of clean, dark-blue cotton around and around my foot. The pressure increased with each layer until my foot throbbed and my eyes ached with unshed tears. I had to use all my willpower not to groan. She continued to wrap the bindings, much more tightly than usual. I tried to pull my foot away. She gripped it harder. 'Stay still,' she ordered.

'Aa Noeng,' I cried. 'It hurts too much.'

'Hush,' she said. 'One day these golden lilies will bring you a good marriage. You will wear silk and live in a house with tiled floors. Best of all, you will *never* go hungry again.'

6

My whimpering faded as she continued to talk about the tasty food that would fill my belly when I become a bride in a well-to-do family. Finally, she eased my foot into my best pair of indigo cotton shoes. She pushed the basin towards me.

'Now you must do the same for your right foot,' she said.

The journey from our village to Canton City took a day on foot. Since Aa Noeng and I could not have walked that distance on our bound feet, Farmer Tang took us on his cart. The wheels churned up hail and mud into a dirty mix. Gusts of cruel wind whipped our faces raw, and though Aa Noeng held me tight against her side, I shivered. At noon, we stopped and the farmer shared his meal with us. The pork bun stung my wind-chapped lips but delighted my stomach. It wasn't until I'd finished my share that I noticed Aa Noeng had barely touched hers, even though we hadn't eaten meat since my father died. The farmer urged her to eat, his gaze full of pity. To be polite, she swallowed fragments of bun, but she looked haggard with sorrow, the way she'd looked in the days after Aa De's death. That, with her strange behaviour this morning, turned the pork bun to stone in my belly.

The grey afternoon sky had darkened further by the time we arrived in Canton City. I had slept fitfully during the journey. Teeth chattering in the deepening chill, I couldn't pay attention to the strange sights around me.

My mother had been silent since our midday meal, but now she roused herself and spoke to me in an urgent voice. 'You're a good girl. I must do this because there is no other way.'

The farmer cleared his throat. 'Must you tell her now?'

'Yes,' Aa Noeng said resolutely. 'She must be told.' She said to me, 'From now on, you will be living in a pretty brick house with the Fongs. They are a nice, rich family.'

I struggled to understand what she was telling me. 'When will I come home?' I asked. 'Tomorrow?'

'I have sold you to the Fong family, as a *muizai*,' she said, her face crumpling. 'The housekeeper has promised you won't be a common slave girl. Lady Fong wants you as a personal maid to her daughter, like Little Green who looks after our village headman's wife and daughters. You won't have to do any heavy work.'

I reached up and pulled her face down to meet my eyes, but she squeezed hers shut. 'Little Green is an orphan,' I said, 'but you will visit me, won't you?'

Opening her eyes, she slowly shook her head.

'When will I come home?' I asked again. My voice cracked and I began to sob.

'You will never come home again. A *muizai* is not like a hired servant. You will belong to your mistress, just like Little Green – even if her parents were still alive, she couldn't leave. You can't leave either.' She heaved a sigh and then another, as if something was trapped inside her chest and she was trying to free it. 'I have to do this. We'll be evicted soon. We need money to pay for Little Brother's carpentry apprenticeship. It's the only way he will get a chance at a decent life.'

I could not imagine never seeing my home again, never seeing my mother or Little Brother. 'Never' was so big it was beyond my imagination. 'But I can't live with strangers,' I said. 'I belong with you.'

She talked on as if convincing herself as much as me. 'Without the money we will all starve. Then who will carry on the Yung name? I need to do the right thing by your father's spirit and our ancestors. You understand what's happened to our family, don't you?'

I shook my head. What did Aa De's death have to do with this Fong family? I did not understand. But I remembered what had happened five months ago. Aa De had returned home from tending the fishponds and taken to his bed, complaining of cramps in his guts. Nothing tempted his appetite, and the little rice porridge he ate came straight back up. He changed from a man with the strength and endurance of a water buffalo to a gaunt invalid. The village *daai fu* prescribed herbs, which my mother boiled into a bitter tea and gave to him by the spoonful, but he couldn't keep it down. He burnt with fever and shivered with chills. This went on for fourteen days until he died. Aa Noeng used our savings to give him a decent funeral.

After that, our lives had crumbled like a crushed biscuit. My mother couldn't manage the farm by herself. We ran behind on the rent, the fishponds became neglected, and no one harvested the mulberry leaves so our silkworms died of starvation. We went hungry, too, despite Aa Noeng's efforts to stretch our rice supply by watering down our congee.

'This is a chance for you,' she said. 'You will be a slave girl but you'll have food to eat and a roof over your head. You'll live better than we do.' Her lips trembled as if she did not quite believe that. 'Be good, grateful and patient,' she said. 'Follow orders and always remember your place. A *muizai* is her mistress's shadow. You are there to do her bidding. Don't ever forget that. You must never argue or disobey orders. Life is easier for those who can swallow bitterness and accept their lot.'

'I'm a very good girl,' I protested. 'Don't send me away.'

She pulled me to her chest, squeezing me tight. 'Can we go home now?' I asked hopefully. She did not reply as she

9

continued to hold me close until we arrived at a big house, the biggest I had ever seen. A huge black plaque with two gold characters hung above the main entrance: a set of red gates, the height of more than two adults, each door guarded by a dragon head. Their red-painted eyes glared at me as our cart rolled past, and they looked as though they'd attack any visitor who dared knock with the thick bronze rings between their fangs.

It seemed an age before our cart rounded the mansion and Farmer Tang pulled the horse to a stop in front of a pair of regular-sized doors, like the ones back home where I used to reach up and touch the lintel when I sat on Aa De's shoulders. Father Tang helped Aa Noeng down from the cart and set me beside her. I clung to her sleeve as she knocked. A lady in a fine quilted coat greeted Aa Noeng and hurried us into a courtyard furnished with a stone table.

'I am Cerise, the housekeeper and Lady Fong's personal maid,' the lady with a fleshy mole on her chin told my mother. 'Dip your thumb lightly into the ink and press it here.' She pointed to a red paper.

'Wait!' Aa Noeng said. 'What does it say?'

'It's just the standard terms of indenture.'

'Please tell me.'

With a gusty sigh, Cerise told her, 'It says you agree to sell your girl to Lady Phoenix Fong, the First Fong *taai taai*. Your daughter will be Miss Linjing's maid unless Lady Fong tells her to serve another. Lady Fong also has the right to sell your daughter to another household.'

'Does it say whether I can buy back my daughter's freedom?'

'I don't know why you ask,' Cerise complained. 'I've worked here for over ten years and no parent has ever come back for their girl. This isn't a pawnbroker.'

'*Please*,' she begged. 'I just want to know.'

'It states that you can buy back her freedom if you return the sale price with twenty per cent interest for every year the Fongs have had to feed and clothe her. Now, are you ready to give me your thumbprint?'

I looked up at Aa Noeng expectantly, hoping she'd changed her mind. Instead, her face sagged. Tears spilt over her lashes before she quickly mopped them with her sleeve. I tightened my grip on her forearm.

Cerise's tone softened. 'Lady Fong is kind and fair. Your daughter will be fine.'

'But she will be allowed to marry eventually?' my mother asked, voice urgent yet doubtful.

'If a *muizai* was lucky enough to secure a marriage offer, then she might be released from bondage. I dare say Lady Fong will find her a good husband when she is around eighteen, if she's hardworking and obedient. Mind you, many *muizai* choose to stay rather than be wedded to a putrid night-soil collector or a cripple. But with bound feet, your daughter might hope for a decent farmer.'

'Is marriage a guarantee?' Aa Noeng pressed.

'There's no certainty in life. But Lady Fong is honourable and kind. Now sign.'

Mother's trembling hand hovered over the contract for a long time before she finally dipped her thumb into the ink and pressed it on the paper. Tears flowed down her cheeks. Two splotches hit the paper, smudging the thick, black characters. But once the agreement was sealed, she dried her face with her sleeve and knelt in front of me with an expression of determination.

'Remember my words,' she said. 'Be patient and obey. Things could be a lot worse.'

Since I would never see her again, I didn't know how things

could be worse. Flinging my arms around her neck, I cried, 'Don't leave me here to be a slave!'

My mother wrenched my arms apart, holding me by the shoulders. I tried to wriggle forth, desperate to latch on to her, but her firm grip kept me in place.

'Listen to me,' she said coaxingly. 'To see me again, you must be extra obedient. Most important of all, you *must* look after your golden lilies so you can marry one day. Can you promise me that?' She tried to smile but it looked like a lop-sided scribble.

'Please, Aa Noeng. I'm scared.'

'If your feet are ruined, you'll never see me again. Do you understand?'

'I need another cuddle,' I cried, stumbling forward, arms outstretched. 'Just one more ...'

But Aa Noeng turned her back on me and strode off faster than I had ever seen her move.

At the gate, she fixed me with a final glance, before she straightened her back and disappeared down the laneway. I tried to run after her, but Cerise's fierce clutch kept me in place. 'Let your mother go,' she said. 'You belong to the Fong family now. Be good and you might see her again.'

I bit her arm. Shocked, she yelped and released me. I bolted off, but teetered on my golden lilies and fell long before I reached the gate. The pain of my fall was far less than the sting of her slap.

'Wipe that insolent look off your face,' she ordered. 'You're a *muizai* now.'

2

Linjing

Aa Noeng told me that Little Flower was her special gift to me. She hoped we would grow up to be like her and Cerise, who had been her *muizai* since they were both six. Having a maid with bound feet made Aunt Brilliance and Cousin Elegance very jealous; even sweet-tempered Second Aa Noeng looked at me with envy. But I hated the way Mother doted over Little Flower, comparing me to her – a slave!

'Linjing,' Aa Noeng exclaimed. 'Look at Little Flower's satin stitches. The blend of carmine and magenta is superb. I would be happy if your work was half as good.'

Though Mother spoke to me, her face was turned to my *muizai*, their heads almost touching as she continued to admire the smooth, even stitches blooming beneath Little Flower's needle, filling the petal motif with a band of muddy green, some patches darker than others. I didn't understand what Aa Noeng meant when she talked about reds or pinks, for everything was a mixture of yellow, blue, dull green or grey, but I was too scared to tell her so. I stabbed my needle through the silk and wrenched the thread out of the other side. The stitch bunched up the fabric by pulling its neighbours with it. From across the round table, I bared my teeth as I slammed my embroidery hoop against the polished wood, waiting for Aa Noeng to notice me. Little Flower looked up first and our eyes met, hers dropping back to her needle as I clenched my hands into claws.

'Linjing, stop behaving like a savage,' Aa Noeng scolded. 'What kind of example are you setting for your *muizai*?'

'She's the savage!' I protested.

A frown puckered my mother's formidable high forehead. I darted over, tugging the edge of my *muizai*'s sleeve with my thumb and fingertip, careful not to touch the crusty stains as I lifted it to show Aa Noeng, who shot me a stony look. It seemed she didn't understand, so I explained, 'Little Flower wipes her nose with her sleeves.'

With darkened cheeks, Little Flower pulled her sleeve from my grip. She hid both hands under the table, hanging her head so low it almost touched her needlework. Instead of scolding her, Mother said, 'Linjing, this is unkind. It has only been one moon since Little Flower left her family. You need to be patient while she unlearns her village manners.'

'But she also yawns without covering her mouth,' I added. 'Once, she even picked up my *caa siu bao* from the floor and shoved it into her mouth, like a dog. Her family must have lived like pigs.'

Fat tears rolled down Little Flower's cheeks, falling onto the petal motif, staining it. Snot dripped from her nose, and her hand lifted halfway to her face, then paused in mid-air before she hid it under the table again, making me feel a little remorseful. I reached for my handkerchief but Aa Noeng got there first, patting Little Flower's back as she dried her face with a crisp square of silk. Little Flower's wet eyes widened as they darted between my mother's smile and my scowl. I wanted to smack her for stealing Aa Noeng's attention but dared not anger my mother further.

'A cruel mistress breeds disloyalty,' Aa Noeng warned me. 'Little Flower is obedient and patient, qualities you should copy if you want to excel in embroidery. It's a real shame that such a girl was born into a peasant family. If you don't work hard to improve your stitches and manners, people might think you're the *muizai*.'

'Do you want her for a daughter instead of me?' I asked, tears welling in my eyes.

'Nonsense,' my mother replied, with a dismissive wave, as though my question was a buzzing mosquito.

'Do you?' I repeated, with a stamp, my throat aching. I wanted Aa Noeng to hug me, let me sit on her lap, tell me she loved me. Second Aa Noeng did that for my half-sisters whenever they got upset. She would even stroke their hair, rocking them until they felt better.

'*Linjing*,' she said, in an icy voice. 'You'll never be as skilled as your *muizai* unless you work as hard as her. Go back to your seat and pick up your hoop.'

'*No!*' I roared, my body lurching forward as my hands balled into fists.

'Go,' she said. Her lips flattened to a thin line, her narrowed eyes were hard as ice, her oval face pale and frosty. Often, I wondered if my real mother was buried beneath that chilly skin, and if I dug down, perhaps I would find a warm soul, like my second *aa noeng*.

'This is your last warning,' she told me. 'Behave like a lady.'

As soon as I could escape my mother, I ran to Aa De's study. He looked up from his paperwork with a frown.

But seeing me, he smiled and beckoned me over. I climbed onto his lap.

'How is my little rascal?' he teased, as he wiggled my nose.

'Aa Noeng scolded me just because I said my slave has village manners. It's all her fault that I'm in trouble. I want another maid, one with *huge* feet so she'll be terrible at embroidery.'

'If you're not happy with your maid, then tell your mother to find you another.'

'She won't listen to me. Please, Aa De, can you make her send Little Flower away?'

'It's not my business to get involved with the women's realm.'

I crossed my arms and pouted. He poked my ribs until I couldn't resist the tickles, then he asked, 'When is your foot-binding ceremony?'

'Next month.'

'That is soon,' he said. 'Would you like to keep your natural feet?'

To be sure Aa De wasn't jesting, I hopped off his lap and turned to read his face. From his expectant look, I knew he wanted my answer to be yes. His smile was so wide that I could see his back gold tooth. His eyes shone with eagerness. Yet he fidgeted with his jade thumb ring, twisting it this way and that. I wanted to please him, but I couldn't lie.

'Only slaves have big feet. I don't want to be like them. I want to be like my mothers.'

'Do you like hopscotch?'

I nodded.

'You also love to climb trees, and you're a fast runner, aren't you?'

'Yes!'

'You won't be able to do any of those things after your feet are bound. Do you want to give them up?'

'No.' I added quickly, 'But I also want golden lilies.' I twisted my hands together. Until now, I had thought of the foot-binding ceremony as a grand festival at which I would be showered with gifts and attention from my aunts and cousins. My mother had promised it would be one of the best days of my life, third only to my wedding day and the birth of my first son. I had been impatient for the day to arrive since it hadn't occurred to me that afterwards I would no longer be able to play my favourite games. Now I did not feel so sure. Still, having big feet was unthinkable, for every lady had golden lilies. People would think I was the slave and Little Flower the lady. I couldn't have that.

I looked to Aa De for reassurance.

'These are modern times,' he explained. 'Some genteel families are beginning to let their daughters keep their natural feet.'

'But Aa Noeng and Maa Maa say big feet are vulgar.'

'Your mother and grandmother are very conservative. Let me show you something.'

He opened a leather box to reveal a photograph. The image showed a young lady a few years older than me, sitting on a swing with big feet poking out of her heavily embroidered trouser hems. Instead of seeming ashamed, she was smiling. I looked at Aa De questioningly.

'This young lady is the daughter of a wealthy merchant. Her family are Christians who no longer bind their girls' feet. One day, all girls will have natural feet. Do you want to be a modern girl, like her?'

'I don't want to look like a slave.'

'Let's go and talk to your mother about this,' he said, patting my head. 'I've asked her to meet me in Maa Maa's receiving chamber. I have an important announcement to make.'

I feared something bad would happen: a visit to Maa Maa's apartments always meant trouble for Aa Noeng and me. Since my grandfather's death four years ago, Maa Maa had moved to a remote wing where she spent the afternoons praying for his soul. Though she had handed the chatelaine of keys and most of the household duties to my mother, Maa Maa was still in charge of the women's realm.

We entered Maa Maa's receiving room to find my mother had already arrived. With her head bowed and her hands clasped on her lap, she perched on a low stool, even though chairs lined each side of the room.

Father greeted Maa Maa with a deep bow. She nodded to the chair next to hers. She did not acknowledge me as I hurried to stand beside my mother. The overbearing smell of sandalwood from the giant coil of burning incense made me want to cover my nose, but the glare on Maa Maa's face warned me against it.

Once my grandmother's *muizai* had finished serving tea to the adults, my father cleared his throat and spoke.

'Honourable Mother, what I'm about to propose will sound radical. But, please, I beg you to keep an open mind.'

Maa Maa arched an eyebrow, fixing him with a hard stare. Despite the cold, his face was flushed as he tugged his collar.

'Proceed,' she told him.

'Linjing's foot-binding ceremony should not go ahead.'

Maa Maa and Aa Noeng stared at him, bewildered.

'The practice is condemned by all Western nations as cruel and barbaric,' he went on. 'It makes China look primitive. I implore you to permit Linjing to keep her natural feet.'

My grandmother slammed her teacup onto the table so hard that it cracked. She gaped at him. I didn't know her squinty eyes were capable of such roundness. Mother and I exchanged a distressed glance. The *muizai* who crept over to mop up the spillage stared at Aa De, dumbfounded by his suggestion.

'Do you wish to dishonour our ancestors?' Maa Maa asked.

'Honourable Mother, please listen—'

'No son would make such a request.'

'This has nothing to do with filial duty.'

'Dear husband,' Aa Noeng said, 'Linjing must have bound feet or she will be unmarriageable. We have already waited too long.'

'Phoenix is right,' Maa Maa said. 'Golden lilies are the hallmark of every well-bred girl. No genteel mother-in-law will have a girl with big feet. Do you want her to be a spinster and shame our family?'

'Times are changing,' he countered. 'Most families will abandon foot-binding in the coming decades. Besides, I have secured a betrothal for Linjing.'

My mouth fell open.

'What's wrong with the prospective groom?' Aa Noeng demanded.

'Is he crippled or soft in the head?' Maa Maa asked.

'Is he mean?' I asked, in a small voice.

Aa De shot me a reassuring smile. 'He is a fine little gentleman, only a little older than you. I'm told he is athletic too. You will like a lot of the same things.' To Maa Maa and Mother, he added, 'Valiant Li is the first son of Lord Li, the Viceroy of Tianjin.'

'Why would a family of such importance want a big-footed bride?' Maa Maa asked. 'And why Linjing?'

'Honourable Mother, please, I beg you to let me finish before you make up your mind.' She nodded grudgingly. 'Lord Li is one of China's most influential statesmen, and one of Emperor Guangxu's most trusted foreign ambassadors and negotiators. A marriage alliance with Lord Li is critical to my career. He has promised me the posting of deputy governor of Shanxi, once we formalize Linjing's betrothal. Lord Li believes the survival of the Qing dynasty depends on modernization. China must not only upgrade her army and navy with modern artillery and steam-powered ships, but the Chinese people must also adopt new ideas. Natural feet is one of them. He sees a future when wives of mandarins will need to socialize with Western ladies, and it is impossible for our ladies to be treated as equals if they still have crippled feet. That is why he has pledged to secure a daughter-in-law with natural feet. But Lord Li has struggled to find a bride from a suitable family. Despite some influential men vowing to prohibit their sons from marrying girls with golden lilies, they cannot convince their mothers and wives to embrace natural feet. This is a rare opportunity for me.'

'Let Lord Li keep searching,' Mother said. 'Our daughter will have no part in his absurd pledge. The anti-foot-binding movement is doomed to failure. Take Linjing's new *muizai* as an example. Even a poor, illiterate peasant understands the importance of bound feet. Such a family must have made significant sacrifices to bind their daughter's feet when she was four. What kind of mother would I be if I failed to bind Linjing's?'

'Phoenix, these beliefs are antiquated,' he retorted. 'They are chains holding China back from progress.'

'Westerners don't have China's best interests at heart,' Mother argued. 'They know opium is harmful, yet they have dumped it on our populace, turning husbands into addicts, destroying families.'

'Their morals are irrelevant,' Father said. 'The West is

prosperous and powerful. We must humour them, learn from them, at least until we're their equal in economic and military prowess.'

'Stop fighting with Aa Noeng!' I cried. 'I don't want big feet.'

'Phoenix,' Maa Maa scolded. 'Keep Linjing in check. A girl should remain silent unless she is spoken to.'

Aa Noeng pinched my arm and warned me to keep quiet. 'There is plenty of silver in our coffers and our tenants are reliable,' she said. 'We don't need your salary.'

'I have been out of work for close to four years. My former aide has been promoted twice and now outranks me. It's humiliating.'

'But you were in mourning for Father-in-law for three years and forbidden to work. Surely no one would speak ill of you for following the law.'

'Phoenix, you are ignorant of the men's realm, so don't embarrass yourself with these idiotic remarks. Our country is in turmoil, under constant siege from rebels and foreign attacks. Hong Kong, Shanghai and Amoy have all been annexed to Western powers. Many of my colleagues are struggling to keep their postings, let alone find new ones. I would be a fool to refuse this opportunity.'

Maa Maa reached for her prayer beads and muttered a sutra. 'I support my son,' she pronounced. 'His career is paramount. If we must sacrifice a daughter, it may as well be Linjing.' Glaring at Aa Noeng, she said, 'In any case, Phoenix, you have waited far too long to bind her feet. Big feet breed wildness, insolence and vulgarity in a girl.'

'But, Maa Maa,' I reminded her, 'it isn't Aa Noeng's fault. The geomancer told us to wait.'

'Hush, Linjing!' my mother snapped. 'You should never contradict Maa Maa.'

'But it's true. The geomancer said—'

Aa Noeng cut off my words with a stinging smack. I looked to Aa De, hoping he would tell Maa Maa that I spoke the truth, for we all knew the geomancer had divined an early death for me if my feet were bound before my seventh birthday. But he turned his face away from us, staring at the wall hangings.

Maa Maa glowered at us as though we were a pile of refuse as she continued to speak. 'A daughter's sin is a mother's liability, just as a mother's sin is a daughter's burden. Linjing is wayward and disobedient. Her needlework is appalling. Crooked stitches speak of a careless and impatient girl with a slapdash attitude. She is far too spirited. You are to blame. If you cannot tame her, I'll seize your chatelaine and give it to your sister-wife.'

Aa Noeng dropped to her knees and crawled towards Maa Maa, pressing her forehead on my grandmother's golden lilies. 'Revered Mother, I beg you to reconsider. Please have mercy on her. She will be tamed once we bind her feet.'

Maa Maa kicked Aa Noeng's forehead with such force that her golden phoenix comb almost flew off. I hissed at her, but Aa Noeng's eyes pleaded with me to behave. Again I looked at Aa De, longing for him to say something to help Aa Noeng. But his eyes were hard and impatient.

'Phoenix, stop making a scene,' he said. 'It is a brilliant match. Linjing will want for nothing, and she will be one of the young ladies to help shape China into a modern nation. It's an exciting future!'

Though I still wished he'd defend Aa Noeng, how could I be angry with him for wanting the best life for me? But could I really still be a lady without golden lilies?

'What if something happens to Valiant Li?' Mother asked.

'There are many years between a betrothal and a marriage. If Valiant Li dies, no one else will want a girl with big feet.'

'That is very unlikely,' he insisted.

'Life is full of illness and misfortune. It would be impossible to arrange another suitable marriage for Linjing.'

'For the sake of my son's career,' Maa Maa declared, 'that is a risk I am willing to take. My word on this matter is final.'

Despite Aa De's cheerful tone and exciting promises, I chewed my bottom lip as the doubts grew in my mind. Big feet were ugly and vulgar. Aa De said I was his favourite daughter, but Maa Maa said I should be 'sacrificed'. If he loved me, why didn't he sacrifice one of my half-sisters instead?

3

Little Flower

My belly was an empty well and fatigue dragged at my limbs like logs. Each morning, I started my day at sunrise, fetching and boiling water for Miss Linjing's wash. The kitchen was so far from her bedchamber that my golden lilies throbbed and my arms shook from the weight of the copper kettle by the time I reached her door.

My stomach grumbled, craving its next ration of watery congee and limp *gaai laan* that was still several hours away. I glanced at a nearby stone bench, wishing I could rest my aching feet, but Cerise had said if I failed to win Miss Linjing's favour quickly, I might be sold to a sing-song house and wouldn't see my *aa noeng* again. At the thought of my mother, sadness climbed onto my chest and settled there. Blinking back tears, I placed one wobbling foot in front of the other as I clambered up to the pagoda, which stood on a manmade hillock. Maybe Miss Linjing would like me if I could keep up with her games. This morning's downpour had made the steps wet and slippery. Ahead of me, Miss Linjing bounded up like a frog. From the top, she shot bamboo dragonflies over the pagoda's ledge, letting them spiral to the ground. When she scrambled down to fetch them, she said, 'You can't get up the steps.'

'Yes, I can,' I said, determined to prove her wrong.

'This game needs strong players and you're weak!'

'You're very good at this game, Miss. Can you show me how to throw the dragonfly?'

Pleasure flashed in her wide-set eyes and a smile tugged at the corners of her mouth, but her arms remained crossed.

'Please, Miss. I really want to play with you.'

'Fine,' she said. 'You can play with me if you make it to the top.'

Taking a deep breath, I trudged on, gingerly placing my feet to avoid patches of slimy moss and small pools of water that had gathered in the grooves of the stone slabs. By half-way up, my thighs were trembling from the effort and I was heaving for breath. There was no railing to rest against. After endless minutes, a dozen steps still stood between me and Miss Linjing, who had by now made two return trips to the pagoda, grinning at me each time she dashed past. I urged on my quivering muscles. In my haste to reach her, I almost slipped and tumbled backwards but windmilled my arms and swung forward instead, landing on my hands. I dared not stand up again for fear of falling and breaking my neck, so I crawled the rest of the way.

'I've made it,' I panted, slowly coming to my feet. 'Can we play now?'

'You took too long. I'm bored.'

'But I just got here!'

'If you snap at me again, I'll tell Aa Noeng to sell you to a horrid place where girls get a disease that rots their noses.'

I dropped to my knees and apologized, banging my forehead against the cold stone. 'I'm sorry, Miss. Please don't do that.'

25

'You don't look sorry enough.'

I clutched her knees and looked up, begging her to forgive me. With a smirk, she tossed the bamboo dragonflies into a puddle, shoving me aside as she skipped down the steps. I snatched one up, snapped it and hurled it down the garden path. If I still had big feet, if my *aa de* was still alive, if I were still a daughter and not a slave, I would chase after Miss Linjing and kick her back. But 'ifs' were not reality and I had been abandoned. Besides, Aa Noeng's words rang in my ears: follow orders, obey, look after my golden lilies; if I did all that, I would see her again soon.

Exhaustion and homesickness fogged my mind as I retired to my dormitory that night, ready to collapse onto my straw pallet. But I must wash and wrap my golden lilies with fresh bindings first, as Mother had said, or I wouldn't see her again. I shared this tiny room with two hostile kitchen maids and Spring Rain, the *muizai* who served Lady Fong's junior sister-wife – I must remember to call her Second Fong *taai taai*, rather than Second Lady Fong, or Cerise would twist my ear again. Eager to finish my task before the other girls returned, I hurriedly opened the drawer that stored my spare set of indigo bandages, the only things I had left from my *aa noeng*. I staggered: they were unravelled, streaked with grease, and smelt of something foul – a mixture of urine and rotten vegetables. Defeated, I threw myself onto the bedding, buried my face in the pillow and sobbed, my body shaking as I called for my mother. I howled until the straw beneath the pillowcase clumped into a sodden mess. At the touch of a hand on my shoulder, I flinched, expecting a slap from Cerise. But it was Spring Rain.

'There, there,' she soothed. 'I'll help you wash them.'

Fearful this might be a trick, I shrank away. Although Spring Rain didn't join in when the kitchen maids called me nasty names, like 'Little Weed', 'Dim Cloud' or 'Lazy Worm', she had also never spoken a kind word to me before.

'The kitchen maids are too mean,' Spring Rain said.

'Why do they hate me?' I asked.

'They are . . .' she paused, then corrected herself '. . . *we* are jealous of your golden lilies. The kitchen maids are so green with envy they might turn into a pickled plum. But ladies' maids outrank kitchen staff and I'm the eldest in our dormitory. Once I give them a scolding, they'll behave.'

'But don't you hate me too?'

She sighed and half smiled, revealing two dimples the size of black-eyed peas as she sat on the edge of my bed.

'Do you?' I repeated.

'Of course I'm jealous. Who wouldn't be? All the girl slaves would kill to have golden lilies. But your sad eyes remind me too much of my little sister. I miss her.' She reached out and brushed the hair from my eyes; this time I didn't flinch.

'Where is she?' I asked.

'Probably sold to another family to pay off my father's opium debts.' Though she said this with a shrug, a rough edge crept into her voice, making her sound much older than ten.

'My *aa noeng* says I'll see her again when I get married. Maybe if you marry, you'll see your sister too.' I tried to keep my voice steady, but it wobbled with doubt as I knew only the poorest family would take a big-footed bride, if at all.

'Maybe.' But she didn't sound convinced. I wanted to make her feel better, so I gave her a tight hug, the type my mother used to give me when my golden lilies ached and I whimpered through the night.

She squeezed me back, then reached into her jacket and

pulled out a pork *bao*. It was huge. 'Take this,' she said, offering me half of it. 'One of my mistress's daughters dropped it on the floor but I've brushed off the dirt. It's still warm.'

I shoved the whole piece into my mouth. Sweetness exploded on my tastebuds. I closed my eyes, imagining the little dots on my tongue skipping and dancing as I chewed.

'Slow down,' Spring Rain laughed, 'or you might choke.'

I thought about the way Linjing and her two half-sisters discarded food so carelessly. 'Why doesn't the family let us eat more? People need a full belly to work.'

'Most of the time, they forget we're people.'

'Do they think we're animals?'

'Not animals exactly,' she said thoughtfully. After swallowing, she added, 'More like tools – a teacup or a comb. Useful but not important. They can always buy another slave.'

'I don't want to be sold again. How can I make Miss Linjing like me?'

'That spoiled brat can't be pleased,' she replied, 'but at least she doesn't hurt you.' Rolling up her sleeves, she showed me bruises the size of thimbles, and further up her arm a cluster of red raw dots festered – fresh burn wounds.

I gasped. 'Did Second Fong *taai taai* do that?' I could never imagine Lady Fong doing such a thing, and Master Fong's second wife had seemed so gentle, too.

'She is a snake in a rabbit's cloak! But I'll get away from her one day.'

'How?'

'If I can marry, or I might . . .' She trailed off as she pulled me to my feet. 'Enough about that,' she said. 'Let me show you a trick that will help you survive.' She tucked her smile away, resetting her lips into a flat line, and she snuffed out the sparkling light in her eyes, leaving a dull stare. 'Now you try it.'

I tried to mimic her vacant mask.

'Not bad,' she said, 'but your eyes are still sad. Try to think of something boring so they look like a blank page. We can't let them know our real feelings.'

Three days ago, Master Fong had announced Miss Linjing's betrothal to the household. The other slaves said Miss Linjing was his favourite child, so I couldn't understand why he would punish her with big feet. Though it was selfish to be happy at her expense, I was thrilled. No lady with natural feet could have a *muizai* with bound ones.

'Aa Noeng wants you to be Cousin Elegance's *muizai* so you can keep your golden lilies,' Miss Linjing told me, as I brushed her hair. The oval mirror reflected her smile, the tip of her tongue poking out between the gaps of two missing teeth. Miss Elegance seemed much kinder than my mistress. But before I could rejoice, she added, 'But I want to keep you. At first Mother said no but Aa De told her slaves don't deserve golden lilies, so now she says yes. Cerise will unbind your feet tonight.'

I dropped the comb and it clattered onto the floor tiles. Miss Linjing swung around on the stool, stretching her lips into a mocking grin as she faced me.

'You'll be able to keep up with my games when you have big feet again,' she said. 'I thought you wanted to play with me. Why are you sulking?'

Tears pricked my eyes as I looked down at my golden lilies. 'Please don't take them away.'

She twirled her fingers through her hair, sucking the ends as she stared at me. I tried to make my face blank but could not stop my lips trembling. At last she stood up, planted a hand on each hip and said, 'No.'

29

'Why not?'

'You're a slave. I don't have to explain things to you.'

'You don't like me,' I reminded her.

'That doesn't matter.'

'If I'm Miss Elegance's *muizai*, then I'll sit with her on the other side of the needlework chamber, far away from you and Lady Fong. You'd have your mother all to yourself again.'

'Mother only likes you because you sew perfect satin stitches, but that'll change after you have big feet again – everyone knows you can't be good at embroidery without golden lilies. If I can't have them, neither can you!'

I dropped to my knees and kowtowed to her. 'Please, Miss Linjing,' I begged. 'I'll do anything if you let me keep my golden lilies.'

She turned around and hopped back on the stool. I crawled to her side, clutched her wrist and pleaded, 'I won't sew satin stitches any more. Please let me keep my golden lilies.'

Without looking down at me, she swatted me away. 'Get up and finish combing my hair,' she said. 'I'm hungry and we are late for the morning dumplings.'

I wanted to hit her but knew I could not. Instead, I picked up the comb and pulled myself up. Thinking of Spring Rain's lesson, I dulled my eyes and smoothed my face as I dragged the sharp teeth through Miss Linjing's tangles, making her yelp.

Cerise unfurled my bindings and plunged my feet into a basin of vinegar and water. She massaged the shattered bones with oil before tugging my toes from their hiding place. As soon as she released them, they sprang back under my soles.

When I cried in pain, Cerise told me, 'This can't be as bad as foot-binding. Stop acting like an infant.'

I continued to cry and call out for Aa Noeng. To stop my toes curling back into golden lilies, Cerise forced rolls of cotton under them before loosely wrapping them in bandages. She told me that once my toes stopped curling, I should sleep without bindings so my blood could circulate. I nodded and agreed to follow all her instructions.

My mind drifted back to my first months of foot-binding. My *aa noeng* had presented me with a series of lotus shoes, each half an inch smaller than the previous pair. She'd cradled them in her palms as though they were sacred gifts. As she eased each new pair onto my shrinking feet, she comforted me with promises. 'As your shoes get smaller, your dream marriage comes closer,' and 'Your future mother-in-law will take one look at your tiny lotus shoes and realize you're a girl of good character,' and 'It is always better to suffer bitterness when you are young so you can enjoy sweetness in your twilight years.' Her words were a balm to my pain. I had chanted her promises like an incantation as my feet throbbed. She repeated the same words as I paced around the room, urging me to take one more step, and then another, and another to make my bones break and form the shape of a graceful lotus. Sometimes, when I whimpered into the small hours, she would cradle me in bed, whispering about the sort of home I would marry into. 'Your perfect golden lilies will take you to a mansion where the floors will be tiled and carpeted. You will never go hungry. Every day you will feast on pork, fish and chicken. Golden lilies will bring you a life of comfort.' Aa Noeng's promises had lulled me into sleep, giving me respite from my aching feet.

Now she was lost to me unless I saved my golden lilies.

That night, after Spring Rain and the kitchen maids began snoring, I tossed aside the rolls of cotton under my toes. In the moonlight, I reached for my indigo bindings and wrapped my feet back into golden lilies. This time, I did not wince from the pain. Using all my strength, I pulled and pulled my bandages until they felt as tight as the bindings wrapped by Aa Noeng's hands. Finally, I collapsed onto the pallet. I lay curled on my side and imagined my mother pressed against my back, wrapping her arm around me, keeping me warm and safe. I breathed deeply, searching my memory for the smell of jasmine and pomelo leaves in her hair. During the day, I would obey. But the adults could not stop me binding my feet in secret. One day, I would see my mother again.

4

Little Flower

I woke to Cerise inspecting my feet. She shook her head and tutted. I sat up, drew my knees to my chest and cradled my golden lilies as I braced myself for a slap. She stood in front of the small window, blocking out much of the faint dawn light, shadows hiding her face.

'Are you very angry?' I asked.

She sucked in a big breath, puffed her cheeks and blew it out, then sat on the edge of the bed and reached for me. I wriggled back from her grasp.

'Come here, child,' she beckoned.

I gripped my golden lilies and shook my head.

'Come,' she repeated.

'Don't take them away,' I sobbed. 'I need them to see my *aa noeng.*'

She reached over and wrapped her arm around my shoulders, resting her chin on my head. Her body was soft and round, like Mother's before we began to go hungry. I continued to hold on to my feet as she talked.

'What you're doing is very naughty,' she said, 'but it's hard

33

to stay vexed with a girl who is so desperate to see her mother again. You've escaped punishment because I pity you. But I can't be your new mother, so don't get used to this special treatment.'

I pushed her away. 'I don't want a new mother,' I cried. 'I want to go home!'

'Well, you can't!' she snapped, throwing her hands into the air. 'Stop pining for the impossible and start looking at your blessings. If you're good, obedient and lucky, when you're ready for marriage, a matchmaker might find a family who want a big-footed bride.

'But a *muizai*'s life is not as bad as you think. I'd rather be Lady Fong's companion for life than be tortured by a cruel mother-in-law. Or, worse, die in childbirth. I've more freedom than the ladies of the house. You and Miss Linjing could be just like me and Lady Fong. And Miss Linjing's betrothed is a first son, which means one day you'll be a housekeeper too, in charge of all the *muizai*. Wouldn't that be good?'

'I'd rather see Aa Noeng.'

'It pains me to say this,' she began, with a sigh, 'but it's time for you to know that your mother lied to you – not to be cruel but to protect you.'

'She never lies!'

'Do you know her full name?'

'She is Aa Noeng,' I replied, frowning, 'and we're Yungs.'

'What is the name of your village?'

'It's the one with an ancient banyan tree in the village square. There is a face of Buddha in the middle of its huge, thick trunk.'

'Little Flower,' she said gently, 'even if you keep your golden lilies, even if you get a marriage offer, you will never see your mother again. Without her full name and the name of your village, it'll be impossible to find her.'

'But Aa Noeng said—'

'I know what she said – most parents say something like that when they sell their children, to make the parting easier. Normally, I let the children believe in that false hope until they are old enough to understand, but you need the harsh truth now.'

She continued to talk as she loosened my bindings, but I didn't listen to her. I had another plan.

Later that day, between the evening meal and our bedtime tasks, I slipped away from the women's quarters, down a path that circled the rockery. Wind tunnelled between the piles of jagged grey rocks, whistling in and out of the nooks and crannies, making the garden sound alive.

I shivered.

Part of me wanted to turn back, but I folded my arms around my belly and hobbled on, for I knew the courtyard where I had first entered the Fong estate with my *aa noeng* lay just beyond this garden. I also remembered Farmer Tang's cart had travelled along a winding river, one with lots of willow trees dangling over its bank. Perhaps a nice grown-up would take me to that river. Then I could follow it until I saw the huge banyan tree. All I had to do was be brave, step through the side gate and start walking down the alleyway. With this in mind, I reached over my head, stretching my arms as far as they would go, but the plank of wood that bolted the doors was beyond my grasp. At the crunch of feet against the gravel, I gasped and turned around.

'Where are you going?' Spring Rain asked.

'I'm going home.'

'You won't get far on those feet. Besides, you'll be kidnapped by a sing-song madam as soon as you step onto the street. They love to snatch little girls, especially ones with fair skin and rosy cheeks, like you.'

'Maybe if I ask nicely one of those madams will help me find my mother. Please, Spring Rain *ze ze*, can you help me open the door?'

Bending to look me in the eye as she touched my cheek, she said, 'Those women are evildoers. The grown-up maids say they'd rather die than end up imprisoned in a sing-song house. There are also beggar tribes that might chop off your limbs or make you blind so you can beg for them.' When I edged away and reached for the gate, she asked, 'If it was that easy to run away, wouldn't I have left by now?'

I still didn't understand why sing-song houses were horrible, but I knew Spring Rain was smart and I trusted her. If she said it wasn't safe to go, then I should listen. Crushed, I sank to the paving, my legs askew, as I stared up at her.

'Does this mean I'll be Miss Linjing's slave until I'm dead?' I asked.

'We can run away together when we're big,' she said.

'But you said we'd be kidnapped.'

'We're too little to take care of ourselves now, but if we wait until we're grown-ups, we can find a way to make money, live by ourselves, eat until our bellies are full, laugh when we want, cry if we feel like it, never have to hide behind a blank face ever again!'

The last word tumbled out in a half-whisper as she finally drew breath. Though dusk fell around us, Spring Rain's eyes were shiny, like new copper coins. Her dimples deepened as she hoisted me up and hugged me tight. Swept up by her happy promise, I smiled too.

PART 2

5

Linjing

My betrothal to Valiant Li had secured Aa De's promotion to deputy governor of Shanxi, a landlocked northern province lying more than a thousand miles from Canton. My mothers, half-sisters and our *muizai* had all relocated with him. In the first leg of our journey, we sailed up the east coast, travelling from Canton to Tianjin, the closest harbour to Shanxi where steamships could dock, but there were still at least three hundred miles between that treaty port and Taiyuan, the province's walled capital and Father's new station.

I remember little of that long, dull sea journey ten years ago, but an encounter with my future mother-in-law, though brief, was branded into my memory. Normally, we wouldn't have met until I stepped over the Li threshold wearing my bridal *qun kwa*. But upon hearing we had arrived in her city, Lady Li summoned us to her receiving chamber, a room with shuttered windows, stiff stools and not a single cushion in sight. While Aa Noeng and Lady Li exchanged pleasantries, I studied my future mother-in-law: a wiry woman with eyes set so far apart they sat almost at the temples of her triangular face. That, combined with her long front teeth, made me think of a mantis, and I felt as defenceless as an aphid when she looked at me with chilling distaste. Afterwards, I had shared my fears with my mother, but she dismissed them, chiding me for my disrespectful imagination, warning me that such impish thoughts might show in my mien and mark me as impertinent, unfit to inherit the role of matriarch from Lady Li. I dared not mention it to her again, but Lady Li's face continued to plague my thoughts and sometimes my dreams, too.

I had spent the rest of that week in Tianjin dreading another summons from Lady Li. Though my fears had not come to pass, I'd been ill at ease until our convoy left the outskirts of the city. During our three-week journey west, I did not see much of my mothers or sisters, for they remained cloistered in palanquins or carriages, while I rode mostly with Aa De, his long arms wrapped around me as his hands held the reins. From him, I learnt the language of horses: flared or quivering nostrils signalled nerves, while a steed enjoying a thrilling ride might have half-closed eyes and a stretched upper lip, but I must be on alert for aggression if I spotted a stallion lowering his head as he waved his neck from side to side. All this and more Aa De shared only with me.

I wished Maa Maa had stayed behind in our ancestral home, but she'd insisted on coming with us, for she wanted to be present when one of her daughters-in-law bore an heir. Over the years, she'd subjected my mothers to countless *daai fu*; some prescribed tonics, others applied acupuncture, but nothing succeeded in producing an heir for my father. Maa Maa had appealed to the gods too: aside from the usual offerings of sandalwood incense and prayers, when I was thirteen she purchased eight hundred and eighty-eight turtles and released them into a river, hoping this act of kindness would finally coax the deities into granting our wish.

But although Aa De married another two wives, he still did not have a son, and Maa Maa blamed my mothers. Her increasing rage towards them fanned my fears about marriage.

It would be another two years before a wedding palanquin would carry me off to my betrothed, but Lady Li was already an incubus that lurked in my mind, and panic squeezed my chest whenever I thought of her. Aside from the frightful encounter in Tianjin when I was seven, her perfunctory letters to Mother since then, each filled with dismissive remarks about modern ladies, suggested Lord Li had forced her to accept my natural feet when she still preferred golden lilies. Would she be just like Maa Maa? Since my first memory, Aa Noeng had sung a certain folk song of warning to me, and Aa De's three minor wives repeated its grim portent to my eight half-sisters:

> *Life as a daughter-in-law is bitter in ten thousand ways; this is your fate.*
> *No matter what time you rise from bed, your mother-in-law will complain it's late.*
> *Tears, suffering and toil. Our bitter fate is impossible to foil.*

These lyrics now echoed in my mind as I knelt beside my half-sisters, all of us trapped in Maa Maa's praying chamber. Our mothers stood in a row at the front of the room, facing us. Their shoulders slumped, and they wore the expressions of guilty children waiting to be smacked by the cane end of a feather duster. Fourth Aa Noeng's lips quivered. Our maids stood against the wall, looking as downcast as I felt. A charcoal burner blazed in each corner, and the woody, pungent

41

scent of myrrh stifled me. Sweat beaded my nose; the room spun when I turned my head. Maa Maa paced in front of my mothers, punctuating each of her sentences with a thud of her cane on the floor.

'Our family needs an heir,' Maa Maa said, 'and none of you seem capable of fulfilling your duty.' She swiped her cane across my mothers' midriffs. 'You are all useless. A sow is worth more than each of you.'

Fourth Aa Noeng's daughter sobbed and waddled towards her mother. Maa Maa slapped her and spots of blood bubbled on her cheek where the tip of Maa Maa's nail guard had grazed it. My half-sister fell silent momentarily, then recovered her breath and shrieked. Her mother stepped forward with outstretched arms, tears trickling down her frightened face.

'Get back in line,' Maa Maa ordered, 'or I will beat your worthless girl until the skin on her bottom is raw.'

Fourth Aa Noeng fell back as her eyes remained fixed on her sobbing daughter, who tried to run to her again, but my grandmother's slave seized her shoulders.

Maa Maa barked at the nursery amah, 'Take this rubbish out of here.'

The amah scooped up my screeching half-sister and hurried out of the room.

Maa Maa addressed me and my remaining half-sisters. 'A daughter's sin is a mother's liability, just as a mother's sin is her daughter's burden,' she told us. 'Your mothers have failed in a wife's fundamental duty and you must share their shame.' She waved her cane over our heads. 'I would sacrifice every one of you,' she declared, 'if it meant I could secure a son to carry on the Fong name.'

Maa Maa turned back to our mothers and stopped in front of Second Aa Noeng, whose hands flew to her swollen belly.

Maa Maa slapped them away and began probing the taut bump, pressing her gnarled fingers into her ribcage.

'Your belly is sitting very low,' Maa Maa grumbled. 'This is not a good sign. Do you still crave spicy food?'

'I am afraid so, Revered Mother.'

'Let's hope you will prefer sour and salty food soon. Regardless, you must take extra care to avoid another stillbirth. I will not pardon you if there is a repeat of last year's disgrace.'

Second Aa Noeng staggered. A bitter taste filled my mouth as I stared at my grandmother's ruthless face; she looked on with indifference as Peony began to cry. The depth of Maa Maa's cruelty shocked me, for I did not think even she would be capable of such heartless words. Second Aa Noeng deserved sympathy, not threats. I pitied her hard fate. She had suffered four small, half-formed births. Worst of all, in her last pregnancy, a healthy boy had died on his way out. During that dark time, she had not left her bedchamber for six months. I thought she would never conceive again, but now she was halfway along her eleventh pregnancy. Despite her stoic effort, Maa Maa still blamed her for my brother's stillbirth.

The warnings in the folk song did not seem stark enough.

As I began to wonder if my grandmother had a soul at all, her junior *muizai* entered the room carrying a tray, which she set down on the desk. She laid out the items: a paperweight anchoring a stack of yellow paper, a calligraphy brush, an inkstick with a dragon engraving, a small jug of water, an inkstone mortar and a knife. At Maa Maa's order, the slave poured water into the shallow well and began grinding the inkstick against its smooth surface. A thin paste filled the dish.

'Phoenix, come to the desk with me,' Maa Maa ordered.

I caught Aa Noeng's eye for an explanation as she followed my grandmother, but she shrugged.

'This is the best cinnabar-red inkstick money can buy,' Maa Maa said. 'The imperial family uses it to copy holy text for the gods. From now until Peony gives birth, we will copy a hundred pages of scripture and burn it to Heaven on the first and fifteenth day of each moon cycle. With luck, the gods will be moved finally to grant us a son.'

'I would be happy to complete this task,' Aa Noeng offered. My other mothers echoed her enthusiasm.

'What I need is your *blood*,' my grandmother declared, as she seized the knife. 'Only the addition of blood to the ink can demonstrate our sincerity to the gods, and you will be the one to sacrifice since you are almost as barren as a mule.'

My mother gasped and stepped back; the bells on her chatelaine cried out in a startled jingle. I lunged forward but her eyes signalled me to remain kneeling.

'Coward,' Maa Maa spat. 'Give me your hand.'

Aa Noeng froze.

'Take mine instead,' I blurted. 'I'm strong and not afraid.'

Cackling, she sneered, 'No doubt your time will come if your fertility *qi* is as weak as your mother's. But not today.'

She gestured for her *muizai* to grab my mother's hand. Aa Noeng did not struggle as the slave pulled her to the desk and held her hand over the inkstone. Maa Maa sliced the side of Aa Noeng's palm, dripping her blood into the mortar. The junior slave continued to mix the ink as Maa Maa squeezed my mother's hand, forcing more blood into the mixture. Aa Noeng's head jerked back, the ruby studs on her phoenix comb glinting. But she did not cry out. My throat ached as I watched her suffer, and I balled my hands into fists, digging my nails into my palms. Fourth Aa Noeng fainted. Her *muizai* hurried over and, using her thumb, applied pressure on the groove between my half-mother's nose and upper lip. Within seconds, her eyes sprang open, and with her *muizai*'s help, she hoisted herself upright again. Her sister-wives covered their mouths with their hands; none had dared to help Fourth Aa Noeng. They looked spellbound and aghast. The slaves' faces were pale as they all fixed their eyes on their shoes. Only Little Flower continued to watch, her eyes filled with pain as she chewed her bottom lip. How dare she behave as if she cared about Aa Noeng, as if Aa Noeng were her mother, not mine? Later, I would remind Little Flower of her place.

Around me, my half-sisters edged towards each other as though proximity would protect them from Maa Maa's cruelty. I envied their ability to take comfort from each other, but at sixteen, I was too old to believe in childish charms. I understood that only sons would save me from my mother's fate. Although I despised Maa Maa, her threat might be a prophecy – the risk of following in my mother's footsteps lay at the root of my nuptial fears. Not only had Aa Noeng failed to bear a son, she had never conceived again after birthing me. Her feeble fertility *qi* might be hereditary. If Maa Maa treated her like this despite the respectable size of her golden lilies, what would Lady Li do to me?

Once Maa Maa released us, I sprinted to the stables in search of Aa De, for I wanted answers, long overdue ones. My lungs ached and my thighs burnt by the time I reached the horses' stalls, but my heart felt lighter. Despite their mannish size, my strong feet brought me the joy of vigorous exercise.

Since Aa De hadn't arrived, I approached Night Pearl. Upon seeing me, she whinnied and nudged her muzzle against my cheek. I smiled and fed her a lump of sugar as the groom strapped my side-saddle onto her back. Once I mounted, the tension in my neck and shoulders loosened and my misery retreated. We trotted onto the arena, taking time to warm up her limbs until I sensed her eagerness for speed and tapped her side to urge her forward. My pulse raced as she speeded up and delight washed away my worries; I gripped the pommel between my thighs to stay in control as she leapt over the first hedge on the obstacle course. Upon landing at the end of the circuit, we panted with triumph. I believed we could fly over even greater heights if Aa De would permit me to use a real saddle, but he had strict instructions from Lord Li to keep me in line with Western ladies' etiquette, and my American tutors, past and present, had confirmed that no well-bred lady straddled her mount. As I lined up Night Pearl for a second round, Aa De appeared at the arena's gate.

He sat tall on his white mount, holding the reins in one hand with the easy confidence of a man used to riding and in full command of his horse. A wide smile spread across his face as he greeted me. But I frowned as this morning's cruelty pushed past my short-lived reprieve, reminding me of the unpleasant conversation ahead.

'Who has dared cross my favourite daughter?' he joked. 'Tell me and I'll have them whipped.'

'It has been an unhappy morning.' I relayed the scene in Maa Maa's chamber. He listened with the same detached look that settled on his face whenever he witnessed my grandmother's malice or heard about it from me. His indifference angered me, but it would have been unfilial of me to say so.

When I'd finished speaking, he said, 'Your *maa maa* is doing what she must to secure an heir for me. Maybe one day you will do the same when you're the matriarch.'

I sighed. Why go to the trouble of telling him about Maa Maa's brutality when he always sided with her? But the foolish part of me still hoped that one day he might defend Aa Noeng. I wanted to ask him whether all husbands left their wives to the mercy of their spiteful mothers, but even I did not dare venture on such an indelicate topic with my father.

'Come,' he coaxed. 'Let's leave the city and ride along the creek. It will help restore your spirits.'

When I remained silent, he offered me a piece of peanut toffee as though I were still a child. The treat did not tempt me, but his affectionate smile won me over, reminding me that I was a treasured jewel, not a worthless girl with shameful feet.

We steered our horses away from the arena, down the alley, joining the throng of pedestrians and carts on the congested Principal North Road as we headed towards the Gate of Truth, the busiest of the eight entrances that separated the crowded streets and laneways of our city from the vast wilderness that lay beyond the impenetrable stone wall. A crowd had gathered to watch a wedding procession: a pair of musicians led the parade, each trumpeting a deafening tune. Combined with the bellows from pedlars – this one touting the merits of his knives, that one hawking the benefits of a tonic of baby mice pickled in rice wine – the clamour rattled Night Pearl, and she raised her forelegs, poised to rear. I bent forward and soothed her with hushes. The pedlar took no heed as he waved the bottle in my face. Eager to get away, I urged Night Pearl into a trot, pushing past the horde, Father riding beside me as we sped through the gate.

We abandoned the paved road, turning east as we broke into a canter, our horses stamping a track through the thick, long grass. Recent rain had swelled the creek. Water babbled over the rocks and pebbles, making a soothing sound. The late-autumn sun warmed our faces as we travelled side by side, and our horses snorted to each other, their ears pointed forward in contentment. Above us a flock of geese flew towards the wetlands south of the city. In the distance, I glimpsed the peak of Erlong *saan*, soaring into the sky; often I looked to those mountains wishing I could scale their heights, see the country beyond Taiyuan, perhaps even venture abroad. But such thoughts were flights of fancy. I dragged my mind back to reality, slowed my pace and signalled Aa De to do the same.

'Why did you choose to betroth me to Valiant Li?' I asked, tugging my horse to a halt beneath an elm tree.

He stopped and turned to me with a look of puzzlement.

'Second Aa Noeng already had two daughters back then,' I pressed. 'Why didn't you choose one of them instead?'

'They are too timid and small-minded to be Lord Li's daughter-in-law. From the beginning he revealed to me his ambition for Valiant. He has plans for his son to be an ambassador for the Emperor. It won't happen for several years after your marriage. Valiant needs to gain enough experience before he can be trusted with such a mission. But when he goes, his wife will need to travel abroad with him and socialize with Westerners. Can you imagine your half-sisters living in England or America?'

I thought about my sisters' fear of photography and knew he was right. All the women in our family except me believed photographs would snatch fragments of their souls. A few months ago, Aa De had invited a foreign photographer to our house, but they had all refused to pose in a family portrait; only I stood beside him in the picture.

'They are frightened of Western ways,' I agreed. 'But they were only four and two at the time. You couldn't have known what they would be like when they grew up.' I hesitated, unsure if I should voice the next thought. Would it anger him? I pushed on. 'This betrothal is fraught with uncertainty. No other family will want me if Valiant Li dies before our wedding or the Li family rescinds the marriage offer. I don't understand why you've chosen to risk my fate like this when you say I'm your favourite child.'

'That is true,' he admitted reluctantly. 'I couldn't be sure of your sisters' characters and there are some risks to your betrothal. But I was certain of your intelligence, courage and spirit of adventure. I needed to pledge a daughter to Lord Li who would make me proud, and I knew without a doubt that you could fulfil my expectations. A lesser daughter would fail, tarnish our family name and ruin my career.'

'Will you still love me if I fail at my duty?' *What if I cannot produce a son? What if Lady Li cannot forgive my natural feet?* These questions perched on the tip of my tongue but I could not say them aloud: they were feminine matters and not to be discussed with a man, even my own father.

He chuckled, but I could not share his humour.

'Will you?' I repeated.

'You are the daughter of my heart,' he said, with a light laugh, 'the pearl in my palm and the only child whom I *respect*. I know you will never fail or disappoint me.'

He smiled at me with such conviction that my protests crumbled before I could voice them. But I couldn't silence the voice inside me, the one calling for him to say he would treasure and protect me always, no matter what happened. He was the only parent who valued me. Little Flower might be a slave, but in my mother's eyes she was the perfect disciple and I was an inept daughter.

6

Little Flower

On the fifteenth of each month, alongside Spring Rain, I relished three hours of reprieve to do as we pleased and go where we liked as long as we returned to the Fong residence by noon. For those with the means, Taiyuan offered many diversions: at the centre of this metropolis, diviners – blind men who shook brass coins in tortoiseshells – crowded the courtyard of the Fire God Temple, each promising to reveal our fortunes; the pavilion alongside West Creek staged lively operas; and behind the Academy of Confucius, rows of stores, tucked in alleyways that pressed against the eastern city wall, sold a variety of trinkets, from jade hairpins and simple gold hoops to brilliant kingfisher combs.

As much younger girls, Spring Rain and I used to skip up and down those streets and lanes, thrilled by the possibilities, imagining all the things we could buy or enjoy if we were ladies. But without any money, this pastime gradually grew tiresome. For the last few years, we would always hurry down Principal South Road, past the crude medicine market and the live-beasts market, turning left at Prosperity Lane then right onto Bright Moon Street before exiting the city via the Gate of Virtue. From there we turned away from the trade road, hiking up a steep path lined with plum trees until we reached the shrine of Jyut Lou. To ensure a swift journey, and to avoid losing our bearings in the maze of alleyways, we seldom diverged from this route.

Today, as always, it was crowded and noisy with the hum of a hundred maidens' voices, each murmuring prayers to the deity of marriage. Standing twice as tall as a man, the statue of Jyut Lou held a sack of red threads in one hand and the book of marriages in the other, his ruby lips partly covered by a flowing white beard as he smiled down at us, his eyes crinkled into crescents.

Since I had long given up hope of seeing my mother again, embroidery, the promise of marriage and my friendship with Spring Rain formed a pyramid of stars in the endless night that had become my life since I was sold. Unlike Spring Rain, who resented her father, I didn't blame Aa Noeng for selling me, for she had done so with the understanding that I could keep my golden lilies and eventually marry into a respectable family, perhaps one more comfortable than ours. Still, I missed her. Even if Miss Linjing had cherished me in the way Lady Fong did Cerise, it would be no substitute for a mother's love. When grief threatened to burst forth, I would escape into embroidery; a veil of serenity fell over me each time my needle glided through silk. With each satin stitch, I retreated further and further into a realm where nothing mattered except the smooth bands blossoming over my motifs, filling the empty space with shades that ranged from the brilliance of flame-orange, yolk-yellow and crimson, to indigo, moss, pine and dove-grey, the colours of the mandarin ducks on my bridal quilt, a prized possession that would become the centrepiece of my wedding trousseau ... if I could secure a marriage.

But art alone wouldn't have been enough for me to survive those long months when the loss of Aa Noeng and my golden lilies had still ached like a throbbing tooth. During that time, Spring Rain would wrap her arms around my small quivering shoulders, holding me until my sobs quietened and grief loosened its grip. With her help, I also learnt to navigate slavery, and of all her lessons, the most valuable one remained the vacant stare. In the span of ten years' servitude to Miss Linjing I had absorbed a critical lesson about my wilful mistress: a blank face was my best armour, one that I had long ago fortified, keeping the corners of my mouth flat and my eyes like mirrors, reflecting only what she expected to see in a *muizai*. But that wasn't enough to safeguard me from her jealousy. As long as her mother compared us, I remained a splinter under her skin and nothing I did ever won her affection or approval. We could never be like Cerise and Lady Fong.

Spring Rain and I still talked about freedom, but even she no longer believed in the fantasy of running away. Life on the streets for young women meant danger: rape, abduction, perhaps even murder. Only marriage offered a safe escape, though what kind of family would choose a *muizai* for a bride I did not know and did not care. I wanted only to escape slavery, for the chance to be treated as a person again. Second Fong *taai taai* had finally promised to engage a matchmaker for Spring Rain in the new year, and though I wouldn't be released until I turned eighteen, Lady Fong had already approached one for me too. To my relief, Miss Linjing had not raised any objections. I looked forward to the matchmaker's visit with equal parts hope and anxiety; after years without bindings, my feet had regained full function, but if she saw their disfigurement she might turn down the assignment.

I picked my way to the front of the crowd, searching for a clearing among the piles of offerings to lay down a posy of chrysanthemums. Looking over my shoulder, I beckoned Spring Rain to follow, but she pointed to the creek and told me she'd wait there. Before I could question her odd behaviour, the throng of maidens had pushed me forward.

Compared to the pyramids of dried persimmons, red bean cakes, bowls of sugar and sweet dumplings, my tawdry tribute seemed hardly worth the deity's notice. Still, I knelt among the other maidens and whispered my wish: 'Jyut Lou, though I'm a penniless *muizai*, beneath your notice, please bestow your blessing on me. Please tie a red string between my ankle and that of a kind man, one like my father. I don't mind if he is pockmarked, simple or even a cripple. All I ask is a marriage to spirit me away.' I placed my hands on the ground, palms facing to the sky as I kowtowed between them, the wet grass seeping through my trousers and a stone digging into my knee. 'Grant me this wish, Jyut Lou, and I'll honour you for the rest of my days. Please let the matchmaker be a compassionate woman, willing to do her best by me.'

Behind me, a young woman cleared her throat several times and her basket thumped against my shoulders each time I rose from a bow. I gave my spot to her and walked over to join Spring Rain. She rested her elbows on the railing of the bridge as she peered into the murky green ripples, determination tightening the corners of her mouth. When I touched her forearm, she winced; no doubt beneath the fabric of her sleeve a fresh wound festered. From her grimace I suspected it was a cut or a burn, another injury inflicted by Second Fong *taai taai*.

'How bad is it?' I asked.

She shrugged. 'No worse than usual. But it doesn't matter any more, at least not for much longer.' She turned to me with a forced smile, lips stretched too tight, two dimples gouged into her wind-chapped cheeks. When she continued, her voice sounded too bright, as though she were trying to sell a lie to both of us.

'I'm running away,' she announced, 'during Dowager Lady Fong's birthday banquet. There will be at least two dozen opera performers, stagehands and a hundred or so guests. It's the perfect time to slip away, and I'm sure the troupe leader will offer refuge. I hear those travelling troupes always need an extra pair of hands and I'm strong, willing to earn my keep. Life with an opera troupe will be an adventure, far freer than life as a wife.' She tilted her chin, squaring her shoulders as she dared me to oppose her.

'Wait for a marriage offer,' I urged.

'I've made up my mind.'

'Don't be rash. You'll regret it!'

'I'm not like you,' she snarled, voice as bitter as bile. 'I'm not a genius at embroidery. I don't have Lady Fong's protection.'

For a decade, we had been like sisters, braiding hair, whispering into each other's ear in the small hours, sharing dreams, secrets and scavenged leftovers. Until now, she had never spoken a word of envy. Hurt and shock stung. I reminded her, 'Second Fong *taai taai* said she'd engage a matchmaker for you at the end of winter. That's only four months away.'

She folded her lips into a dainty pout, and her hand swayed as though she was holding a handkerchief before she rested it lightly on my arm. The uncanny resemblance to Second Fong *taai taai*'s mannerism unnerved me. I took a step back, but she gripped me tight, digging her nails into my tunic-blouse.

'Let me teach you a lesson, Spring Rain,' she said, mimicking her mistress's cloying tone. 'If you wanted to get married, you shouldn't have let me know. If *I*, a lady with perfect golden lilies, can't get what I want – to have a son and be first wife – then why should a *muizai*'s wish be granted? To punish you for your stupidity and your presumption, I had planned to keep dangling this false prize before you. But I'm tired of that game, so take heed, for I shall say it only once. I will never let you go.' Reverting to her own voice, Spring Rain released me and said, 'That is what she told me this morning. I'd often feared she was only taunting me, but you've always told me to be patient, that she couldn't be that wicked. Now, surely, even you can't deny I have no choice. Join me or help me, but don't lecture me about the dangers.'

'Please, Spring Rain *ze ze*,' I said. 'Don't treat me as a foe.' I reached for her hands. 'We're sisters. What can I do to help you?'

Her flared nostrils relaxed and her face slackened. 'Keep my secret,' she said. 'Help me raise funds and pray for me.'

'Of course. I won't tell a soul. And I'll find a way to get money. This I swear on our friendship.'

'I'm sorry,' she said, drawing me into an embrace, her wet cheek pressed against mine. 'My ill fate isn't your fault. I shouldn't be cross with you. Forget my harsh words.' The sharp tang of liniment mixed with the earthy scent of herbal wound dressings filled my nostrils. When she was gone, her smell would linger in my memory, far longer than her face, just as the fragrance of pomelo and jasmine still reminded me of Aa Noeng though her features had faded years ago.

7

Linjing

My English and Western etiquette lesson with Miss Abigail Hart wasn't due for another half an hour, so I was surprised when Little Flower ushered her into Aa Noeng's private sewing room.

Miss Hart walked briskly inside, her strides long and purposeful, her head high, her spine straight and her chest thrust forward, like Aa De. The contrast between her stable gait and my mothers' golden-lilies mince accounted for the obvious difference, but I had natural feet – so did all our *muizai*. None of us carried ourselves, though, with the same assurance, and our presence didn't fill the room as Miss Hart's did. Her sonorous voice commanded attention, and even her hair, a haphazard nest piled high on her crown, defied convention, the curls fighting the hairpins.

Miss Hart peeled off her damp cloak, fur hat and gloves, handing them to Little Flower with a brief smile that revealed small, neat teeth, which sat at odds with her stout frame and exceptional height. She stood half a head taller than me, and I was the tallest woman in our family.

'I hope you don't mind my impromptu visit, Lady Fong,' Miss Hart said, in Cantonese, as she stood in front of Aa Noeng's embroidery frame. I abandoned my hoop to the side table, eager to see how Aa Noeng would treat Miss Hart; if she had her way, I would have nothing to do with white ghosts, but Lord Li had insisted on a Western education for me.

'Not at all, Miss Hart,' my mother replied, her tone clipped. Though she seemed vexed with Miss Hart, she frowned at me. 'Have you come to voice a concern about Linjing's behaviour or progress?'

I dug my nails into my thighs. Having stowed Miss Hart's belongings in the drying room, Little Flower returned to her spot sitting opposite my mother, for they were working together on a landscape with willow trees draping over a lake. As soon as Little Flower pulled the first stitch through the silk, her posture loosened, and when she looked up to change thread, her glazed eyes saw nothing but her embroidery. Aa Noeng smiled as she glanced at my *muizai*, but the frown returned when she looked back at me. I wished Little Flower would stab her finger with a needle and bleed all over the silk.

Behind her spectacles, Miss Hart's eyes twinkled as she fixed me with a reassuring smile. 'Not at all,' she said, with an easy laugh. 'Linjing is a quick study, my best student. It won't be long before she is fluent in English.'

'My daughter lacks patience and discipline,' Aa Noeng insisted. 'If she doesn't conduct herself with the strictest decorum, you must report to me immediately.'

I leapt up. Miss Hart patted my shoulder; her firm hand was comforting and this unexpected kindness quelled my anger.

'Lady Fong,' she said, 'I have come to ask a favour. I'm looking for a sewing teacher for the older girls in our orphanage. Nothing too fancy, just some fundamental embroidery. It's important for them to have employable skills once they leave our care. It would be only a couple of hours a week. I thought Linjing might enjoy the diversion, and it would be inspiring for our girls to meet a Chinese lady with natural feet.'

Aa Noeng exchanged a grimace with me. In spite of our differences, neither of us considered my big feet an inspiration, but saying so to Miss Hart might offend her Western sensibilities. Instead, my mother said, 'I'm afraid it isn't possible. Linjing is cursed with colour infirmity. She cannot see red or green.'

'*Aa Noeng!*' I cried. 'My curse is a family secret.'

'Miss Hart is your tutor. She'll notice sooner or later.'

My cheeks flared with shame and anger.

'But,' Miss Hart began, her pale brows twisted in a quizzical knot, 'I've seen examples of Linjing's embroidery, and many of them have shades of red and green.' She pointed to the half-finished peony in my hoop. 'If she cannot see colour, how does she manage?'

Aa Noeng looked to Little Flower. 'Fetch the pattern book and silks,' she told her, 'and tell Miss Hart about your colour-coding system.' To Miss Hart she said, 'Little Flower's method is ingenious. It might inspire you to help Linjing in other aspects of her learning where colour is unavoidable.'

Little Flower's needle paused in mid-air as she looked from my mother to me, mouth agape, eyes dull, waiting for my approval. I glowered at her, daring her to carry out Aa Noeng's order.

'Linjing,' my mother rebuked, 'you cannot blame Little Flower for your misfortune.' In a completely different tone, she said to Little Flower, 'Don't fret, my dear.'

Little Flower rose, bowed to me but obeyed my mother.

I stared down at the taut damask stretched across the

rectangular frame. The needlework on each half of the fabric was smooth and identical; it was impossible to distinguish where Aa Noeng's stitches ended and Little Flower's began. Their concordance taunted me. It was a struggle not to seize a pair of scissors and drag them through their project, not to stain the flawless landscape with black *pu'er* tea, not to tip the brazier's blazing coal onto the delicate silk, reducing the mocking colours to ashes.

Little Flower returned with the items my mother had requested and laid them on the round table in the centre of the room. My mother took a seat at the table and invited Miss Hart to join her. Little Flower stood to her left. I slumped onto the remaining stool.

'Explain your method,' Aa Noeng encouraged Little Flower.

'I label each silk skein with a number,' she began. 'Five belongs to fire-cracker red, four to pomegranate, three to pillar red, two to lotus pink and one to maiden's blush.' She opened the pattern book to the peony motif I had been working on. 'The palette on the tray is specific for this pattern.' She pointed to the flower. 'The centre of each petal should be filled in with fire-cracker red, so I have assigned it to number five. The next section is pomegranate, so it is coded with number four. Each segment gets progressively lighter, until the border is filled with maiden's blush.'

'May I?' Miss Hart asked, holding out her hand.

Little Flower gave the book to her. As Miss Hart thumbed through the pages, her face, which had earlier smiled in praise of me, now beamed at my slave. I reached over and snatched the book from Miss Hart, curling it into a tight scroll which I squeezed between my fists.

'There is nothing extraordinary about Little Flower's system,' I said. 'I dare say I would have thought of it myself if I

59

cared enough for embroidery.' I glanced away, unable to meet the disapproval in Aa Noeng's glare, for this statement wasn't entirely true. Though needlework dulled my mind in the way that fatigue blunted my senses, it was a feminine virtue second only to golden lilies. I would have given anything to have Little Flower's sight, to sketch, paint and sew with the natural ease of spiders spinning their webs, to exchange my ungainly hands with her nimble ones. But to say so would yield power to a slave and admit defeat. My pride couldn't stomach it.

'Did you think of this solution on your own?' Miss Hart asked Little Flower.

She nodded.

'Is it a recent creation?'

'I came up with it when we were ten.'

Until now, Little Flower had been as insignificant as an ant to Miss Hart; now she gazed at Little Flower as though she had seen her for the first time. It was the same expression I'd seen on Aa Noeng's face all those years ago when Little Flower completed her first band of perfect satin stitches while mine looked like overlapping teeth. Even before Miss Hart spoke, I had guessed what she wanted, and I would have none of it.

'I forbid it,' I told Miss Hart.

'I beg your pardon?' she said, puzzled.

'You can't have Little Flower. She is my *muizai* and I need her.'

'It will be only one afternoon a week,' Miss Hart said. 'You'd scarcely notice her absence.' Turning to Little Flower, she asked, 'Could you still manage all your tasks if you came to the orphanage to help me once a week?'

Little Flower bowed her head, shoulders slumped.

'It pains me to quarrel with you, Miss Hart, but you must

understand that Little Flower's opinion doesn't signify. She is my slave, my property, and I say no.'

Aa Noeng drew breath but Miss Hart spoke first. 'Linjing.' Her voice was a bent twig, poised to snap. 'People are not objects, slaves are not machines, even a *muizai* is entitled to speak her mind.'

'Lady Fong,' Little Flower said, her face suddenly alert, like a horse about to leap over a hedge. 'I will work twice as fast to complete my chores. Miss Linjing won't be inconvenienced, I promise. Please, madam, it would give me such joy to teach the little girls.'

Stunned by her boldness, I was dumbstruck. I stared at her, wanting to see behind the blank face she always presented to me, but she looked past me into the distance. Was there a hint of defiance in her eyes? It flared like the spark of a match, too quick for me to be sure before she snuffed it out. Perhaps misinterpreting my silence as consent, Aa Noeng said, 'Very well then, you may go. They will be blessed to learn from you.'

I dashed over to my mother and shook her arm. Her jade bangles smashed against each other. 'How could you side with her against me?'

'Little Flower's behaviour is impeccable,' Aa Noeng said. 'She deserves some respite. Let us speak no more on this trivial subject.'

'A truly virtuous maiden, especially a lady, shouldn't take more than three steps outside her home,' I said, quoting an adage that Aa Noeng often used to admonish me whenever I wanted to explore Taiyuan on foot.

From behind me, Miss Hart asked, 'What has that to do with Little Flower?'

'As my handmaiden, her behaviour is a reflection of my reputation and our family's decorum.' I straightened and turned to face my naive tutor. 'We have lesser servants to do errands. Little Flower is expected to shadow me, and if I were matriarch I would forbid the three hours' leave that she already enjoys each month.' I pointed to the perimeter wall beyond the open window and added, 'She should stay within these boundaries, not expose herself across town, mixing with orphans or worse.' Turning around, I stooped over Aa Noeng and said, 'Surely you agree with me now.'

'I have given my permission,' my mother said, face rigid. 'Do not challenge me again or you will sorely regret it.'

I had lost this battle, but I would make Little Flower pay for her insolence, for Aa De had told me that slaves were like weeds: at the first hint of leniency, they would grow wild. Though Little Flower had been exceedingly obedient all these years, her behaviour today cast my authority in doubt, reminding me to govern her with a firmer hand.

8

Little Flower

From Miss Hart's study, a chamber adjoining the orphanage's workroom, I glanced over my shoulder. It was my third lesson with the little girls and already they had progressed to blending two colours, the green of bitter gourd interwoven with coriander. Their faces were as intent as a sparrow's when searching for grubs in the dirt, some with the tip of their tongue poking out, all determined to guide needle and thread over and under their hoops to form a seamless band of satin stitches. Pity swelled in my chest. Five of the six girls suffered a physical affliction. The eldest, a child of eleven, wore her thick hair loose with a side parting to the right in an attempt to hide the purplish-black birthmark that stained half of her cheek and temple, spilling into her hairline. Hare lips marred a pair of twins, the fourth girl lacked eyebrows – the skin where they should have been was pink and shiny – and the spine of the fifth child curved and bulged like a tortoiseshell. Only Blossom, the youngest, remained unmarred, her thick fringe framing a round face with no remarkable features, and I wouldn't have given her much thought if not for her golden lilies.

'Take a seat, Little Flower.'

I turned back to face Miss Hart. She patted the empty spot on the settee next to hers, and with her other hand she proffered a steaming cup of tea. The sun shone on Miss Hart's hair, the bronze and gold strands glowing like hot iron in a blacksmith's forge. I wanted to sketch her portrait, to capture the blazing curls with needle painting, but no metallic thread in my palette could match their likeness.

'Sit down,' she repeated.

'*Muizai* are not permitted to sit beside a lady.'

'Here, you're a teacher, not a slave. The girls will be fine on their own for a little while. Take some tea with me.'

I clasped my hands around the cup but still did not sit, fearing this might be some sort of test. By coming here, I was taking a chance on Miss Hart, but I had to tread carefully. Ladies were like wild cats: one never knew when they might strike. Though escaping Miss Linjing for an afternoon each week was delightful, I wouldn't have vexed her for this reason alone. I had done it for Spring Rain. I needed to raise funds for her escape, and I could think of no other means than to sell my embroidery. Since approaching a pawnbroker directly would draw attention and endanger Spring Rain, Miss Hart might be our only ally – if I could trust her, if she could be persuaded to help us, without being privy to Spring Rain's plan. Despite these uncertainties, a tiny thrill of excitement – a novel sentiment – lightened my fears. I had bested Miss Linjing, won a sliver of leisure time and, most importantly, I now had a chance to help Spring Rain. For the first time since becoming a *muizai*, choice and, dare I say, even *power*, which had seemed as distant as the moon, now felt almost within reach.

'Sit,' Miss Hart commanded. 'I insist.'

I lowered myself, perched on the edge and sipped my tea,

waiting for her to speak. She lifted the lid of a delicate sugar bowl, its borders gilded, and added a spoonful to her cup, then stirred in slow circles, seeming in no hurry to talk. To steady my nerves, I studied the illustration on the opposite wall, behind Miss Hart's desk. Though illiterate, I had seen the characters for Taiyuan above the city gates enough times to recognize it as a map of our city. From this distance, the streets and laneways looked a blur and all the tiny characters added to my confusion, but drawings of the landmarks dotted across the countryside beyond the city walls awed me. In the lower right-hand corner, two eight-tiered pagodas soared above a forest, while a peanut-shaped lake dominated the opposite corner. Villages, farmland and larger estates were scattered around the other sides of the map, some surrounded by mountains. Amid the vastness, would there be a sanctuary for Spring Rain?

Miss Hart had still not spoken. With only seven weeks until Dowager Lady Fong's banquet, I needed to become better acquainted with Miss Hart quickly, to decide if she could be trusted, to win her affection, so that she might grant me a favour.

'May I ask you a question?' I asked.

'Certainly, ask me anything.' She rested the spoon on a saucer, angling her body towards me. I set my cup on the table and did the same; our knees almost touched.

'I thought Westerners considered bound feet primitive,' I said. 'Why does Blossom have golden lilies?' Other questions hovered on the tip of my tongue, but they might be too intrusive, too provoking; best to be careful, like a foot testing an icy path.

Her blouse puffed over the bodice of her waistcoat as she drew breath. When she spoke, it was in a rapid, defensive cadence. 'Foot-binding is mutilation and torture, and our church is against it. But the pastor, my brother, has fallen prey to his wife's persuasions, upholding her sentimental views over logic and progress. Sarah spends far too much time with the village women, so much so that some of her values have gone native. The other girls, poor souls, could never marry, so their feet are spared. But Sarah thinks that Blossom might have a chance at a respectable match if she has golden lilies.' Her mouth twisted as though biting into a sour plum. 'Even that term is mocking and deceitful. There is nothing beautiful about crushed bones and rotting skin.'

I fixed my expression, keeping it neutral. I would have done anything to save my golden lilies, but I mustn't agitate her. As I searched for the right response – not a falsehood, but something that would endear me to her – I pressed my thumbnail into a chilblain on the side of my index finger, scoring the swollen skin with tiny crosses. 'Foot-binding is excruciating and some girls die of blood poisoning. Yet, without it, a girl's marriage choices would be severely limited, if any at all. Spinsterhood is not only shameful but also condemns a woman to poverty and likely homelessness too.'

'That is also my sister-in-law's argument.' A furrow settled between her brows, her pupils narrowed to pinpoints and she swivelled away from me, glaring out of the lattice window. I scrabbled for something agreeable to say, but finding none, I settled on frankness.

'Why did you speak up for me?' I asked.

She turned back to me. 'Foot-binding is cruel, but slavery is wicked.'

'Don't you have slaves in your home country?'

'In America, slavery ended in 1865.' Pride lit her moss-green eyes. 'My father and uncles fought in the war that helped end that abominable practice. It is also illegal in most Western countries. I hear some members of the Qing court are debating similar legislation, and Lord Li is an advocate for the anti-slavery movement. He wants China to be respected by the international community. Linjing ought to embrace more progressive views before she joins the Li family. Admittedly, I was rather curt with her. But I intend to speak to her again, albeit in a less confrontational manner.'

'Please do not vex my mistress.'

'As a future daughter-in-law to Lord Li, Linjing has the power to help topple the *muizai* system. I must open her mind, challenge her presumptions, make her see you as a person.'

I doubted Miss Hart's chances, for Miss Linjing was as blind to our cause as she was to seeing shades of red and green. Keeping these impertinent thoughts to myself, I said, 'I am grateful for your sympathies, but this type of talk will make things harder for me and the other slaves. Besides, Master Fong will instantly dismiss you if he hears a word of support for the anti-slavery movement.'

Obstinacy stiffened her face and her mouth flattened into a mulish line. She reminded me of Miss Linjing, and I wondered if I had been wrong to come here. I tried another strategy. 'Please, Miss Hart. Coming here is my only reprieve. If you upset Miss Linjing again, she'll find a way to put an end to it.'

'Sometimes power must be snatched, not begged.' She leapt up, splayed her feet and punched her right fist into her left palm. Conviction blazed in her eyes, but underneath it, there was also a hint of blame, an edge of exasperation, towards me. 'To be meek is to be weak. Linjing might respect you if you stood up to her.'

I stood up too. 'I'm a *slave*, not a foreigner protected by a privileged birth and a powerful nation that holds mine to ransom.' A swoosh of regret seized my throat, constricting it like the drawstrings of a sack pulled too tight, for surely my untimely outburst had ruined the only means to help Spring Rain.

Miss Hart's mouth fell open, her cheeks and neck reddening. Any moment now she would scold me, perhaps even strike me. I flinched as she reached for me, squeezing my clammy hands in her hot, dry ones. 'Forgive me, Little Flower. I have been thoughtless and insensitive.'

I shook my head vehemently. 'The fault is all mine. I shouldn't have lost my temper with you.'

'You spoke with candour. Never apologize for that.' She released my hands and gestured for me to sit as she lowered herself back onto the settee. From a tray of pastries she selected one and placed it on my saucer. I wanted to resist, but hunger overrode my scruples and I took a big bite. She smiled. 'Of course you cannot openly defy Linjing. I promise I won't speak to her about this provoking topic again, for I am loath to distress you.

'But I don't regret the inroads our treaties have made. Without them, we can't bring Christianity into the heartland of China, but it has cost lives and livelihoods, and for that I'm sorry. I'm grateful you had the courage to remind me about the darker side of Western influence. Can you give our friendship another chance?'

I nodded and smiled.

Although Miss Hart might be naive to my lot and condescending towards our beliefs, she also seemed amenable and kind. She could be persuaded to help us – I felt almost certain of it.

*

68

That afternoon, I returned to find Miss Linjing in the poky room I shared with Spring Rain. Never before had my mistress set foot in the slave quarters. She was waiting in a chair by the window. On the side table, a dish of roasted chestnuts sat at her elbow; next to that a pair of scissors glinted. Shells littered her feet, a mess that I would have to sweep away later. Upon seeing me, she stood up. With the toe of her boot she crushed the shells, grinding the husks into the grooves of the floorboards.

'Ah, Little Flower, you are home at last.' Her voice tolled with malice, like the taunting noises a cat made when it toyed with prey, moments before the kill. Unlike poor Spring Rain, I'd never had reason to fear my mistress before, but now my skin prickled. Still, I took care to present a blank face, hoping that it was only my guilty conscience, stemming from my conversation with Miss Hart, that made me misread my mistress's tone.

'Have you a task for me, Miss?' I asked.

'Oh, yes. But it won't take long.' She cast her eyes around the room, first frowning at the sight of a chipped porcelain washbasin and tarnished kettle, next glancing at a pair of trousers that hung on a bamboo rack, then tutting at the patched quilt, as if all these things offended her. All the while, she made a show of searching for something, but from her knowing half-smile, I suspected she had already found what she wanted, and this was an act to stoke my unease. Finally, her eyes settled on the trunk tucked under the bed I shared with Spring Rain: my wedding trousseau filled with bridal quilts, bedsheets, fragrant pouches and other nuptial accessories that I had been sewing since I turned fourteen, in readiness for marriage. So much embroidery took time, and Miss Linjing only permitted me to work on them before she woke and after she went to bed as all the daylight hours were devoted to her own trousseau.

'Take out your trunk and open it,' she commanded.

Stones of foreboding settled in my belly; still, I hoped to deter her. 'There is nothing of interest in there for you, Miss, and most of the pieces are unfinished.'

'I will decide what is of interest once I look inside.'

I remained rooted to the floor.

'Do as I say.' Her voice was a whip.

I walked to the trunk and dragged it out. The hinges protested as I lifted the heavy lid, and a pungent waft of star anise struck my nostrils. My folded wedding quilt sat on the top of the pile; in the centre a pair of mandarin ducks swam side by side. I used my body to shield them from Miss Linjing. She pushed me aside, grabbed the quilt and threw it across my mattress.

'How long did it take you to embroider all this?' she asked, hand sweeping over the mandarin ducks, the circle of eight goldfish, the lily pads, lotus flowers and border of cherry blossoms.

'Two years,' I replied.

'Impressive,' she said, but her tone did not imply praise. 'Your future mother-in-law would be pleased with such fine embroidery. Would you say it is one of your best works?'

'It was not easy.' Sensing a trap, I tried to keep my voice indifferent, but a note of anxiety had crept in. I clasped my hands in front of my *ou*, squeezing my fingers tight as I waited.

She stroked the smooth satin bands with her index finger as tenderly as one might pet a rabbit. I wanted to snatch the quilt, to tuck it back inside the trunk, but I dared not move. Perhaps if I stood motionless, mute, played dead like a prey animal, she might lose interest and spare me. But she sprang from the bed, darted to the side table and seized the scissors, gripping them like a dagger as she walked back to me. She shoved them into my hands, the metal chilling my palms.

'Cut up the quilt,' she said. 'I want it shredded.'

'Please, Miss, don't make me do it.'

'This is the price you pay for disobedience. Never forget that I'm not a mistress to be trifled with.'

I dropped to my knees, the scissors clattering on the floor. 'I will gladly accept another punishment.' I kowtowed three times, each one loud and firm. 'Please, be merciful. Spare the quilt.'

'No.'

'I am deeply sorry, Miss Linjing. Please forgive me.' I slapped my cheeks. One. Two. Three. Four. Five. With each blow, my skin grew hotter, but I did not feel the sting. 'I won't defy you again, I swear.'

Her face was a shuttered room, closed off from pleas and compassion. 'Get up.' She pointed to the quilt. 'Destroy it, and I might forgive you.'

Having no other choice, I took the scissors and stood up, my knees aching as I hobbled to the bed. Tears dripped down my face and chin, and I bit my cheek to keep back the sobs.

Miss Linjing had gone too far. I would strike back.

9

Little Flower

Miss Linjing's cruelty made me more determined to help Spring Rain. If one of us escaped, it would be a triumph for both.

The next time Miss Hart fetched me for the orphanage, I stuffed half a dozen of Miss Linjing's silk handkerchiefs into my inner pocket. All were double-sided embroidery – clusters of peonies or camellias bloomed at the centre of some, pairs of mandarin ducks or golden carp swam in the corners of others. She had so many and was so careless with them that she wouldn't even notice they were missing. Besides, I had embroidered them all, so it wasn't thievery. Each handkerchief could fetch one, perhaps two strings of copper coins for Spring Rain.

Once I'd settled the girls into their lessons, I went to the adjoining room where Miss Hart sat at her writing desk, quill in hand, ink-stains dotting her palm. Her spectacles had slipped down her long, slender nose, the end of which tilted up like the tip of Second Fong *taai taai*'s lotus shoes.

Doubt sprouted in my heart – could I trust this Western lady? Miss Hart looked up, adjusted her glasses with the back of her hand and smiled, the kind of smile that spread across her whole face, lighting up her eyes.

'Come inside,' Miss Hart said. 'I see you're troubled, perhaps I can help.'

When I still hesitated, she pushed aside her half-written letter and rose to lead me over the threshold, guiding me to the settee.

'Your hands are freezing,' she remarked. From a side table she reached for a peach-shaped handwarmer and pressed it between my palms, a thin swirl of floral smoke drifting out of its vent. A sigh escaped my lips as I wrapped my stiff fingers around the warm porcelain.

'How can I help?' she prompted, patting my knee.

I returned the handwarmer to the side table and clasped my hands together as I turned to look at her. 'I need to ask a favour,' I began, 'but you must promise to keep it between us. If word got back to Miss Linjing, I'd be punished, perhaps sold.' I swallowed and added hurriedly, 'I don't have a right to ask you for anything, much less to keep a secret from my owners, but a dear friend is in need. She is a sister to me.'

She glanced at the door. 'Your conversation won't cross this threshold.'

I reached under my jacket and pulled out the handkerchiefs. Miss Hart tilted her head, her gaze a question. 'Could you help me sell them?' I asked. 'My friend needs some urgent funds, as much as possible and before the twentieth of next month. I'd be so grateful if you helped us.'

She leant in, and a pale vein pulsed beneath her left eye, its beat matching the ta-dum, ta-dum of my anxious heart.

'This dear friend,' she said, voice gentle and light, like a hand soothing a skittish horse, 'is she also a *muizai*?'

'She is like me.'

73

'Is she unhappy with her situation?'

I slowed my breath, allowing my slave mask to cover my thoughts. For me, happiness was a foreign shore, glimpsed from afar, never reached.

'Forgive me, that was a silly question,' she said, smacking her palm against her forehead. 'No one could be happy in slavery. What I mean is: if your friend wants to leave, if she wants freedom, the church will help.'

'Miss Hart, it isn't what you think.' To steady my wobbling voice, I glanced away, drummed five beats against my thigh before I spoke again. 'My friend is loyal to the Fongs and grateful for her position. We both are. The money is for something else, a private matter.'

Her eyes darkened with solemnity as she clutched her pendant, a small cross of gold. 'Slavery is a blight against the Redeemer's teachings, and I'm not alone in the fight against it. We don't have an expansive underground railway here, but we can smuggle your friend out of Taiyuan to a safe place with shelter, food and employment.

'It takes immense planning and endangers our Chinese Christians, so I only make this offer to worthy candidates.'

I frowned.

'Quick-witted young women,' she explained, 'who have enough shrewdness and tenacity to strike out and survive. I do not know your friend, but I trust you wouldn't befriend a simpleton. This is enough for me to offer her protection.'

I wanted to know more, but clamped my lips, for I still couldn't be sure if I should trust Miss Linjing's tutor. Yet her ancestors had fought to get rid of slavery, and she seemed to have nothing to gain from hoodwinking me. Still, whether to tell Miss Hart was Spring Rain's decision, not mine, so I dropped my eyes to my lap and buried my fingers among the handkerchiefs. Miss Hart placed a hand on my knee and said, 'Devotion to Christ is all we ask in return for liberty.'

Fearful I might betray my eagerness for Spring Rain to be safely under her protection, I avoided Miss Hart's eyes as I pressed the handkerchiefs into her lap and repeated my request. This time she agreed, promising to get the best price possible. I excused myself and hurried away. Before I stepped back into the workroom, she called, 'If I'm right about your friend, come back to me.' And then she muttered, so quietly that I couldn't be sure if I'd heard correctly, 'I could save you too.'

That night, as soon as I slipped into the bed I shared with Spring Rain, I told her about Miss Hart's offer. Though no one else slept in our room, I kept my voice low and spoke into her ear. We huddled together, each of us wearing cotton wadded jackets, a quilt wrapped around our shoulders as we leant against the brick wall; still, without a brazier, the late-autumn chill burrowed through the layers and my teeth chattered as I spoke. The candle on the side table burnt low, its flame flickering, the small pool of light scarcely able to reach us, but it was enough for me to see the curl of Spring Rain's upper lip, her chest rising and falling with short, sharp breaths.

'Why are you upset?' I asked.

'I'll never accept charity from those foreign devils,' she said, slamming her fist against the wall. Her corner of the blanket slipped.

'Miss Hart's offer sounds much safer than your plan. Why not consider it?'

'I wouldn't be a slave if not for the white ghosts.' Bitterness contorted her face, and her voice was sharp, like the blade of a scythe.

'But it was your parents who sold you. Why do you blame Westerners?'

'The foreign devils are hypocrites – people like Miss Hart go about wanting to save "the poor Chinese", but their armies attack our cities, demand access to our ports so they can sell poison all over our country. If there were no opium dens, my father wouldn't have spent our savings, borrowed from money-lenders to feed his addiction, and I would still be at home, probably a wife and mother by now.'

'I'm sorry about your father,' I said, 'but Miss Hart isn't like that. She has nothing to gain by helping you.'

'I don't trust her and I won't turn my back on our deities.' I opened my mouth to reply but she interrupted: 'I've seen pictures of the skeletal man on the cross, the one they call Son of God. How could such a pitiful man be the saviour of the poor and the weak? No mighty god would allow his only son to suffer such a horrific death.' She leapt off our bed, marched to the doors and flung them open, letting in a blast of wind as she pointed to the posters above her head, a pair of door gods, each clad in armour, facing each other, one bearing a sword, the other a spear, both burly and fierce. 'These are gods that I respect and trust.' She bowed to them, murmured a quick prayer, closed the doors and returned to our bed, sitting down with a heaviness that, despite her clenched jaw, betrayed exhaustion of spirit.

'The Christian god does look helpless,' I admitted, 'but that doesn't signify, not when his teachings have inspired people like Miss Hart to sympathize with us. Please, put aside your hatred of foreigners. Let her help you.'

'My mind is made up,' she replied. She kicked off her shoes

and lay down on her side of the bed, pulling the quilt over her shoulders and neck. 'We have so little time left,' she said, her eyes pleading as she gazed up at me. 'I don't want to quarrel. Please, let me do it my way.'

Knowing I couldn't change her mind, I assured her that I'd soon have money for her, then blew out the candle and joined her, our backs pressed against each other. Her breaths lengthened to sleep and I stared into the darkness. Aside from Spring Rain, the thought of Miss Linjing also kept me awake, for tomorrow presented an opportunity to hurt her. Would I have the courage to act?

10

Linjing

'This sample is appalling, even for you, Linjing,' Maa Maa scolded. Repugnance carved deeper lines into her furrowed face. She let out a sour breath and tutted. I struggled not to wrinkle my nose.

It was a fortnight before our pilgrimage to a mountain nunnery, a bid to secure a son for Second Aa Noeng. Aside from my mother, one of us would be chosen by Maa Maa to embroider a lavish offering for the son-bestowing goddess, a long panel of silk damask outlined with infant sons and young boys playing in a garden. A border of pomegranates framed this motif, each so ripe they burst open, revealing segments of seeds. Second Aa Noeng's swollen feet forced her to lie down for most of the day, but the rest of us wanted to be selected, so Maa Maa had set a contest where we each had to sew a sample of the fruit in the time it took for an incense stick to burn. I wanted to be chosen, for my mother to be proud, and I felt quite sure this sample was my best work: all the stitches were even and delicate, sewn with filaments of silk finer than my hair.

Maa Maa took another glance at my pomegranate before tossing the hoop back to me, slamming the wooden frame into my chest. I studied it but found no obvious flaw.

'What is amiss, Maa Maa?' I asked.

'A pomegranate should be fresh, vibrant, enticing.' She jabbed a gnarled finger at my work. 'These reds are the colour of cooked pig's blood, of bruises. Your colour infirmity must be getting worse. What a blight it'll be on our family's name when Lord and Lady Li discover your curse!' She shot a scorching glare at my mother. 'All these years, you have only birthed a useless daughter and even she is marred. Heavens, why am I punished with such a hapless daughter-in-law?' She banged her walking cane against the rug, the veins on her neck bulging as if they might burst through her mottled skin. Collapsing onto her throne-chair, she continued to glower.

From the opposite side of the room, Aa Noeng hurried over, the keys on her chatelaine jangling in distress. She peeled the hoop from my white-knuckled hands. Concern creased her brow as she examined my needlework; the tassels on her hair comb jittered. I wanted sympathy, but when she looked up, I saw disappointment.

'I don't understand ...' I stammered. 'I followed Little Flower's colour codes.' I spun around and demanded an answer from my maid, but the stupid, blank look on her face made it impossible to read her thoughts. I stormed up to her. 'What have you done?'

By now, my three half-mothers, all my younger sisters and their *muizai* had abandoned their sewing, necks craned like vultures. Little Flower shook her head, eyes wide with feigned innocence. But I knew she must be the culprit.

I dashed back to my sewing table. The shaded pattern Little Flower had drawn looked unremarkable: the numbers in each segment of the pomegranate matched the tags on the bundles of threads I'd used. But of course they would! The problem wasn't in the numbering. Rather, she must have assigned the numbers to those rotting shades of red, and I couldn't tell the difference. Tears of frustration pricked my eyes. What had I done to deserve this horrid affliction? *Outwitted by a slave, I'm a fool.* I seized the bundle of threads and raced back to my mother and Maa Maa.

'Maa Maa, Aa Noeng! These are the colours Little Flower's pattern instructed me to use.' I held them up to their faces. 'You see, it isn't my fault. I was tricked.'

Maa Maa's lip curled and she hawked into the spittoon. Aa Noeng looked at me with pity, but now I wanted vindication, not sympathy. She touched my arm and lowered it. 'There is nothing amiss with these silks.'

'But they are the same ones I used for my sample.'

'Linjing, these are the right shades for a pomegranate, but they are not the same as the colours in your work.' Aa Noeng pointed to the remaining skeins on the palette tray. 'Those are the shades of red you have used.'

'But there are no number tags on those bundles.' I spun around and gripped Little Flower's shoulders. 'You sly vixen! Admit it, you changed the tags when I wasn't looking.' Her head flopped back and forth as I shook her. 'When did you do it?'

She did not answer. Instead, her fearful eyes darted to my mother. A look of understanding passed between them, a secret code that excluded me. Aa Noeng said, 'I believe Little Flower. Release her.' Her tone was gentle but her bias smarted.

My other mothers and sisters stared at me, their faces enthralled by the drama. Some of them coughed to hide a thrilled giggle. Anger and embarrassment roiled in my chest, choking me.

'Confess!' I dug my thumbs into the tender nooks of Little Flower's shoulder joints. She winced. 'Speak now or I'll order a manservant to whip you.'

I expected her to crumple, drop to her knees, beg for mercy in a gabble of remorse. Instead she said, 'To quell your anger, I'll willingly submit to it.' Her voice was steadier than the columns that supported the chamber. When she lifted her chin to meet my eyes, I saw a resolve that I had never thought possible in a *muizai* and I understood further threats would be futile: she would endure pain and flayed flesh rather than admit her guilt.

A stirring of respect wedged through my rage. For certain, she was guilty, but that no longer mattered, at least not as much. I sharpened my gaze, pinned hers in place with it. Since childhood, I had dismissed Little Flower as too dull, too docile, too weak, and even though I appreciated her colour-coding system, I had made light of it. Back in Canton, I'd insisted on keeping her because I couldn't bear to see her with golden lilies as *muizai* to Cousin Elegance when I had big feet, but I wasn't fond of her the way my mother treasured Cerise. Earlier this year, when Aa Noeng had told me another *muizai* would replace Little Flower as my dowry handmaiden, I hadn't given it a second thought – I'd assumed the new slave could easily fill her shoes. But now I saw that Little Flower had more than artistic ingenuity: she possessed pluck and cunning, which, if I could yoke and tame them, would be indispensable weapons to help me survive Lady Li. I must convince Aa Noeng to let me keep her.

I glanced sideways at my mother, trying to gauge her mood, as we strolled through the covered walkways that

81

linked the north wing to the south. Her cheekbones jutted from her long, pale face, and the line between her brows had become permanent. Spots of blood seeped through the bandage around her palm, a fresh cut to feed the ink for this morning's scripture. With each step, the keys on her chatelaine rattled fretfully. I shared her worry: what would Maa Maa do to my mother if Second Aa Noeng birthed another girl?

A light drizzle fell onto the pots of *pun zoi* that flanked the outer edge of the pavement. Even though we were still in the eleventh month, frost already covered the leaves. She paused and inspected each one, assessing its profile and inspecting for pests. Frowning at an elm *pun zoi*, she removed the scissors from her chatelaine and snipped off several new shoots. I preferred the soaring oaks and elms but Aa Noeng adored their stunted cousins.

She said, with mild irritation, 'I must remind the gardeners to be more vigilant with their pruning, and they should move the *pun zoi* into the greenhouse soon. Winter will be upon us before the month's end, and I think it will be a brutal one.' She straightened, shivered and plunged her hands into her muff. I breathed deeply, my headache receding as the frosty air filled my lungs. Would the horizon at Tianjin be as expansive as here? No doubt Lady Li would keep me cloistered indoors until I bore a son and I'd have little chance to see the sky. Despite Aa Noeng's dismal spirit I must forge ahead.

'Aa Noeng,' I began once she resumed walking, 'I want Little Flower as my dowry handmaiden. Can you please revoke her marriage rights?'

'I have already given my word,' she replied. 'Besides, I have spoken to your fourth *aa noeng*, and she agreed to allow her *muizai* to be your dowry handmaiden. Aa Sap is reliable, hardworking and already too old for marriage. It'll be an ideal arrangement.'

'Aa Sap is slow-witted. I need Little Flower.'

'Aa Sap is more than adequate.'

'But her embroidery skills are humdrum and she can only follow other people's patterns. She'll be useless to me.'

Reluctantly, she admitted, 'Aa Sap isn't as bright as Little Flower. But loyalty and willingness to serve are far more important than a sharp mind. A forced ally is likely to turn hostile.' She gave me a pointed look.

'What?'

'I know what happened to Little Flower's bridal quilt.'

I rolled my eyes. 'Of course she would tell you.'

'Little Flower didn't complain. Cerise overheard Spring Rain grumbling about it to some other maids.' She turned to me, eyes narrowed with reproach. 'It was childish and unfeeling of you. One day you'll manage a household with minor wives, sisters-in-law and *muizai*. Unless you become mature and fair-minded, no one will respect you, and your sister-wives might even collude to harm you.'

'But Maa Maa does whatever she wants!'

'Is that the type of matriarch you want to become?'

'Of course I won't be brutal like her.' I drew my shoulders back. 'But I also won't be like you. I'll never love a *muizai* more than I love my only daughter.' She reeled back as if my words were a blow, and her lotus shoes skidded on a pile of soggy leaves. She would have fallen if I hadn't reached out to steady her, but I stepped away as soon as she regained her balance, keeping a body length between us. My face and neck flushed. I should have stopped, but I could not. 'I certainly wouldn't conspire with a slave to shame my own flesh and blood. You must have known Little Flower was guilty, yet you defended her. Why?'

'I defended Little Flower because I believed her.'

I scoffed and shook my head. 'Trusting her over me is worse. Can't you see that?'

She rubbed her temples and exhaled a long sigh. 'Linjing,' she began, in an exhausted voice, 'I always act in your best interests. This is why I refuse to tell Lady Li about your curse as I fear it would give her a reason to rescind your betrothal. Of course, once you live under her roof, it won't be long before she learns of your colour infirmity, but—'

'That's why I need Little Flower!' I leapt over a puddle to get ahead of Aa Noeng and blocked her path. 'She is the only one who can help me conceal my curse for as long as possible . . . maybe until I have a son.'

'It'll be impossible to hide your defect after you're married,' Aa Noeng countered. 'I expect the Li household will have a needlework chamber similar to ours. No secret can exist in such a confined space.'

'Well, aside from embroidery, I still want Little Flower.'

'But you don't like her.'

'I might like her more,' I snapped, 'if you praised her less! But you always compare us. It isn't fair, not with my curse. Do you want her as a daughter instead of me?'

My allegation had the opposite effect to what I had intended: instead of remorse, anger froze Aa Noeng's face, and her glare was as icy as a blizzard. 'An indulgent mother risks destroying her daughter's future. I criticize you so you can improve – become a flawless lady who is *above reproach*.'

Fearing I had pushed her too far, I wrangled my voice into one of deference. 'Please, Aa Noeng. Little Flower is clever and resourceful. There is no other *muizai* like her. I need her.'

Her anger had thawed, vanishing as quickly as it had come, and her face slackened. She took a step towards me. 'Little Flower is not like Aa Sap or Cerise. They are canaries, happy to be kept in a cage.'

'Didn't you forbid Cerise to get married?'

'Certainly not! She has been a free woman since we were of marriageable age, but she chose to stay with me. I reward her loyalty with a salary and privileges denied to other servants.'

Excited, I clapped my hands. 'Couldn't you offer the same advantages to tempt Little Flower?'

'Little Flower is a wild goose,' she said, with a firm shake of her head. 'It's impossible to keep a wild bird in captivity for ever. If you try, she will either wither away or eventually attack you. A resentful *muizai* may even be tempted to betray you to gain favours with your sister-wives. I cannot protect you in the Li household, so I must send a reliable handmaiden who is willing to stay in servitude. Only then will my mind be at ease.'

She reached over and placed her hand on my cheek. Her fingers were chilly, and my face stiffened from shock, for we were never affectionate towards each other. After a moment, she buried her hand back into the muff. The warmth and concern in her eyes made me regret my earlier outburst, but I still believed she wanted to fulfil Little Flower's wish more than she wanted to protect me. Yet she was right. It was wiser to be tactful.

'Aa Noeng, if I could persuade Little Flower to change her mind, would you allow her to marry out with me?'

She lifted her muff to her face, covering her nose and mouth as she considered, her eyes staring past me.

Finally, she agreed but warned, 'I won't allow Little Flower to be your dowry *muizai* unless I'm convinced that is what she wants too, which I doubt.'

I would prove her wrong: Little Flower might be clever, but she was still a slave. Surely I could win her loyalty.

11

Little Flower

Miss Linjing did not whip me, but I wished she had. I'd been disloyal – had tricked and embarrassed her. The punishment, though harsh, would have been justified, and I would have preferred the swift lashes over her ominous appraisal. Her eyes were a pair of scales, assigning half a *gan* for defiance and audacity, eight *loeng* for usefulness.

To dispel my unease, I focused all my hopes on the match-maker as she hobbled into Lady Fong's receiving chamber, leaning heavily on her ivory cane. One of her golden lilies looked longer than the other, and both feet were at least six inches. A gale rattled the lattice frames and heavy rain pelted against the gauze window screens. Water sprayed into the room, forming puddles on the tiles; after this meeting, I would have to fetch a bucket and mop to clear up the mess. The stout matchmaker sank down onto the seat next to Lady Fong, breathing heavily. A soft whistle accompanied each breath as she toasted her plump hands over the small furnace in the centre of the table.

'Madam Hung,' Lady Fong said. 'Thank you for keeping

this appointment despite the freezing rain. It is a testament to your conscientious conduct.'

'Oh, Lady Fong,' she purred, 'you're too kind.' She huffed a sigh. 'Hardship is expected for a blacksmith's widow, yet I used to be the daughter of a merchant's clerk. I wouldn't be in this situation if my mother had done a better job of binding my feet.' Her voice was bitter, as though she spoke of a recent injustice. After swallowing a mouthful of tea, she added, 'Still, I am grateful to have this business. It's not much. But it keeps starvation at bay.' Her belly bulged beneath her brocaded silk *ou*, and three chins perched atop her high collar, straining against the knotted clasp at her throat.

'You're too humble,' Lady Fong said. 'Every family knows you are one of the best matchmakers in this city.' Madam Hung grinned.

I fetched the water-chestnut jellies and served them. She attacked her piece with gusto, but my mistresses did not touch theirs. My mouth watered as I sucked in my hollow belly.

Lady Fong gestured to me. 'Little Flower has been Linjing's *muizai* since they were six,' she said. 'She is a capable and obedient girl of sixteen. I would like you to help her find a suitable husband, but you must negotiate for a long betrothal. We cannot release her for another two years.'

Madam Hung said, 'Come here, girl.'

I stepped forward for her inspection.

Leaning on her cane, she stood up and stepped towards me. She brushed my fringe aside. 'Thank heavens you do not have a broad forehead!' she said. 'No mother-in-law wants a strong-willed girl. Your mouth is on the large side, but not so wide that a mother-in-law would fear you might eat the family poor.' Then her eyes travelled to my feet. 'Take off your shoes and socks,' she instructed.

Alarmed, I glanced at Lady Fong.

'Is this necessary?' she asked.

'The peasant families want a thorough description of a girl's feet. I cannot accept this business if the girl has a collapsed arch or other deformities that will make her useless for fieldwork.'

Lady Fong told me to obey.

'*Aiya!*' Madam Hung cried. 'This is a thousand times worse than a girl with natural feet.' Her triple chin wobbled in dismay.

My feet were two gnarled logs, huge and appalling. They had regained their function, and my toes no longer curled under, but they still looked like snapped branches pointing in haphazard directions. Hastily, I shoved my feet back into my socks and shoes, cheeks burning with shame and bitterness. I stared at the rug as I struggled to tuck my fury behind my slave's mask, just as I hid thread ends among the satin stitches of double-sided embroidery, ensuring no ugliness showed.

'Is it hopeless?' Miss Linjing asked, voice thick with pity as she strode over to us, dispersing some of my anger with her unexpected sympathy.

Madam Hung stared at Miss Linjing's big feet, and her mouth opened and closed, like that of a gasping fish. Curiosity wrestled with propriety as she looked questioningly at Lady Fong, but she did not utter the question that must have been burning on the tip of her tongue. A storm of vexation and embarrassment swept across Miss Linjing's face. Even Lady Fong struggled to remain composed as she told Madam Hung about Miss Linjing's betrothal. The matchmaker fixed her lips into a polite smile, but she could not keep the note of pity and disbelief out of her voice. 'I'm deeply sorry for you,' Madam Hung commiserated. 'You must be—'

'If you cannot find a husband for Little Flower,' Miss

Linjing interjected, 'then you should tell us the truth to save her pining for the impossible.'

Pride straightened Madam Hung's spine and she stood to her full height. She opened her mouth to speak, but Miss Linjing interrupted again: 'I suspect not even the poorest peasant would want a girl with half-broken feet.' To me, she added, 'Don't look so worried. You'll always have a home with me.' Her words were warm, like an embrace, and she cast me a reassuring smile. Tempting as it was to believe her, I couldn't forget my shredded quilt.

'I wouldn't say that,' Madam Hung objected. 'I've always found a match for my clients.'

Embers of hope kindled in my heart. 'Please help me,' I beseeched. 'I would be eternally grateful, and I will accept anyone. I hope only for a home.'

'I want to help,' she said tentatively. 'But Miss Linjing might be right. I am concerned that mothers-in-law will be put off by your feet.'

'They are stronger than they look. I can stand and walk all day.'

'It would be difficult to convince the families I have in mind for you. They need strong, healthy brides.' To Lady Fong, she said regretfully, 'I am so sorry, my lady. Perhaps I ought to forgo this assignment. A matchmaker's livelihood depends on her reputation, and my competitors always deliver a marriage proposal for their clients. This is what distinguishes us from lesser matchmakers. My business will suffer if I'm no longer ranked in the top tier.'

Lady Fong nodded thoughtfully.

'If I'm not suitable for a peasant family,' I ventured, 'perhaps I would be useful to a tailor's family or a manufacturer of soft furnishings.'

Madam Hung scoffed. 'They would be even more selective. The sun will rise in the west before such families accept you.'

Touching my arm, Miss Linjing said, 'Little Flower, though you're disappointed, please be realistic. Wishing for the impossible will lead only to heartache.'

I continued to plead my case. 'My embroidery skills are exceptional. I will be an asset to my husband's business.'

'But you don't even have bound feet,' Madam Hung objected, 'and everyone knows golden lilies go hand in hand with excellence in needlework. I don't doubt you can manage basic embroidery, but there are limits to a *muizai*'s talent.'

I cast about the room until my eyes landed on the embroidered portrait of Gun Jam that I'd completed last summer. I dashed over to the open cabinet and snatched up the circular frame, whispering a prayer to the goddess of mercy's image, willing her to help me.

Heart pounding, I returned to the table and set it before Madam Hung. 'This is proof of my skills,' I said.

'But this isn't embroidery,' she protested. 'The subject is Chinese, but it is done using a white-ghost technique. Look at the light and shade on Gun Jam's face. Her skin is contoured. No embroidery can achieve this three-dimensional effect.'

'Little Flower speaks the truth,' Lady Fong said. 'I was equally amazed when she presented it to me.' She picked up the frame and handed it to Madam Hung. 'Touch it. You will feel the subtle texture of her sublime stitches.'

With reluctance, the matchmaker ran her forefinger across the surface of Gun Jam's portrait. Disbelief shifted to delight as she cried, 'But I have never seen anything like it! Are you sure it is the work of a slave?'

At her astonishment, satisfaction bloomed on my face, tugging my lips into a proud smile. Though Madam Hung still struggled to credit me, her rounded eyes were praise enough. I might be an illiterate *muizai* with big feet, but I had surpassed even Lady Fong's embroidery skills. No one could rob me of this achievement.

Lady Fong glared at Madam Hung. Though she did not speak, her piercing eyes made the matchmaker squirm.

'Pardon me, my lady. I did not mean to question you.'

'She has a lady's eye when it comes to embroidery,' Lady Fong said evenly. 'This technique is her own invention.'

'How did you come up with it?' Madam Hung asked.

'Master Fong has a collection of foreign oil paintings. The people and animals in those pictures don't look flat. It took a long time, but eventually I managed to create a similar effect with a mixture of shaded satin stitch, slanted satin stitch and split stitch. I call it needle painting.'

'Needle painting! What a notion! Never heard the like before.' From her inner sleeve pocket, she pulled out a pair of armless spectacles and perched them on her nose as she continued to examine the portrait.

Lady Fong asked, 'Do you think Little Flower's embroidery skills could compensate for her big feet?'

'Oh, I don't know if I can guarantee that!' She looked alarmed. 'I got carried away with this new-fangled artwork, but I'm not sure if I can risk my reputation for a *muizai*. Suppose no mother-in-law takes heed of my proposal? What then? I would be a laughing-stock to my competitors.'

'My father often tells me that it takes a lifetime to build a good reputation,' Miss Linjing said gravely, 'but only a single act to destroy it – especially for a woman.'

The matchmaker's jowls trembled in fierce agreement. She grew restless, pushing her teacup away as she readied herself to take leave.

'Madam Hung,' I stammered. 'Your prominent cheekbones are evidence of your warrior spirit. A woman like you is destined for success.' I dropped to my knees and clasped her golden lilies. 'Please, I beg you to take on this challenge. Only a champion like you can help me.'

She stared at me for several heartbeats. 'Very well,' she said grudgingly. 'But keep your expectations *very* low. I'll look for a minor son who is club-footed or has a hare lip. Not even the poor want their daughters to marry a man who might pass on defects to the next generation. Nevertheless, I make no guarantees.'

12

Linjing

The feeble late-autumn sun struggled to push through a band of tyrannical clouds. In the central courtyard of the Temple of Eternal Tranquillity, a dusting of fresh snow covered the pavement. This nunnery housed a statue of the famed Sung Zi Gun Jam, the deity my grandmother had pinned all her hopes on to grant us a son. The odds seemed slim, for Second Aa Noeng's insatiable appetite for spicy food suggested she would have another daughter. But no one dared douse Maa Maa's hopes. Instead we all prayed for a miracle.

The white-jade goddess perched on a lotus throne with one crossed leg, and the bare foot of her dangling leg peeped out from her voluminous gown. A plump, smiling, naked boy-infant sat on her lap. The statue was mounted on a raised platform, looming over us. Maa Maa told us this miracle idol was only on loan for two seasons before it would be moved to a temple in the next city. According to Maa Maa, Sung Zi Gun Jam had granted at least ten thousand wishes since she'd started to travel across China, and we should thank Heaven that she'd arrived in time for Second Aa Noeng's confinement.

But the deity's heavy-lidded eyes seemed to look down at us with apathy, and I feared she might have grown indifferent to the countless women who beseeched her for a son. For all our sakes, I hoped she had enough compassion to grant one more wish.

The chill distracted my thoughts from prayers. The nuns had covered the windows with a thick fabric, and a heavy quilt hung at the entrance, blocking out the worst of the cold and the wailing wind, but the candle flames still flickered, like nervous faces. Dozens of large incense coils were suspended from the vast ceiling, filling the chamber with the fragrance of agarwood and frankincense; smoky swirls snaked across the room. The heady scent ought to have calmed and soothed me, but my body was stiff with tension and discomfort. The frigid air blasted through my cotton wadded jacket, cold sweat prickled my back and my nose ran. As soon as we had arrived, Maa Maa had instructed the abbess to confiscate all our fur-lined jackets and mantles. Sniffles from my other mothers echoed in the room and Aa Noeng's teeth chattered. A small charcoal burner blazed between Maa Maa and Second Aa Noeng's chairs, but its limited heat failed to reach the rest of us kneeling in the middle of the cavernous room. My mother faced the altar, Third and Fourth Aa Noeng formed a tri-angle behind her and I knelt in the third row, beside Meilian, my thirteen-year-old half-sister. Our maids were lined up on each side of the room, Little Flower's hands burrowed into the sleeves of her coat. Coughs, sniffles and sighs rose and fell, a wave of misery rolling over all of us.

The prayer session had only just begun, but my knees already ached from pressing against the hard tiles. I glanced down at my chain watch and groaned inwardly – another two hours of devotions to endure before the evening meal

95

at five. I longed for the heat of my handwarmer to ease my stiff, icy fingers, but Maa Maa had forbidden us this essential item too, and she had refused the nuns' offer to light the central brazier.

'Phoenix,' Maa Maa commanded. 'Strip down to your cotton *ou*.'

My mother clutched the fastenings of her outer jacket but did not move.

'Take off your jackets,' Maa Maa said. 'We are here to pray for a son. Sung Zi Gun Jam will bestow her blessing only on the faithful. Suffering is proof of one's devotion. As first wife, you should suffer the most and set an example of fortitude.'

At Maa Maa's signal, her junior *muizai* rushed over and draped another fur stole over her shoulders.

Hypocrite.

'You will pray until dawn if I have to repeat myself,' Maa Maa added.

With unsteady hands, Aa Noeng unfastened the knot at her throat. Her nose leaked, and she shivered. From the corner of my eye, I glimpsed Little Flower's face stiffen with concern as she sucked in air but dared not speak.

I stood up, struggling to straighten my stiff knees as I walked over to Maa Maa's throne. A hand brushed my skirt, and I glanced down to see Aa Noeng shaking her head, warning me to stop. But I had to protect her. I bowed before my grandmother. 'Maa Maa, please spare Aa Noeng and let me take her place.'

She thwacked her cane against my thigh and a yelp escaped before I could clamp my mouth shut. I resisted the urge to rub the sore spot.

Maa Maa said, 'That is for getting up without my permission.'

'Please,' I tried again, 'it is far too cold for my mother. I'm younger and in better health.'

Maa Maa curled her upper lip. 'As I've told you before, your time will come if you prove as barren as your mother. Now, step aside.'

I dropped to my knees. 'Sung Zi Gun Jam is merciful. She would be moved by my filial sacrifice.'

'No.'

From behind me, Aa Noeng tried to speak, but her chattering teeth rattled her words into gibberish.

Little Flower rushed over to my side. She lowered her chest to the floor and extended her arms as she banged her forehead against the brutal flagstones, three strikes echoing around the room. When she rose to her knees, a darkened lump bloomed on her forehead. Maa Maa glared at her with disgust.

'*Lou taai taai*,' Little Flower said. 'You are most wise. Nothing is gained without sacrifice. But I fear for Lady Fong's health. It might be a bad omen for the birth of your grandson if she falls ill or . . .' She did not say 'dies' but looked up to the deity with her palms in prayer before glancing back at my grandmother. Second Aa Noeng wrapped her arms around her belly as she turned to Maa Maa, her face tight with alarm.

I quickly added, 'The goddess might be angered if a life is harmed in her name.'

Maa Maa's eyes wavered. She looked from Second Aa Noeng's belly – its roundness so taut that the side fastenings on her fur waistcoat gaped – to my mother, who had by now taken off her outer jacket. Mother's complexion was snow-white, the tip of her nose dark grey as it continued to drip.

'Maa Maa, please have mercy.' I reached out and clutched one of her golden lilies. Following my lead, Little Flower wrapped her hands around the other. We exchanged a look of solidarity.

'Ill fortune comes in pairs or threes,' Little Flower said, voice quiet but grim. 'If Lady Fong's weakened spirit summons a cow-head horse-faced demon, they may also be tempted by . . .' This time, her gaze fell on Second Aa Noeng's swollen bump.

Maa Maa seized her prayer beads, closed her eyes and muttered a string of sutras. When she opened them, she said, 'Phoenix, wrap yourself up and come here.' To her senior *muizai*, she instructed, 'Bring another chair, place it beside me and ask the nuns to light a brazier next to it.'

My shoulders slackened with relief. I released Maa Maa's foot, and in the same instant Little Flower let go too. I smiled at her. Perhaps not accustomed to my goodwill, she stared. No matter, I would soon convince her I was a mistress worthy of her lifelong devotion. I couldn't control my fertility, and cruelty at my mother-in-law's hands seemed certain, but the hardships would be less daunting if I could keep Little Flower, especially now we were on the path to becoming friends.

13

Little Flower

I carried a basin of warm water to the chaise where Miss Linjing sat waiting for me to wash her feet. She smelt of horses, wet grass and sweat, but her eyes sparkled with delight; spending time outdoors always put her in good spirits. After removing her boots and socks, I put her feet into the water and began to scrub them with a soft towel. I tried to focus on my task, but my mind slipped back to my worries. Tomorrow would be Dowager Lady Fong's birth feast and Spring Rain planned to flee during the closing performance of the opera. She was still convinced the opera-troupe leader would offer refuge, but I couldn't share her optimism, though I hoped the five taels from the sale of the handkerchiefs would help persuade him.

A splash of water in my face dragged me back to my chore. Miss Linjing's bare foot knocked the basin of water again, flicking droplets onto my *ou* and the rug. She glared at me.

'Little Flower,' Miss Linjing said, with an edge of impatience that she tried to disguise with a quick laugh, 'I have called your name three times.'

'I'm sorry, Miss.'

I laid out a towel on the rug and she stamped her feet onto it. As I dried them, I braced myself for her to continue to berate me, but instead she said, 'I have a gift for you.' She pointed to her fox-fur mantle draped over a rack, drying in front of the brazier. I gaped up at her.

'Why don't you fetch it and slip it on?'

I had often burrowed my hand into the thick, soft pelt, and once I'd even wrapped it around my shoulders, the warmth hauling me back to a time when I'd nestled beside my mother, cocooned in her protection. Bitter longing had smothered me. Since then, I'd avoided the mantle, touching it only when I dressed Miss Linjing and to clean it.

'It's too fine for a slave,' I said.

She shooed my comment away with a flick of her wrist. 'Nonsense, I want you to be the envy of all the *muizai*,' she cooed. 'Wouldn't that be nice?' She clapped in delight as though she was the one about to receive an exquisite gift. When I still did not move, she grabbed my wrist and stood up, pulling me with her. She lifted the mantle and flung it around my shoulders. I hunched under the weight of it as she wheeled me around to stand in front of her dressing mirror.

'There now, isn't this lovely?' she asked, patting my shoulders from behind. In the reflection of the mottled looking-glass, her eyes sparkled as she grinned, expecting me to be overjoyed too.

'This is your best fur,' I said. 'Why are you giving it to me?'

She spun me around. 'I want this gift to mark the beginning of our new friendship – so we can be like Aa Noeng and Cerise.' I shrugged a shoulder out of the mantle, but she shoved it back inside and fastened the ribbon around the closure, double knotting it.

'I have no use for it,' I said. 'Such finery belongs to a lady.' I tried to loosen the fastening. It was a noose.

'Keep it, I insist.' Her brow crinkled in puzzlement, and I struggled to keep mine smooth as frustration threatened to crack my mask. 'Little Flower, I want you as my dowry handmaiden.'

Panicked, I struggled with the knot again, but the harder I tugged, the tighter it grew. 'I want to marry.'

'Even if the matchmaker secures a marriage for you, it'll likely be a terrible match.' She shuddered. 'Do you want to spend your life sweating in the fields?'

Charcoal crackled in the brazier.

'You would be much better off staying as my maid.'

I stayed silent as my fingers continued to tug at the ribbons and one knot loosened.

'You're living a pampered life with me.' She parted the mantle like a curtain and gestured to my *ou* and trousers as though they were an exquisite ensemble instead of discarded garments from her wardrobe that had faded from peach to dull beige. The shoulder seams drooped, for I was much narrower than her, and I'd had to take up the hems by several inches. Despite the alterations, I looked like a cat drowning in the skin of a tiger. 'The wife of a peasant farmer would never wear silk,' she said. 'Such a pitiful creature would be lucky to wear patched homespun cotton.' She seized my hands and turned up the palms. 'These soft hands will thicken with calluses within the first moon of your marriage, and you will have no time to embroider. Only a fool would trade the easy life of a lady's maid for a lifetime of drudgery, and you're not a simpleton!'

'I still wish to marry,' I replied.

'Why are you so stubborn?'

'I want to be free.'

'But you *are* free! All you have to do is look after me.'

'I'm still a slave.'

'A lady's maid is not really a slave, especially not with me,' she said, with a dismissive laugh. 'I don't keep you in chains or lock you up. Your skin is not branded, and I don't even beat you. You're my treasured handmaiden. We could be like my mother and Cerise. I shall promote you to housekeeper once I become the matriarch in the Li family. Won't that be wonderful?'

She was a pedigree horse wearing blinkers, only able to see the safe, privileged path she trod. How could she understand that a slave's life was a tightrope? Miss Linjing could be as dismissive as she liked, but she was not the one who must bend to the will of another day after day. I wanted to tell her all this, but I pushed down the urge and swallowed it.

Switching to another approach, I said, 'Aa Sap can fill my shoes. I can train her to be equally helpful to you.'

'But I need you!'

'I am so sorry, Miss, but I cannot change my mind, and Lady Fong has agreed to release me into marriage.'

At last, I untied the fastenings. I slipped out of the fur and draped it back on the rack. She did not stop me, but I couldn't read the expression in her darkened eyes.

14

Little Flower

Spring Rain had disappeared last week, on the evening of Dowager Lady Fong's banquet as she'd planned. Second Fong *taai taai* had sounded the alarm and fallen into hysteria, demanding Master Fong bring her back. 'No other *muizai* can replace Spring Rain! I love her like a daughter. I must have her to care for me in my confinement.' Her lies sickened me. I avoided her eye: my hatred would be as transparent as glass. Like naive children, Miss Linjing and the family pitied Second Fong *taai taai*, commiserating with her, indulging her with sweet words. Lady Fong even fed her spoonfuls of pearl powder mixed with honey to soothe her nerves.

Master Fong's guards combed the city, hunting for Spring Rain. With each passing day, worry loosened its grip and my pulse slackened. On the fifth day, I dared to hope she might have left the city. Still, every night, I crept into the praying chamber and knelt before the goddess of mercy's altar. With nothing else to offer, I pricked my fingers and squeezed blood into the ashes, one drop for each day Spring Rain remained in safety. I would continue this sacrifice until Master Fong terminated the search.

When I next travelled with Miss Hart to the orphanage, I could almost relax.

Miss Hart hopped into the cart and extended her hand for me. 'Come along.'

I climbed up and sat next to her. With a light tug of the reins and a soft command, she urged her horse into motion. It let out a cheerful whinny and set off at a jaunty pace. The midday sun sparkled above our heads, but frosty fingers tunnelled through gaps in the thin cotton wadding of my jacket and trousers. My ears ached. The tip of Miss Hart's nose reddened and she shivered despite her cloak.

'It seems Spring Rain has made a successful escape,' she said, 'but you must miss her.' She glanced sideways at me.

'I do, but I'm happy for her. Besides, we always knew we'd part once I married.'

'About that . . .' She reined her horse to a halt and turned to me. Concern darkened her eyes from moss to dried jasmine leaves as she took my chilled hands into her gloved ones. The cold leather offered no comfort. 'About that,' she tried again. 'Linjing told me she is set on keeping you.'

'It is not up to Miss Linjing,' I countered. 'At least, that's what I hope. Lady Fong has engaged a matchmaker for me, and if she finds a suitable marriage then I will be freed in two years.' I recounted the matchmaker's visit, adding, 'Madam Hung is a proud woman who values her reputation. I think she won't let me down.'

'It doesn't sound promising,' she said, 'and you'd know better than I that Linjing is relentless.' Dropping her voice to a whisper, she added, 'There is a vacant spot in one of our safe houses. You would have to stay there only for a week or so.

104

Then I can arrange a ride for you out of the city. After that, we would help you find employment at one of our orphanages, or you could work as a sewing amah. You could be as free as Spring Rain. Perhaps we might even find a way to reunite the two of you.'

I struggled to conceal my shock and reproach – I had come to trust and respect this foreigner, consider her a confidante, yet she was asking me to abandon the safety of marriage for what? I looked down at my hands and did not answer, for I could think of nothing that would not sound offensive.

'Marriage is another type of slavery,' she persisted, 'especially in China. Independence is the only true freedom for women. This is a modern era. Many women can earn a living and support themselves. I am one of them. The wages I earn from tutoring are generous, so I don't need a husband to support me. I go where I please, answering to no one.'

I snapped my head up and stared at her. 'Do you wish to stay a spinster?'

'I will not marry unless I meet a deserving man.'

Dumbfounded, I repeated, 'A *deserving* man?'

'One who treats me as an equal,' she explained, her voice bright with idealism. 'He would be a friend with whom I could converse for hours, or not at all when we preferred a companionable silence. Most importantly, he would see me as a person with free will, not as his property.'

'Does such a man exist?'

'My late father was one, and my brother treats his wife with the same consideration. Until I meet someone like them, I will not wed. You should hold yourself to the same standard. Wait for a deserving man.'

'Women in China cannot be independent,' I replied. 'Only widows are permitted to live alone. Spinsters must stay with their families, and I don't have a family any more. I would be homeless if I left.'

'But you will have the church! Christian charity has no bounds. We will house you and keep you safe.'

'I am grateful for your offer. But please try to understand that I feel a marriage contract has far more security.'

'I urge you to think on it. My offer remains open. It is never too late to change your mind. And you mustn't be afraid. I've already helped free eight *muizai* since the beginning of this year. They are all safe and settled in their new situations.'

Her face was a sea of possibilities, and her eyes shimmered with hope and optimism. I envied her independence and admired her courage, but her lofty ideas would likely get me killed. She lived in a world with boundless streams and rivers, each waterway feeding into another until they converged in a vast ocean of opportunity. I inhabited a shallow, fenced-in pond, and my only hope lay with Madam Hung.

'What took you so long?' Miss Linjing demanded, as soon as I entered the needlework chamber. She pushed aside her sewing and sprang to her feet, agitation crowding her face. Before I could answer, she seized my elbow and dragged me back over the threshold. 'The guards found Spring Rain. All the slaves are in the back courtyard, except you. Maa Maa is livid and—'

My heart plunged down a waterfall of terror, drowning the rest of Miss Linjing's words. I broke free from her grip and sprinted, not stopping until I pushed through the crowd of slaves and saw Spring Rain slumped on the paving, flanked by two guards. I lunged towards her, but Miss Linjing, who was close on my heels, pulled me back. 'There is nothing you can do for her. Please, stay out of trouble. Maa Maa will force my mother to issue a punishment soon and I can't bear to see you hurt too.'

Reluctantly, I heeded her warning. Scratches covered Spring Rain's face, her lip was split and swollen, and her collar flapped open. I tried to catch her eye, but she stared into the distance.

'This treacherous slave will be punished according to the Fong *Gaa Faat*,' Dowager Lady Fong announced. She chopped the air with the *Ancestral Book of Domestic Rules*, then handed it to Lady Fong. 'It is the first wife's responsibility to issue the punishment.'

Lady Fong hesitated.

'Open it,' Dowager Lady Fong snapped.

Lady Fong looked stricken as she consulted the *Gaa Faat*.

'Be decisive,' Dowager Lady Fong said. 'Show me you're worthy of your position.'

Lady Fong closed her eyes and drew a long breath. When she opened them again, I saw emptiness, as though her true self had fled.

'Take her right eye,' Lady Fong told Cerise. They exchanged a sombre look and Cerise hurried away. Dowager Lady Fong glanced at Lady Fong with something that bordered on respect. Miss Linjing covered her mouth and her eyes bulged.

I had expected a whipping, followed by several days of confinement in the cellar, perhaps without food, *not this*. Even Second Fong *taai taai* looked uneasy. Spring Rain begged for mercy, and I pleaded too.

But Lady Fong did not waver. As punishment for my daring to speak out, Dowager Lady Fong ordered a manservant to hold me in place, forcing me to witness Spring Rain's terror. Cerise returned carrying a length of rope with a knot in the centre. She positioned the knot against Spring Rain's right eye and tied the rope at the back of her head before sliding a rod into place. I watched in a stupor, unable to grasp the unfolding scene. Before I could make sense of Cerise's actions, my friend had lost her gentle and intelligent eye. Mercifully, Spring Rain fainted. I vomited and collapsed to the ground.

Miss Linjing stared down at me, mouth agape. Her voice was as faint as mist when she spoke. 'I . . . I didn't know that could happen.'

I turned away from her, wiped my chin with my sleeve and stumbled over to Spring Rain. A bitter toll rang in my heart, warning me that all *muizai* were expendable, even to a mistress as kind as Lady Fong.

I pushed a copper coin into a hot hardboiled egg and wrapped it in a handkerchief. Gingerly, I rolled it across Spring Rain's swollen lid. The bruised skin was the colour of trampled perilla leaves. She winced and squeezed her good eye shut, tears flowing down her cheek.

'How do you feel today?' I asked. It was a stupid question, but I wanted to encourage Spring Rain to talk and could think of nothing else to say.

She shrugged. I lifted the cooling egg and set it aside, next to the half-eaten bowl of congee. 'Do you want the rest of your evening meal or perhaps some tea?'

She did not reply. Her good eye glanced at me, hollowed of hope and expectation. The damaged one blinked, and the scooped socket moved in the same direction. I rose and turned away from her. A trembling breath gushed from me, and I stifled a sob with my hand: I had no right to indulge in tears. No, Spring Rain needed a protector, not a snivelling girl. I straightened my back and turned to her with what I hoped to be a convincing smile. 'Sleep will help speed your recovery.' I lifted the corner of our quilt and gestured for her to lie down.

She slipped onto the mattress and I tucked the quilt around her. Within moments, she drifted off. Since the horror, she readily took refuge in sleep. I whispered a quick prayer, thanking the gods for this small mercy. I remained sitting at the edge of her pallet, blazing with anger at our helplessness, but I had no way to vent my fury.

Like always, I must endure, bide my time – until when? I wasn't so sure any more. Even if Madam Hung secured a marriage for me, who could love a wife with mangled feet? Which family would truly accept a slave for a daughter-in-law? I would be the epitome of a pebble in a shoe, a nagging reminder of their poverty, their failure to secure a respectable bride for their son. At best, I could expect to be saddled with the worst chores – be it cleaning the latrines or washing the bones of their ancestors – but more likely I would be the brunt of their disappointment, a target for fists, sharp nails, canes or worse. Yet I would be freer than I was here, wouldn't I? A slave's life was eternal darkness. Life as a daughter-in-law would be tough, but hope glimmered in the distance: if I bore a son, my twilight years would be comfortable and secure. Like a drowning soul, I had always clutched at this branch of hope, but the currents of despair threatened to cast me adrift.

I startled as Spring Rain screamed, her arms thrashing across the quilt. She bolted up, then immediately collapsed back onto the mattress. Panic scorched her good eye as she stared at me, but she wasn't truly awake. I rested my palm on her chest. 'You are safe now. Go back to sleep.' She closed her eyes and drifted off.

My mind turned to Miss Hart's offer. Should I accept her

help? And take Spring Rain too? No, she was far too fragile to attempt another escape. Besides, what kind of life awaited us? I wanted to believe Miss Hart's blithe words, but we were Chinese women, bound by Chinese rules.

At the sound of a knock, I jumped. Miss Linjing poked her head around the door. I should have stood up, greeted her with a bow, but I did not. Instead, I watched her tiptoe towards the bed, her arms groping empty space as her eyes adjusted to the dimness.

'How is Spring Rain?' she asked.

'She doesn't complain.'

'Poor soul.' From her pocket, she withdrew a square paper parcel, tied with red strings, and held it under my nose. 'Can you guess from the smell?' A smile danced on her lips, the type that foresaw applause.

I said nothing.

'It's ginseng flakes,' her voice faltered, 'to restore Spring Rain's health. But Maa Maa mustn't know.'

I took the parcel from her and laid it on my lap. 'Thank you, Miss. We are most grateful.'

She plopped down on a nearby stool and sighed. 'Little Flower, I am shocked and appalled by our *Gaa Faat*. The brutality is monstrous, and I would have stopped it if I could, but I am as powerless as you. Do you see that?' She leant forward. In her eyes, I saw conviction – she wasn't lying to win my forgiveness: she truly believed in her lies. She wanted me to praise her scruples, to declare she was nothing like them, but I couldn't lie.

'Maa Maa is to blame, perhaps Aa Noeng too, though she was only following orders. But I'm not like them, and when I become matriarch, you will be under my protection. I vow that no harm will come to you.'

'As you say, Miss.'

'Little Flower.' Vexation made her voice brittle. 'I'm soliciting friendship. Why are you resisting my goodwill?'

'I deeply appreciate your visit, thank you.' I stood up and bowed to my waist.

She stood too. 'Look at me.'

I straightened my back and lifted my chin.

'I'm going to be frank with you.' She crossed her arms. 'I must have you as my dowry handmaiden, but Aa Noeng won't approve unless you agree to it. What will it take for you to devote yourself to me?'

'I am sorry, Miss. I want to be a wife and a mother. I won't change my mind.'

'Neither will I!' Her arms flew out, hands like claws, but her fingers curled into fists before they grazed my shoulders, and she wrestled them back to her sides. Without another word, she turned, stalked out and slammed the door. Her obstinacy strengthened my resolve. Though I would be sorry to abandon Spring Rain, I must do whatever it took to escape Miss Linjing.

15

Linjing

Little Flower was born in the year of the pig, but her stubbornness belonged to an ox. I had shown her compassion, patience, had even reined in my temper, but it still wasn't enough for her to abandon marriage. Since Aa Noeng refused to change her edict, I must find another way to convince Little Flower. Better yet, if the matchmaker failed to secure a betrothal, she must concede to her fate with me. A twinge of guilt stirred at this uncharitable thought, but I swiped it away impatiently.

Madam Hung arrived, carrying a basket in the crook of her arm as she hobbled into Aa Noeng's receiving chamber. I scrutinized her puffy, rouged face, hoping for signs of defeat. But I couldn't read her distracted expression as she stared at the new rosewood lantern hanging from the ceiling beam. Red tassels dangled from the dragon heads that rose from each corner of the hexagon. She tilted her head, mesmerized by the floral images painted on the frosted-glass panes. Finally, she remembered her manners and addressed my mother.

'Lady Fong,' she gushed, 'this is exquisite!' She proceeded to point around the room. 'I adore all the red paper cuttings,' she cried, 'especially this pair of carp and the lotus pod. The patterns are so intricate and cut with such precision. But it is too early for New Year decorations. What is the happy occasion?'

'Second Fong *taai taai* delivered our heir,' my mother said.

'A thousand congratulations! This is splendid news indeed.' She clasped her hands and bowed three times, obliging my mother and me to rise and reciprocate the formality.

'Miss Linjing is your only child, so I suppose you'll foster Second Fong *taai taai*'s son and raise him yourself?'

'This matter has not been decided yet.'

'*Ah*, but you must insist! We sonless first wives must safeguard our futures by taking possession of the heir. Besides, it is our legal right. I did so with my sister-wife's two sons. You must seize the infant as soon as can be and rear him in your apartments.'

Aa Noeng's face stiffened as she brushed some invisible lint off her sleeve. She asked, 'What news do you have for us?'

'The best news!' Madam Hung exclaimed with a grin. 'I have received *three* offers!'

A look of gladness flitted between Little Flower and my mother, making a sham of Aa Noeng's assurances to me.

'At first I didn't have much luck,' Madam Hung said, turning to Little Flower. 'As soon as I explained your circumstances, the first batch of tailors' families cut the meeting short, giving me no chance to show your work. But your luck changed when I switched strategy and presented a sample even before I told them your name.' From the basket, she pulled out the embroidered portrait of Gun Jam. 'You should have seen Madam Wang's eyes,' she continued. 'They were as big as full moons! She wanted to know if the maiden responsible had noble blood. She grew a little doubtful when I told her about your situation, but she still agreed to a marriage with her third son. He has a limp, isn't sharp, but he has a full set of front teeth. The Wangs are a very respectable tailor's family, one of the most successful on the Street of a Hundred Grandsons. The apartment above their shop is a little poky but not shabby.'

'This is wonderful news,' Little Flower gushed. 'Thank—'

'Wait until I tell you the other two offers. The Sung family's business is twice as big as the Wangs', and they do not live over their shop. The family has a house with two courtyards on the outskirts of the city. Madam Sung was so impressed by your skills that she offered to take you as the second wife for her first son.'

Little Flower opened her mouth to speak, but the matchmaker silenced her with a raised palm. If I could, I would have gagged Madam Hung and sent her away.

'Wait,' she said excitedly. 'I still haven't shared the best news. For a lark, I approached a banking family with an eligible first son, expecting a polite rebuke. No matter, I thought, even if the mistress laughed in my face. I was so buoyed by success that I wanted to test the limits of your luck.

'The Zhu family have been bankers for six generations. But they converted to Christianity a few years back. I cannot understand why a prestigious family would fall prey to the ways of the white ghosts. But I saw it as an opportunity for you, since not many respectable families would want a Christian groom for their daughters. You should thank the heavens that I took the risk!

'Madam Zhu said that only a maiden of exceptional virtue, intelligence and fortitude would have produced such astonishing work. And she wept when she heard about your background. Madam Zhu thinks strength of character is far more important than bloodline or breeding, and she feels a daughter-in-law who has risen over hardship is bound to instil excellent morals in her future grandchildren. She immediately agreed to marriage with her first son as his *first wife*. What do you say of that?' She slapped the table with triumph. Eagerly, she looked around at us, expecting praise and applause.

I wanted to slap the grin off her face. All would have been well if only she had given up after the first round of refusals. Aa Noeng smiled and indulged Madam Hung with compliments. Happy tears streamed down Little Flower's face. My head pounded with annoyance: Little Flower would never forgo such a brilliant match. But without her, I wouldn't survive Lady Li.

At Miss Hart's instructions, two menservants hauled a trunk into my study, setting it next to the round table where I took my refreshments. At another time, I would have been excited to see the contents, but now frustration outweighed curiosity as Little Flower opened the lid and rummaged through the collection of Western dinnerware and cutlery. She handed each item to Miss Hart, who stacked them in a pile on the tablecloth. There were two plates, a soup bowl, three wine glasses, a water goblet, and a stash of knives, forks and spoons, along with a salt cellar and a butter dish. Once done, Little Flower scurried away to prepare our afternoon tea.

'I have set you a practical task today,' Miss Hart announced. 'You have ten minutes to arrange a table setting for one person, according to the formal dinner-table setting advice in the *Ladies' Home Journal*. But you mustn't refer to it. This is a test of your memory.'

'I'm not in the mood for games,' I said.

Miss Hart studied me with her shrewd eyes. 'Let us sit for a while,' she suggested, as she drew me to the settee. Carefully,

Miss Hart said, 'Lady Fong has told me about Little Flower's marriage offer. She wants me to speak to you.'

'Aa Noeng has enlisted you to plead Little Flower's case?' Incredulity and anger squeezed my throat.

'Your mother means well.'

'Her sympathy is with my *slave*.'

'Listen—'

'No. Save your breath. I don't need to hear you repeat my mother's excuses. It won't change my mind. I need Little Flower.'

'Please rest assured that I am not here to convince you to let her go.' I shot her a sceptical look. 'I know Little Flower is very helpful and important to you,' she continued, 'and I understand your fears about Lady Li. But . . . perhaps . . .' She cleared her throat and tried again. 'Have you thought about not marrying?'

'Is this what my mother asked you to propose?'

'No.' She let out a nervous laugh. 'No. Not at all. She wanted me to help you accept Little Flower's good fortune. But I want you to know that you don't have to marry against your will.'

'There is no greater shame for a woman than spinsterhood. An unmarried woman cannot even die in her natal home for fear her ill-fated ghost will haunt her family. Worst of all, she will have no spirit plaque. Do you know what this means?'

'No.'

'A ghost without a spirit plaque cannot receive offerings from the living. She will become a hungry ghoul, roaming the earth until she has faded to a vapour. Even then, she cannot enter the wheels of reincarnation. I don't want that fate.'

'Do you really believe these superstitions?' She tried to

remain respectful, but a trace of contempt crept onto her face, and I knew she considered my beliefs primitive.

'Insult is not the way to win me over,' I warned.

'I'm sorry,' she said. 'Prejudice has affected my judgement again. Nevertheless, pray – please consider my advice.'

I opened my mouth to protest, but she held up her hand. 'We are on the cusp of a new century.' She was breathless with fervour. 'More and more occupations are opening to women. We can be teachers, nurses, secretaries and journalists. Lots of us have the means to support ourselves, so we can marry for love and companionship, not just for security. We can afford to wait for a deserving man, one who treats us well. I acknowledge Chinese women do not have such choices yet, but it is only a matter of time. You're only sixteen. You can wait and search for a better path.'

'This arranged marriage is my only path,' I said.

'That isn't true,' she countered. 'Perhaps in a few years you can travel to Shanghai and find work as an interpreter in the International Settlement. I can help make introductions. There are so many possibilities! Besides, you're more fortunate than your peers. Of all my students' fathers, Master Fong seems the most liberal-minded. The proof is in your natural feet' – she looked pointedly at them – 'and you often say he loves you best. I think he would accept your choice to stay unmarried if you spoke to him about your fears and concerns.'

Her face lit with feverish resolve and she gripped my hands as though the gesture might impart the same passion for revolution to me. Sweet, naive Miss Hart. She might be my teacher and several years my senior, but her knowledge of Chinese society was as innocent as a child's. Perhaps her views were progressive and rational in her country. But here they were lunacy. She meant well, so I promised to give her advice some

117

serious thought. But the truth was, I could never contemplate spinsterhood. The shame would kill me and taint Aa Noeng as well. Maa Maa would send us both to a nunnery if I voiced such an outlandish request. Besides, Aa De's career depended on my union with Valiant Li. Asking him to sacrifice such a connection for me was impossible. But, thanks to Miss Hart, I knew what I must do. She had reminded me of my importance in Aa De's heart. Knowing that he rarely intervened in domestic matters, I hadn't approached him earlier, but now he was my only hope.

My parents were huddled together on the chaise adjacent to Aa Noeng's canopy bed. Aa Noeng had taken Madam Hung's advice, after all. Though she could not remove my brother from his birth mother until he was weaned, she had installed a secondary cradle in her room and insisted on taking care of him in the afternoons. Second Aa Noeng had objected, but Maa Maa had sided with my mother, reminding Second Aa Noeng that she must submit to the rules that governed first-wife privileges. I pitied her. But for once, I agreed with my grandmother. Soon I would be a first wife, and I certainly did not want to be treated the same as my husband's junior wives. Hierarchy and distinction between our statuses gave meaning and order to our lives, underpinning the stability of our society.

She cradled my half-brother. For the first time, she had removed her nail guards, and the inch-long nails on her fourth and fifth fingers had been trimmed and filed down to a minimum length. A tiny dimpled fist escaped the baby's heavy swaddling. Aa De offered his forefinger and Fei grasped it, forming a tight fist.

'He is strong!' Aa De exclaimed, delighted. Fei cooed.

'He knows you're talking about him,' Aa Noeng said, 'and he agrees.'

They both laughed. The playful tone in my mother's voice belonged to a stranger, one who did not carry the burden of fertility failure. Much of the tension in her face had drained away; even the line between her brows had softened. My father could not stop smiling. Though I stood near them, neither noticed me. Would Aa De continue to treasure me now that he had a son? Like a prying neighbour, I hovered at the edge of their intimacy. But seeing their relief and joy reminded me of my own plight. I must produce a son, but my mother's blood flowed in my veins.

'Aa De,' I began, 'I need your help.'

He didn't respond.

'I need to speak to you,' I said.

He glanced up. A trace of impatience puckered his brow.

'I want Little Flower to be my dowry handmaiden,' I blurted.

My mother jerked her head up, frowning.

He said, 'You must have whoever you need.'

I wanted to catch his eye, but he had already turned his attention back to Fei.

'She does not want to come with me.'

Without looking up from my half-brother, he said, 'A *muizai*'s duty is to obey. She goes where you go.'

'I have agreed to release her when she turns eighteen,' Aa Noeng said. 'She will marry out just before Linjing's wedding. I've arranged for another maid to accompany Linjing to the Li household.'

'You see,' I pressed, 'Aa Noeng refuses to let me keep her. Little Flower is clever and resourceful. No one can replace her.'

119

I tried to keep my voice calm and level, but it rang with frustration. Fei screwed up his face and cried. My mother swayed him back and forth, but he refused to settle.

'You've upset little Fei,' Aa De snapped, glaring at me. His sharp tone stung like a slap. He had never lost his temper with me before.

When the infant's cry climbed to a shriek, Aa De ordered Cerise to take him back to Second Aa Noeng for nursing. Cerise glanced at my mother for approval. Aa Noeng gave her a resigned nod.

'About Little Flower,' I ventured, 'can you—'

'Enough about your *muizai*,' Aa De interrupted. 'A slave is property, no different from a piece of furniture. She does not deserve an ounce of our attention.' To Aa Noeng, he said, 'Let Linjing have her. I do not want to be troubled with this trivial matter again.' He rose to his feet. Relieved to secure his support and craving his affection, I reached for his arm, then shrank back as annoyance flared in his eyes. Had my brother filled the space in his heart that used to belong to me?

'But Linjing needs a willing ally,' Aa Noeng insisted, 'and—'

'Enough! I am the master of this family and I say this slave will be part of Linjing's dowry.'

16

Little Flower

With a copper kettle in the crook of my arm, I trudged to the well. Snow had saturated my cotton shoes and socks by the time I reached it. After resting the lantern and kettle on the ground, I picked up the long pole lying against the wall. My hands ached from the cold as I gripped the frozen wood, plunged the pointed end into the shaft and cracked the crust of ice into shards until I could swish the pole in the water. By now my fingers were numb. I pressed them against my lips and blew air onto them until a faint warmth returned. I was winching up a bucket of water when the approach of a glowing lantern distracted me.

I recognized Cerise's purposeful gait first, but when she drew near I saw that her face sagged with uncharacteristic pity. The winch handle slipped out of my hand and the bucket crashed down the well.

She shivered and drew her cloak tighter across her chest. 'It gives me no joy to be the bearer of bad news.' She sighed. 'But I must fulfil my duty, even the unpleasant kind.' She touched my shoulder. 'Lady Fong has written to the matchmaker to revoke your betrothal. You have become part of Miss Linjing's dowry and will travel with her to the Li household.'

Her hand remained on my shoulder. It felt like a rock crushing me. I wanted to shake her off but despair paralysed my limbs.

'What happened?'

'Miss Linjing spoke to Master Fong. It is his edict. There is nothing Lady Fong can do for you.'

Be good, grateful and patient. Follow orders and always remember your place. My mother's parting words echoed in my head. *A* muizai *is her mistress's shadow. You are there to do her bidding.* Despite following her mantra, I had lost my golden lilies, and now my only means of escape had been crushed too. The time for obedience was over. Cerise's mouth was opening and closing, but I could not hear her over the fury that exploded in my mind. Miss Linjing would do anything to hold on to me, her indispensable tool. I had seen her treat Night Pearl with more kindness and consideration than she had ever shown to me, a living, thinking person. To her, a tool could not think or feel. She would keep me enslaved until I was no longer useful. And Master Fong would give my spoilt, selfish mistress whatever she wanted. My eyes felt as dry as ash. I stared past Cerise into the darkness.

With an exasperated shake of her head, she picked up her lantern and turned to go. Though I hadn't heard what she'd said, I could guess at her sentiments. She would have repeated the same reassurances she'd uttered when she'd unbound my feet. I knew she wanted me to regard my fate as good fortune. But I could not share her love of servitude, not with my mistress. I could endure slavery but I could not stay in it. Bondage tattooed Cerise's soul and she had accepted the branding willingly. For me, this life had always been like soot, to be scrubbed away once I'd earned my liberty through marriage.

Life as a *muizai* was full of hunger, suffering and humiliation, and I'd endured it all. All these years I'd pushed my anger and longing deep, deep down inside me because I'd expected this life to be temporary. My mind was an overflowing vault into which I'd pressed more and more pain and sorrow. I could still force the door shut and slide the bolt against the teeming anguish. As long as that vault remained locked, I could carry on with my duties and submit to Miss Linjing's whims; I could bite my tongue and bend my will. But not any more. Now my feelings burst out and I no longer wanted to keep them inside. I must escape. And Miss Hart was my only ally.

Impatience and anger made the time drag until I could visit Miss Hart later that day. I must give no hint of rebellion, since doing so could rob me of the chance to see her, and I must speak to her as soon as could be.

I stood behind Miss Linjing, dressing her hair into a tight braid before pinning a crescent-shaped horsehair pad above each ear and combing sections of her natural hair over it.

From her jewellery collection, Miss Linjing selected a silver butterfly hair stick inlaid with kingfisher feathers. She told me to insert it above her right ear. It took all my self-restraint not to stab her scalp. My cheeks flushed with suppressed fury. I wanted to hurt her, make her pay for her theft of my betrothal. But I must remain calm. Breathe in: one, two, three, four. Breathe out: one, two, three, four. The silent counting steadied my pulse and kept my blank expression in place.

'You have taken the news very well,' Miss Linjing

commented. 'I thought you would be more upset. I half expected you to fall sick and take to your bed for a day or two.'

Upset? Her offhand tone suggested that I'd missed something trivial, like the chance for half a day of rest from my duties. Not trusting myself to speak, I gave her what I hoped was a resigned shrug.

'Well, it seems Cerise has made you see it is all for the best. I'm glad of it. No wonder my mother values her so much. She is a treasure, just like you.'

Her attention returned to the velvet tray of hair accessories. She hesitated between two hair sticks: a cluster of rubies in a peony motif, and five bats inlaid with kingfisher feathers, ending in five strings of pearls with coral beads. She picked them up, holding them to the window light. After returning the one with rubies to the tray, she proffered the other towards me.

'I hope you'll like this better than the fur mantle,' she said. 'It matches the one I'm wearing. This is a token of our new beginning. Let us be allies and friends rather than mistress and *muizai*.'

I did not move.

'Take it,' she urged. 'Do not be worried that it is too precious for your station.'

To avoid rousing her suspicion, perhaps it would have been wise to feign acceptance and gratitude. But I could not. I pushed away her hand.

'I see,' she said. 'You are angry with me after all. I know your heart was set on marriage. But I truly believe this path will bring you more freedom and happiness. Just think, you will never have someone like my *maa maa* to terrorize you. Isn't that a relief?'

'Madam Zhu sounded kind.'

She stood and thrust the hair stick into my braids. 'In time you'll see I have made the best decision for you.'

I wanted to snap it in half and throw it back at her.

'It looks marvellous on you,' she said. In her smugness, I saw the satisfaction of someone who believed they had acted with selfless generosity.

'I have some sewing to finish,' I said curtly.

Without waiting for her to dismiss me, I hastened out of her bedchamber. If I didn't leave immediately, I would say or do something that could cost me my life. I didn't go to the needlework chamber but to the side gate and into the alleyway. Tall red walls hemmed in both sides of Green Dragon Lane; the Fong perimeter rose on the right and the neighbours' smaller courtyard houses bordered the left. The two mouths of the alleyway opened onto busy thoroughfares. I walked to Five Prosperity Street, where carriages rattled through the snow. The cold had driven most people indoors, and the few men who ventured out had wrapped themselves in padded coats that made them look bloated.

Beneath the eaves of a noodle shop, a beggar woman and a girl huddled together, each wearing a frayed and patched jacket. Clumps of cotton stuffing burst out of the little girl's armhole seams. Scarves wound around their faces left only their eyes and the reddened tips of their ears exposed. Perhaps it was a small mercy that the harsh winter had lulled them into a stupor. Maybe they would enter an eternal sleep and be freed from their sufferings.

The sight of them turned my thoughts to Aa Noeng, and memories of our last day together flashed before me. I hoped she was tucked in a thickly wadded coat, sitting beside a warm brazier. My brother would be thirteen now, almost a grown man who could take care of our mother. Perhaps one day he would open his own carpentry workshop and keep Aa Noeng in warm clothes, with plenty to eat as she aged. I found comfort in knowing that my sacrifice had saved us from falling into the same pitiful state as the beggar and her daughter. All at once, an urge to sprint away seized me. I wanted to leave *now*. I could disappear into the streets of Taiyuan and take my chances with the world. But Spring Rain's missing eye reminded me that I could not afford to be impulsive. I must wait and plan with Miss Hart. With great effort, I turned and walked back into the compound.

'Are you still willing to help me escape?' I asked Miss Hart.

She pushed her papers aside. Her eyes danced with excitement and an eager smile flashed across her face. Her demeanour unsettled me: my life would be at stake and I needed her to be prudent. But she had already saved others before me. Besides, I needed to trust her.

'This is wonderful,' she said, 'I am so proud of you! What made you take this leap of faith?'

I told her about Master Fong's edict.

'He is a hypocrite,' she said. 'He picks and chooses from whatever Western values suit him best. I can excuse Linjing's selfishness, for she is genuinely terrified of marriage. But he ought to have more compassion! If it would not endanger your escape, I would give him a piece of my mind.'

'I will lose my eye if I'm captured. How will you protect me?'

'You will not be captured, I promise. All of our previous rescue missions have succeeded. There is no need to worry.'

'I want to leave as soon as possible. Can it be arranged?'

'You will be baptized as soon as you are out of this city,' she said, grasping her cross. 'Are you willing?'

'If your Christian God can spirit me away to freedom, I will devote my life to his worship.' Raising the three middle fingers on my right hand and punching the sky, I vowed, 'I swear on my life.'

'I don't need you to pledge your life, but I do need absolute devotion to our Redeemer. Are you capable of recanting all the Chinese false deities?'

'I'll offer my soul to the Redeemer in gratitude for your help.'

She clasped my hands, squeezed them and smiled. 'There are several safe houses around the city,' she explained. 'Each one belongs to a Chinese-Christian family who support the anti-slavery cause. They have taken a vow of secrecy. But to avoid their neighbours' suspicion, each family can only host one runaway per year.'

'Does this mean there is no place for me?'

'You're in luck. The Tung family can take you in. They live in a two-storey courtyard house on Beansprout Lane, behind Shengmu Temple. Are you familiar with that area?'

'Is that the one behind a large stone bridge and an ornamental lake?'

'The very one.'

'But the alleyways there are a maze.'

'Do not fret. I will arrange a guide. We must make haste and get you out while the moon is still waning. The darker the night, the safer it'll be for you.' She unfastened her chain watch, pressed it into my hands and asked, 'Can you wait for him at the corner of Green Dragon Lane and Bronze Pavilion Avenue at two in the morning, tomorrow night?'

'*Tomorrow?*' I gasped. Though I wanted to get away as soon as possible, the suddenness alarmed me.

'It is best to make haste. The longer we wait, the more likely you are to lose your courage. Or, worse, betray your intentions to your mistress.'

I nodded.

'Bring nothing with you save the clothes on your back,' she instructed. 'It is easier to move without luggage. You will stay at the Tungs for a week or two, three at the most. We will smuggle you out with the next merchant convoy headed south. They are all Christian-Chinese too and you will be safe travelling with them. Our sister church is about five days by horse and cart. They will take you in, immediately baptize you, and keep you safe until we find a permanent situation for you.'

My head spun. I could scarcely follow her words, but I forced myself to focus. I needed to be sharp and alert.

'How will I recognize the guide?'

'He will ask you a question: "When were you last at ease?" You must answer, "Not since the ink on my indenture paper dried." Repeat the sentences three times. I need to be sure you'll remember.'

I did as she asked. She squeezed my hands again and fixed her eyes on me. 'I hope we will meet again one day,' she said. 'But I'm afraid it won't be soon.'

'Oh, I didn't realize this would be our last meeting. I thought . . .' My voice trailed off, for I didn't know what I had thought. Only that I wasn't ready to part with this kind friend.

'My Western features draw attention wherever I go,' she explained. 'The neighbours will grow suspicious. Let us pray for your safe delivery.'

With that, she recited a prayer and I repeated the words after her.

17

Little Flower

Clutching Miss Hart's chain watch, I stared into inky night. Drums of fear beat in my heart, but steadfast conviction gave me courage: I was ready to turn against Aa Noeng's warnings, shape my own destiny and slash the bonds of slavery. Spring Rain cried out several times but did not wake. Usually she slept like the dead, but tonight she tossed and turned as if sensing my imminent departure, though I had not revealed my plans to her. The less she knew, the safer she would be. My nerves were on the brink of tearing.

At half past one, I rose and dressed, putting on as many layers as I could manage. Though Spring Rain could not hear me, I whispered a farewell. If Fate gave me the means, I vowed to buy her freedom. I pressed my lips to her forehead and wished her safety and good health.

In the courtyard, a gale whipped up the fresh snow into stinging pinpricks on my face. All around me, the wind seemed to howl dire warnings. Despite all my layers, I shivered. But I was grateful for the bitter cold, for it would keep everyone else cocooned in their beds. Fearing the pounding of running feet would draw attention, I put my panic on a leash and walked through moon gate after moon gate, turning down one walkway after another until I reached the side gate.

From the laneway, the crunch of boots came towards me and the metal clang of a night-watchman's gong pierced the wailing wind. He stopped on the other side of the gate. I froze and held my breath.

'Watch out for fire!' he slurred. 'Lock your doors. Be mindful of thieves.'

He banged his fist against the gate doors and cursed. Oh, no, not a drunken fool. In an even louder voice, he garbled the same warning phrases several more times. I held my body rigid and waited. A sour stink of vomit sailed through the gaps between the doors. He retched twice more. Finally, he stumbled off.

But it was too late.

His shouting had woken one of the Fongs' guards from his sleeping quarters, which lay a short distance from the gate. Inside, someone lit a lantern. Whoever it was opened the door and headed in my direction. Had he already seen me? I dashed beneath a stone table, making myself as small as possible as I crouched low, wrapped my arms around my knees and hoped the table's thick, hexagonal leg would conceal me. With terror, I saw his trouser hems approach the other side of the table. I pressed my hands against my trembling mouth as tears tumbled onto my frozen fingers. He set the lantern on the table, and it threw a cage of light around me. Any second now, he would reach down and haul me out. But he unfastened his waistband. I gasped, and the sound would have given me away but for my hands against my mouth. He urinated against the tree beside the table, cursing the cold as his nightwater steamed up the trunk. With a loud yawn, he picked up the lantern and staggered back towards his dormitory. When at last he had blown out the flame, I released a long, shaking breath. With wobbling legs, I struggled up and headed back to the gate.

Once out in the laneway, I forced myself to walk slowly to the appointed corner. By now, cold sweat drenched my back and underarms. To steady my heaving stomach, I collapsed against a wall, resting my clammy brow on my forearm.

A huge hand clamped over my mouth, stifling my scream.

'When were you last at ease?' a male voice growled. 'Keep your voice low.'

I nodded, and he removed his hand.

'Not ...' I stuttered. 'Not s-since ... since the ink on my indenture paper dried.'

'Take my hand and obey my directions.'

When I hesitated, he grabbed my hand and started marching away, dragging me with him. Many times, I stumbled over the uneven paths, but his fierce grip steadied me. The moon was a thin sliver, drifting into and out of clouds. All the shops and houses lay in a thick darkness like black sesame paste. I failed to make head or tail of the streets, soon feeling lost. This could have been another town, such was my disorientation. But he seemed to have an owl's eyes, only lighting a torch every now and then to confirm we were still on the right track.

'Stop.' He pulled me to the ground, where we pressed ourselves against a fence as another night-watchman approached.

'Who's there?' the watchman asked. 'Show yourself.'

His tone was harsh and alert. Within moments, he stood before us. My guide rose, pulling me to my feet. The watchman held his lantern to our faces. I pressed my lips together to fence in my panic.

'What are you doing out here?' he demanded.

I turned to my guide, expecting to see a look of defeat. But his square, lined face was a blank slate. He reached into his sleeve pocket and pulled out a small silver coin, which he offered to the watchman.

'A payment for your silence,' he said.

The watchman weighed the ingot in his hand. 'It's not enough,' he grumbled.

'Three taels is generous.'

My guide remained as calm as a stagnant lake. But I almost wet my trousers from fear. The two men glared at each other. At last, the watchman waved us off. On and on we tramped across the city, turning this way and that, walking uphill and down. I could not fathom the distance we'd travelled – I felt as though we'd walked for hours.

At last, we reached a two-storey house. He tapped on the back gate five times, followed by one beat, then two. The door slid open.

'May Our Lord keep you safe,' he said. With that, he pushed me inside and disappeared into the night.

On that first night at the Tungs, I did not expect to sleep. But exhaustion plunged me into an abyss of nightmares as soon as my head hit the pillow. I woke to find a woman smiling down at me. Dark crescents circled her eyes, and her dry skin was like brittle autumn leaves. But her steady gaze shone with charity and goodwill.

'I am Tung *taai taai*,' she told me, 'and you're sleeping in the servants' room. You are safe here. All I ask is that you help with the housework and hide in here as soon as anyone knocks at the door.'

I nodded.

'You can stay as long as it takes Miss Hart to arrange a safe ride for you. As soon as you are out of the city, you will be baptized and become one of our flock. Are you sure you are ready to accept the Redeemer?'

'I have no doubt.'

'Good,' she said, patting my hand as she nodded.

'Why do you help me?' I asked.

'Slavery is a breach of our Christian values. My husband and I must do what we can to help eradicate it. I am proud to say we do not keep any *muizai*. Both of our servants receive a wage and may come and go as they please.'

Her words touched me. Perhaps the Christian God might be more compassionate than Chinese deities, who demanded tribute and sacrifice in exchange for protection. Again, I vowed to give my heart to this foreign god if I reached a permanent place of safety.

Over the next few days, I felt like a piece of driftwood stranded on an exposed beach. Knowing my absence would have been noticed the morning after I left, I grew anxious for news.

'Tung *taai taai*,' I said, 'is the Fong family looking for me?'

'Do not fret about such things. You are safe as long as you stay inside. Taiyuan is a big city. Your masters' guards cannot search from house to house.'

'Please, I need to know.' When she still hesitated, I said, 'My mistress is determined to keep me, and she has her father's ear. Not knowing keeps me awake at night.'

'There are posters,' she said reluctantly, 'with a sketch of your face. But it is a poor likeness. No one would recognize you from the image.'

'Have they offered a reward for my capture?'

She nodded.

'How much?'

'Fifty taels.'

I gasped.

'Do not be frightened. You're safe here. We would never betray Miss Hart's trust.'

She fixed her sincere eyes on me as she spoke. I had no reason to doubt her, and Miss Hart would not entrust me to a greedy family, so I did not question her further. To repay the family's kindness, I took on the most disagreeable tasks. I washed the clothes, scrubbed the infant's soiled napkins and even cleaned the latrine. The other housemaid, a former orphan from Miss Hart's mission, welcomed my stay, for she struggled to keep up with the work. Apart from the cook, she was the only servant in the house. My hands were red and raw, but I did not mind.

When I'd first arrived, shock and panic had dulled my observations. After a week had passed, I began to wonder whether the Tung family had suffered monetary troubles in recent years: their house seemed to be a skeleton of its former glory. Red paint peeled from the pillars, support beams and rafters. The house had two wings, which included a large hall, two studies and seven bedchambers, but each room was sparsely furnished, and the rugs were threadbare. Tung *taai taai* wore faded clothes and many of the children's garments were patched. Only Master Tung's gowns looked passable.

A household of this size needed at least another two servants. But there was no talk of hiring more staff. Instead, Tung *taai taai* helped with mending clothes and preparing the vegetables for pickling. She also taught her two older boys to read and write, even though children of their background should have attended one of the city's scholar academies. Though curious, I refrained from poking into their affairs; neither the

134

housemaid nor the cook offered any explanation, so I kept my questions to myself, thankful they had agreed to help me despite their struggles. Surely they would have exposed me by now if they wanted the reward. Again, I reminded myself that Miss Hart should be a good judge of character. Yet, fifty taels was a large sum – enough to paint the house and pay for tuition and new clothes.

Despite my misgivings, I did not question Tung *taai taai* when she ushered me into a cart one morning, a fortnight after my arrival. She said the driver would take me out of the city. She'd packed a parcel of biscuits and dried meat for my travels. Into my hands she also pressed a flask of warm tea. She even gave me a thick blanket that I feared she could not spare. I tried to thank her, but she brushed me off and hurried back into the house.

The driver warned me not to lift the window flaps until we reached our destination. I nodded, though the caution was unnecessary. No matter what Tung *taai taai* had said about the poorly sketched poster, I could not risk being identified. I settled back on my bench and braced myself for a long journey. The stuffy cart and the bumpy ride made me queasy. I opened the flask to take a sip, hoping to settle my stomach with some tea. The bittersweet tang of ginseng hit my tastebuds. I could not fathom why Tung *taai taai* would offer me such an expensive concoction. Her excessive generosity made me ill at ease. But the drink soothed my nausea and calmed my nerves. I turned my attention to the street noises. Only the occasional neigh of horses as our cart passed another added to the rhythmic clopping of the horses' hoofs on the pavement. I leant into a corner and closed my eyes, hoping to fall asleep and save my energy for whatever awaited me at the next destination.

A moment later, the cart pulled to a halt. The driver pushed the door flap aside and ordered me to come out. Though confused by the short journey, I obeyed. He gripped my wrist, yanking me to the ground and into the blinding sunlight. I blinked and recognized the stone lions guarding the Fong residence.

A pair of guards dragged me to the back courtyard, the same one that had witnessed Spring Rain's return and punishment. They kicked the back of my legs, and my knees crashed to the pavement. The icy snow failed to cushion my fall. Even though I did not struggle, the guards held me down, bruising my shoulders. I thought I had experienced true terror on the night of my escape. But I was wrong.

Real terror numbed my senses and drove a wedge between reality and perception. Though I still breathed and my heart pounded in my chest, my spirit had detached itself. I saw and heard the next moments as one would watch the horrors befall another person. *This is not happening to you*, my mind consoled me. To endure what would come next, I must believe the delusion.

I was a sacrifice in a circle of horror. Those who gathered to watch ought to have been familiar faces, for they were the *muizai* and menservants I had worked alongside. But they were strangers to me now. Dread transformed their wide-eyed stares into the eyes of prey that feared it would be the next victim. No one looked at me with friendship or kindness. They huddled together, and a few of the maids held each other's hands. But everyone kept a wide berth from me. I searched the crowd for Spring Rain and found her good eye pressed against the shoulder of the *muizai* belonging to Third Fong *taai taai*. Like a wounded animal, she clung to her companion.

Her other lid was squeezed shut as though the empty socket still contained an eye. A gush of panic escaped my bladder and flooded my trousers.

Dowager Lady Fong's predator eyes blazed with the glee of an approaching kill; her gnarled hands were talons as she gripped her cane and stalked towards me. I shrank from her, but the guards pushed me back into place. Behind her, Lady Fong's face was pale and puckered with wretchedness. Miss Linjing crouched in front of me and shook my shoulders.

'You silly, silly girl!' she cried. 'Why did you run away?'

'You robbed me of hope.'

'I am a kind and decent mistress. Life as my handmaiden is no hardship. Why did you make such a stupid, dangerous choice?'

I could think of nothing to say that she would understand.

'You'll lose your eye,' she went on. 'How can it be worth that?'

I stayed mute. By now Dowager Lady Fong and Lady Fong had reached us. Throwing herself to the ground, Miss Linjing pressed her forehead to the snow and clasped her grandmother's bound feet.

'I beg you, Maa Maa,' she said, 'please spare my *muizai*. She needs her eyes. Whip her or starve her instead. Please have mercy.'

With the tip of her cane, Dowager Lady Fong shoved her away. Lady Fong pulled Miss Linjing to her feet.

'It is too late,' Lady Fong said. 'Do not pester your grandmother.'

'But—'

'You must stop before you anger Maa Maa further. Even I cannot save Little Flower.'

Cerise approached with the same rope she'd used on Spring Rain. Flecks of dried blood still clung to its fibres.

'Take it away,' Dowager Lady Fong barked. She bent down until I could smell her meaty breath. 'I have something else planned for you,' she told me, with a cruel smile.

Terror drained the blood from my head and I swayed. One of the guards slapped my cheek, the sting jerking me awake. I tried to get to my feet, but they forced me down.

Dowager Lady Fong ordered her two slaves, 'Bring the tools.'

They scurried over, one of them carrying a chopping board, the other a mallet and a narrow piece of wood. The senior *muizai* slammed my right hand onto the chopping board. I tried to form a fist, but she pressed the piece of wood on top of my three middle fingers, leaving my thumb and last finger exposed. Now I understood their intention.

'No, no, no!' I begged. 'Take my eye instead. Please, it is all I have left to live for.'

'Do it,' Dowager Lady Fong ordered.

A manservant raised the mallet. I closed my eyes.

18

Little Flower

In the aftermath of the mallet, I couldn't keep count of how many times the moon cycled through the sky while I remained in my bedchamber. I slipped in and out of awareness as I huddled in the cot. Often Spring Rain spoke to me in a steady, calming voice, but her words failed to push through the fog induced by the numbing medicine. Still, seeing her made me feel safe.

Miss Linjing made a habit of visiting me in the early afternoons. What did she want? I did not care to know. Her presence was a barb, needling me, when all I wanted was oblivion. Each time she visited, I turned my face to the wall and shut my eyes. But she persisted. I could not stop her intrusions, but she could not force me to speak. In this way our battle of wills played out. It satisfied me that each time she visited, my silence wore out her patience, forcing her to retreat.

Once again, Spring Rain was my protector as she nursed me back to health. Several times a day, she hauled me out of bed and led me to the chamber pot. Afterwards, she fed me thin gruel, followed by more of the sedating brew.

One day, an intense pain in my hand jolted me awake. I rolled over, cradling it in my good one. For a moment, I thought I was back at the execution block. But I found the three fingers bandaged against a splint.

Confused, I looked to Spring Rain.

'I'm sorry,' she said. 'Dowager Lady Fong found out about the numbing draughts. Lady Fong won't be able to smuggle any more for you.'

'But I need them.'

'It has been a fortnight. Dowager Lady Fong says you must resume your duties.'

I stared at her, unable to fathom the thought of leaving this room.

'I'll help you,' she soothed. 'You'll need to train your left hand to do all the heavy lifting. Until then, I can help you haul water for the kettles and arrange Miss Linjing's hair.'

'Is my hand crippled?'

'Lady Fong and Miss Linjing wanted to call for a bonesetter. But Dowager Lady Fong forbade it.' She glanced at my hand and added, 'I did what I could, but you should not expect to use those fingers again. It is a miracle they have not turned gangrenous. At least they won't need to be amputated.'

She looked expectantly at me, but her words did not console me. I wanted to crawl back into the abyss of sleep, if that would even be possible without the draught. She walked over with a basin of water and began to unfasten my tunic-blouse.

'You need to wash and change your clothes.'

I did not protest as she helped me undress. She pressed a soapy towel into my good hand and instructed me to sponge myself. I was happy to obey. Following orders comforted me; I did not want to think for myself. I bent my head and let her pour water over my greasy hair. Her gentle fingers massaged my scalp, reminding me of Aa Noeng's maternal touch. All at once, misery pierced me: grief for the mother I would never see again, bitterness for my stolen liberty and anguish for the loss of needle painting – the one thing that would have consoled and sustained me.

I started to sob, collapsing against Spring Rain, crying so hard I struggled to breathe.

'All will be well again, I promise,' she soothed.

Unable to believe her, I continued to weep.

Winter gave way to spring, and soon the summer heat descended upon our city, but I was still frozen with despair. Gratitude towards Spring Rain was all that propelled me forward each day. I learnt to sweep and dust using only my left hand. Though my smashed fingers had healed, I kept them bandaged because I could not bear the sight of them. To pour water into the teapot, I lifted the kettle with my good hand and wrapped my right forearm in a towel to support the heavy bottom. At first, Spring Rain fed me, but after a month had passed, she forced me to pick up chopsticks with my good hand. Left to myself, I would have refused all meals, for even sweetmeats tasted like ashes, and my appetite had fled. But I could not bear to distress my kind friend, so I mastered it for her sake. I did all my tasks with my good fingers, even managing to open and close knotted fastenings with one hand. As much as possible, I tried to keep my crippled hand out of sight.

On the surface, I stayed biddable and proficient, as capable as I could be with a useless hand. Inside, despair echoed. Miss Linjing continued to hope I would shake off my despondency, as one might dust soil from one's hands. To her, a *muizai* must be as simple as a beast of burden, too stupid to experience real

141

grief. I ought to have lashed out at her. But I withdrew into apathy. I didn't even care to know how the Tung family had betrayed me, which was just as well, since Master Fong had dismissed Miss Hart and I never heard from her again.

Exhaustion was my constant companion, and I might have stumbled through the rest of my life in this way. But one evening at the beginning of summer, my feet led me to the well, the one that Cerise and I had stood by when she'd delivered the ill tidings of my broken betrothal. I leant against its curved wall, pressing my palms against the warm bricks. For the first time since my loss, peace settled on my heart. I climbed onto the ledge of the well and stood. The toes of my shoes protruded over the edge. One step, that was all it would take, just one, and I would be free from pain, loss and despair. I lifted my face to the setting sun, closed my eyes and readied myself for the leap.

A pair of arms grabbed my waist and pulled me backwards. I tumbled to the ground. Seizing my shoulders, Spring Rain shook me hard. 'Why didn't you talk to me?' she demanded.

'I don't want to be here any more.'

She loosened her grasp and I slumped back. She knelt in front of me and gripped my shoulders again, holding me at arms' length, as though afraid I might flee back to the well.

'We cannot let them win,' she said. 'They own our bodies but they will never have our souls. Those are *ours*, always. Your misfortune woke me. Seeing you suffer was like looking at my own reflection. You made me see that I shouldn't lie down and take Second Fong *taai taai*'s abuse.' From beneath her *ou*, she whipped out a poppet. 'I have filled its body with my mistress's hair and nail clippings.' She pointed to rusty spots in the centre of its chest and forehead. 'This is my blood, my payment to the lords of foul magic,' she explained. 'Luck won't always side with her. Soon, this will work. I'll have my revenge and win. This is how you should think too.'

'They've already won,' I replied. 'We lost all hope of a future when our parents signed the indenture paper. I shouldn't have tried to escape, and neither should you. Freedom is for white ghosts, not us. A slave must endure, endure and suffer to the bitter end. I have nothing to live for. Why shouldn't I hasten that end?'

'You have me. Stay for me.' Her voice trembled with pleading. Tears pooled in her good eye. 'Promise me you will never try to take your life again.'

I wasn't sure if I could keep such a promise. Years and years of slavery stretched before me, each as empty as a dry riverbed. One step was all it would take to end my misery. The cool water at the bottom of the dark chasm beckoned me, promising oblivion. I didn't want to abandon Spring Rain, and I might have been able to endure a lifetime of servitude, but embroidery was my lifeblood. Without it, my soul was a wasteland of grey, leached of all hues that used to give me joy.

As though reading my mind, Spring Rain seized my right hand, unfurled the bandage and thrust my hand in front of my face. I looked away. With her other hand, she turned my head back. The sight of my disfigured fingers appalled me. I wanted to shut my eyes, but her commanding glare held me captive, forcing me to take stock of my impairment. Until now, I'd avoided looking at my deformity, always working quickly to change my bandages. Now I saw it all. The first joint of my forefinger was bent in a permanent hook, my fourth finger lay collapsed against its taller neighbour, and the shattered bones around the middle joints had grown over each other, forming a hideous mass that reminded me of barnacles on a rock. Never again could I form a fist, for these three fingers were as stiff

143

as the dead. I tried to snatch my hand away, but Spring Rain tightened her hold around my wrist.

'Why do you torment me?' I shouted.

'You must confront your new situation.'

'Let go.'

She responded by tightening her grip again. 'You still have a thumb and one finger that works,' she said. 'Make use of them.'

'My hand is crippled.'

'Dowager Lady Fong wants to see you shattered,' she said. 'She feeds on other people's misery. Don't indulge her.' When I did not respond, she added, 'If you can't find the will to live for my sake or your own, then at least try to stay alive to spite that black-hearted crone. Better yet, you must do whatever it takes to thrive at needlework again. That will ruin her glee! If you hate Miss Linjing more, find a way to hurt her. Show them that your resolve is stronger than their malice.'

I understood Spring Rain's thirst for vengeance. Anyone who had witnessed her cuts, bruises and burns would sympathize with her need for a reckoning. But hatred was a beast with a bottomless stomach, a beast that would eventually gorge on her kindness and generosity too; it would eat and eat until she might be as bloodthirsty as Second Fong *taai taai* and Dowager Lady Fong. Already Spring Rain's face had begun to look strange and hostile, and though her enmity was not directed at me, it made me shudder. Grateful as I was for her care and affection, I did not want to become like her. Besides, I didn't hate Miss Linjing. Yes, I resented her, blamed her for my fate and would never absolve her, but I did not wish her to suffer, at least not at my hands.

*

Despite our differences, Spring Rain's words had succeeded in motivating me. Afterwards, the heaviness I'd lugged around lightened.

That very night, I pulled out my sewing basket and laid it on the small table in my bedchamber. Opening the lid, I began to examine the tools. Bundles of silk thread rested between layers of rice paper; none had rotted from neglect. A couple of needles showed signs of rust, but the scissors remained serviceable. A length of white silk damask had begun to yellow at the edges. No matter, it would do for practice. Before starting, I took a long look at my hands. Should I retrain my thumb and little finger to hold the needle or start afresh with my left hand? Either way, I suspected the journey would be gruelling. I asked Spring Rain for her opinion. She put down her mending and looked up. The candlelight flickered on her thoughtful face. Finally, she said, 'It is ill-fated to be left-handed. To survive this life, you will need as much luck as possible. You must retrain your injured hand.'

Knowing she was right, I held a needle in my left hand and tried to thread it with my thumb and little finger. Success on the first attempt gave me a little thrill. But gripping the threaded needle with the same fingers quickly sapped my newfound excitement. Unaccustomed to use, my smallest finger struggled to hold the needle and began to cramp after only three simple stitches. Time and time again, my thumb longed to be reunited with my pointer finger, its natural partner. Many times I pulled the thread too far, losing the end as it slipped through the eye of the needle. Rethreading proved much harder than the first fluke. The candle had all but burnt to the wick by the time I'd managed a dozen or so stitches, each as crooked as an infant's first steps. I vowed to continue. Liberty was out of reach, but I had time to spare and I would not quit. To live as well as I could within the confines of slavery would be my best revenge. Even without the certainty that I would regain my mastery over needle and thread, I must trudge forward and keep trying. A life without my art was not worth living.

As for Miss Linjing, I had no desire to hurt her, but our relationship needed to be on more equal terms. I must find a way to make her treat me with as much respect as Lady Fong did Cerise. Only then would a lifetime of slavery be bearable.

PART 3

19

Linjing

Over the last two years, my dread of marriage had continued to mount. My wedding ceremony would take place in a month's time at Lord Li's estate in Tianjin. Travelling directly there would have been easier since Tianjin was much closer to Shanxi than to Canton. But Aa Noeng longed to see her natal family, and Maa Maa wanted to parade my brother before our relations, so they'd decided to host the pre-wedding bridal celebrations back in our hometown.

Aa Noeng had invited her only sister to come ahead of my other maternal aunties and cousins, who would arrive tomorrow and stay for a month of festivities until I departed for Tianjin. Mother and I waited for Aunt Sapphire under the pavilion by the lake, where the breeze off the water ought to have cooled our skin. The sight of a fat carp swimming languidly around lily pads should have been calming too. Yet, despite the bamboo woven undervest I wore to increase airflow, sweat clung to my underarms and back.

Earlier, I'd asked Little Flower to prepare some towels soaked in peppermint water, but she had not returned with them yet. I twisted about on the stool, failing to find a comfortable position. I envied Second Aa Noeng's serenity. At the far end of the pavilion, she sat in a rocking chair nursing Fei. She looked as cool as a dish of shaved ice; every now and then she tickled his belly, making him giggle. He should have been weaned by his second birthday, three months ago. But when he was in a petulant mood, only nursing could settle him, so Maa Maa had allowed him to continue until I set off for Tianjin. She worried his tantrums would reflect badly on our family's breeding to our relatives.

The change in Second Aa Noeng's appearance astonished me. Since giving birth and throughout the journey back to Canton City, she'd looked exhausted: blotchy patches had covered her waxy skin and grey crescents had marked the area under her eyes. We'd been back for scarcely a fortnight, but now she glowed. There was a fresh energy to her movements and her bright eyes glinted with new confidence. I could not fathom this metamorphosis, for after my wedding she would have to surrender Fei to my mother. With this in mind, I would have expected Second Aa Noeng to look wan and dejected, yet she was the picture of good health. Perhaps she still hoped for a miracle.

When Fei turned away from his mother's chest, Aa Noeng beckoned him over with a new toy train and a piece of marzipan. He squealed with delight, ran over and climbed onto her lap. She popped the sweet into his mouth and stroked his downy hair as he pushed the train back and forth on the table.

Without turning to look at Second Aa Noeng, my mother told her, 'You may go now, Peony. Cerise will return Fei to you when he is ready for a nap.'

'No. I prefer to stay.'

My mother's head snapped up. She shot her a look that

could have stopped a charging horse, but Second Aa Noeng did not flinch. 'I will stay,' she repeated.

The corners of my mother's mouth twitched as she glared at her sister-wife, who stared back with a polite but determined smile. I was stunned: my father's minor wives had never treated my mother with such blatant defiance. She did not seem to know how to respond. Second Aa Noeng must be overwrought from her efforts to conceal her misery as she counted down the days until she would have to give up Fei. Sympathy prompted me to speak in her support.

'Why not let her stay?' I said to Aa Noeng. 'She can soothe Fei if he gets fussy, so you can speak to Aunt Sapphire in peace.'

My mother might have objected and upbraided me for impertinence, but at that moment, Aunt Sapphire approached from the garden path, accompanied by Cerise. My mother set Fei on the floor, where he began to push the train along the perimeter of the pavilion. She rose to meet her sister.

Despite having golden lilies, Aunt Sapphire still managed to walk with firm, assured steps. Unlike my mother, who always wore long, full skirts cut from coloured silk, Aunt Sapphire's black habit comprised a knee-length tunic and matching trousers. A motif of bamboo leaves, woven into the black damask with silver threads, shimmered like armour in the morning light.

She was a much taller and broader version of my mother. Aa Noeng, whom I'd always perceived as poised and regal, swayed like a fragile bamboo sapling next to Aunt Sapphire's sturdy frame. My aunt stood a head taller. I had, of course, met Aunt Sapphire several times each year before we moved to Shanxi, but I was only six years old when I had last seen her. In my memory, she was an outspoken black-clad figure. I didn't know much more about her except that she was the mother superior at a Celibate Sisterhood. Those women always wore black, never married and worked long hours reeling silk in a factory. It sounded like a miserable life.

A jade hair stick speared Aunt Sapphire's wiry grey bun. The tiny silver bells attached to Aa Noeng's chatelaine chimed as she pulled my aunt into an eager embrace. When they finally released each other, their hands remained linked while they stood at arms' length, studying each other.

'It's been too long!' Aunt Sapphire cried. 'One month is scarcely enough time to make up for twelve years.'

'Dear Sapphire *ze*, I have missed you!' my mother exclaimed. 'I'm so happy you could spare the time away from your duties. Does the sisterhood mind your absence?'

'Oh, don't be concerned about me,' my aunt replied, with a blithe laugh. 'There is nobody to order me about. I come and go as I please.' She squeezed my mother's upper arm and waist. 'You have grown thinner. I thought you'd merely lost the youthful plumpness in your cheeks. Now I see you are thin indeed. Is something troubling you?'

'Dear sister, you always have such a keen eye. I am troubled about Linjing's wedding preparations.'

'Whatever could be the problem?' Aunt Sapphire asked, noticing me at last. I rose to greet her with a deep bow as she walked towards my seat. She acknowledged me with a warm smile before turning back to my mother. 'This is a month of festivity!' she cried. 'It's your last chance to enjoy Linjing's company before she joins another family. And it's an opportunity to sew, eat and converse with our aunts, cousins and nieces. Why do you look so glum?'

'I am troubled by Lady Li,' Aa Noeng explained. 'She should have sent shoe patterns or samples of existing shoes to us at least six months ago.'

'Why do you need them?' Aunt Sapphire asked.

'It is their marriage custom,' I replied. 'Lady Li expects me to present a pair of embroidered lotus shoes for her and each of the ladies of the Li household on my wedding day. During the ceremony, the shoes will be displayed on tasselled silk beds for inspection.'

'I am glad we do not have this custom,' Second Aa Noeng said. 'Shoes are the ultimate test of a bride's embroidery expertise and feminine virtues.'

'*Shoes* as wedding gifts?' Aunt Sapphire all but shouted. 'That is ill-omened.'

'They speak Mandarin in the north,' my mother reminded her. 'The character for shoes might sound like a sigh in Cantonese, but it has no ill association in Mandarin.'

'I see,' Aunt Sapphire said. 'Still, I do not approve of it.'

'There is nothing to be done about it,' Second Aa Noeng chimed in. She quoted an adage: '*Marry a chicken, live like a chicken. Marry a dog, live like a dog.* It is a woman's fate to yield to her husband's and mother-in-law's whims.'

Even my mother nodded in agreement.

'If it is so important to them, why hasn't Lady Li provided the shoe patterns?' Aunt Sapphire asked.

'It troubles me deeply. I have written on three occasions to prompt her.'

'What did she say about the delay?'

'Nothing,' Aa Noeng said. 'That is to say, I have received half a dozen letters from her about trivial matters. But not a word about these shoe patterns.'

I added, 'We don't even know how many pairs are needed.'

Aunt Sapphire's brow gathered into a thoughtful knot. 'Lady Li is going to be a spiteful mother-in-law. I am certain it has something to do with Linjing's big feet. By withholding the patterns, she ensures that Linjing can't make the shoes.'

153

'You've voiced my worst fears,' my mother said. 'I always suspected Lady Li would not approve of natural feet. Dear Sapphire *ze*, what should we do?'

'Nothing can remedy the situation,' my aunt said gravely. 'Linjing had best learn to swallow bitterness. There will no doubt be years of hardship ahead of her. That is the fate of brides.'

Aunt Sapphire's eyes filled with pity as she looked at me. My mother slumped onto a stool and I sank down beside her.

The next morning, a breathless Little Flower hastened into my bedchamber, carrying a rectangular shoe-storage chest.

'This has just arrived,' she said. 'It was delivered by a man-servant who said he works for Lady Li.' She set it on the table.

'Oh, Little Flower, I have an awful feeling about this.'

'If it is bad, we had better find out sooner rather than later. Do you want me to take the shoes out?' Her calm voice and sensible words steadied my nerves, and in her eyes I saw genuine understanding, not like the mask she used to hide behind. Over the last two years, we had become like Aa Noeng and Cerise, and our friendship gave me courage. Knowing Little Flower would find a solution, no matter what trap awaited me in the box, I gestured for her to open it.

I wrapped my hands around a teacup, gripping it tight as I watched Little Flower. She removed both halves of the lid and placed them on the table, then opened the doors. Now the chest looked like a display cabinet. Four small red silk parcels sat on the top tier and another four identical parcels peered out from the second. She unfurled the wrappings to reveal eight tiny pairs of exquisite shoes and bootees. All had arched wooden heels covered with ivory silk, and the sloping vamps curved downwards, like the beak of a parrot. Tiny gold sequins adorned the tip of the most graceful pair: bootees fashioned from black silk, with a blooming water lily in the centre of the uppers, flanked by mandarin ducks. The quality of their embroidery alone would have been enough to intimidate me, but each pair also fitted into the palms of our hands. My mother-in-law and all the ladies of the house had four-inch golden lilies!

'One pair of four-inch golden lilies could be good luck,' I cried. 'But *eight perfect* pairs?'

'That could only be achieved with fierce willpower and fortitude,' Little Flower said.

'How could a family of such exacting standards accept my big feet?'

'There is also a letter,' she said solemnly.

With shaky hands, I picked it up.

'Go on,' Little Flower urged softly. 'Open it.'

My hands tightened around the paper, but I could not bring myself to break the wax seal.

'We have already seen the worst of it. Why do you still look so frightened?'

I opened my mouth but could not speak, as though giving voice to my worries would make them true. I thrust the letter into her hand. 'Please, you read it,' I said.

'But, Miss, I know only a few characters.'

'Yes, of course.'

She broke the wax seal, opened the letter and placed it in my trembling hands.

First Daughter-in-Law,
I do apologize for the belated delivery of these shoe samples. Alas, it could not be helped, for my fourth daughter's golden

lilies did not achieve their ultimate four-inch length until recently. We live in Tianjin, but my natal family is from Shandong province. We place the greatest importance on bound feet; even poor peasant women who work in the fields have six- or seven-inch golden lilies. So, you see, I knew it would be only a matter of time before my youngest daughter earned this vital feminine virtue, just like all her sisters and aunts. I did not want you to waste your time and energy on making shoes that would be far too large by the time you presented them to your youngest sister-in-law.

I eagerly look forward to seeing the fruits of your labour. My manservant will remain in Canton City and collect the shoes from you before you commence your journey to Tianjin. He will ride ahead of the wedding convoy to deliver the shoes to me before you step over our threshold. A month is not a long time; you must make haste.

Yours sincerely,

Lady Li

I lifted my eyes from the page to find Little Flower looking as thunderstruck as I felt.

'Lady Li will never accept me!' I cried. 'Her rebuke is clear – she despises big feet. I will be treated like a leper!' My voice rose to the point of cracking. I pressed my lips together to stem my panic. I needed calmness, not hysteria. But I continued to shudder with fear.

For the first time in my life, Aa De's high opinion of me seemed like a curse, one far worse than my visual infirmity. My half-sisters' golden lilies would help safeguard them against some of their future mothers-in-law's enmity. But Lady Li's letter had confirmed my worst fear. She must resent Lord Li's decision to impose a daughter-in-law with natural feet on her family, yet a man was beyond reproach. I would be defenceless once I entered her sphere of power. If it were possible to drown in panic, I would have been dead. I covered my face with my hands and struggled to steady my breathing. Little Flower stroked my back until my ragged breaths slowed to a calmer rhythm. I dropped my hands and she turned me to face her.

'There is nothing we can do to fix your feet,' she said. 'But I have an idea that might help us finish the shoes in time.'

'How can we? It takes at least a week to embroider and assemble just one pair,' I protested. 'There are only . . .' I paused and counted '. . . twenty-eight days until Lady Li's manservant returns. I can't spend my days sewing. I need to entertain the guests. There isn't enough time! And I am sure Lady Li will know if the shoes are made by different hands.'

'It won't be easy,' she admitted, 'but we must try. Lady Li wants to humiliate you on your wedding day. We can't let her succeed without at least trying to do something about it. Do you want to hear my plan?'

Though doubtful, I nodded.

'We must divide and conquer,' she said. 'It will be a tight schedule, but if we each make four pairs of shoes it might be possible. I know your needlework well enough to imitate your stitches. To keep it simple, I will create only two designs. For Lady Li's shoes, I'll use a chrysanthemum motif since all older ladies prefer a symbol of longevity. The other seven pairs will be decorated with lotuses. It's a safe choice that will ensure no one is offended. Most importantly, all the flowers and leaves must be embroidered with solid colours. The end result won't be sophisticated, but it'll make it easier for our needlework to be indistinguishable. Your visual infirmity won't matter. What do you think?'

What a treasure she was!

I had been right to keep her. Again, she had proven her worth. No one else could fill Little Flower's shoes: she was creative and resourceful – even if she'd never been able to embroider again, her ingenuity would have been valuable to me, but I was relieved she'd regained her skills.

A pinprick of remorse stabbed me as I recalled how close I'd come to losing Little Flower's talent. Maa Maa had proven to be the mistress of cruelty when she'd punished Little Flower. For most people, I suspected that losing three fingers to save an eye would have been a good trade. But Maa Maa had known Little Flower valued embroidery more than her life. In the months after her foolish escape attempt, I'd begun to think I'd made a mistake in forcing her to stay as my dowry handmaiden. I'd endangered her life and reduced her to a common *muizai*, like Aa Sap. Perhaps I should have asked Aa Noeng to salvage her betrothal. Yet no other handmaiden could match her ingenuity, so I'd clung to the hope that she'd regain her former creativity.

One day, about six months after the punishment, I visited Little Flower's room. I found her alone, sewing on her bed. A bunch of rudimentary stitches crisscrossed the fabric. I'd never known a person to embroider with only thumb and little finger, but if anyone could do it, she would.

'Little Flower,' I said, 'I'm very glad you have taken up embroidery again. You must believe me. I didn't want to hurt you.'

I sat down on her bed and waited. After several minutes, she finally put the hoop and needle aside and looked at me. 'Are we speaking as mistress and slave?' she asked. 'Or person to person?'

For a moment, I didn't know how to reply, then I said, 'We

are bonded for life now, destined to live side by side. I hope you will see us as friends, like Mother and Cerise.'

'They are not friends.'

'Of course they are.'

'Lady Fong is a kind mistress, but Cerise is still a servant.'

Her comment made my statement sound foolish.

'Why did you run away?' I asked. I'd asked this question many times before, but she hadn't given me a satisfactory answer. When she remained mute, I said, 'Do you think I'm as cruel as Maa Maa?' She still hesitated. 'Let us speak person to person,' I said. 'As equals, even if it is only this once. I need to know the truth.'

'Your grandmother is as black-hearted as a demon,' she said. 'You are not like her.'

'Then why did you run away?'

'I need to be free.'

'Life with me will be far better than the false liberty you would have gained as a wife. Look to Cerise. Her life is easy, and she reigns over all the servants. Doesn't she have more freedom than my mothers?'

'Lady Fong would never force Cerise to do anything against her will. You don't treat me with the same consideration.'

Her voice was calm and sure – like mine. Her bold accusation stunned me into silence. I tried to look away, but her condemning eyes locked me in place.

I admitted, 'I haven't always treated you fairly.' Uncertain how much of my thought I ought to reveal, I paused. Saying too much might erode my authority, but I must say enough to gain her loyalty.

'Sometimes it is hard for me to see Aa Noeng treat you like a daughter,' I continued. 'It pains me to be compared to you. But I promise I will not punish you any more. From now on, you will find a fair and considerate mistress in me, I promise. Can we please start again?'

She half smiled and did not resist when I embraced her.

Over the last two years, I'd watched her closely and now felt almost certain that she bore me no grudge. She'd continued to apply herself to her embroidery with fierce resolve, and her tenacity won my respect. I needed an incorruptible ally in the Li household. Many obstacles and hardships lay in wait for me, but Little Flower was unlikely to be one of them.

20

Little Flower

Since my candid talk with Miss Linjing, I had laid aside my grief and loss, pushing them into the recesses of my mind. We'd reached a sort of harmony as I tried to make peace with a life-time of servitude. But Miss Linjing's bridal festivities threatened to dredge up the past. All over the Fong residence, scarlet paper cuttings festooned the walls, lattice windows and door frames. In every direction I turned, my eyes would land on a provoking image: characters for 'double happiness', cut to look like a couple linking hands; duos of mandarin ducks swimming in circles of bliss; and pairs of dragons and phoenixes soaring towards the heavens. Overhead, vermilion silk streamers hung in waves across the rafters; the fabric at each crest had been gathered into a pompom the size of a watermelon. Wide ribbons in the same colour draped the support columns and all the entranceways. I was drowning in a sea of red. The wedding motifs mocked my lost betrothal, and it took all my self-control to restrain my bitterness and focus on the task at hand. Giving way to despair would lead me down a destructive path; I'd promised myself that I would not visit that dark place again.

With immense exertion, I forced my mind to swim away from the whirlpool of lost dreams and crawl onto the shores of reality. With only thirteen days until Miss Linjing and I set out for Tianjin, Cerise said it was time for me to learn how to create a married lady's chignon. The four of us gathered in Lady Fong's bedchamber. Miss Linjing and her mother sat side by side on stools in front of a large trifold looking-glass that sat atop her dressing-table. Cerise and I stood behind our mistresses. On a nearby counter, I'd added a handful of nanmu woodchips and drops of tea-seed oil to a basin of cool water. Cerise and I each picked up a small brush that had been soaking in this mixture for the last quarter of an hour. We combed our mistresses' hair, moving slowly from the roots to the ends to allow the lotion to seep into the follicles. But the mixture struggled to tame the frizzy hair around Miss Linjing's temples. I had to wet the brush twice more before I managed to wrestle it into sleekness. Miss Linjing's fidgeting didn't help, for she absentmindedly scratched the sides of her head as she struggled to stitch the uppers of a shoe to the sole. So far, Miss Linjing had finished Lady Li's lotus shoes, and I had completed three other pairs. To reach our goal, I'd have to sacrifice more sleep to bridge the gap left by my mistress's slow progress. Not only was she frequently called away from shoemaking to socialize with her relatives, but her nerves also made her fingers clumsy. Her stitches often bunched together, forcing her to unpick her work as she was doing now. She scratched her head, messing up her hair again.

'Miss,' I suggested, 'perhaps you should take a break from sewing.'

'I can't spare the time,' Miss Linjing objected. 'We still have three pairs of shoes to make, not counting these.'

Her voice, which was usually low and steady, took on a

shrill, frenzied edge whenever we spoke about the shoes. At moments like this, I could almost forgive her theft of my freedom. No doubt her insistence on keeping me was selfish, but it was not wicked: she had acted out of fear. She'd also upheld her promise to treat me with fairness and as much respect as a lady could bestow on a slave.

'Little Flower cannot dress your hair if you don't hold your head still,' Lady Fong said. 'She must learn a married woman's style before you leave home.'

'We will finish a lot faster if you don't move,' Cerise added, 'and please try to keep your hands in your lap.'

With resignation, Miss Linjing put the upper and the sole aside and adopted the position Cerise had suggested.

Cerise split Lady Fong's waist-length hair into three sections, with a centre parting down her scalp; I did the same with Miss Linjing's. I tied the front sections into two bundles, keeping them out of the way as I worked on the back of her hair. Mimicking Cerise, I pinned a large, bean-shaped horsehair pad on the crown of her head and spread her natural hair over it, creating considerable height. With ten deft fingers, Cerise was able swiftly to twist and twirl Lady Fong's hair into a smooth chignon. I could not hope to do the same, for my three stiff fingers would not hold any hair in place. I fetched a pair of clean ivory chopsticks. Cerise cast a questioning glance at me.

'I think I can use them to create a braided bun for Miss Linjing,' I explained, 'like the sort that Miss Hart sometimes wore.'

'That is not traditional,' Cerise said. 'A Han Chinese lady's chignon should be smooth.'

'Would you object to a braided bun?' I asked Miss Linjing.

'I don't mind what you do, as long as you finish quickly

163

so we can get back to the lotus shoes. There are only thirteen days left until Lady Li's manservant comes to collect them!'

Cerise opened her mouth to object, but Lady Fong said, 'Let's see what Little Flower can achieve.'

Lady Fong gave me an encouraging smile, which I returned in earnest. Though I sometimes struggled to contain my bitterness for Miss Linjing, I harboured no resentment towards her mother and would be sorry to part from her. Like Miss Linjing, I dreaded the ill-treatment that would befall us at the Li household. As a *muizai* I might be beneath Lady Li's notice, but my fellow servants would take their cue from her treatment of my mistress; it seemed Miss Linjing would have a hard time of it, which meant I should brace for ridicule too.

I inserted a chopstick into the midsection on top of the pad and aligned the second stick horizontally below it, leaving a finger gap between the two. I wove Miss Linjing's hair over and under them, creating a four-stranded braid as I moved each stick down the length of her tresses. They acted like a third hand, helping to keep the strands in place. Finally, I rolled the braid under itself and tucked the coil at the nape of her neck, using several pins to fasten it. The effect looked far more intricate and elegant than I had dared hope. I picked up a hand mirror and held it behind Miss Linjing. She took a distracted glance and waved the mirror away.

'Hurry,' she said. 'Please finish so we can resume sewing.'

'Cerise, can you please fetch my gift for Linjing?' Lady Fong asked. Turning Linjing around so they faced each other, she said, 'It is time I deliver an important lesson to you.'

Cerise opened a drawer and gave my mistress a long, narrow, lacquered box. Upon opening it, Miss Linjing found a gold ornamental comb with a phoenix motif, identical to the one on the crown of Lady Fong's head.

'I had it replicated by the best jeweller in Canton City,' Lady Fong explained. 'Your maternal grandmother did the same for me, and her mother gave her the same comb just before she married. It is a symbol of your first-wife status. Your father's minor wives know they must never wear a phoenix motif or copy my signature hairstyle.

'Your maternal grandmother told me that it is not enough to have the title of Lady Fong or, in your case, Lady Li: you must also find ways to remind your sister-wives that you are the principal wife. Only then will you retain control over them. I suggest you follow my example and set down the same rules as soon as your sister-wives enter your household.'

'But it is only hair.'

'It is a sign of their submission to you.'

Miss Linjing continued to look sceptical.

'*Aiya*, Miss Linjing!' Cerise cried. 'You mustn't doubt your mother's wisdom. Your *maa maa* was far stricter. You are too young to remember this, but when Old Master Fong's two minor wives were still alive, Dowager Lady Fong forbade them to use false hair even though both of them barely had enough to create a simple bun. Only Dowager Lady Fong was allowed to look dignified.

'I've urged your mother to adopt the same practice. But she is kind-hearted. This is why the other Fong *taai taai* can do as they please, as long as they do not mimic or upstage my lady's coiffure.'

Understanding dawned on my mistress as she nodded solemnly. But unease settled in my stomach like a stone as I recalled a remark Spring Rain had made a few days ago. She'd mentioned Second Fong *taai taai*'s sudden interest in emulating Lady Fong's signature style with a similar ornamental comb. It seemed odd, for Second Fong *taai taai* had never fussed about her hair, wearing it in a simple bun with a fringe cut high above her wide forehead. She didn't even bother to use padding to add volume to her sparse hair.

Neither Spring Rain nor I had been privy to the covert understanding between Lady Fong and her sister-wives, so we'd thought it was a harmless fixation on the part of Second Fong *taai taai*, perhaps a way of distracting herself from the impending loss of Young Master Fei. Now I saw her behaviour with wary eyes. Whatever she was planning, it couldn't be good for Lady Fong. I must share my concerns with Spring Rain.

With only seven days left, I would rather have worked on the lotus shoes but was often needed elsewhere. Along with the other young ladies' *muizai*, I huddled in Miss Linjing's bedchamber, standing shoulder to shoulder with my neighbours as we listened to her cousins talk about their marriage woes. Clarity *taai taai*, a woman with thick wrists and sausage-like fingers, reclined on a daybed, her pregnant belly stretching the seams of her tunic-blouse. Beside Miss Linjing sat Lavender *taai taai*, a woman with a twitchy face. On the other side of the circle, Harmony *taai taai* chewed her nails. All three ladies had been married for less than a year.

'Oh, Linjing,' Clarity *taai taai* said, 'you must treasure these last days of maidenhood. It's a blessing to sleep alone. My husband has a horrid, lustful appetite. Even though I'm heavy with child, he gives me no rest.' She shuddered before continuing, 'I'm sick to death of his pawing. I beg him to spare me, at least until the child is born, but he won't listen.'

Miss Linjing, along with her maiden cousins, stared at Clarity *taai taai*, their eyes wide, cheeks scarlet. Like me, the other *muizai* grimaced, but we also looked relieved. Perhaps there were some consolations in remaining a slave.

'But,' Miss Linjing began, 'I thought we didn't have to perform wife duties during pregnancy.'

'I thought so too!' Clarity *taai taai* cried. 'I complained to my mother-in-law, but she says it is my job to satisfy her son.'

'My mother-in-law says the same to me,' Lavender *taai taai* said. 'Obey. Obey. Obey. That's what I hear all day. But no matter how much I try to please her, it's never enough. She criticizes my sewing, scolds me for serving tea that is too hot or too cold, and strikes me every time my red aunty arrives. My wedding anniversary is fast approaching. If I don't fall pregnant soon, she might cast me out.'

'At least you are both the first wife of an heir,' Harmony *taai taai* mourned. 'Linjing, you are fortunate too – once you become the matriarch, all this suffering will have been worth it. My husband is the youngest son, so I must please my mother-in-law and all my senior sisters-in-law. At mealtimes, I only get to eat meat if everyone else has had their fill, but there is often not enough. I also get the least stipend. I can scarcely pay for my toiletries, let alone any treats.'

Miss Linjing's cousins and adolescent sisters dispersed into small groups as we served refreshments. Miss Linjing drew Lavender *taai taai* and Clarity *taai taai* aside, speaking to them in hushed tones. As I poured tea for them and returned with trays of sweetmeats and fruit, I caught snippets of their conversation. Miss Linjing asked Lavender *taai taai* about remedies that might help conceive a child faster, but the lady replied that nothing seemed to work. Next, she wanted Clarity *taai taai* to share more details about wife duties. My mistress's complexion flickered from deep blushing to ashen as she listened to her cousins' tales. At one point, I thought Clarity

167

taai taai said her husband even forced his male organ into her back entrance, but I couldn't be sure, for I caught only the tail end of the story, and I'd never heard of such a thing before. I grabbed the empty kettle and hurried out of the room. In some ways, a wife endured more indignities than a *muizai*.

At the well, I met Little Grass, Harmony *taai taai*'s maid, who was hauling water to fill a basin. Her faded *ou* hung loose on her weedy frame. From the way she'd swallowed when she watched our mistresses eat, I knew she must be hungry. Poor thing – she reminded me of my former self. I reached inside my pocket for the parcel of peanut brittle Miss Linjing had given me as a reward for finishing the fifth pair of lotus shoes.

'Would you like a piece of sweet?' I asked her.

She snatched it out of my hand, tore the wrapper and shoved it all into her mouth. She didn't speak until she'd finished it. 'Do you have more?' she demanded.

'Your thanks?' I said.

'Why should I thank you?' she mumbled, as she licked the crumbs from the wrapper.

'Why are you so hostile?'

'Don't pretend you're ignorant of your privileged position,' she scoffed.

I frowned at her.

'Miss Linjing will become a matriarch,' she said. 'That means you'll be a housekeeper and lord it over all the other *muizai*. But I'll always be a low-ranked slave. Why should I be nice to you?'

Without waiting for my reply, she shoved me aside and walked off. Despite her rudeness, her words rang true: my prospects were brighter than hers, especially if I could help Miss Linjing evade Lady Li's traps.

21

Linjing

The disturbing conversations with Clarity and Lavender sickened me: marriage seemed far worse than I had imagined. Though I had been in the company of visiting young gentlemen, sons of Aa De's colleagues or distant relations, I had no understanding of their characters. As for Valiant Li, I had only one photograph of him and the image offered no reassurance. Would he be kind, or a beast like Clarity's husband? In another six days, Lady Li's manservant would collect the lotus shoes and I would leave home for ever to meet my fate.

Heart heavy, I stared at my embroidery. I should be finishing the petal motif on the shoe vamp, but my eyes felt dry and gritty. I pushed my sewing aside and stepped outside. I needed to walk. At this hour, most of the guests were napping, so I had the garden to myself. I ran down the slope that led to the lake's edge, took off my shoes and socks, and plunged my feet into the cool water. If I'd had golden lilies, I wouldn't have been able to enjoy this simple pleasure, and though I still longed for them, this was a small but delightful recompense.

One of the golden carp swam over and nudged my toes with its mouth. As I reached into the water, it darted away.

If only I could remain at home! My thoughts drifted back to Miss Hart's radical advice about women who married only if they met a deserving man, or not at all. At the time, I had dismissed it as lunacy. Now I wished I could emulate her. Should I broach the subject with Aa De? No, rejecting the marriage, especially at this late stage, was impossible. But suppose he was as open-minded as Miss Hart had suggested? I needed to know. At the very least, I needed his reassurance that he would protect me, no matter what lay in store. I dried my feet and hastened to his office.

I found him at his desk, reading a scroll. He looked up and beamed, the corners of his eyes crinkling. He reserved this type of smile only for my brother and me.

'Ah, Linjing, you have come in time to take tea with me,' he said, getting up and walking to the refreshment table. 'My manservant will return with cakes soon.'

I sat on a stool beside him. My throat felt dry.

'You look worried, my pet,' he said. 'Tell me what troubles you. Perhaps I can help.'

'I'm scared of marriage,' I began.

'That is perfectly natural. All respectable young ladies are reluctant to leave their natal homes.'

'Aa De ... would it be ... could I stay a maiden?' I blurted.

Disbelief darted across his face as he pushed away from the table, distancing himself from me. Even as I braced for his reprimand, I said, 'Marriage terrifies me! I'd rather devote my life to serving you. Please, Aa De, let me stay.'

At this confession, his eyes softened and an indulgent smile spread across his face as he pulled his stool closer to mine. 'Your loyalty to me does you credit,' he said, patting my hand,

'and your fear about marriage is proof of your modesty and superior breeding.'

'Will you grant my wish?' I asked, gripping his forearm.

'Oh, Linjing,' he said, voice rich with fondness, sounding like he used to before Fei's birth. 'Marriage is the best path for you. I would be a negligent father if I stopped your marriage to protect you from these very natural but *unwarranted* fears.'

'But I have real cause to believe Lady Li will torment me.' I proceeded to tell him about the eight pairs of four-inch lotus shoes and the accompanying letter. 'Surely that is proof of her prejudice against natural feet.'

'A wife must submit to her husband. This same rule applies to Lady Li – since Viceroy Li supports natural feet, she must yield and embrace you. For her to give you trouble would be an act of insubordination. No high-born lady would commit such an offence.'

His words were no comfort. I dropped my eyes to the table-cloth, picking at loose beads as I struggled to find the means to make him understand the complexity and dangers within the women's realm.

'Valiant Li is on the cusp of becoming one of China's ambassadors,' he said, pushing a cup of tea into my hands. 'In a few short years, you will accompany him to a splendid modern city like London or New York. Wouldn't that be wonderful?'

'I'd love to go abroad,' I admitted, lacing my fingers around the cup. 'But ... if things should go awry ...' I swallowed. 'If there are problems in my marriage,' I tried again, 'if I cannot bear a son, will you protect me?'

'My pet,' he said. 'You'll always have a protector in me.'

22

Little Flower

According to Spring Rain, Second Fong *taai taai* had started adopting Lady Fong's hairstyle, albeit only in the privacy of her bedchamber. Spring Rain was eager to discover her motive, hoping to have a chance to expose her cruel mistress. We considered telling Lady Fong, but it would be Spring Rain's word against Second Fong *taai taai*'s denial, and we couldn't risk the latter's wrath. Instead, Spring Rain did her best to eavesdrop and search for suspicious items in Second Fong *taai taai*'s apartment.

Meanwhile, time was running out to finish the lotus shoes. Dowager Lady Fong had summoned an opera troupe to stage three days of performances as a finale to the pre-wedding festivities, which kept Miss Linjing confined to the viewing pavilion from mid-afternoon until well into the night. The looming deadline kept me awake until the small hours. Fatigue brought on headaches and compromised my sewing.

Such was my exhaustion that I must have dozed off as I waited in the rockery alcove for Spring Rain, who'd told me earlier that she had news about Second Fong *taai taai*. She shook me awake.

'I found something,' she said.

She reached into the concealed pocket of her tunic-blouse and pulled out a sheet of folded paper; the red wax seal had been cracked. 'I found this in the false bottom of my mistress's cosmetics box.' She handed the missive to me. 'It must be important if she hid it.'

I opened the paper and tried to decipher the characters. As part of Miss Linjing's attempt to win my loyalty over the past two years, she'd been teaching me to read and write. It was a privilege that few slaves received. But between my *muizai* duties and the time I'd devoted to retraining my hand, I'd only managed to learn some elementary characters and phrases.

'Well?' she urged. 'What does it say?'

'I can only make out a few characters,' I said. I pointed to the ones I understood and read them for her: 'good progress', 'mother', 'daughter', 'search', 'servant yet to agree', 'payment' and 'Phoenix'.

'That's a strange jumble of words,' she said, tugging her braids.

'It's about Lady Fong, that much I can be sure. But the rest doesn't sound threatening. It could be an innocent letter between Second Fong *taai taai* and her natal family with some trivial complaints about Lady Fong.'

'Why would she keep something innocent in a secret drawer? You must show the letter to Lady Fong. She'll pay attention if it comes from you. If my mistress has done something wicked, I want to see her punished.' From beneath her *ou*, she wrenched out the poppet, pulled a pin from its forehead, pricked her finger and smeared its faceless head with her blood. 'And if that fails, foul magic will eventually make her pay.'

She glowered, daring me to challenge her. Despite Spring

Rain's faith in the poppet, nothing supernatural had happened to Second Fong *taai taai*, but I didn't have the heart to try to dissuade her from believing in it. A wave of sadness washed over me as I compared the hatred blazing from her eye to the gentle person she used to be. Spring Rain thought slavery couldn't rob us of our souls, but she was wrong: it had already blighted hers with bitterness. Life had treated her cruelly, and I understood her rage. Sometimes I felt it too. I'd once thought of vengeance as a beast with an insatiable appetite. Now, it seemed more like poison ivy with far-reaching tendrils whose touch tainted everything. If I let my guard down, it might find a foothold in me too, for there were moments when I still mourned the loss of my liberty.

Spring Rain repeated, 'Show her, tonight.'

Though reluctant, I agreed.

That night, when the household had finally settled into sleep, I went to Lady Fong's bedchamber. I had to knock several times before footsteps approached and the door opened.

'What is the matter?' Lady Fong asked. 'Is it Linjing?'

'I have something to tell you. May I please come inside?'

With a solemn nod, she led me into the recess of her bed-chamber and told me to sit on a chaise longue. After lighting a lamp on the side table, she blew out the candle and sat beside me. Her formidable forehead creased with concern.

'It is about Second Fong *taai taai*,' I said. 'Spring Rain found a letter hidden in the false bottom of her cosmetics box.'

I told her what Spring Rain had observed about Second Fong *taai taai*'s sudden desire to imitate Lady Fong's hair-style and relayed the few characters from the letter that I'd understood.

'Do you have this letter?' she asked.

I pulled it from my pocket and placed it on her lap. She sat motionless, staring as though it were a sleeping viper that might awaken at the slightest vibration and attack. Finally, she picked it up and read it in silence. Her rigid face betrayed little of her thoughts; when she'd finished, she crushed the paper, squeezed her eyes shut and let out a long, shaky breath. When she opened her eyes again, I saw resignation, tinged with another emotion that I couldn't interpret. But she didn't appear angry or shocked.

'Are you all right, my lady?' I asked.

'You must keep this to yourself,' she told me, 'and implore Spring Rain to do the same. Do not tell a soul, especially not Linjing. We mustn't add to her worries.'

'What . . .' I hesitated, feeling intrusive even though I had been the messenger. But curiosity got the better of me. 'What did the letter say?'

'All will be well,' she said. 'I will address the matter in private.' She tried to reassure me with a smile, but her trembling lips offered no comfort. She looked past me to the shadows as though an answer lay there. 'Can we trust Spring Rain to keep quiet?'

'Second Fong *taai taai* treats her ill. She is eager to be of service to you. I know she will obey your orders. All she asks in return is to be reassigned to a kinder mistress.'

'Good. Good. I am glad of it. Now, go to bed.'

'Please, my lady. Won't you tell me what it says?'

In response, she walked to the side table, tossed the ball of paper into a bowl, lit a match and burnt it. Within a moment, the flames had swallowed the transcript. She ordered me to go. When I did not move, she took a step forward, lingering at the edge of the circle of light cast by the lamp.

With her face half in shadows, she said, 'I am sorry for your lost freedom, but I hope you can forgive Linjing. It is an unfair request, I know, but I ask as a helpless mother. Soon I will be unable to protect her. You will be her only ally. Linjing doesn't know it, but she is fragile. Your spirit is fierce and enduring. Hers is crafted from glass, showy but brittle – perhaps this is the curse of a privileged upbringing and a lenient father.' She bent over so our eyes were at the same level. 'Promise me that you'll be loyal and kind to Linjing,' she implored, 'even if she doesn't always deserve it.'

Stunned, I could not reply straight away. Lady Fong had spoken many words of encouragement as I struggled to retrain my hand, but she'd never shared such thoughts with me. In this moment, I didn't feel like a slave. She was wrong about Miss Linjing, though. Her will was a cannonball, blasting any obstacle that dared to stand in her way. Hadn't she shattered my hope of liberty to secure her own goal? I wanted to say so to Lady Fong. Yet I knew I must make the pledge: it would be my gift for her kindness.

'I will be to Miss Linjing as Cerise is to you,' I vowed. And I meant to keep my word, as long as Miss Linjing continued to uphold her end of the agreement to treat me with respect.

'Then my mind is at ease,' she replied, as she reached across and touched my cheek. Switching to an upbeat tenor, she said, 'Now, we must sleep. Tomorrow will be another busy day.'

I still wanted answers, but seeing the resolve on her face, I knew she would say no more. She had spoken with conviction and I wanted to believe her. But danger lurked behind her forced cheer.

23

Linjing

In one more sleep, Little Flower and I would set off for Tianjin. Despite my best efforts, I'd managed to sew only two pairs of shoes, leaving Little Flower to make the others. The last pair still needed some finishing touches to the embroidery before the uppers could be stitched to the soles. Little Flower had promised to stay up all night if need be. Fearing she might fall ill, I had fed her plenty of chicken and ginseng broth. Poor girl, her eyes were red and her complexion pale. I didn't enjoy burdening her, but no one else had the skills to save me from Lady Li's spite.

Our guests had retired to their apartments for an afternoon nap, so I returned to my bedchamber to sew the upper to one sole as Little Flower finished the embroidery on the other shoe. But energetic knocks on the door interrupted us before long. It was Spring Rain. She was panting and her fringe stuck to her sweaty brow.

'Miss Linjing, my mistress and Master Fong want you in his quarters. You must come straight away.'

I signalled Little Flower to accompany me.

'Sorry, Miss,' Spring Rain said. 'Only you.'

I stepped over the threshold of Aa De's receiving chamber and into an incoherent tableau. My father sat alone at the round table where he often took his afternoon refreshments. Instead of a teapot, cups and a platter of sweets, seven rice bowls half-filled with water formed a circle. Within it, the sharp blade of a knife glinted in a shaft of light from the nearby window. Father looked rigid and tense, like a horse about to rear. A muscle in his right cheek twitched.

Second Aa Noeng perched on a settee surrounded by her six children. Agitation hung about her like a swarm of bees. Her plump cheeks were flushed and her forehead was damp. She rarely spoke a harsh word to my half-siblings, but today she pecked at them like a ruffled hen. One moment she blamed Meilian's spots on her weakness for fried food; in the next breath, she chided another half-sister for having messy braids. She smacked my three youngest half-sisters and confiscated the paper dolls they were fighting over. 'Go and sit on the stools,' she told them, 'and do not utter a sound.' Fei climbed onto her lap, asking to be nursed. She pushed him off and shoved a sweet into his mouth before he could bawl.

My mother was sitting in the shadows, slumped in a chair like a wilted flower. A kingfisher hair stick dangled from her dishevelled chignon, and the phoenix comb that she had worn throughout the festivities lay at her feet, several of its teeth bent. A dark stain sullied the white lotus on her crumpled *ou*. Was it blood? I darted to her side.

'Aa Noeng, are you ill?'

She did not answer.

I looked about the room. Where were the slaves? Aa De's manservant ought to have been on standby, poised to take orders from his master. And why hadn't Spring Rain followed me into the room? Aa De stared with vacant eyes, like a marionette.

Second Aa Noeng leapt into action, her face calm and determined, and the sudden change heightened my misgiving. 'Gather about the table,' she ordered her children. 'You too, Linjing.'

I glanced at my mother. She remained motionless.

'Go on,' Second Aa Noeng repeated, as she came over and pulled me away.

Meilian hoisted Fei onto a footstool and we all crowded around the table.

'Why are we standing here?' Meilian asked.

'Hush!' Second Aa Noeng chided. 'Good girls do not ask questions.'

Fei reached for the knife. Second Aa Noeng slapped his hand away and twisted his earlobe. He shrieked and called for my mother. But Aa Noeng continued to stare at us, as lifeless as a doll.

'What is happening?' I asked Aa De. 'The children are frightened. Tell me what's going on.'

'Husband,' Second Aa Noeng interjected. 'We should make a start.'

My father nodded and heaved himself up as though he were a frail man of seventy. Holding his left hand over the nearest bowl, he grabbed the knife and sliced open his palm. A drop of blood splashed into the water. My siblings and I all gasped. Fei wailed and my little half-sisters began to sob too. Only Second Aa Noeng did not look alarmed.

I clutched Aa De's sleeve and said, 'You are scaring us. What

179

is this all about?' He cast me a perturbed look but did not speak. 'Is Aa Noeng ill? Or is it you?'

Instead of replying, he passed the knife to Meilian. 'Cut yourself,' he commanded, 'and let your blood drip into the same bowl.'

Looking up at Second Aa Noeng, Meilian beseeched, 'It'll hurt. Please don't make me do it.'

Second Aa Noeng seized the knife and nicked Meilian's finger before she had time to protest. She was so stunned that she didn't even cry out. The drops of her blood embraced his in the water. Second Aa Noeng shot Meilian an approving smile. My father's expression remained tense as he let another drop of his blood fall into the second bowl. Second Aa Noeng grabbed her next daughter's hand. My half-sister tried to pull away, but she couldn't overcome her mother's strength. With the swiftness of a butcher, Second Aa Noeng sliced her finger too, her droplet again meshed with my father's larger one.

He repeated the strange ritual with the remaining children, his blood merging with theirs each time. Even Fei was not spared, though Second Aa Noeng had to nick his heel, for he bit her when she tried to seize his hand. Fei glared at Second Aa Noeng afterwards and ran to my mother. I thought Second Aa Noeng would order him back, but her eyes were fixed on the bowls. Fei buried his face in my mother's skirts and she rested a hand on his head. Frightened, I walked towards my mother with the intention of demanding answers from her. But Second Aa Noeng grabbed my arm, the sharp tip of her nail guard piercing my sleeve.

'It is your turn.'

The cut on Aa De's palm had begun to congeal; he sliced it again and dripped a fresh drop into the final bowl. Then he handed the knife to me. He clasped his hand over mine, gripping it tight, as though he was delivering me into the bridal palanquin and did not know when we would meet again.

With great interest, Second Aa Noeng peered into the bowl as I cut my palm and let a red drop fall. Father looked equally spellbound. I expected our blood to mix, just like it had for my siblings.

But it did not.

Instead, it drifted apart.

'What does this mean?' I asked.

Rage and shame burst across his face. Shame tried to throttle rage, but the latter would not be choked. It consumed my father's eyes, turning them into two orbs of hatred. His fury frightened me. What had I done to provoke it?

Then, the first inkling of what had just come to pass gnawed at me. No, it could not be. It was impossible. I shoved the thought down, down, down. My father opened his mouth to speak but snapped it shut again.

'It is me, Linjing,' I said, in a small voice, 'your cherished pearl.'

I stared at him, willing him to cast aside this misunderstanding, whatever it might be, to hold on to the love and esteem he had for me, to refrain from any rash words or actions.

He overturned the table, sending the bowls crashing to the tiled floor.

After Aa De's violence, my mother straightened, tucked the rogue strands back into her chignon and smoothed her skirt and tunic-blouse. By now, I had sunk to the floor, paralysed. The bells and keys on Aa Noeng's chatelaine tinkled rhythmically as she walked towards me. I took her extended hand and dragged myself up. In a firm, calm voice, she said, 'Linjing,

181

listen to me. Return to your bedchamber immediately. Stay there until I come.'

'Why?'

'I must speak to your father.'

Aa De was slumped in a chair, his body turned towards the window and his face buried in his hands. A strange calm had settled on Second Aa Noeng, who sat at a side table, sipping a cup of tea as though nothing was amiss. She must have ushered the children out, or perhaps their amahs had come to collect them; only the four of us remained in the room.

'Linjing,' Aa Noeng repeated. 'You must go.'

'I want to stay.'

'You must go now. I will explain everything tonight.'

She drew me into an embrace and repeated her order. I shivered. Something appalling was happening. Again, understanding nudged to the surface, but I forced it back as I hurried to my quarters.

Long after the sun had disappeared over the horizon, Aa Noeng finally came to my bedchamber. With a shock, I realized that her chatelaine was missing. The symbol of her first-wife status had accompanied her everywhere for as long as I could recall. Now it was gone. I wanted to ask her where it was but was too afraid of the answer.

We sat together at the table.

'That blood ritual,' I said. 'I think I know . . .' But I could not finish the sentence. 'Aa Noeng, I'm afraid.'

'I'm sorry I couldn't protect you,' she said.

She squeezed my hand and looked at me with sorrow. Even in the candlelight, I saw with a shock that her face was bare of rouge, lip paint and eyebrow charcoal. I'd never seen her unpainted face before and it unnerved me. She looked vulnerable. The rest of her toilette added to my dismay. Her hair was swept back into a neat chignon held together by a plain wooden hair stick. She had changed into white silk, with only a border of pale-yellow chrysanthemums to differentiate it from mourning clothes.

'Why are you dressed like this?' I asked.

'Listen closely to the story I am about to tell you,' she said, 'and do not interrupt me until I finish. Can you do that?'

A part of me wanted to beg her not to speak. If she remained silent, I could pretend nothing had changed. But I knew the truth could not wait, so I nodded.

'Every bride hopes to become pregnant soon after her wedding day. Her life is full of humiliations and the only hope of reprieve is if she bears a son. I shared that hope when I married your father, but one year went by, then two, without a sign. Your *maa maa* said I was barren, ill-fated and cursed. She forced me to drink all sorts of fertility remedies, but nothing worked. By the summer of the third year, she gave me an ultimatum: I must be pregnant before the new year or her son would divorce me. Your father did not try to defy her. It seemed I was doomed to return to my natal home in disgrace, to live the rest of my life as an object of contempt and derision.

'Cerise told me that sometimes a woman's fertility *qi* was not compatible with her husband's, but that did not mean she was barren. I was desperate. I knew what I must do.'

Her voice cracked as she continued. 'I returned to my natal home for the Autumn Moon Festival. On the journey, Cerise and I discussed which of my distant male relatives would be most likely to help me and, most importantly, remain silent about it. We made our choice. There is no need to name him. Cerise acted as matchmaker and he agreed.'

'Am I . . .' I choked '. . . am I not Aa De's daughter?'

'You are not,' she confirmed.

Aa Noeng's confession was an earthquake that shook everything from its foundation. All that I had taken to be irrefutable facts were tethered to lies. In this moment, I could believe the sun rose in the west and set in the east, rivers ran upstream and spilt water could be salvaged, such was my dwindling faith in the order of the world.

Two women existed in my mother's body: one had devoted her life to rules, discipline and virtue; the other had cast all caution to the winds, committing adultery, a woman's ultimate sin. I had been raised by the former, and her fixation with rules and feminine virtues had driven a wedge between us. The latter woman, I'd only glimpsed. Could I have shared a deeper connection with her? Which one was her true self? And could I forgive her? I didn't know. Her boldness awed me, but Maa Maa's favourite reprimand warned me that I would also pay the price for her recklessness. *A daughter's sin is a mother's liability, just as a mother's sin is a daughter's burden* – I would be as tainted as Aa Noeng now.

Yet Aa Noeng's admission about my true birth origins did not shock me as they would have even that morning. Despite my refusal to admit it even to myself, I'd guessed the truth some hours ago. Although I'd been ignorant at first, Aa De's violent reaction had forced me to understand that the ceremony was to test my bloodline. Could I still call him 'Aa De' or would he become 'Master Fong' to me? I didn't know. Questions about my future and my mother's fate jostled in my mind.

'Who exposed you?' I asked.

'Peony.'

'But Second Aa Noeng wouldn't hurt a fly.'

'I underestimated her too. I thought she was a rabbit, but she has turned out to be a viper. For many years after your birth, I lived in fear that your *maa maa* would grow suspicious about my inability to conceive again. If she did, she never said anything, and eventually I felt my secret was safe. Early last year, someone in Peony's natal village used the same ploy to conceive and was discovered. Peony's mother told her about it and planted the suspicion in her mind.

'She paid for an investigator and her mother helped. Together, they found a manservant of my distant relative, your natal father, who knew the truth. A few days ago, Little Flower gave me a letter that alerted me to Peony's plans. It said the manservant still refused to give his testimony. He had sworn to his master to take his secret to the grave. But this letter was from some time ago, and it seems that recently he succumbed to bribery when his master died. He provided a witness statement and agreed to appear in person, if needed. Peony revealed the secret to your father today, but he did not believe her and insisted on the blood ceremony.

'I didn't care what happened to me, but I needed you to be safe. So, I wagered with Fate. I believed the best way to protect you was to do nothing and hope you'd be well on your way to Tianjin, or even married, by the time Peony had enough proof to expose us.'

She reached over and took my hand in hers again. Tears fell on them. At first I couldn't be sure they were hers, for I had never seen her cry. I touched my cheeks, but they were dry. My mother's endurance was ebbing; she looked crushed.

'I have tried to keep you safe,' she croaked. 'After ... after my transgression, I followed every feminine rule. I was convinced that only rules and fortitude could keep a woman safe. My newfound rigidity soured your father's affection. I'm sorry for everything. You have the right to hate me. I deserve it.'

Despite her brave words, I saw pleading in her wet eyes.

'I don't hate you,' I said. 'But I wish you'd done something to stop Peony, or at least talked to me about it. Together, we could have found a solution. Now what will happen to us?'

'Leave that until the morning. We'll think of a way forward. Come with me.'

She dried her face and led me to my bed.

'I can't sleep,' I objected.

'You'll feel better after a rest.'

I obeyed and she pulled the quilt up to my chin, tucking the edges under the mattress as she had when I was a little girl. In this snug cocoon, I could pretend all would be well again.

'Close your eyes.'

I did so, my lids suddenly heavy. She smoothed my hair as she sang a lullaby, one I'd long forgotten. The lyrics cast me back to a time when facts were solid and worries were foreign to me. Just before I drifted off, she whispered, 'I will fix this.' Sleep claimed me before I could ask her what she meant.

24

Linjing

Someone shook me by the shoulders, the jingle of bells and keys chiming with each jerk, and I opened my eyes, expecting to see my mother. But it was Second Aa Noeng who peered down at me, her round face twisted with contempt and Mother's chatelaine dangling from the top knot of her tunic-blouse. Behind her, a *muizai* held a lantern. I sat up, alert and fearful. Last night I'd noticed the chatelaine's absence; now I understood Mother had surrendered it to Second Aa Noeng. How quickly things were falling apart! I hadn't thought my mother would be stripped of her status even before the wedding guests had left. Panic mounted in my chest. Had everyone heard about my shame already? Before I could ask questions, Second Aa Noeng slapped me three times. 'Get up!' she ordered. 'Stand before me.'

Resigned, I obeyed. She stood so close I could smell the stale perfume on her neck.

'Who made my mother give you the chatelaine?' I asked.

'Didn't Phoenix tell you?' she sneered. 'Your *maa maa* snatched it off your disgraced mother as soon as I reported the scandal to her. The old crone wanted to carve "whore" onto her forehead, but my husband objected and said it was too cruel. Men can be so weak.'

Another wave of panic swelled in my chest as my mother's last words rang in my mind: *I will fix this*. What had she meant? I blamed myself for falling asleep when I should have stayed up and helped her solve our predicament.

'Where is my mother?' I asked.

'I have come to fetch you so you can join her.'

The contrast between her sweet tone and the menace in her eyes made me shudder. Why hadn't my mother come herself? I tried to keep my face blank and my voice even. I needed answers from Peony, and hysteria wouldn't help.

'Will my wedding go ahead?' I asked.

'Of course not,' she replied, with a cackle. 'I'm surprised you've asked such a thick-witted question. We've told everyone that you and your mother have smallpox. All the guests will leave tomorrow.'

'What will you tell Lord and Lady Li?'

'My husband will tell them you didn't survive the disease.'

'What will happen to us?'

She answered me with a taunting smile but refused to elaborate, despite my repeated questions. The more frustrated I became, the more she seemed to enjoy herself. Stunned that someone's character could be so altered, I grew speechless, unable to reconcile this spiteful face with the meek woman I had known. I could no longer think of her as my second *aa noeng*. The woman who stood before me was Peony, a ruthless stranger I feared more than Maa Maa, perhaps even more than demons. Yet, I needed answers that only she could provide, so I pressed her with a different line of questioning.

'Do you think a secret of this magnitude can be contained?' I asked.

Her face twitched, and I knew I'd struck a nerve. I persisted: 'You know that a man who cannot control his family will not be trusted to govern a province. Aa De might lose his post if Lord Li discovers the truth. But you still chose to expose us at this critical time. Why?'

My question triggered a burst of mania. Her eyes widened, showing so much white that she looked deranged. 'Damn his career! Damn your mother and all first wives! Why should I give up my *son*, my flesh and blood?' Spittle flew from her mouth, some of it landing on my face. I stepped back, but she seized my *ou*. 'Most minor wives are weak,' she continued, 'but not me. Sons are not ripe fruit to be plucked by anyone who wants them. My husband and his brother were sons of minor wives, but their mothers forfeited them to your *maa maa* without a fight. That is why that hag is so keen to uphold first-wife privileges. I have endured and survived *eleven* pregnancies to get a living, breathing son. I would sooner smother Fei than surrender him to your mother.'

Her confession had the effect of a purge. Almost at once, the manic blaze in her eyes faded. She still scowled at me, but she no longer looked crazed. Pity flooded me – for Aa Noeng, myself and even Peony. I could never forgive her cruelty, but I understood what had driven her to the edge of madness. All this anguish, grief and tragedy had been for a son. Was Aa Noeng that much different from Peony? They'd both taken extreme risks to protect themselves, and the cycle might have continued with me after I'd married.

Until now, I hadn't known Maa Maa was not Aa De's birth mother. Things might have turned out differently if she hadn't felt compelled to side with Aa Noeng. If all children belonged

189

to their birth mothers, then Aa Noeng wouldn't have pushed Peony into desperation by claiming her son, and I would still be Aa De's beloved daughter. I would have given anything to reverse this twist of Fate, but I was powerless. Drained, I didn't protest when Peony called for two guards to escort me to Aa Noeng's apartment. I wanted only to be with her now.

I didn't recognize the menservants who shoved me over Aa Noeng's threshold, slammed the door and bolted the lock as they stood guard outside. Their bulky shadows filled the paper-lined lattice panels of the door frame, silent and intimidating. Given that Maa Maa had confiscated the chatelaine so swiftly, I'd expected she might also have stripped my mother's bedchamber of furniture and luxuries. But nothing looked amiss: here stood a bunch of camellias in an antique vase; there lay an embroidery hoop with a half-finished pair of huge tiger eyes, to be made into an animal hat for Fei. A blanket lay crumpled on the daybed and an open book poked out from the heap. At a side table, a teapot sat beside two cups. In short, all the usual domestic comforts remained untouched. But where was my mother?

'Linjing.'

I jumped and almost dropped the candle in my hand.

'Linjing,' the voice repeated, 'come to me. I've been waiting for you.' The soft call came from the back of my mother's sleeping alcove, but it wasn't her voice. A woman sat on a stool at the head of the bed, her face hidden in darkness.

'Come to me,' she repeated.

As I crept closer, the candlelight fell on Aunt Sapphire's face. She looked haggard. Aa Noeng's sleeping form came into view. She lay on her back beneath a heavy quilt, which was tucked firmly under her chin, and her eyes were partly open, as though she was about to wake. I touched her cheek and called her several times, but fear filled me when she remained motionless and her chest did not seem to be rising and falling. I looked a petrified question at my aunt.

'Your mother took hemlock about four hours ago,' she said. 'I stayed with her until her last breath before I reported her death to Peony and your *maa maa*.' She reached out to me, but I reeled away, dropping the candle onto the quilt. My aunt snatched it up before the quilt caught fire and placed it on a table. The room tilted sideways. I clung to a bedpost until the floor stopped tipping. Still I refused to believe my aunt's words. I lurched across the bed and pushed down on my mother's *jan zung* meridian point with both thumbs, hoping she would revive like Fourth Aa Noeng had from her faint when her *muizai* had done the same. But she did not move. My aunt placed her hands on my shoulders and gently pulled me away.

'Why didn't you stop her?' I asked. 'Why didn't you send for a *daai fu*?'

'Let me help you to a seat. Then I will tell you everything.'

I shook my head.

'You need to understand the truth.'

'I have heard too much already. I can't bear any more horrors.'

'Please, for *your mother*.'

She offered her hand again. This time, I took it. She led me to the daybed and sat beside me, stroking my back as she talked. A feeble dawn light stole through the gauze window screen.

'Phoenix came to me soon after her conversation with Little Flower,' she explained. 'She wanted my advice, and I agreed that—'

'How long have you known this secret?'

'Phoenix and I were together in our natal home during the Autumn Moon Festival when you were conceived. She confided in me after the fact.'

'Oh, Aa Noeng! If only I'd known earlier, if only . . .' Guilt, pity and gratitude wedged my throat, silent tears streaming as I stumbled back to the bed and slumped over Aa Noeng's body, pressing my wet cheek against her chest. All my life, I had craved her approval, wished for her affection and resented her rigidity. But she had carried this crushing load all on her own, sparing me. If I hadn't been ambivalent the previous night, if I'd reassured her of my support in her plight, then perhaps she wouldn't have taken her life. Instead I had fallen asleep, leaving her to face Peony and Maa Maa alone. It was too late to save her life now, but I could still ease her path into the afterworld, ensure she had the means to cajole the ox-headed demons and secure their aid. This would be my last gift to her. I sat up, wiped my face with my sleeves and strode towards my aunt.

'I'll speak with Aa De,' I said. 'Only he can ensure a grand burial for Aa Noeng, with all the necessary sutras, offerings and enough joss-paper money to safeguard her passage through the courts of Hell.'

My aunt rose, wrapped her arm around my shoulders and pulled me back onto the daybed. Once seated, she turned to face me, gripping my hands.

'I must make haste,' I said, twisting away, but she refused to loosen her fingers. 'There is no time to waste, the vigil should already have commenced. Please let me go.'

Still she held tight.

After a deep breath, Aunt Sapphire told me, 'Your father will not see you.'

I pulled away, and this time she let go.

'You're mistaken,' I said. 'He promised he'd always protect me.'

'I'm sorry, Linjing. Your father has discharged his duty to you.'

'*Discharged*,' I repeated dumbly. 'People discharge criminals from jail, soldiers from an army, patients from infirmaries, but not daughters from their lives.'

'Those were his exact words.'

'Did he have another message for me?'

She shook her head.

All my life, I had worshipped him, even as I'd witnessed his indifference to Aa Noeng, even as he'd neglected me for my brother. But he had used me, sacrificed my right to golden lilies, dismissed my fears, all for his career. Crushed by the weight of his callousness and my misplaced faith in him, I sank to the floor.

My aunt knelt beside me and laid a hand on my arm.

'You think you've lost everything,' she said, 'but that's not true. You still have me and the Celibate Sisterhood. Peony wanted to confine you to a remote nunnery. Your mother used her death to force your *maa maa* to overturn Peony's insistence. She wrote them a letter, saying she would haunt this family unless your *maa maa* agreed to let you become my responsibility. In time, you might come to see this turn of events as a blessing in disguise.' I stiffened and pulled away. She added quickly, 'No, no, no. I don't mean your mother's death. Of course I didn't want to lose her.'

'Then why did you watch her die?'

'I saw no other path for her. Once a woman has lost her virtue and been exposed, death is the only way to atone.'

'How can you say so?'

'I can't blame Phoenix for the risk she took. She had no choice. A barren woman can be turned out by her husband's family. If her natal family had refused to take her back, she would have ended up on the streets. And now, I supported her decision to end her life in an honourable way.'

'Did you give her the poison?' I demanded.

'Yes. I procured it for her. We decided the best plan of action was to wait and watch. As you know, she hoped you'd be safely married before Peony exposed her. But she wanted to have the hemlock on hand for the day she would need to use it. Sadly, this day came too soon.'

I leapt up and cried, 'You pushed her to her death! I would still have a mother if you hadn't fed her that poison. You're as much to blame as Peony.'

With a heavy sigh, Aunt Sapphire reached into her jacket and pulled out a letter.

I reached for it. The brushstrokes were shaky and smudged. They bore little resemblance to my mother's usual crisp, clean hand.

Dearest Linjing,

I pray you will not grieve for too long. Do not waste your life on things that cannot be changed. I can't bear to live in disgrace, but my death will not be in vain, for it will save you from the nunnery, where you would be cloistered behind high walls, cut off from the outside world and compelled to recite sutras for most of your days — the monotony would rob your sanity.

Oh, daughter — how I wish I had accepted my fate instead of fighting it. Remember me as a cautionary tale: we can only find peace in this life if we obey and accept our lot. Go with your aunt; she is your protector now. Life at the sisterhood won't be easy. You will need to make compromises and endure many hardships, but compared to the nunnery, I believe it will offer more freedom. You will earn an income, and if you're disciplined, in time you may have enough savings to do as you please, perhaps even travel abroad. I beg you to accept your fate and live a long, contented life. Take care of yourself.

Your loving mother,
Phoenix

Aa Noeng's love overwhelmed me. In her darkest hour, she had sought to protect me.

25

Little Flower

'Yesterday I was fretting about shoes,' Miss Linjing said. 'Now my mother is dead.' She stared at me, eyes huge and bewildered, like a child seeking reassurance from a night terror. I wished I could tell her it was only a dream. Her hand hovered over Lady Fong's face, like a puppet suspended in motion. When she clenched her fist, droplets of perfumed water from the linen towel she was holding trickled onto her mother's lips, then slowed to a drip. One. Two. Three. Four. Five. I counted each drop, hoping against reason that the next would wake Lady Fong. Although Madam Sapphire had told Cerise and me everything as soon as the guards had ushered us in here, I couldn't yet accept the truth. Lady Fong's arm, which I was easing into the first layer of her burial clothes, was stiff but still warm.

'Cerise, stop!' Miss Linjing and I turned at Madam Sapphire's shout. She was struggling to wrest a pair of scissors from Cerise's grip, and hanks of hair lay scattered on the rug. Cerise pushed Linjing's aunt away and sheared another fistful of her own hair, cutting so close to her scalp that blood stained the blades.

'Why are you hurting yourself?' Madam Sapphire asked.

With her free hand, Cerise pounded her chest. 'It's my fault. Lady Fong would still be alive if I hadn't instigated that wicked plan.'

'You are not to blame.' Madam Sapphire touched Cerise's shoulder. 'Phoenix was an intelligent woman. She knew the risks.'

Cerise shook her head and sobbed. 'She wasn't just my mistress, we were true-hearted friends, as close as blood sisters. Now I'm all alone.' I winced at the raw pain in her voice and dropped my eyes to my hands, avoiding Miss Linjing's searching stare. Though my mistress remained mute, I understood her silent question: *Do you love me as Cerise does my mother?* Of course I pitied her, and once again our fates were hinged together like the links of a chain, but we were not like Lady Fong and Cerise. I was her *muizai* because I had no other choice, and I would follow her to the sisterhood for the same reason.

Madam Sapphire wrapped an arm around Cerise's shuddering shoulders. 'Why don't you join us at the sisterhood?'

'No, I must atone.' Cerise wiped her eyes with her sleeve and took several deep breaths. 'I will surrender to a nunnery after you leave with the girls.'

'Phoenix does not blame you, I'm sure of it.' Madam Sapphire appealed to my mistress. 'Linjing, please help me persuade Cerise.'

'If she wants to go, why should I detain her?' Miss Linjing's voice was dull and hard, like pewter. She turned back to her mother and resumed sponging her face and neck.

Madam Sapphire heaved a sigh but did not continue to press Cerise. Instead, she led her to the dressing-table and helped her cut her hair. The trifold mirror multiplied Cerise's grief-stricken face. I couldn't bear to look at her any more, for the image hauled me back to the day the four of us had sat in front of the same looking-glass as Cerise taught me to dress Miss Linjing's hair. In the space of a fortnight, our lives had altered beyond recognition, like a desert reshaped by a windstorm into an incomprehensible landscape. I'd promised Lady Fong I'd be loyal and kind towards Miss Linjing at the Li household, but I wasn't her dowry handmaiden any more. A part of me yearned for the safety of that lost future, for I'd come to accept it and even to look forward to becoming house-keeper one day, with the hope of wielding my modest power to ease the lives of the other servants. Yet, another part of me wondered if the Celibate Sisterhood would bring me closer to liberty, and though I didn't know what to expect in that new life, I hoped at least to be on equal footing with Miss Linjing.

Madam Sapphire championed Lady Fong's need for a soul-exoneration ritual. She quarrelled with the guards, threatening them with a curse upon their bloodlines until they agreed to escort her to Dowager Lady Fong's quarters, where she per-suaded her to hire two nuns. At first glance, these taciturn, elderly sisters appeared heartless. But when they clasped Linjing's hands and looked into her eyes, I saw compassion and a wisdom that transcended mortal understanding. Their occult powers gave me hope: if anyone could pardon Lady Fong's soul, it would be them. For the next seven days, they arrived each morning and remained until sunset, chanting the Buddhist sutras that would travel to the afterworld and cush-ion Lady Fong from some of the sufferings that awaited her.

Emptiness descended upon us after the menservants carried the coffin away for burial on the fourth day, leaving only Lady

Fong's spirit tablet behind. Miss Linjing refused to speak of the future, but over our last evening meal there, Madam Sapphire broached the subject of the Celibate Sisterhood again.

'Did your mother tell you why I joined the sisterhood?' she asked.

Miss Linjing shook her head.

'My fiancé died the week before our wedding,' she said. 'He contracted a brain fever, and everyone blamed me for his death. People said my *qi* was too strong, that I had too much *yang* in my spirit, that I'd cursed him. My father was rich enough to secure another marriage for me, albeit to a lesser family. But I didn't want to take my chances with a husband and a mother-in-law. I chose to live a free life as a celibate sister. Now, you will follow in my footsteps. This is what I meant when I said you may one day see this tragedy as a blessing in disguise.'

'Do you ever regret your choice?' Miss Linjing asked.

'I would not trade my freedom for anything.'

'I have nowhere else to go, but I cannot see how I will be happy there. I hear silk reeling is hard. It is a peasant's life.'

'It is gruelling, that's true. The hours are long. The factory is hot and humid. A silk reeler must have excellent coordination and a delicate touch. Every sister must contribute to the communal economy. We do not tolerate slothfulness, but we support each other.'

Miss Linjing eyed Madam Sapphire's golden lilies. 'How can you work long hours?'

'I don't have to. I contributed enough silver to add another building to our sanctuary.'

'I have nothing to give.'

'Don't worry about that,' Linjing's aunt told her. 'You're strong and healthy. I'm sure you'll get used to the work.'

199

Miss Linjing glanced at me. 'At least I'll have you to ease my burden.' She squeezed my arm. 'I expect you'll take to silk reeling the same way you conquered embroidery and be able to help with my share of the work too.'

'Well, Miss, I'm not sure I'll ...' I wanted to say 'remain your *muizai*', but the rickety smile on her face stopped me. Since the tragedy, she'd scarcely talked or slept, and her skirts hung loose on her hips. I would wait.

PART 4

26

Little Flower

One moon cycle had passed since Miss Linjing and I had started our silk-reeling apprenticeship in Chan Village. In the factory, the steam used to power the engines choked the air, and the fishy reek of boiled silkworms turned my stomach. Around me, rows and rows of black-clad celibate sisters laboured at their individual stations. Some of them fished out colanders of cocoons from troughs of boiling water; others bent over the reeling machines, coaxing silk from six, eight or even ten cocoons into a single filament to be threaded through the eyes of porcelain buttons. No matter their tasks, their flushed, sweaty faces were fixed in concentration, just like mine. The skin around my split cuticles throbbed and itchy red rashes tormented the webbing between my fingers, caused by the frequent exposure to water. Madam Sapphire had given us a greasy ointment mixed with crushed cicada shells to rub into our inflamed hands, which I diligently applied before work, during our midday break and at bedtime. But relief was temporary, for our wounds had no time to heal.

From my workbasket I scooped a handful of cocoons, tossed

them into a copper colander, then plunged the colander into boiling water. Using a brush made from a bunch of dried twigs tied together, I swirled in slow, large circles until strands of silk unwound from the cocoons, catching on the ends of the brush. Next, I distributed the boiled cocoons among the three warm-water baths on the workbench. Selecting ten at a time, I dropped them into a bath of cool water that ran from one end of the station to the other, found the thread leads from all the cocoons, rubbed them between my thumb and little finger until they merged into a single strand, and fed it through a small hollow in the centre of a porcelain button. I fed the strand through a series of holes until it reached the end of the working reel, rubbed the existing strand together with the fresh one until they were one, and turned the machine on. The ten cocoons bobbed about in the water bath as the motion of the reeling wheel tugged them into an orderly dance. I moved to the second reel and repeated the process, but this time the silk lead snapped several times, slowing me as I mended the break. Before moving to my third reel, I glanced at Miss Linjing's station.

She was taking too long to fetch supplies from the storage room and had left her reel unattended again. Three of the six cocoons in her water bath had ceased to move, but the reel continued to turn; a segment of her silk thread would be thinner than the rest. If this continued, her reels would fail the quality inspection at the end of the day, since uniformity was critical. Gritting my teeth, I hurried over and switched off her machine. From my own supplies, I fetched three replacement cocoons and rubbed their leads with Miss Linjing's existing strand before reactivating the reeling wheel. A few moments later, she sauntered towards me, carrying a basket in the crook of her arm as though she was collecting flowers instead of working. I marched up to her. 'You've taken too long!' I shouted, above the engine's clatter.

She shrugged. 'I knew you'd look after my reel.'

I inspected her basket, plucked out five cocoons, held them in my palm and pointed to the beige spots, evidence of insect bites.

'You'll have constant snaps in your silk thread if you use them,' I said. 'I've told you this many times before.'

'It isn't my fault and you shouldn't scold me.'

She stared at me, expecting an apology. I'd had enough of doing her job as well as mine. Eventually I planned to tell her that I couldn't be her *muizai* any more. But the thundering noise made a long conversation impossible. Besides, pity for her and my promise to Lady Fong were reins that checked me. I turned away and flung the defective cocoons into a waste bin. She darted over, blocking my path as I tried to return to my reels.

'I will have words with you tonight,' she warned.

'I have something to tell you too.'

Now that the words were out, I knew it was time to take the leap. Miss Linjing would never be ready to let me go, so I must be the one to break free.

'What do you mean?' she asked.

Without answering, I walked back to my station and resumed working on my third reel. From the corner of my eye, I caught Miss Linjing's vexation but refused to acknowledge her. Halfway through threading a new lead into a porcelain eye, a male voice, low and commanding, interrupted me. I looked up to find a gentleman towering over me. His face reminded me of wooden wall panels, all rigid lines and sombre shadows. Beneath his drawn brows, his grave eyes peered down at me with disdain.

'I must speak with you,' he shouted above the racket.

Startled, I didn't know how to respond, for I was unaccustomed to speaking to men, especially one from his class.

'What is your name?' he demanded.

'Little Flower.'

'Step outside with me,' he ordered.

He headed towards the worm-rearing room, which had a door that opened by a canal. To keep up with his long, impatient strides, I half ran. At the pier, a stream of farmers were arriving with basketfuls of cocoons balanced at each end of a pole across their shoulders. A long queue snaked out of the side door into the courtyard, which backed onto the canal. Boats jostled for space on the narrow waterway. Young men wearing simple, sleeveless cotton vests rowed the boats laden with brimming containers of mulberry leaves or cocoons. One by one they docked at the pier to unload. Each new arrival waited in turn for his cargo to be weighed by a foreman. After weighing the baskets, the foreman wrote down the figures in a ledger and counted out copper coins in exchange.

The stranger led me away from the factory to the shade beneath a scholar tree with cascades of small white blossoms covering its branches. At this distance, the stench of the boiled silkworms receded, replaced by a whiff of fragrance as a breeze rustled the tree and dispersed the flowers' scent. I inhaled with relief, and so did he. For a moment, his face relaxed, but upon fixing his eyes on me, the frown returned.

'I am Noble Chan,' he said, 'your employer and the proprietor of this filature. You may address me as Noble Siu Je.'

'How can I help you, sir?'

'We expect all our silk reelers to have impeccable fingers. Your right hand is . . .' He gestured awkwardly at my infirmity.

'Crippled,' I supplied.

206

He cleared his throat and glanced down. After adjusting the chain watch that hung from the toggles of his purple robe, he fixed me with a determined glare. 'You will not be able to manage a full quota without two good hands,' he said. 'Your apprenticeship cannot continue.'

His unjust assumption rankled, chasing away my timidity. I took a deep breath and straightened my back, though doing so still left me a head shorter than him, obliging me to tilt my face up to meet his eyes. With steadier nerves, I replied, 'Sir, please do not judge my right hand by its appearance. The injury is old and the middle fingers do not cause pain. I have retrained my thumb and little finger to compensate.'

'We do not employ women with impairment. My clerk, Ming, should not have made an exception for you. I would not have allowed it if I were here when you were hired.'

'Ming did not mention this rule to me, and I showed him my infirmity during our interview. Madam Sapphire can attest to this.'

'My word is final. I can dismiss you without notice. But on account of my respect for Madam Sapphire, I am willing to offer you a job in the worm-rearing room if you can manage a cleaver with your other hand.'

Fat white silkworms slithered in my mind, and I shuddered; their segmented bodies made my skin crawl. Besides chopping mulberry leaves to feed the worms, those workers also collected droppings. The thought of using my bare hands to rummage through the piles of squirming vermin soured my mouth. These ghastly creatures had not only six real legs but five pairs of false ones on the rear of their bodies. I recoiled at the thought of one crawling up my arm. But I doubted sharing my disgust with Noble Siu Je would help my cause.

Instead, I said, 'That is half the wages I can earn reeling silk.'

207

'It is a fair amount for unskilled work. Many women end up there when they are short-sighted.'

'My vision is perfect and I'm a quick learner. Please, sir, give me a chance.'

'Apprentice work is slow-paced. You will have to work much faster once you look after a full quota.'

'I've been here a month and I can already look after three reels. I'll move to four tomorrow. According to Madam Sapphire, this is fast.'

'My mind is set. You can either accept my offer or leave.'

Determined to safeguard my job, the first that rewarded my skill and labours, I searched for a counter argument and found it in the factory's reputation.

'I have been told your filature prides itself on fairness,' I reminded him, 'and I have done nothing to deserve dismissal or a demotion. Let me prove myself to you by my progress.'

He stepped forward, closing the space between us. From his sash belt he pulled out a folded fan but did not open it. His fault-finding eyes narrowed as he tapped the fan against his thigh. I wanted to step back from his scrutiny but forced myself to stay put.

'Very well,' he said at last. 'You may stay. But if you cannot keep up, I will not be lenient a second time.'

'Thank you, sir.'

After a swift bow, I fled back into the factory. Noble Siu Je's warning made it imperative for me to stop doing Linjing's job for her. Yet guilt and pity curdled in my belly. By abandoning Linjing, I would not only be defying my mother's parting words, again, but also breaking my promise to Lady Fong. I was only a little girl when I agreed to follow Aa Noeng's mantra, but my pledge to Lady Fong was scarcely two moons old. Could I truly turn my back on her daughter?

27

Linjing

Each day felt like purgatory, with no end in sight. Here, I worked from seven in the morning until sunset, and almost every waking moment was spent in the company of others; I had even descended to sharing a dormitory with nine other women. The only recompense for being deprived of all privacy was that I dwelt less on my wretchedness.

By the time the whistle sounded for the end of the workday, my feet screamed for a seat. In my old life, I had begged to be released from the confines of the needlework chamber. Now, I would welcome it. All I wanted was food and sleep. In the fading light, I joined the horde of celibate sisters streaming out of the factory's main gate. Dressed in matching black gummed silk tunic-blouses and trousers, they looked like dung beetles crawling through a small crack in the wall. A few laywomen were scattered among the mix, their coloured garments setting them apart. In our bereavement white cotton, Little Flower and I stood out too, for we would not take the So Hei vows and adopt the black habits until our year of mourning finished.

We all dragged our feet, our backs hunched, and every step

hurting as we trudged the half-mile back to the Hall of Eternal Purity, the sanctuary for our sisterhood. Along the way, other wretched souls packed up for the evening: the noodle vendor, a woman with underarm stains on her patched tunic-blouse, tossed a bucket of filthy water – the same she'd have used to rinse her bowls and chopsticks – into the canal that flowed alongside this principal road. I vowed never to eat from her stall. Further ahead, a scribe yawned as he gathered his brushes and inkwell. A fishmonger carried baskets of salted whitebait from the display counter back into the shop; the queue coiled around his head had loosened, slipping over his clammy forehead. They all looked tired, but none as weary as us.

Damp hair clung to our foreheads too, and even Joy, our youngest novice, sagged as she plucked wilted sprigs of jasmine from her braids and tossed them to the ground. Little Flower rubbed the rims of her swollen eyes, but that only aggravated them further and soon she gave up. Her wretchedness dispersed some of my earlier vexation – poor girl, silk reeling would be gruelling even if she didn't have to shoulder my share of the work, but she was diligent in her efforts to lighten my burden, making factory life sufferable for me. In spite of our heated words earlier, I felt charitable again. No doubt she needed a scolding, but I'd keep it short. I didn't want to spoil the harmony we'd established in the last few years, and she was my only friend . . . If I could, I would buy another slave to do the rough work, leaving Little Flower free to attend me, but I couldn't afford my own bedchamber, let alone a new *muizai*.

Back at the sanctuary, I collapsed onto a stone bench in a far corner of the courtyard beneath a cotton-flower tree. Although I couldn't see its flame-red colour, I still appreciated its full bloom, especially after a day at the stifling factory. I rolled my neck and stretched my shoulder joints as I waited for Little

Flower to bring me a basin of water infused with frangipani flowers and pomelo leaves. As one of the newest members of the sisterhood, Little Flower had to wait until the eighteen other sisters had had their turn at the well. Though we were all weary, we never skipped this washing ritual. Nothing could rid us of the fishy reek that burrowed into our pores, but the frangipanis' heady sweetness and the citrus tang of the pomelo leaves helped mask the stench.

When at last Little Flower returned with the scented water and a towel, I plucked a handful of flowers from the basin and pressed them to my nose. For a moment the fragrance spirited me away from my situation. I expected Little Flower to sponge my face, neck and arms before removing my clogs to wash and massage my feet. But she stood motionless as she chewed a corner of her lower lip.

'My feet and calves are throbbing,' I told her. 'I desperately need a long kneading. Be quick about the wipe down so you can spend more time on them before Cloud *ze* strikes the gong for the evening meal.'

'No,' she said.

'*No?*' I repeated, incredulous.

'I will not be washing your feet any more.'

'I know you're tired, but that doesn't mean you can shirk your duties. I'm still your mistress.'

'I'm glad you have brought up this subject. It's been on my mind for a while now.'

Little Flower sat down on the opposite bench, something she'd never done before without my permission. One of the lanterns from the nearby refectory cast a pool of light over her determined face.

'Our situation has changed,' she said. 'In memory of Lady Fong and to help you cope with your grief, I've continued to look after you this past month. But this arrangement must stop.'

'But you're my best friend,' I said. 'We're like my mother and Cerise. Why would you turn against me?'

'Lady Fong and Cerise were never real friends.'

'If they were not friends, then why did Cerise surrender herself to a nunnery out of grief?'

Little Flower straightened her spine, tilted her chin and said, 'Lady Fong issued commands and Cerise obeyed. That's not friendship.'

'But I don't bark orders.' She raised an eyebrow. 'Well,' I said, colouring as I remembered my behaviour back in Taiyuan, 'not any more. I speak to you with courtesy – it's been years since I shouted at you.' Little Flower shook her head. I went on: 'Earlier, I was just thinking that if I could afford it, I'd buy another *muizai* to do the rough work and cover my shift at the factory, so you'd only have to look after my toilette.' At this, she bowed her head and rubbed her temples. Suspecting she doubted my sincerity, I added, 'I still have a few pieces of jewellery. They aren't worth much, but if I sold a ring, perhaps we could hire a charwoman for a week or so. Wouldn't that be a nice break for you?'

'Linjing,' she said, with a gusty sigh. Before I could object to her use of my name without the honorific, she added, 'This gesture, though kind, fails to address the chasm that prevents us from being friends.' She took a deep breath and resumed. 'As long as you see yourself as my mistress, we can't be friends – and I can't be your maid any more.'

I crossed the courtyard and stood over her as I reached under my *ou* and pulled out her indenture paper from the pocket of my inner garment. Since Aa Noeng's passing, I'd taken to keeping this piece of paper with me at all times. It had become a sort of talisman to ward off despair, for having a *muizai* was all that kept me from sinking into true penury. Holding it before her eyes, I said, 'It seems you've forgotten about this contract of sale, and though it might injure our friendship, I must remind you that you're my property.'

I expected she'd crumple with remorse and it pained me to distress her.

Instead, Little Flower snatched the paper and ripped it in half, the pieces fluttering to the ground before I had time to react. My mouth fell open, but I closed it again without a word. Little Flower rose to her feet and took my unresisting hands. In a gentle tone that made a mockery of her mutiny, she said, 'My mother sold me to the Fong family, but you are *not* a Fong.' Her words stung more than Peony's slaps once had. She squeezed my hands and added, 'I am sorry for your loss, but it is time for me to live my own life. I can't do your work any more. But, if you like, we could help each other, as friends and equals.'

'How dare you?' I spluttered. My hands shook as I pulled them out of her grip. 'You' – I pointed at her – 'are low-born. I'm a lady. These facts are as solid as the ground we stand on.'

She stared at me for a long beat. I expected an apology, but she walked off without another word. I sank back on the bench, my chest heaving. How many more times would the foundation of my world be shattered? I'd already suffered more shock and disgrace than any reasonable person could endure. Yet, it seemed Fate had more torment in store for me. *Oh, Aa Noeng, if you'd known about the grinding work and Little Flower's impending rebellion, would you still have made the same choice for me?*

*

213

No matter what Little Flower claimed, she should always defer to me; I just needed my aunt's help to remind her of this irrefutable fact.

I hurried to the south wing, which housed Aunt Sapphire's apartment. She was the only person at the sisterhood with a room to herself. The darkness from within told me she was elsewhere. No matter, I would wait for her return. I stepped inside and left the door ajar, allowing moonlight to guide me until I found the lamp and lit it. Though this room was far smaller than Aa Noeng's quarters and only half the size of my former bedchamber, it felt like a palace compared to the upstairs dormitory lined with two rows of cots where I now slept. A set of drawers separated each bed, but I could touch Little Flower's hand if we both reached over the narrow space, which we'd done often when we first arrived as I sobbed into the small hours and recalled Aa Noeng's final words. If that wasn't proof of real friendship, then what was? I sighed and turned my attention back to this room. Here, my aunt could entertain guests in a sitting room furnished with a round table and four elegant stools, and along each wall, a set of chairs flanked a side table. A thick rug lay in the centre of her inner chamber and beyond a moon arch nestled an alcove bed. I ran my hand along the lacquered tabletop and took off my clogs to feel the carpet between my toes. All these comforts had once belonged to me. Now I had nothing. I slumped into a chair and wept into my hands. I would do anything to live as a lady again.

At the sound of footsteps, I lifted my head.

'Little Flower told me what happened,' my aunt said, as she approached. 'Your disappointment is reasonable, but it's not all bad. She is still willing to help you until you can manage on your own.'

'Can't you order her to remain my *muizai*?' I asked.

'I'm afraid that is impossible.'

'Isn't your word like an empress's edict here?'

She laid her feather fan on the side table and sat in the chair adjacent to mine.

'The sisters are peasants, but I don't own them. There are plenty of other sisterhoods they can join if they don't like it here. At worst, they could vote to cast me aside and instal another leader. I can't support myself without their earnings. Little Flower has logic on her side, and the sisterhood will support her cause too. Any attempt on my part to interfere with your situation would be seen as biased and in violation of one of our So Hei vows.'

'Which one?'

'The sixth. I've sworn to "love and respect my sisterhood", treating everyone as an equal. No matter their background, once a woman takes her So Hei vows, she has as much right as any other sister – this privilege applies to novices too. I didn't interfere while Little Flower seemed willing to serve you, but now she no longer wants to be your *muizai*. Who could blame her?'

'We are not equals,' I objected. 'You live in this comfortable chamber while everyone else is crammed into two dormitories.'

'This is the privilege of the mother superior. If you want to live like me, then aim to inherit my position.'

'How can I do that? I have no dowry.'

'Not every mother superior comes to the sanctuary with a bag of silver. My predecessor was a peasant, but she attained this coveted status with her shrewd economy and her diligence. For more than a decade, she was the top earner for this sisterhood, before too much dampness settled in her lungs and she struggled to breathe inside the factory. By then, she'd already secured her sisters' respect and support.'

A decade. I shuddered. 'I detest silk reeling! It's torture, especially for a lady. I'll never be good at it.'

'You must swallow your pride and accept your reduced circumstances.'

'Easy for you to say. You've never spent an hour in that stinking place. And you don't share a hovel with nine other women. I won't accept your hypocrisy.'

'Then leave.' She pointed to the door. 'Search for your own destiny. But heed my words: the outside world is far crueller than the trifles you've endured here.'

Her words were like a bucket of icy water, waking me from my petty grudge. At once, I understood I'd made a grave mistake in irritating her. Without her protection, I would not survive more than a few days on the streets, if at all. Terrified I'd lost her affection, I knelt and clasped her golden lilies. 'Please, Aunt, forgive me. Grief and exhaustion have clouded my judgement.'

'Get up,' she ordered, 'before we upset Phoenix's spirit.'

Her voice was edged with annoyance, but it had softened enough to give me the courage to press on. I continued to kneel, my eyes beseeching hers. 'Help me. Having a slave is the only privilege I have left. I was raised as a *lady* – I'm not destined for drudgery.'

She peered down at me with a mixture of gravity and compassion. 'Listen carefully, Linjing,' she said, 'for I will say this only once. I'm honouring your mother's request by giving you refuge. I promised her you would be safe, warm and nourished. But I did not pledge a genteel life for you. Doing so would have been a fallacy, and I can't lie. You must learn to make do with your new destiny.'

216

To appease my aunt, I bowed my head in a facsimile of submission. I would have to rely on myself to find an escape out of this dismal place. But how?

28

Little Flower

I did not grieve for Lady Fong like a daughter – no one could replace Aa Noeng in my heart – but for a time her death left me almost as bereft as it did Linjing. Both our mothers had bidden me to obey Linjing, to be her shadow, and neither had paid heed to my feelings. In their eyes, that was the natural order. But the Celibate Sisterhood sat outside that hierarchy, so I took comfort in thinking that if they were here, at least my mother – if not Lady Fong – might approve my stance against Linjing.

As the sorrow for Lady Fong began to recede, I discovered something else in its wake: if she had the courage to defy her destiny, then perhaps I could do the same with my life, for despite her tragic end, she had until then ruled as first wife. Her courage gave me hope that I might carve a different future for myself. Living as a freed woman ought to be enough, but I yearned for more, and I did not share the other sisters' reverence for an independence gleaned from gruelling hours and mind-numbing work. To me, the sisterhood was another kind of prison, albeit a much larger one.

Today was Joy's So Hei ceremony, and Madam Sapphire had negotiated a holiday for us. The main hall, a large rectangular chamber that served as a refectory at mealtimes, and a living room once the plates and bowls were cleared from the tables, was usually a sombre space with no paintings, wall hangings or rugs to soften its austerity. The stools and chairs, though carved from first-rate rosewood, lacked seat-pads; it seemed that Madam Sapphire had selected furniture to discourage slothful habits. But today no comfort was spared. We sat on plush cushions embroidered with silver and gold threads, and a thick rug covered the floor. Wall hangings with couplets depicting the virtues of chastity draped the walls: *Blessed are those women with the purity of jade. A chaste daughter honours her parents and brings glory to her clan. Better to live a simple life of liberty than risk a brutal husband in an extravagant home.*

Scarlet garlands with pompoms bedecked the rafters and support beams. Crimson satin tablecloths with fringes of long tassels covered the two tables; another five had been hired and set around the courtyard in readiness for Joy's family and other guests who would attend the afternoon banquet. Vases of red peonies sat on the side tables. Apart from the red paper cuttings, which were of the goddess of mercy and lotus flowers instead of double happiness and mandarin ducks, the trimmings mimicked those of a wedding. That a ceremony to denounce marriage should mirror one struck me as ironic, suggesting that beneath their bluster the sisters yearned to be wives, but I kept my thoughts to myself lest I offended them. The overall effect ought to have been festive, but its eerie reminder of Linjing's ill-fated nuptials dampened the mood for me. Linjing had barely spoken a word to me since our confrontation and had largely retreated into herself. Like a lost child, she wandered among the decorations in a stupor, at times blinking rapidly as she swiped the corners of her eyes. Knowing she would likely misconstrue my sympathy as an insult, I didn't comfort her. But seeing her so pitiful, I resolved to befriend her if she reached out first.

I expected Joy to look excited since Madam Sapphire and all the other sisters had told me this day was the best of a celibate sister's life, the day when she would commit herself to a life of independence from men. But she picked at her rice bowl and responded to the congratulations with a rigid smile. The other sisters' shrill voices filled the room as we gathered around two circular tables for a celebratory morning meal, the first festive activity in honour of the day. They were busy recounting stories about their decisions to join the sisterhood. After Madam Sapphire told her history, a sister with small, flitting eyes said, 'My mother died of childbirth fever. Two of my older sisters also perished trying to bring their first infant into the world. Their labours were long and bloody, and all for nothing. This sanctuary has saved me from the same fate.'

'Have you always known you wanted to join the sisterhood?' I asked Joy.

'My father gave me up to Aunty Cloud to raise when I was eight,' Joy replied flatly. 'It was a path chosen for me.'

Puzzled, I looked between Joy and Cloud *ze*. The older woman's ruddy face and flared nostrils bore no resemblance to Joy's delicate features.

'It is our village custom,' Cloud *ze* said. 'Most men who have several daughters give one to a celibate sister to raise. My eldest brother has five daughters and Joy is the youngest. So Hei nieces are expected to take the celibate vows too.'

'But . . .' I ventured '. . . can a niece refuse to take the vows?'

'Nonsense,' Cloud *ze* said. 'Who wouldn't want to be a celibate sister?'

Joy shoved a lump of rice into her mouth. I searched her face for the truth, but she'd drawn a curtain over her eyes, revealing nothing as she chewed. Her blank expression reminded me of the face Spring Rain had taught me to master, the mask all those like me used when we were forced to bend to the will of others. I missed my dear friend and suspected the worst had happened to her. No one else seemed to notice Joy's sadness.

'I want to be respected,' a sister with a square jaw declared, as she slammed her fist onto the table. 'On festive days, the village headman gives my family an extra share of roast pork in my honour, as if I am a son. No other women command the same respect.'

'That's right!' Bing Bing, an outspoken sister, agreed. 'We make so much money at the silk filatures that even fathers and brothers must kowtow to us. I get to lord it over my family whenever I visit.' Her eyes danced gleefully. 'I'm treated like a revered mother-in-law. Only it's much better, since I don't have to suffer for twenty years as a daughter-in-law first. My mother cooks all my favourite dishes. My father and brothers talk to me as an equal. As for my sisters-in-law,' she chortled, 'those poor wretches! They positively quiver with fear and awe in my presence.'

'Why are they afraid of you?' I asked.

'I'm their money tree! My sisters-in-law are extra mouths to feed. But my wages are almost equal to my entire family's earnings. They live in comfort because of me. My brothers wouldn't hesitate to thrash their wives if they dared to vex me. My whims are my sisters-in-law's commands.'

I shuddered. Her attitude was no better than Dowager Lady Fong's, and it breached the sisterly solidarity I thought sat at the heart of the Celibate Sisterhood. I had no family with whom to share the rewards of my hard work, but Bing

Bing could have chosen to be kinder to her sisters-in-law, treating them with the respect she enjoyed so that her path of independence brought joy to others too. I expected Madam Sapphire to rebuke Bing Bing, but she looked at her with approval. Did she care only for women who took the So Hei vows, no matter how they treated others?

At the auspicious hour of the horse, we formed a circle around Joy as she offered joss sticks to the goddess of mercy and kow-towed to the deity nine times. Afterwards, Madam Sapphire guided her to a chair that sat in front of a small mirror. A basin of water, two combs and a length of red cord lay next to it. Our circle shifted and tightened. Two elderly sisters, summoned from another sisterhood, began to unwind Joy's braids.

'We're very lucky to have Luk *ze* and Hei *ze*,' Madam Sapphire said. 'These blessed sisters have kindly agreed to comb up Joy's hair. They will bestow on Joy their longevity and the constancy of their celibate vows.'

Luk *ze* and Hei *ze* grinned; both were missing most of their upper teeth.

'Before we continue,' Madam Sapphire pressed on, 'I must emphasise the gravity of Joy's vows. This is also important for my niece and Little Flower to hear.' She fixed us with a stern look. 'The same standard applies to you. As novices you may change your minds about the vows and leave the sisterhood, with my permission, but if you shame us while you live here, you will be disciplined in the same manner as a full-fledged sister.'

Linjing and I responded with a solemn nod.

'The punishment for losing your maidenhead is execution by drowning,' she told us, peering from Joy to Linjing and me as she slowly enunciated each word. 'There is no clemency, no matter the reason. Guard your virginity with your life.'

Dumbfounded, we all stared at her.

'*Aiya!*' Luk *ze* cried. 'You're frightening the poor girls.'

'They need to be told,' Madam Sapphire replied. 'It's my duty to make them understand.'

'Not in such frightening tones,' Hei *ze* said. 'Besides, there hasn't been an execution in our village for as long as I've been alive. The last sister who fell pregnant was sent into exile by our late mother superior.'

Madam Sapphire opened her mouth, perhaps to protest, but Luk *ze* silenced her with a raised hand.

'Let us begin the ceremony,' Luk *ze* insisted, 'lest we miss the auspicious hour.'

With a vacant half-smile pinned to her face, Joy's reflection stared back at us as Hei *ze* and Luk *ze* took turns in combing her hair. Each stroke symbolized a commitment or a hope. Luk *ze* and Hei *ze* chanted in unison:

> *First stroke is for good fortune.*
> *Second stroke asks for conviction.*
> *Third gives freedom and peace.*
> *Fourth stroke binds you to chastity.*
> *Fifth hopes for determination and constancy of heart.*
> *Sixth stroke is a commitment to love and respect your sisterhood.*
> *Seventh ensures good tidings, and the eighth stroke prays for a life without suffering.*

By the eighth stroke, they had swept Joy's maidenly fringe back from her forehead and coiled her hair into a plain bun at the nape of her neck, securing it with red cord. Joy's shoulders sagged as she looked at her austere reflection. Oblivious to her mood, the sisters cheered and applauded, and Madam Sapphire led the way, coming forward to give Joy lucky red pockets.

After our bellies were full to bursting from the lavish banquet, which included a roasted suckling pig, chicken and duck, the last guests took their leave in the mid-afternoon, leaving us free to do as we pleased for the rest of the day. Madam Sapphire, Linjing and some of the sisters retreated for an afternoon nap; others gathered in the courtyard to play *maa-zoek* and I took out my embroidery supplies. I often thought about my art during the long hours in the factory, but at the end of each day, my eyes were too gritty to sew. Now, all I wanted was to embroider, even if I had time only to create a cluster of blossoms for a handkerchief. Once the table inside the main hall had been wiped down, I laid out two small hoops, three needles, scissors, a length of grey silk, a pile of motifs I'd designed, and a handful of indigo, apricot, crimson and moss-coloured silk thread. I longed for my embroidery frame, but Second Fong *taai taai* had confiscated most of our belongings and it had been too large to hide among my clothes. I'd managed to smuggle out only these meagre supplies and the portrait of the goddess of mercy. I lifted it from its linen wrappings and showed it to Joy and a few other sisters, who were eager to see my embroidery when I told them about my afternoon plans.

Joy traced the image with the tips of her fingers. 'Did you really make this?'

The other sisters echoed her astonishment. Glad to see Joy's spirits lifted, I cut off a section of the grey silk and fitted it into an embroidery hoop, then split the apricot thread into six strands and pushed one into the eye of a needle.

'This portrait is created by a mixture of different stitches,' I explained. 'Let me show you how it works.' Joy and the other sisters stood over me as I sewed. I embroidered a coin-sized sample with split stitches, shaded satin stitches and slanted satin stitches.

'I call this needle painting,' I said, as I held up the hoop, tilting it towards the light. 'See how the stitches reflect or absorb light? Can you imagine how it would look if the sample had only smooth satin stitches? The use of light is the key to making an image come alive, but contrasting texture is also vital.' I took a breath, ready to tell them more, but one of the sisters raised her hand.

'Slow down,' she said. 'I can't keep up.'

'Sorry,' I said, blushing. 'I shouldn't be talking so fast.'

'You should approach Noble Siu Je and offer your services to his shawl project!' Joy declared. 'I heard that he is looking for sewing amahs to help him design something unique for the white-ghost market. That's all I know. But after seeing your work, I'm certain you can create whatever he needs.' The other sisters nodded in agreement.

At the mention of Noble Siu Je, his angular face rose in my mind. Since confronting him a fortnight ago, I'd learnt he was the first son of the principal family of Chan Village, named after his ancestors who'd laid its foundations, and was only twenty-six, though his solemn bearing made him look older. My stomach dropped at the thought of another encounter with him, but my heart fluttered at the possibility of creating new designs and escaping silk reeling.

29

Linjing

With each passing day, I grew increasingly frantic to find a way to flee, but I needed a better alternative than life on the streets. Pride compelled me to refuse Little Flower's offers of assistance, for help from her now felt like charity. But I missed her services, and her companionship. I wanted to restore that bond, but it meant I must treat her as an equal, and if I did that, wouldn't I be a peasant too? How could I still claim to be a lady if I kowtowed to the whims of my *muizai*? After hearing about our falling-out, the sisters sided with Little Flower and shunned me. In the factory, I worked alone. During meal breaks, the sisters and Little Flower huddled together, chatting and laughing while I crouched on the fringe of the courtyard. Back at the sanctuary, no one spoke to me except out of necessity, and even Aunt Sapphire addressed me in clipped tones. I felt more alone than ever.

Days of poor sleep had dulled my senses, making my head thick and my fingers clumsy. At my workstation, I fought down the lump in my throat when yet another of the finicky silk threads snapped as I carefully fed it through the nooks and bobbins. My colour infirmity added to my troubles: in a world of greys, blues and yellows, it wasn't easy to see the beige spots on the cocoons that signified insect bites. How would I ever manage a full quota of twenty-five reels? It was beyond me, and that left me with only one option: worm rearing. At the thought of touching those grotesque creatures, saliva pooled in my mouth and nausea gripped my stomach. I ran for the nearest side door. In my haste, the raised platforms of my wooden clogs skidded on the slimy entrails of a squashed silkworm and I stumbled backwards, my arms flailing as I braced myself to smash against the filthy tiles. A pair of strong hands caught my shoulders, breaking my fall. Regaining my balance and taking deep breaths to calm myself, I turned to face my rescuer. It was Noble Chan. He stepped back, his posture regal as he placed one arm behind his back and the other across his sash belt. In response to my gasped thanks, he reciprocated with a well-bred, masculine smile, one that didn't show his teeth. Until now, I'd seen him only from a distance and we'd never spoken before. Up close, I noticed that his broad shoulders and chest filled out his clothes, much like a hand fitted a glove. At my full height, we almost stood eye to eye. I wondered if he enjoyed riding, like me.

'Miss Linjing,' he said. 'I'm well acquainted with your aunt, so it's a pleasure to meet you, though it must be hard for you to adjust to factory life.'

At this unexpected kindness, my eyes filled with tears, which I tried but failed to blink away. He offered a handkerchief, a snowy square of pressed linen. Grateful, I accepted it with a shaking hand.

'Come,' he said.

With his hand on my shoulder blade, he guided me out of the back door into the courtyard where we usually took our midday meals. He pulled out a stool from beneath a table and urged me to sit, telling me he would return soon with a soothing drink. Gradually, my sobs subsided and by the time he came back, my eyes were almost dry. He poured two cups of tea and offered one to me. I inhaled the sweet scent of chrysanthemum and took a long sip, allowing the delicate petals to linger on my tongue before I swallowed. All the while, he tapped his nails against the tabletop, drumming out a steady rhythm as he stared at a spot above my head. Despite my limited encounters with gentlemen, I had watched enough operas to know that his understated concern was perfect decorum.

'How do you know of me?' I asked.

'I often discuss business with Madam Sapphire,' he replied. 'During one of our recent meetings, she spoke of you and asked me to be lenient with your performance. I am sorry to hear of your misfortune. Please let me know if I can be of assistance.'

Alarmed, I asked, 'What did she say?'

Heavens, please, please don't say my aunt has been foolish enough to expose Ah Noeng's shame.

'I know she is your natal aunt, and she said you've fallen on hard times. But she did not mention the particulars.'

I let out my breath.

'Please rest here as long as you need,' he said, 'but I must return to my office.'

I wanted him to stay, but before I could say anything more, he bowed and strode back into the factory. Through the window, I saw him take the staircase that led to his office on the floor above our workstations. My dismal mood lightened as I watched him bound up two steps at a time.

*

The fleeting pleasure I'd enjoyed from Noble's thoughtfulness vanished that evening as I dipped a rag into a bucket of murky water, wincing as the heat and soap stung my split cuticles and irritated the ringworm patches on my forearm. I scratched until my skin broke and bled. At the sanctuary, we took turns to mop the refectory, a tedious chore that had to be done every evening after everyone had retired to bed. Little Flower used to do my share, but now it fell on me. My back ached as I shuffled on my hands and knees across the tiled floor, going up and down the length of the hall. With gritted teeth, I completed another section before I flung the rag aside and kicked the bucket, toppling it. Water spilt across the floor. I sank into the puddle and wept, not caring that my trousers would be soaked and need laundering, another task that had become my wretched lot.

Little Flower approached from the courtyard, her face etched with pity. I turned away, not wanting her to see my tear-stained cheeks. She crouched down and put an arm around my shoulders. I should have pushed her away, but instead I buried my face in her neck, sobbing. She stroked my back, just as she'd done when I'd panicked about the lotus shoes; the familiarity was too comforting to resist. When I could finally speak, I croaked, 'Oh, Little Flower, this life is too horrible. I can't cope without a maid. Please help me.'

She let go of me and stood up, half poised to leave. Gazing down at me, she said, 'I have come to offer my help because I can't bear to see you so miserable. But I can't be your *muizai* again.'

There was no venom in her tone, but it was unyielding. I hauled myself up and took her hands. Her fingers twitched and she frowned but didn't pull away.

'Thank you,' I said, squeezing her hands. 'I should have

accepted my reduced circumstances long ago. Instead I continued to live like a lady at your expense. I didn't understand the burden I was to you until forced to do this rough work myself. Please, forgive me and let us start again as *friends*. I've been so lonely. You're the only link to my past – I miss you.'

She pulled away from my grip and stepped back as she searched my face. 'Let us sit for a moment,' she suggested.

I nodded, following her to a bench in the courtyard.

'If we're to be friends,' she began, 'I must speak frankly and set out expectations.'

'Of course. I will treat you with equal respect.'

'I'm happy to help you until you get used to the physical demands of silk reeling and domestic work. But I'll decide when and how much assistance I can offer. Your words aren't my command any more.'

'I understand. Is that all?'

'Linjing,' she said, with a deep sigh. 'I hope you are not lying to me.'

'I'm sincere.'

She stood up, pinning me with a probing stare.

'Only a fortnight ago you insisted I was still your slave. Now you say we're equals. Are you capable of such a drastic shift?'

With my right hand, I held up my middle three fingers and lifted my arm high above my head. 'I swear it to the gods. Heaven be my witness, if my pledge of friendship is false, then let me die a painful death and return in my next life as a slave. No, worse yet, as a *sing-song* girl.'

Little Flower's eyes widened, though from disbelief or awe, I couldn't tell. I lowered my arm and pulled a hair stick from my braids. With it, I stabbed my finger, pressing deep until a droplet of blood appeared. I held the hair stick towards her, but she hid her hands behind her back.

'Let us swear a blood vow,' I urged. 'You've heard my pledge, all I ask is that you agree to be friends.'

She still didn't take the hair stick from my opened palm.

'Please, Little Flower. We must let go of our grievances and become true-hearted friends.'

Instead of coming towards me, she walked to a table, placing it between us.

'No,' she said. 'Too much has happened between us. I can't make such a solemn vow . . . at least, not yet. But I will try to be your friend if you agree to another condition.'

'Anything.'

'You mustn't wallow in your grief. I know you hate silk reeling as much as I do. But it's up to us to find something else, a better way to sustain ourselves and contribute to the sisterhood's economy.'

'Tell me what I must do and I'll pursue it.'

'I don't know how to advise you.'

'Do you have a plan for yourself?' I asked. With her ingenuity, I expected she might see a way out already.

She told me about her confrontation with Noble, along with her intent to approach him about the sewing amah position. I smiled, recalling his kindness as I in turn shared our earlier exchange with Little Flower.

'Strange,' she said. 'The man you describe is at odds with the master who threatened to dismiss me.'

'Perhaps it's because . . .'

I meant to say, *perhaps it's because he sees me as a lady*. But I couldn't finish the sentence. Doing so would antagonize Little Flower and shatter our friendship before it could even begin. We might be similar in age and have grown up together, but our fates were as distinct as copper and gold: one metal was destined to be cast into kitchenware, while the other would be crafted into jewellery. Little Flower was born to toil, but a finer life could still be within my reach. I couldn't alter my sentiment, but I would change my conduct: outwardly. I would treat her as an equal – surely the latter mattered more. Lest Little Flower read my mind, I turned back into the refectory, saying, 'We'd better finish the job as soon as possible.'

30

Little Flower

Linjing's contrition left me wary and hopeful in equal parts. I wanted to believe her, but our past was a fading scar that lingered, and I didn't know whether it could vanish altogether. I pushed aside these thoughts as I clutched my basket and ascended the stairs leading to Noble Siu Je's office.

Nerves jangling, I knocked on the door and waited. Footsteps approached. I smoothed my *ou* and took a deep breath, determined to remain dignified, no matter how much Noble Siu Je's grave eyes bored into mine. But it was Ming who stepped onto the landing and greeted me with a warm smile. I gave him a low bow. 'I'm afraid I might have got you into trouble with Noble Siu Je. Did he scold you for hiring me?'

Ming dismissed my concern with a wave of his hand.

'He seemed very vexed that you'd overlooked my infirmity,' I said. 'I'm most grateful for your kindness and hope you didn't suffer for it.'

'Noble Siu Je and I go back a long way,' Ming replied, with a quick laugh. 'M-my family have been w-working for the

Chans for th-three generations. Noble Siu Je and I w-were playmates. Old M-master Chan didn't w-want a stammering clerk, but Noble Siu Je refused to set m-me aside, so don't w-worry about m-me.'

I nodded as I mulled over this new information about Noble Siu Je. So far, I had three accounts of his character. According to Ming and Linjing, he was tolerant and considerate. Did he hold a personal grudge against me?

'Wh-what can I do for you t-today?' Ming asked.

'I would like an interview with Noble Siu Je about his shawl project.'

With an arched brow, Ming glanced at the broken fingers on my right hand.

'Please, Ming. Give me a chance to speak with him. That's all I ask.'

For several seconds, Ming squeezed his eyes shut. When he opened them, he gestured for me to step over the threshold. Inside the office, wood panels lined the walls, dark and sombre like Noble Siu Je's manners towards me. Once Ming shut the door, the factory racket receded. Smoke from incense burners masked the fishy odour with a sweet, refreshing scent. Artwork and photographs covered the walls, and I longed to examine them but did not have time, though I noticed one was a portrait of Noble Siu Je wearing a Western suit with a tall hat. I followed Ming through the curtain of beads that hung in the moon gate, separating the small reception alcove from the inner quarters. Noble Siu Je sat at his desk, head bent over an abacus as he flicked its counters with undue force. *Tack, tack, tack.* The wooden beads smashed against each other as though in protest.

'Pardon m-me, Noble Siu Je,' Ming announced. 'Little Flower, of M-Madam Sapphire's sisterhood, w-wishes t-to speak to you.'

Noble Siu Je frowned at Ming, who flashed him a sheepish grin and shrugged before retreating to his own smaller desk.

Noble Siu Je pushed away the abacus and leant back in his chair with an elbow on each armrest, his hands coming together to form a steeple. His brow lowered, like a band of foreboding clouds, and my confidence could not keep from swaying. To steady my nerves, I gripped the handle of my basket, my knuckles turning white. With as much poise as I could muster, I declared, 'I have heard you are looking for unique designs for your shawl project. I'm a gifted embroidery artist. I can help you.'

He crossed his arms. 'I am impressed by your ambition.'

The band of clouds lifted, and I smiled.

'But you've a nerve to think you can hoodwink me. Only women with golden lilies are capable of exquisite embroidery. This is a universal truth. You have big feet.'

To stifle a weary sigh, I pressed my lips together, closed my eyes and readied myself for a battle.

'Your doubt is reasonable,' I replied, as I opened my eyes, 'but I've worked as a handmaiden for Linjing since I was six, up until recently. Her mother was a generous tutor who encouraged me to practise my needlework.'

'The ladies' maids in my household all have bound feet, albeit not very small ones. Even so, their embroidery is inferior to that of my mother and sisters. Golden lilies are only one requirement; to excel in needlework, a lady also needs an artistic eye. You wouldn't have had the same high breeding and opportunities.'

From my basket, I pulled out a circular picture frame and laid it before him.

'This portrait of the goddess of mercy is my original creation,' I told him. 'I designed the motif and invented the needle-painting technique to mimic Western oil paintings. Please, sir, I would be grateful if you would look at it.'

He picked up the portrait and studied it. With his fingertip, he touched the surface, and a gasp of awe escaped his parted lips. My pulse quickened.

'This is extraordinary! I have never seen such a thing.'

'Thank you, sir. Your esteem means a lot to me.'

He laid the portrait back on his desk and pinned his eyes on mine. 'I am tempted to believe you, but this can only be the work of an exceptional lady. There is nothing like it in the genteel homes I have visited, or on the export market. I wish to meet this remarkable artist.'

'Sir, *I am the artist.*'

Despite my resolve to appear composed, my voice shook with indignation and my cheeks flushed. I glared at him. The haughty certainty in his eyes shifted as I willed him to believe me. He picked up the portrait and examined it again, turning it this way and that as his fingers continued to explore the satin stitches.

'This portrait is an expression of artistic flair,' he insisted, 'and that could only be the product of an elegant mind, that of a high-born lady. A peasant is not capable of such finesse, particularly one without golden lilies.'

I lifted a collection of patterns from my basket and laid them on his desk.

'These are samples of my sketches,' I told him. 'Among the floral designs, you will find the various drafts I made in the process of selecting the best pose for the goddess. I implore you to inspect them.'

My skin burnt as Noble Siu Je flicked through the patterns and studied the ones relating to the portrait: the first had the goddess standing on a floating lotus platform; in the second,

236

the deity hovered above rolling waves with a golden carp leaping out of the water; and in another, a plump infant sat on her lap. There were different versions of her face within each composition: in some she looked at the viewer and in others her face tilted down towards a child. In between examining each sketch, Noble Siu Je glanced up, and each time our eyes met I saw both gravity and scepticism in his gaze. My courage faltered. The former *muizai* in me begged to flee, but I stayed, for it was time I chased my dreams, rather than surrender to the roles society and Fate had allotted to me.

'These sketches are works of art within their own right, and I am convinced they are drawn by the same hand,' he said. 'But that does not prove you are the artist. I have seen you at work. Although you are good at silk reeling, it is impossible to believe you can excel at embroidery with three damaged fingers.'

'I can embroider in front of you. Right now! I have supplies in my basket. I need only half an hour of your time. I—'

'That won't be necessary.' He gestured to the pile of shawls on a nearby table. Some had a border of tassels, others were trimmed with strings of finely braided knots; the one on top depicted a garden with peonies, stone bridges and an eight-tiered pagoda. 'I need something novel that will outshine these existing samples and appeal to Western taste, for the export market. I doubt you'd have a solution for me.'

'I don't,' I admitted. 'But I am confident I will meet your expectations if you give me a chance.'

'No.' With that, he sprang to his feet and walked over to a bookcase, where he pulled out a volume bound in black silk and thumbed through its pages. With his back turned to me, he addressed Ming.

'Kindly see Little Flower out,' he said. 'In future, do not

allow workers to interrupt me. If any of them has a grievance or a question, tell them to speak to their mother superior.'

Crushed, I followed Ming out of the office. He patted my shoulder and promised to help if he could. I thanked him, but his words offered little comfort. Once I stepped over the threshold, my legs felt like two blocks of tofu. I sank onto a bench on the landing around the corner, beneath an open window. As I tried to compose myself, the short, sharp tones of an argument penetrated the fog of my thoughts. It was Ming and Noble Siu Je, their voices carrying through the door to his chambers.

'What?' Noble Siu Je snapped.

'Why did you t-turn Little Flower down?' Ming asked. 'I believe her.'

'You are *not* a fair judge of character when it comes to others who have physical impairments.'

'I admit I have a soft spot for kindred spirits.'

'Enough said!'

Pulse quickening, I knew it was wrong to eavesdrop, but curiosity overcame my scruples.

'I broke your rule because I took p-pity on her, I'll admit that. But I w-would wager a m-month of my salary th-that she is not an impostor.'

'Only ladies with bound feet can embroider,' Noble Siu Je asserted.

'She has given ample p-proof of her skill. Isn't it a bit antiquated of you t-to doubt her just because she has natural feet?'

'The correlation between excellence in embroidery and golden lilies is a universal truth. Even middling sewing amahs have respectable feet. Your mother and wife will side with me if you appeal to them.'

'The w-women in my family still worship golden lilies, that's t-true. But unlike us, they haven't been t-to London. The English ladies all have natural feet, but I recall seeing some exquisite needlework th-that is on par w-with Chinese embroidery.'

'Chinese embroidery is far more intricate than Western needlework. But it is more than aesthetics. For a Chinese lady, embroidery is an expression of her high breeding, patience and fortitude – qualities a woman can't achieve without first binding her feet.'

'Are you sure you only rejected Little Flower because she is a peasant?' Ming asked.

'What the devil are you implying?' Noble Siu Je growled.

'I m-mean no offence,' Ming said. 'Only I do not w-want you t-to overlook a rare artist, that's all.'

'Little Flower cannot be the artist,' Noble Siu Je insisted, 'because she does not have golden lilies.'

Noble Siu Je's tenor was of the forbidding sort designed to remind Ming who was in charge. Yet beneath the show of command, a hint of hollowness implied Noble Siu Je was parroting a phrase he'd learnt by rote. I sighed. Clearly, it would take an exceptional event to overcome his entrenched prejudice. Pleading would not work, and I suspected even an endorsement from Madam Sapphire would fall short. What would be enough?

31

Linjing

Since Noble's kindness to me, I couldn't stop thinking about him. In this bleak life, he was my only spot of brightness. To glean a better understanding of him, I paid heed to factory talk and asked questions of my fellow workers. According to them, his visits to the factory floor were perfunctory, never lasting more than a quarter of an hour, and he rarely spoke to his employees. His air of gravity frightened many of the young maidens, while the older women complained of his arrogance. If displeased with an employee's performance, he would instruct his clerk to issue disciplinary measures. When an issue escalated, Noble would approach the mother superior in charge of the offender's sisterhood and discuss matters with her. In short, Noble rarely condescended to speak with peasants, which accounted for his dismissal of Little Flower.

Of course I felt badly for her. Poor girl, she was so dispirited by Noble's rejection that the quality of her silk reels suffered. These days, many of her skeins were rejected by the daily quality checker. Distracted by the shawl-project obstacle, she often neglected to merge the existing thread with new leads when the cocoons in her water bath had run out of silk, exposing a dead worm. To be a worthy friend, I tried to commiserate with her, but it was hard to be solemn when I felt buoyant for the first time since Aa Noeng's disgrace. I couldn't be certain yet, so I dared not utter my conjecture to a soul, but the increased frequency of Noble's visits to the factory floor suggested he might be seeking me out.

To confirm my hope, I observed him closely. He often stared at the workbench I shared with Little Flower, but there was a clear distinction between the frowning disapproval he cast at her and the civil bows he bestowed on me when I raised my hand in greeting. He also stopped to talk to me when our paths crossed. On one occasion, he asked when Little Flower and I would take our So Hei vows; another time he wanted to know when I'd first met Little Flower and whether we were still mistress and *muizai*. He seemed so interested and concerned for my welfare.

In the cocoon storage room, he'd been talking to his clerk, only to stop mid-sentence when I entered with Little Flower. He took a step in our direction but, with visible effort, turned and resumed his discussion. The clerk's brow quirked, questioning his master's odd behaviour. As the two men conversed, Noble's gaze drifted to the corner where we were selecting cocoons for our workbasket. When our eyes met, he quickly looked away and turned to face the canal. Could he be struggling with his feelings for me? Perhaps he wished to speak to me but felt inhibited by my novice status. I walked over to him.

'Good day to you, Noble Siu Je,' I said. 'The breeze is a relief.'

241

He replied with a deep bow and similar pleasantries. I smiled, encouraging him to continue the conversation, but he lapsed into silence. He stood upright, his hands clasped behind his back and his eyes looking into the distance. Often, people did not live up to their names: my poor *aa noeng*, for one, couldn't rise above the ashes of her downfall like a phoenix, and I was far from a piece of serene jade. But Noble's highborn profile – with an angular jawline and a striking nose – was worthy of his namesake. Hoping to build on our acquaintance, I ventured on the one subject we had in common.

'Have you reconsidered hiring Little Flower for the shawl project?' I asked.

'I've no such intent,' he said, voice tight with displeasure.

I cursed myself for bringing up a topic that vexed him. 'I don't mean to pry,' I said hurriedly. 'Only Little Flower is crestfallen by your dismissal. It's very hard for me to see her so miserable. I thought perhaps you might give her a chance.' *For my sake*, I wanted to add.

Noble's mouth flattened into a rigid line as he looked at Little Flower and shook his head before bowing at me. 'Excuse my abruptness, Miss Linjing,' he said. 'I didn't intend to offend you. I suppose she asked you to plead her case.'

'Oh, no—'

'My mind is made up. I'd be much obliged if you would convey the finality of my decision to her. Good day to you again, Miss Linjing. Please send my regards to your aunt.'

With a brusque nod, Noble strode outside, his clerk scurrying behind. I stood at the threshold, shading my eyes from the sun as I watched him disappear down the canal path. He carried his height with the conviction of a general. At the next pier, he turned back, but distance made his face inscrutable. I blamed myself for our clumsy tête-à-tête, but my efforts had not been futile: I had further proof that he considered me a lady, worthy of gallantry.

The next day, as I looked above my head to shoo away a pestering fly that seemed drawn to me, I caught sight of Noble peering down from one of his office windows. Again his gaze rested on our corner of the factory. He leant against the window frame, rubbing his jaw as though ruminating on a puzzle. I waved to him, but he was too deep in contemplation to respond.

Could it be true that he esteemed me despite my natural feet and reduced circumstances? Might he be thinking about the obstacles that lay in our way? After Aa Noeng's disgrace, a part of me had been relieved to be freed from the matrimonial pressures I had so feared ... but now everything had changed. Unlike Valiant Li, who was a stranger, I felt I knew Noble, admired him, even desired him, and marriage to him would restore my status. *Oh*, how I wanted him to feel the same, but I needed more evidence of his regard before I dared to voice my hope to Little Flower.

Soon it would be the Seven Sisters Festival, on the seventh day of the seventh month. Aunt Sapphire summoned us to the refectory for a meeting and addressed us from the front of the room, standing beneath a six-foot-wide black plaque inscribed with 'Hall of Eternity Purity'. The words ought to have served as a kindly reminder of our mantra, yet the thick characters seemed to glare down at us like a scornful mother-in-law.

'The Seven Sisters Festival is in twenty-three days,' Aunt Sapphire told us. 'It has been four years since we last took the

243

title of Outstanding Sisterhood. I am determined for us to outshine the other nine sanctuaries in Shuntak and seize the first prize of . . . a dazzling thirty taels!'

A collective gasp echoed around the room. Though the prize money would be wonderful for the sisterhood, I was more interested in the prestige of winning. If my conjecture about Noble's feelings was true, then belonging to an exceptional sisterhood might elevate my status in his family's eyes. I sat up and paid attention, and Little Flower mirrored my posture.

'That's ten taels more than last year!' Cloud *ze* exclaimed. 'The other sisterhoods will do anything to win.'

'The competition will be fierce,' my aunt agreed. 'But we are as worthy as them, and if we work extra hard, I am certain the goal is within reach. As always, the three sisters who produce the best dioramas will take the biggest share of the prize money if we win.'

'What about the embroidery contest?' Bing Bing asked. 'I don't think we should bother with that. The prize for the Commoners' League is hardly worth the effort.'

Little Flower raised her hand and asked Bing Bing, 'Who can enter this contest?'

'Each year, the mother superior from each sisterhood nominates a representative for the embroidery contest, which is hosted by Madam Chan at the Chan residence, since they're the principal family in Shuntak. Madam Sapphire usually selects the sister who makes the most exquisite figurine for the offerings to the celestial sisters.' Bing Bing shook her head. 'Madam Chan and the mistresses of the other filatures preach fairness and opportunity, saying any maiden can enter either the Ladies' League or the Commoners' League contest. But none of us have the skills to compete with the rich girls. The Ladies' League gets a silver hairpin decked with rubies or jade and we get a tawdry imitation made from cheap *baak tung*. Oh, you should see Madam Chan's patronizing face when she presents the prize to the winner of the inferior league. It's so insulting!'

'Bing Bing is right,' Cloud *ze* echoed. 'It's enough to make me want to boycott the contest.'

'Yes!' a third sister shouted. 'I say we shun it and ask the other sisterhoods to do the same.'

'What is needed to enter the Ladies' League?' Little Flower asked.

'The contestants must be skilled in double-sided embroidery,' Bing Bing told her. 'Even some ladies cannot do that, let alone us.'

'It's the dishonesty that I hate,' Joy said. 'Why can't Madam Chan openly admit she wants to exclude peasants from winning the fancy prize?'

'I can represent us in the Ladies' League,' Little Flower said.

'I vouch for Little Flower,' I said at once. 'Her double-sided embroidery is second to none. With her on our side, we'll be sure to win.'

My aunt readily agreed, and the sisters clapped and cheered. I turned to Little Flower and grinned. At first, she looked at me with confusion, but surprise soon gave way to gladness. For the first time since the lotus-shoes project, we shared a mutual goal.

For the next few weeks, the Hall of Eternal Purity changed into a beehive of activity as the sisterhood devoted every spare moment to preparations for the Seven Sisters Festival.

Most of the sisters worked on dioramas, replicating the scene where Zikneoi, the youngest of the seven celestial princesses, was separated from her lover, a mortal cowherd. Zikneoi's outstretched arms reached for the cowherd as two soldiers held him back with spears crossed over his chest. Above them, the white-bearded Jade Emperor stood on a suspended platform of clouds, pointing an accusatory finger at his wayward daughter, who had stooped to marry a human. To the left of him, the Queen Mother of the West clutched a long hairpin, poised to scratch a Silver River into the sky to separate the lovers. Aside from these key characters, the dramatic scene needed an entourage of serving maids, divine guards on horses and the magical ox who had sacrificed himself, allowing the cowherd to fly on his hide to the heavens in his bid to rescue his wife.

With the majority of the sisters engaged in the detailed scene, Little Flower and I made figurines that depicted the Seven Sisters in their respective duties: Zikneoi sat in front of a loom, the eldest sister held an embroidery hoop, the next strummed a zither, another sewed clothes, and so on. We made the dolls and props from papier-mâché and fashioned their gowns from silk scraps donated to us from the filatures' mistresses. Each maiden also needed a minuscule pair of lotus shoes.

As we sat together on a bench at the far side of the court-yard, sewing in the fading summer light, my heart was bursting to confide in Little Flower. I shuffled closer to her, looking around and over my shoulders, before I lowered my voice and whispered to her.

'I want to marry Noble Siu Je.'

Little Flower gasped, and her hand stopped mid-stitch.

I suppressed a giggle. 'I know it sounds ridiculous, but hear me out.' I told her all that I'd observed over the last fortnight. As I talked, she fidgeted with her embroidery, picking at the loose threads. 'Do you think he likes me?' I finished.

'I have noticed Noble Siu Je's attention,' she agreed, 'and it is clear he treats you as a lady.'

Beaming, I hugged her, but she peeled my arms away. Her brow puckered with doubt.

'What's the matter?' I asked.

'I'm not convinced he is romantically interested in you.'

'Our first meeting is proof of his affection – only a man in love would act with such consideration.'

'I agree that was very kind of him. Yet his subsequent conversations with you don't seem to hint at secret yearning. It's difficult to read his impassive face . . . but I suspect Noble Siu Je is more likely trying to find fault so he can be rid of me.'

'Yes, he glares at you a great deal. But that doesn't negate my conjecture. We work side by side, so he can't help but see you as he searches for me, can he?'

She resumed sewing but after a few stitches, looked up with a teasing smile and said, 'Be careful what you wish for – he is already far too serious for his age. Imagine what he'll be like when he is an old man.'

'*Oh*, he only appears sombre because he observes the strictest propriety. He won't be like that in the privacy of our bedchamber.'

She arched an eyebrow and widened her eyes.

I protested, 'I'm not thinking about . . .' too embarrassed to continue, I mouthed '. . . wife duty.'

'I didn't say you were,' she replied, with a laugh. 'Though it seems the idea wouldn't be disagreeable to you.'

'He is dashing,' I admitted, as I cupped my flaming cheeks, 'and muscular and tall.'

She responded with a vague hum.

'Even if he is plain and dull,' I told her, 'marriage to him will be my escape from all this misery.' I waved my arms around and kicked the dirt; our shabby courtyard that I loathed at the best of times was now insufferable. I added, 'I want to wear silk, sleep until I naturally wake, go riding – be a *lady* again.'

As we conversed, Little Flower had continued to sew, albeit intermittently, but now she set aside the hoop and turned to face me, her countenance subdued. 'I know you are miserable and desperate,' she said gently, 'but that makes you vulnerable to seeing affection when there is only civility.'

'I'm not a fool! He singles me out because he likes me, I know it.'

'Even if your instinct is right,' she said, 'it's impossible for him to marry you. His family is very conservative. All the Chan ladies and their handmaidens have golden lilies. They would never accept a daughter-in-law with natural feet, especially one with a murky past.'

'There are some obstacles in our way, that's true, but he's a resourceful man of integrity. Besides, I always get what I want. Nothing is impossible if I put my mind to it.'

'How can you be sure of his disposition?'

'It is in his earnest eyes, his speech and his general air. Besides, Master Chan wouldn't allow him to manage the family business at such a young age if he lacked sense or courage.'

The corners of her mouth turned down with scepticism.

I added, 'I heard he sojourned in London for a year and only returned to China earlier this year, which is probably why he doesn't mind my natural feet.'

'I feel as though we're talking about two different men. To you, Noble Siu Je is a flawless hero from a romantic opera. To me, he is severe and intractable. Either you are wrong or I am.'

To protect our budding friendship, I refrained from speaking my mind: it was apparent that Noble's inconsistencies lay not with his character but with the difference in status between Little Flower and me.

'Do you know he is already affianced?' she continued. After a pause, she added, 'I hear they will wed in the tenth month this year. Even if it were possible to marry him, you wouldn't be first wife.'

'His womb betrothal to Miss Prudence Tsui is common knowledge,' I replied. 'The gossipmongers say it's a business match set up by their fathers, who want to strengthen their ties. But Madam Tsui didn't have a girl infant until Noble Siu Je was ten, hence his late marriage. None of this bothers me. Miss Prudence might be first wife, but I would be the one he prefers.'

I could see that Little Flower remained unconvinced.

'If I become second wife, I might provide for you too,' I reminded her. 'Maybe you could live with me, not as *muizai* but like a sister, and I could persuade him to give you a chance at the shawl project. This is my only escape . . . my one chance to return to gentility. Help me find a way to win his family's approval.'

Her gaze dropped to her feet as she plucked at the fabric in her lap.

'Help me,' I repeated. 'You're my only ally. I need you.'

'It isn't a matter of willingness,' she replied. 'I just can't see how I can be useful. But I have one piece of advice. If you're in earnest, find a way to win over his mother.'

At this, we exchanged a grimace and laughed.

32

Little Flower

When Madam Sapphire summoned me for a talk in her apartment, my thoughts flew to Linjing's desperate scheme. Had she caught wind of her niece's outlandish ambition? If so, I hoped she didn't see me as an accomplice. To protect Linjing's feelings, I didn't tell her that I thought her conjecture was lunacy. Hope was hope, even if it was false. Linjing needed a crutch to support her until she could accept her new life; I didn't have the heart to crush her with the weight of reality.

At a round table in the centre of her receiving chamber, Madam Sapphire was poring over some accounts, checking the recorded calculations with her abacus. Upon noticing me, she set aside her spectacles and beckoned me to sit on the opposite stool. I obeyed and clasped my hands on the table, wondering what she had in mind as she poured two cups of tea and served one to me. Both of us blew on our steaming brew while she studied me with a scrutiny that made me feel as if I were sitting too close to a brazier. I shifted in my seat but dared not look away, lest I offended her. At last, she said, 'Little Flower, I have high hopes for you.'

Stunned, I asked, 'Why?'

She listed my virtues, checking off each one with her fingers. 'You are talented with silk reeling and embroidery,' she began, unfolding her left thumb. Next, her index finger rose as she said, 'It took courage to seize your liberty from Linjing.' Finally, she tapped her middle finger. 'More importantly, you didn't gloat afterwards. All these are leadership qualities, putting you in good stead perhaps one day to become my successor.'

I spluttered, spraying droplets of tea onto the account book. Aghast, I used my sleeve to mop it up. Madam Sapphire laughed, a mirthful chuckle that assured me she wasn't the sort of lady who took offence at trifling matters.

'Ma'am, you've overestimated me,' I said. 'I know nothing about the management of a sisterhood.'

'I'm a good judge of character,' she replied, 'and I say you have the essential virtues. Experience would come with time. But I'm also frank and cautious, so I hope you won't mind my questions.'

I blinked at her and tilted my head.

'Don't fret,' she said, patting my arm. 'I only wish to help you examine your thoughts. Safeguarding you from danger is my principal duty.'

'Yes, of course,' I muttered, though I was still perplexed.

'I am aware of your eagerness to be hired as the designer for Noble Siu Je's shawl project. But you'll be frequently in his company if you succeed.'

She looked at me expectantly.

'Are you proposing to recommend me to him?' I asked, hopeful.

'He has made it clear he doesn't want to hire a former slave, but that would likely change if you win the competition.'

Again, she looked at me expectantly. When I remained silent, she asked, 'Is this your way of setting your cap at Noble Siu Je?'

I jolted and shook my head vehemently.

'You wouldn't be the first novice to abandon the sisterhood in favour of marriage,' she continued. 'While I don't condone the practice, it is a forgivable transgression if you seek my approval first and do not disgrace us before you leave the sisterhood. But you have less sense than a village idiot if you think a man of his class will make a decent offer, or any offer at all, to you. Madam Chan is a proud, haughty woman – she would never accept a former *muizai*, not even as a *cip si* of the lowest rank.'

In a low, measured voice, I said, 'Ma'am, I have no desire to be anyone's concubine. All I want is the time and space to pursue my art in a way that will also earn a respectable livelihood within the sanctuary. If possible, I hope to earn more than a silk reeler and thereby make a bigger contribution to the sisterhood's economy.'

She picked up her tea, taking a long drink as she peered at me over the rim of the cup. Again, her intense scrutiny unnerved me, but I dared not look away. I folded my hands together and waited.

'Let me be clear,' she said. 'By working with Noble Siu Je, you will be breaking with custom. Celibate sisters do not work closely with men, even if they are gentlemen of upright morals. I hold Noble Siu Je in great esteem. But he is still a man with male urges.' The last word hovered in the air like a miasma. Grievances from Linjing's cousins hurtled into my mind: *sick to death of his pawing, her husband even forced his male organ into—* I snapped off the sordid memory and grimaced. Madam Sapphire raised one eyebrow and her lip quirked in a way that looked like approval, yet she continued her lecture. 'You are a pretty maiden, the sort to tempt a man. I'm confident he will behave honourably, but if he fails, it will be up to *you* to maintain propriety at all times. If there is a scandal, you will be blamed and I will be the first to denounce you for the sake of our sanctuary's reputation. There will be no mercy, no exceptions. Given my warning, you must think carefully. Are you capable of remaining true to the So Hei principles?'

'Embroidery is my lifeblood. I can't live without it.'

She pressed. 'If there is a shred of doubt in your heart or a quaver of temptation, now is the time to abandon your ambition and retreat to the safety of silk reeling.'

'I love my art,' I insisted. 'Nothing else matters.'

Madam Sapphire tilted her face to the open window, eyes thoughtful as they looked into the distance, fingers flicking back and forth against the tablecloth as though working an abacus.

'Very well,' she said, fixing her attention back on me. 'If you can persuade him to hire you, I'll be happy to negotiate the terms on your behalf. Noble Siu Je is a shrewd businessman, so we need to ensure the conditions are favourable to you and the sisterhood.'

I stood up and bowed to my waist. On my way back to the refectory, I mulled over Madam Sapphire's words. Her warnings rang true, at least with regard to the danger of gossip for a woman. As for Noble Siu Je, I was confident that nothing untoward would transpire between us. If anything, I wished he liked me a little more.

33

Linjing

On the day of the Seven Sisters Festival, the central court-yard in the Chan estate was transformed into an exhibition hall. Trestle tables ran down the length of the northern and southern walls. Each diorama was guarded by the rep-resentative of the sisterhood who had created it. The beads and metallic threads from the figurines' costumes glinted in the early-afternoon sun. On an elevated stage, a young woman played a jaunty tune on a zither, the delicate notes barely audible above the collective chatter. While Little Flower dedicated herself to the Ladies' League embroi-dery competition, I waited impatiently for an opening to address Noble, his mother and sisters. The four of them flitted from one display to the next as they paid respect to each sisterhood.

When the family finally gathered at a nearby pavilion, I took a deep breath and strode towards them. Madam Chan sat at a round table, flanked by Noble and Miss Yi Yi, the elder of her two daughters, who was studying the contest-ants' progress through a pair of opera glasses. Miss Pui Pui sat beside her sister, nibbling a piece of confectionary. At my approach, they all stared.

'Noble Siu Je,' I said, as I curtsied in the Western fashion and addressed him in English, 'I overheard that Miss Yi Yi is betrothed to a gentleman in Hong Kong, and I thought—'

'What is this peasant saying, Noble?' Miss Pui Pui interjected.

Before Noble could translate, Madam Chan said, 'This pavilion is reserved for our family only. Who invited this intruder here?'

Their hostility cut, and I regretted flaunting my English. Too mortified to speak, I wrung my handkerchief in my hands. They might not have been so rude if I'd been wearing silk damask as I used to, but Peony had confiscated all my elegant clothes, leaving me with nothing but cheap cotton *saam fu*, and though I no longer wore bereavement white, this plain light blue *ou* with matching trousers was a world apart from the Chan ladies' heavily embroidered silks.

'Mother,' Noble replied, 'this is Madam Sapphire's niece, Miss Linjing. I believe she wanted to demonstrate her English skills and wishes to be of use to us.' He nodded to me and said, 'Please continue.'

Madam Chan and her daughters glanced between my feet and my face with unbridled disdain and confusion.

'But she has slave feet,' Miss Yi Yi objected. 'Why isn't Madam Sapphire's niece a lady?'

'I am of genteel birth, Miss Yi Yi,' I explained, and turned to catch Madam Chan's eye. 'But my father arranged a marriage for me with a progressive family who wanted a daughter-in-law with natural feet.'

'Are they one of those half-breed families?' Madam Chan

255

asked. 'There seem to be more and more of those hotchpotch unions these days.'

'No. My betrothed was Chinese, but his family was progressive.'

'Did you do something scandalous?' Miss Pui Pui asked.

'Is that why you are a novice now?' Miss Yi Yi added.

I bristled at their cruel questions. In their bright eyes, I saw hunger for gossip.

'*Girls*,' Noble reproached, 'it is ill-mannered to ask such probing questions and Miss Linjing deserves sympathy, not suspicion.'

Oh, how he cared for me!

Cowed but not contrite, his sisters pouted, while their mother continued to glare at me with distrust.

For Noble's sake, I quashed my pride and went on: 'My fiancé died of a sudden brain fever,' I lied, 'just before our wedding. My mother fell victim to smallpox too, so my second *aa noeng* convinced my father to send me to a nunnery since no other genteel family would have a girl with big feet. She'd always wanted to be first wife, and to be rid of me too.'

To my relief, Madam Chan's face softened into one of empathy. I glanced at Noble, hoping this admission would make him even more sympathetic towards me, but he had turned to stare at the embroidery contestants. Though annoyed, I did not show it.

'You poor girl,' Madam Chan said. 'My father's minor wives were equally scheming. I thank Heaven that, unlike my brothers-in-law, Master Chan never took a second wife. How did you escape your second *aa noeng*'s wicked plot?'

'Aunt Sapphire rescued me and gave me refuge here. I will always be indebted to her, but I was not raised for rough work. I wish to earn my living teaching English to other young ladies, and I would be much obliged if you would be my first employer.'

'How tragic!' Miss Pui Pui exclaimed, laying a palm against her chest as her eyes twinkled. 'A lady besieged by misfortune. It is positively like a heroine in an opera. Of course you shouldn't be trapped in that nasty factory.'

'Oh, Mother,' Miss Yi Yi gasped. 'It'd be such a diversion for me. Please, can we hire Linjing?'

'Do say yes!' Miss Pui Pui chimed in. 'I'd love to learn English. My friends will be so jealous. None of them can speak a word of that slippery tongue, not even the stuck-up Lady Guo, who thinks she is better than us.'

'I am not sure how I feel about you learning English,' Madam Chan told her daughters. 'I wouldn't like you to be corrupted by modern ideas.' She glanced down at my feet. 'I especially do not want my daughters to be indoctrinated with perverse arguments against golden lilies.'

Noble finally turned his back to the contest and addressed his mother. 'The next century belongs to the West,' he said. 'English would be an excellent accomplishment for my sisters, especially Yi Yi, who might mingle with British expatriates in Hong Kong.'

To convey my gratitude, I held his eye and smiled. He nodded and the faintest half-smile flitted across his lips. His understated sentiments again marked him as a man of superior masculinity and high breeding, making him even more attractive to me. With effort, I tore my thoughts from him to placate Madam Chan, for her lips remained pursed.

'Please give me a chance, ma'am,' I implored. 'Having natural feet has ruined my life, so I am the last person to preach against the virtue of golden lilies. If you would like to join our lessons, I would be honoured. There will be nothing I say to your daughters that cannot be repeated to you.

'Besides, you are the principal lady of this district. My aunt tells me no other estate in Shuntak compares to the Chan residence in grandeur or elegance. All of the other ladies look to you for guidance.'

'Linjing is right, Mother,' Yi Yi agreed. 'When you set a trend, the other *taai taai* always follow. She'll never get a position in a genteel home unless you hire her first.'

'If nothing else,' I said, 'please consider it to be an act of charity. Heaven will reward your kindness with good fortune and longevity.'

'A lady shouldn't have to work in a factory,' Noble added, 'and Madam Sapphire is a businesswoman whom I esteem. Consider it a favour to her.'

Madam Chan eventually agreed. I wanted to leap into the air – winning her approval might not be half as difficult as I'd feared.

My heart was light as I joined my sisters to observe Little Flower's progress on her double-sided goldfish motif. The thread was split into so many filaments that each was as fine as a spider's web. With a swift flick of her wrist, Little Flower threaded the needle and guided it through the cream silk. Once again, her grace astonished me, for I couldn't sew half as well even with intact fingers. The goldfish that appeared on the surface of the silk looked livelier than a real fish. One of its fins seemed to be waving at us, and the swish of its tail gave the impression of playfulness. If this fish were a person, it would be clever and full of mischief, much like my childhood self.

At the sound of a gong, marking the end of the two-hour period, Little Flower and the ladies all stood and submitted their work to Madam Chan's *muizai*, who carried it to a long table at the front of the courtyard and laid each item next to a card labelled with the respective competitor's name. One by one, the contestants formed a line adjacent to the table, and we crowded in front of them.

Noble and his sisters followed their mother as she and two other ladies judged the ten exhibits, starting with Miss Prudence's sample. Miss Prudence was not what I had expected: her wan, clammy complexion signalled a feeble constitution. Sweat beaded on her brow and nose, and her eyes darted from Noble to the judges and the crowd, resembling a petrified mouse trapped in a circle of cats. Though it was not charitable, I couldn't help but feel relieved: she would be unlikely to pose a threat to me if we became sister-wives.

'Prudence,' Madam Chan began, 'your goldfish is exquisite and flawless! There is not a knot or a loose thread in sight. You've blended the colours seamlessly. Well done! I might as well give the prize to you and save us some time.'

Little Flower's eyes widened with anxiety.

'*Oh, no*, ma'am,' Prudence protested. 'That would not be fair to the other ladies.' She looked nervously to Noble for support.

'Mother,' he said, 'please do not distress Prudence. She is far too considerate to be the cause of the other contestants' antipathy.'

Madam Tsui, who was one of the other judges, said, 'You mustn't show such partiality to my daughter. The other contestants have all worked so hard. We must look at all the exhibits before we decide.' Her calm manner sat at odds with her daughter's nervous disposition.

'Very well, Prudence,' Madam Chan said. 'I shall heed your and your mother's advice.' Turning to Madam Tsui, she added, 'Prudence's talent and modesty are a credit to you.'

'Not at all,' Madam Tsui insisted. 'Prudence is indebted

to you. She would not be half as accomplished without your tutelage over the years. My middling skills are not much use to her.'

The third judge, a plump woman with a broad, shiny forehead, agreed. 'Oh, yes, Madam Chan. Miss Prudence takes after you. Never before has there been a better-matched pair of mother and daughter-in-law!'

I winced at her toadying manner and thought I saw Noble grimace too, but Madam Chan looked pleased. I'd better get used to giving false compliments and grovelling, I thought. Yet I couldn't dismiss this woman's words: if her claim was true, I must brace myself for bias against me if I lived under Madam Chan's rule.

'You are too smooth with your words,' Madam Chan said, laughing. 'Pray, stop this flattery and let us go on with the judging. I am sure the young ladies are eager to know their fate.'

Madam Tsui and the third judge followed Madam Chan's lead, proceeding to examine the other entries, but none except Little Flower's were as refined as Prudence's sample: some were blemished by visible knots on the underside of the silk, others failed to blend colour fluidly, and two were unfinished. Noble lingered over Little Flower's work, the tip of his finger tracing the goldfish's outline, but I couldn't tell if he was pleased with it. Madam Chan frowned as she picked it up.

'This motif is unconventional,' she announced. 'We do not embroider a goldfish in this manner. There is something impertinent about its eyes and fins.' She walked up to Little Flower and said, 'I asked for a goldfish, but yours has the air of a fiend. It looks like a creature who sucks a man's *qi* in its bid to be human, like a fox spirit. Are you trying to bewitch us?'

'I have no such intention, ma'am,' Little Flower said. 'Indeed I couldn't even if I wanted to. I only embroidered what I thought would be pleasing to the eye. I thought you wanted us to create a lively goldfish.'

'Yes, I did say "lively", but I did not want a fish fiend. Your needlework is second to none, I'll not begrudge you that. But Prudence's classical motif is the winner.'

'I agree,' the toady judge chimed in. 'Embroidery is an expression of a young lady's mind.' She scowled at Little Flower's feet and added, 'This girl is not a lady. From her goldfish, it is clear that her mind isn't pure.'

'What are your thoughts?' Madam Chan asked Prudence's mother.

Madam Tsui glanced down at Little Flower's embroidery. 'There is an artistic flair in this girl's work that is lacking in my daughter's stitches. It has a three-dimensional quality that makes it look almost real enough to swim in a pond. But . . .' She looked at Little Flower. At the same moment, Noble was studying Little Flower too, and I worried he would agree with his mother, for he opened his mouth, looking poised to object. Then Madam Tsui hastily concluded, 'But I agree with you. The motif is too unconventional for this contest.'

Prudence cast a look of incomprehension at her mother. Noble seemed equally puzzled, mirroring my confusion. For a moment our eyes met, and in his I saw concern. He must be recalling our conversation from the worm-rearing room and be worried that I'd be upset by this unfair treatment of Little Flower. What a gentleman!

'This is not fair!' Cloud *ze* shouted.

'The rules didn't say it needed to be conventional,' Bing Bing cried.

'Let the best needlework win!' Joy declared.

261

My aunt said, 'Madam Chan, for the sake of harmony, I implore you to be impartial.'

Madam Chan smirked and ignored her.

Little Flower appealed to the judges, 'Please, my ladies. I have followed all the rules. Please find it in your hearts to make the *right* choice in the spirit of fairness.'

To my amazement, Noble stepped forward.

'Mother,' he said, 'I beg your forgiveness for my interference. But I must speak on behalf of Little Flower and her sisterhood. It is apparent that she is the rightful winner. I say this for the sake of impartiality, even if it injures Prudence.'

He glanced at Prudence with an apologetic smile, which she did not return.

'Our decision is final,' Madam Chan retorted, 'and a man's opinion carries no weight in this contest.'

Noble drew his mother to one side and spoke to her in a murmur. The sceptical look on Madam Chan's face did not shift as he talked while glancing every few seconds at the rowdy crowd for emphasis. By now, our sisterhood and others had begun chanting, 'We want fairness! Fairness! Fairness!' Mother and son carried on for several terse minutes before she returned to address us and announced Little Flower as the winner of the Ladies' League.

My conviction of his regard for me soared. First, he'd implored his mother to hire me. Now for my sake he'd publicly challenged her and upset his betrothed. Moreover, his readiness to stand up for fairness and integrity thrilled me.

34

Little Flower

Noble Siu Je was the last person I'd thought would speak up for me. His appearance had given me a fright when I'd spotted him glaring at me as I waited for the contest to begin. I'd worried he would call me a charlatan and forbid me to participate.

Despite Linjing's assertions and Noble Siu Je's strange behaviour, I was still not convinced of his attachment to her. Yet, his support sat at odds with his stubbornness during our interview in his office. Whatever his motive might be, I felt grateful for his help – and, I must confess, I saw his solemnity and resolve in a different light when it was directed at Madam Chan and not me. Once I realized he intended to be my champion, I began to appreciate the firmness of his resonant voice, the perception in his keen eyes and his striking height, which all combined to give him an air of irrefutable authority. Having all these traits on my side was comforting, and the way he'd glanced apologetically at Miss Prudence showed he was thoughtful, too. No wonder Linjing had fallen for his charm! Noble Siu Je's character was like a heavily guarded palace with myriad inner chambers. Beyond the outer wall of pride and sombreness, there appeared to be a man who also valued artistry, integrity and much more. I hoped he might be open to hearing my proposal to help with his shawl project again.

At that moment, seeing him walk down my aisle in the work room, I summoned my courage and waved him over to my station. He stopped in front of me and arched an eyebrow in question. I dropped the colander of cocoons back into the water trough and cleared my throat.

'Noble Siu Je,' I said, 'may I please speak with you?'

'Very well,' he replied. 'Follow me outside.'

On the other side of our station, Linjing's smile was too wide and obliging. I felt embarrassed for her excessive partiality; I had witnessed enough flirtation between other *muizai* and menservants to know she ought to be more reserved. I caught Joy's eye as she disguised a laugh with a yawn. What had happened to my proud, dignified mistress? Noble Siu Je acknowledged Linjing with a bow and a cursory nod, but from his impassive face I couldn't tell if he noticed her fawning eyes.

I hurried to keep up with his long strides. He didn't stop under the scholar tree outside the worm-rearing room as I'd thought he would. Instead he continued walking until we reached a quieter bend in the canal. At this distance, the cool breeze and the serene waterway made it almost possible to forget about the factory. Beneath a frangipani tree, he sat down on a stone bench and gestured for me to join him. I hesitated. We'd already drawn the attention of the farmers who were loading basketfuls of cocoons and mulberry leaves from the pier and carrying them into the worm-rearing room. Though we were now out of their field of vision, we could still be observed by passing boats. Knowing Noble Siu Je had never before condescended to sit beside one of us, I didn't want to be the subject of gossip.

'Sit down, Little Flower,' Noble Siu Je said. 'I expect you wish to discuss business with me. I am accustomed to speaking with my business associates at the same level.'

Still standing, I asked, 'Sir, why did you speak up for me?'

'Perhaps my mother is right. Your goldfish cast a spell on me.' A smile seemed to tug at his lips, but his tone was flat, confusing me.

'Sir, if I am a sorceress,' I replied, 'you wouldn't have had the power to refuse my initial proposal.'

For the first time, he beamed, flashing even white teeth. It transformed his grave face into one of affability. A petal of hope unfurled in my heart. Tentatively, I smiled in return.

'I am not one to break with tradition,' he said, 'especially not in regard to rules that govern the feminine realm. But your innovation reminds me of the impressionist artists who faced immense criticism when they first introduced their new method of painting to the art world. Such is the way when one challenges custom and convention. My father and I are having a similar debate. I want to open the first department store in China, but he is afraid of Western ideas and reluctant to give me the capital I need.'

'What is a department store?' I asked.

'Imagine a three-, four- or five-storey building filled with every conceivable luxury item you could ever want: silk gowns, fine porcelain, perfume, cosmetics, jewellery and much more. But that's not all. These marvellous establishments also have restaurants, sometimes even an orchestra. Everything is under one roof. Each floor is covered with plush carpet. One does not need to navigate dusty roads or worry about foul weather. A person can spend half a day inside without feeling the passing of time. Wouldn't every lady wish to go to such a place?'

Excitement rendered his face inviting, emboldening me to speak my mind.

'I think they will like it,' I said, 'if there are also private rooms for ladies only, with recliners where they can rest, since golden lilies cannot endure much walking. It might also help to have plenty of wheelbarrow seats available as a complimentary service. But you will need sturdy female staff to push the ladies around. The presence of unfamiliar menservants following at close proximity might discourage mothers from allowing their maiden daughters to accompany them.'

His brows climbed as I spoke, and his eyes widened with surprise and another, more complex, sentiment that I couldn't decipher. I shifted my weight from one foot to the other, unsure whether he would scorn my advice. Finally, he said, 'It's difficult to believe peasant blood runs in your veins.'

'You speak as though it is shameful to be a peasant, but silk reeling depends on women like me. No lady can endure the heat, the stench and the long hours. Without peasants, your family's business would collapse. Where is the shame in that?'

Though I was shocked by my audacity, I did not regret speaking the truth. Again, he stared at me, brows drawn together but not in anger. Yet, I couldn't name the expression on his face.

'How did you become a *muizai*?' he asked.

'My tale of woe is not original. Any *muizai* can tell you a similar story.'

'Tell me anyway.'

Seeing genuine interest in his expression, I told him, 'When I was six, illness carried my father to an early grave, so my *aa noeng* sold me to save herself and my brother. I ended up as Linjing's handmaiden. It's a typical fate for countless girls when misfortune befalls their families.' I did not mention the loss of my golden lilies.

'Common as it is, I am sorry for your loss.' He held my eyes for a beat too long.

Unnerved by his searching stare, I steered our discussion back to my embroidery skills. 'You compared my goldfish to impressionist art. What is it?'

'Have you seen a Western oil painting?'

'Yes.'

'Were you able to distinguish the brushstrokes in the paintings?'

I closed my eyes and reached back into my memory before answering. 'No,' I replied. 'The surface of those images was smooth and they were very life-like.'

'Ah, what you've seen is likely traditional oil paintings. Impressionist artists use short, broken brushstrokes that barely convey forms. Up close, the images are often a blur, but magic happens when one looks from a distance of five or six feet. Somehow it all blends together to create a fresh, vibrant picture that is equal to, if not better than, the older style. But my description doesn't do it justice. You should see the one hanging on my office wall.'

Swept up by his enthusiasm, I finally sat down next to him. '*Oh!* Those brushstrokes sound like the random long and short satin stitches that I use in needle painting to create depth and light – it seems a little disorder is needed to push the boundaries of art.'

'Indeed!' He laughed up at me. 'The thought crossed my mind when I was studying your portrait of the goddess.'

'So you do believe me, after all. I hope you're not too proud to apologize for what you said to me during that meeting.' Stunned by my boldness, I pressed my lips together. I had never spoken with such playful ease.

'I would be a hypocrite not to believe you now. But I cannot apologize for my initial doubt. If our situations were reversed, you would have been equally sceptical.'

'Will you hire me for the shawl project?' I asked.

'You are exceptionally talented,' he began, 'but I cannot make promises until you show me some designs. And, first, we need to discuss the potential employment terms and conditions. Come to my office tomorrow at ten.'

Madam Sapphire and I arrived at Noble Siu Je's office at the appointed time, only to find his face was a brooding storm when he greeted us. With brusqueness, he said, 'Madam Sapphire, I was not expecting the pleasure of seeing you today. I have set aside this hour for a meeting with Little Flower. Perhaps Ming can schedule another time for you.'

'Little Flower is my novice. All her endeavours are my concern.' Without waiting for Noble Siu Je's invitation, she planted herself on the corner settee and gestured for me to follow suit. I perched next to her, struggling to keep my hands from fidgeting. Noble Siu Je joined us on the opposite seat and signalled Ming to serve tea, all the while continuing to glower at us. What had changed since yesterday?

'Let us begin,' Madam Sapphire said, 'by discussing your intentions for Little Flower.'

'Intentions?' Noble Siu Je repeated. Ming coughed, flicking a bemused glance towards Noble Siu Je as he set down the teapot before retreating to his own desk.

'How do you plan to remunerate Little Flower?'

Her question dispersed the cloud of alarm from Noble Siu Je's eyes. He relaxed back against his chair, placing his right foot on his left knee as he lit a pipe, inhaled and blew out a plume of smoke, filling the space between us with the heady scent of tobacco.

'I intend to pay Little Flower the same wages she would earn as a full-fledged silk reeler for the duration of the design period.'

'Do you mean three hundred copper cash a day?' Madam Sapphire asked.

'No. That is the top rate. Few workers can earn that wage. I offer two hundred and seventy copper cash. That is generous, considering the average silk reeler earns two hundred and fifty.'

'Your offer is an insult.'

'My offer is fair.'

'A silk shawl sells for three or four times the price of a reel of silk. At the very least you need to pay Little Flower one tael of silver each day.'

'Impossible! None of the sewing amahs have demanded half as much.'

I spoke up. 'Those sewing amahs have not provided you with a satisfactory design. If they had, we would not be having this discussion.'

'That might be so,' he said, facing me, 'but neither have you.'

'Give me seven days,' I said, 'and I will deliver something to your satisfaction. I will commence today if you agree to our terms and provide me with a comprehensive briefing of the project's goals.'

'I can give you only three days.'

'I need five, especially if you want me to embroider sample designs.'

'Very well,' he said. 'Let us settle on five days and a payment of one silver tael per day, but only if you create a design that meets with my approval. In the event that the American buyer awards the contract to me, I will pay you another five silver taels as a bonus, but thereafter your designs belong to me and we shall have no further obligations towards each other.'

'This negotiation is heading in the right direction,' Madam Sapphire said, 'but Little Flower is not seeking a one-off transaction.' Without taking her sharp eyes from Noble Siu Je's face, she took a sip of tea and watched his reaction. He sat up, splayed his legs and planted his palms on his thighs. I felt like a deer trapped between two tigers.

'Here is my proposal,' Madam Sapphire declared. 'Little Flower will accept the five silver taels for her five-day endeavours. But if you secure the contract, you must also agree to hire my sisters to embroider the shawls, with Little Flower as their mentor and supervisor. We can readily set up a workshop at our sanctuary. I want each of my women to receive five hundred copper cash per day. Little Flower will get twenty-five per cent of your profits.'

Noble Siu Je laughed, the volume jarring. 'This is akin to robbery,' he said. 'Besides, I have no intention of entering a long-term partnership with Little Flower.' Addressing me, he asked, 'Is this your idea or Madam Sapphire's scheming?'

'Embroidery is my passion,' I replied, 'and the only thing that gives me joy. I am not seeking a temporary diversion. I want a livelihood out of this as much as you want to open a department store.'

I had spoken with conviction but they sounded like words from a stranger. Only three months ago I had been a *muizai* with no rights, and now a well-respected lady, one with an astute business mind, was negotiating on my behalf. If we succeeded, my designs would be a source of long-term income. Could the stars truly align for me?

Noble Siu Je leant forward and studied my face. His inscrutable stare made me feel as if I were lost in a maze of alleys, the path shifting each time I thought I'd found my way. My pulse raced as I waited for him to speak, but he got up and paced the room. At the window, he turned away from us and let out a long breath.

'Noble Siu Je,' Madam Sapphire said, 'I recall you telling me this shawl project is critical in your plan to open a department store. Does my memory serve me right?'

'Yes,' he replied tersely, as he returned to his seat. 'I depend on its success to convince my father to provide the capital. Had I known you would use it against me, I would not have mentioned it.'

'In the grander scheme of things,' Madam Sapphire continued, 'five hundred copper cash and twenty-five per cent of your profit is scarcely a drop in the ocean. On the contrary, if you do not take a chance on Little Flower, I am afraid Master Chan will not take a chance on you.'

'You've trapped me,' Noble Siu Je conceded, 'but the price you name is too steep. My final offer is four hundred copper cash for the sewing sisters and fifteen per cent for Little Flower.'

'Four hundred and fifty copper cash and twenty per cent for Little Flower,' she countered. 'Any less and I will forbid her to help you.'

Madam Sapphire stood, peering down at him. Alarmed by her ultimatum, I reached up and squeezed her wrist, willing her to see my unspoken distress even as I tried to wrestle my face into calmness. I would gladly have accepted fifteen per cent, or even five, if it meant I could escape silk reeling. Surely Madam Sapphire knew how much I wanted this

271

position – why was she being so difficult? From the corner of my eye, I thought I saw concern flit across Noble Siu Je's face. It disappeared behind his aloof mask.

'You drive a hard bargain,' he said, voice flat with resignation, 'but I agree to your terms, provided Little Flower can deliver her proposal in five days' time by six in the evening.'

I let out my breath.

As Noble Siu Je gave me a detailed briefing for the shawl design, he spoke as though chased by a spectre, scarcely pausing until Ming had finished drafting the contract. Noble Siu Je stamped his seal on the agreement first, then Madam Sapphire added her imprint to finalize it. As we waited for the cinnabar ink to dry, she made a peculiar comment.

'We've had many dealings,' she remarked, 'but I have never seen you negotiate so hard for a petty sum.'

'Any businessman worth his salt would have done the same.'

'But the shawl project is only a stepping stone to your real ambition,' she said. 'Are you certain business is your only concern?'

'Business and family honour are of paramount importance to me. Nothing else matters.'

His answer seemed to satisfy Madam Sapphire. She nodded, rose to leave and ordered me to follow.

35

Little Flower

I had been foolishly lulled into a false sense of certainty by Noble Siu Je's easy manner when we spoke by the canal. His hard bargain reminded me of the chasm between our stations. Smiles and shared ideas meant nothing. Only an extraordinary design would compel him to hire me.

Madam Sapphire excused me from silk reeling so I could dedicate myself to the project. Noble Siu Je also lent me his collection of shawls, allowing me to study them in detail. One by one, I shook them out, draped them on bamboo drying racks and stepped back, taking stock of each design. The first was a motif of peonies and phoenixes, embroidered in white against indigo silk. The choice of white seemed odd, for the design was too garish for a mourning shawl, but then I recalled Miss Hart had once explained to Linjing that in the West this was the colour for weddings rather than bereavement. The second shawl depicted a garden with figures of mothers, infants and children playing against a backdrop of pavilions, bridges and trees. A crane dominated the third sample, its sweeping wings spread across a cluster of lotus pods. Though vastly different in their subjects, they all shared a similar level of complexity, which would take an artist weeks to complete. Noble Siu Je had dictated three criteria for me: the designs must be innovative, but to be competitive, the cost of production should be lower than those currently on the market, which meant the motifs could not be as complex as the ones I saw before me; he had also stipulated that the finished appearance of the shawls must not be cheapened by the reduction in labour time. These contrary demands jostled in my mind, loud and insistent, like street vendors bellowing for my attention, each claiming to be more important than its neighbour. How would I find a solution in time to meet Noble Siu Je's deadline?

I paced around the courtyard, too restless to pick up my pencil and notebook. My tunic-blouse clung to my back and chest, and clusters of limp hair stuck to my forehead. I longed for nightfall – perhaps the cooler air would bring inspiration. But the late-afternoon sun blazed, hot and domineering, in no haste to give way to twilight.

My dismal state of mind worsened with each passing day. No suitable imagery arrived. Creating embroidery motifs had never been difficult for me, but now my mind was as barren as an aged hen. Hour upon hour I sat with pencil poised over paper, yet no sooner had an idea sprouted before I faltered, scribbling out the beginnings of a chrysanthemum, a pair of mandarin ducks, a cluster of pomegranates, a peacock feather ... No matter what I drew, the same problem remained: how could I create an exceptional design that would be simple enough to complete in half or a quarter of the usual time?

I rummaged my mind for an answer while sweeping the refectory, while wringing out laundry, while walking along the canal, while Linjing prattled to me about Noble Siu Je.

But inspiration had fled, taking my appetite and sleep with it.

At night, I tossed and turned, staring into the darkness as I waited for sleep to claim me. Noises from the other sisters in our dormitory had never bothered me before – exhaustion was a potent sedative – but now the rise and fall of their snores, their sniffles and the creaking of the bamboo frames as they shifted on their straw pallets boomed in my overwrought brain, jolting me awake as soon as I managed to snatch a moment of sleep. My red, dry eyes gained no reprieve.

In this manner I squandered three days. By the fourth morning, my head pounded and spun, queasiness seized my stomach and I needed to tighten the drawstrings on my trousers to stop them falling down. Unable to sit without my eyes swimming, I lay down again, hoping to regain my equilibrium. With the sisters at work, peace descended upon the dormitory. I closed my eyes, my breaths lengthening as I slid into a nap.

Someone was calling my name and tapping my face. I rubbed the crust of sleep from the corners of my eyes but was still too drowsy to open them. The voice called my name again. I peeled my eyes open to find Joy leaning over me, her brow knitted with worry and a pile of cloth draped over one arm.

'Are you ill?' Joy asked.

It took several blinks for me to realize these were Noble Siu Je's silk shawls. I sprang up.

'What time is it?' I asked.

'About seven in the evening,' she replied.

My skin flushed hot, then cold. I slapped myself. 'How could I have slept all day?' I cried. 'Tomorrow is the deadline!'

Joy backed away, a shawl sliding onto the floor.

'I'm sorry,' I said. 'It isn't your fault.' I wanted to reassure her with a smile but failed.

'Here, take these,' she said, holding out the remaining shawls to me.

I frowned.

'You left them hanging on the clothes racks and a few had bird droppings on them, so I brought them inside for safekeeping.'

I accepted the crumpled heap and flung them onto my pallet. Joy bent to pick up the one from the floor and stroked it. 'These shawls are so lovely. I wish I could own just one, even if it wasn't as fancy as this. The other girls would be so jealous of a Western accessory like this. But they're too dear for the likes of me.'

Like a migratory goose, inspiration flew back, nesting in my mind again. I threw my arms around Joy, squeezing her tight as I spun us around. She squirmed away and looked at me askance as she pressed her palm to my forehead.

'Are you sure you're not suffering from a brain fever?' she asked.

'Oh, Joy! You have given me a solution for the shawl project.'

'Truly?'

'Yes! Thank you. Thank you. Thank you. I'll be sure to show my gratitude in a more meaningful way if Noble Siu Je accepts me.'

'Teach me to embroider,' she replied. 'I want to escape silk reeling too.'

I promised she'd be the first apprentice chosen if I succeeded. With that, I gathered my pencils, sketchbook, fabric and sewing kit. I would not rest until I had captured my vision on paper and silk.

36

Linjing

Patience had never been one of my strengths. All my life, I'd been expected to be tranquil, to sit, to wait. Well, I'd had enough of waiting. Now that Noble was willing to give Little Flower a chance, I felt certain he loved me. From Little Flower's account, he had acquiesced only after a drawn-out negotiation. Why else would he hire my former *muizai* if not to please me? Since it was indecorous for a man to broach such a topic with a novice, it would be up to me to take the necessary steps to initiate a marriage contract. The burden of requesting my aunt's permission to leave the sisterhood lay with me. Ignoring a small voice of doubt, I decided to forge ahead. If I was wrong about his feelings I'd be humiliated, but the thought of forfeiting the chance to be a lady again was far more devastating.

Not wanting to waste another minute, I waited at the sanctuary's gate for Aunt Sapphire's return from a trip to a neighbouring sisterhood.

Anxiety churned my belly as my aunt's palanquin approached. As soon as the bearers lowered the litter to the ground, I swept back the curtains and poked my head inside. Aunt Sapphire tilted her head in puzzlement. She took my proffered hand, leaning on me as she stepped out of the palanquin. 'Goodness, Linjing. What is the matter?'

'Oh, Aunt! I wish to speak to you immediately about Noble Siu Je.'

At the mention of his name, two of the bearers looked up, eyes bright and alert for gossip. My aunt sent them away and turned to me with a disapproving shake of her head. 'One day your thoughtlessness will get you into serious trouble,' she warned. 'Gossip sticks to women like mud. You must learn to be more restrained.'

'I don't want to be a novice any more,' I blurted.

'Hush! We cannot speak of such things in public.'

She shot me a look of exasperation but did not protest when I took her by the arm to help hasten her steps into the sanctuary. She was walking as fast as her golden lilies permitted, but it was still far too slow for me, and at times like these, I was grateful for my natural feet. It seemed an age before we reached her quarters and stepped over the threshold of her apartment.

As soon as I closed the door, I said, 'I don't want to take the So Hei vows. Noble Siu Je loves me, and I want to be his second wife. Please, Aunt, will you help me and set me free?'

My aunt tripped on the fringe of the rug, staggering forward. I reached out to steady her before leading her to the nearest chair. She slumped into it and rubbed her temples. Hovering in front of her, I tapped my fingers against my thighs as I struggled to stay silent and wait. At last she looked at me, taking a deep breath before she spoke. 'Linjing, have you lost your mind?'

'I'm not mad! Noble Siu Je is attached to me, I'm sure of it, and I adore him too.' I knelt before her and clasped her hands. Looking up at her, I said, 'Please, Aunt. Don't dismiss my claim until you've heard all he has done for me.' When she didn't object or snatch her hands away, I launched into my observations of Noble. As I talked, she shook her head and closed her eyes. She opened them to peer at me with pity, as one looks at a ranting beggar. Her mounting incredulity not only hurt and angered me but also shook my conviction: she and Little Flower were intelligent, yet neither agreed with me. Could I really be wrong? No. I mustn't allow anxiety to stand in the way of my salvation.

'I don't need you to believe me,' I said. 'All I ask is for you to approach Madam Chan and act as my matchmaker.'

She pushed me away and scoffed. Weary of grovelling, I leapt up and planted my hands on my hips. 'You made a pledge to Aa Noeng and agreed to care for me,' I reminded her. 'Honour it.'

'As I've said before, I promised Phoenix to keep you safe and give you a home. I did not agree to condone outlandish schemes. And I certainly didn't vow to risk my reputation for your sake.'

'Why would it risk your reputation? As you said, I wouldn't be the first novice to have a change of heart.'

'I'd have no qualms about releasing you from the sisterhood if I thought you had a genuine chance of marrying Noble Siu Je. But I'm certain that neither Master Chan nor Madam Chan would accept a big-footed wife or daughter-in-law. Besides, your conjectures are just that – a fantasy created by a spoilt young lady, too proud to accept her reduced circumstances and to work for a living. Noble Siu Je is no fonder of you than he is of me.'

'If he doesn't love me, why would he speak to me so often? Why does he glare at Little Flower and bow to me?'

'He is civil, giving face to me.'

'What about when he supported me to be his sisters' tutor?'

'He did so because he admires Western ideas and foreign inventions. Having an English tutor will help draw his conservative family into modernity.'

'And Little Flower?'

She heaved a huge sigh.

'Ah, so you can't deny he would hire her to please me?'

'Stop it, Linjing. This is absurd. Noble Siu Je is desperate to win the shawl contract, and Little Flower is the most promising candidate. It's just business.'

'We don't have to see eye to eye. But, please, do this favour for me – that's all I ask. Do it for Aa Noeng's sake.'

Instead of answering, she reached over to the side table and picked up a mandarin, weighing it in one hand then the other. With the tip of her thumbnail, she pierced the skin and peeled it methodically, one strip at a time. Then she lifted a segment, stripped away the pith, popped it into her mouth and chewed slowly. All the while, I wanted to snatch the fruit and demand an answer.

Finally, she replied: 'If I approached Madam Chan, the family would see me as a fool, or worse, an ageing woman losing her grasp on reality, not fit to govern a sisterhood. My duty as mother superior is my first priority. Not even our blood bond can surpass it. Don't ask me again.'

My mouth fell open. I had expected a lecture about the merits of remaining a celibate sister, the advantages of independence, perhaps a severe warning against the trappings of marriage, but not a refusal. Without her to act as matchmaker, I did not know what to do.

37

Little Flower

I didn't finish embroidering the final shawl sample until half an hour before the deadline, forcing me to run to Noble Siu Je's office. When I arrived, my lungs were aching, my cheeks were flushed and the sheen of exertion dampened my forehead. With no time to spare, I tucked the locks of stray hair behind my ears and stepped inside, boots of exhilaration and dread marching in my chest.

'You almost missed the deadline,' Noble Siu Je said.

He stood up from his desk, adjusted his waistcoat, refolded the cuffs of his sleeves and approached me. His bright, eager eyes contradicted his dismissive words. I was certain I saw relief scurry across his face when he acknowledged me.

'Forgive me, sir,' I replied, still breathing heavily. 'This idea came to me only last evening. I have stayed up all night and just finished the samples. I sprinted here.'

Noble Siu Je gestured to the settee. 'Sit.'

I collapsed onto it, placing the basket I'd been clutching on the floor beside my feet. He glanced towards the seat beside me but opted for the chair opposite. To steady my breath, I sucked in air from my nose and exhaled through my mouth. A wisp of hair escaped my braids, floating back and forth as I breathed; no sooner had I tucked it back than another strand broke free. Noble Siu Je watched me keenly; his hand reached out, then paused mid-air before he abruptly extended it overhead and clicked his fingers three times. 'Ming, please serve tea and some refreshments.'

Ming poured, but there was only enough tea for one cup, so Noble Siu Je instructed him to serve me first. I accepted it and drank deeply. To stop myself fretting, I wrapped my hands around the empty cup and rested it on my lap. Ming excused himself, promising to return with a fresh pot soon.

'Show me your designs,' Noble Siu Je instructed.

'I have studied the existing shawls for many hours,' I began, 'and it seems there is little room for innovation. We can't reduce the time needed to embroider these shawls without lowering their quality. But something my friend Joy said has sparked an idea. She loves these shawls but their cost is prohibitive and she wishes there could be something more affordable—'

'I can't see how this will help me win the bid,' he interrupted.

'Sir, it's important for you to hear my reasoning before I show you my samples.'

He gestured for me to continue.

'Linjing used to have an American lady tutor for English and Western etiquette,' I resumed. 'From her, I learnt that Western women from all classes wear similar fashions, although the maids, seamstresses, cooks and other working women dress plainly, in cheaper fabrics, like cotton and calico. A shawl, especially one in silk, is decorative for the ladies who can afford it, but for ordinary women it is a practical item, often in plain brown or grey wool, with no grace or beauty. Yet the heart of a working woman beats with passion and longing too. They also yearn for love, luxury and beauty. My designs will take a quarter of the time to make but still give their wearers a taste of opulence. The seller can price them within reach of lower-class women, not ladies, but the maids who serve them.'

'Do you crave these things?' he asked, leaning forward.

My hand shook a little as I set down the teacup. 'Forgive me, sir?'

He cleared his throat, shifted in his seat, glanced away, then back at me. 'I would like to know whether you and Joy long for these things too,' he said, 'since you are a reliable representative of peasant women. Do you pine for things that belong to a lady's lot?'

'I can't speak for Joy,' I replied guardedly.

'What about you?'

'I do not dwell on things that are out of reach. Doing so makes reality unbearable.'

His questions made me dizzy. I wished he would stop, yet I couldn't help but answer them.

'So you are not a dreamer?'

'I have learnt to be careful with my dreams.' After a pause, I added, 'I keep my expectations pruned, like a *pun zoi*. Unruly thoughts are dangerous, perhaps even fatal for a woman in my position. This is how I survived slavery.'

'Most people would hide a disfigurement, but you are not ashamed. What happened to you?'

'I tried to escape but was caught. The matriarch smashed my hand as punishment.'

'Tell me more.'

I shook my head. 'I doubt it would interest you.'

'Let me be the judge of that.'

I told him what had transpired in Shanxi, from my lost

283

betrothal to Miss Hart's involvement in helping me escape, followed by the Tungs' betrayal and the moment the mallet had crushed my hand. But I omitted telling him that my embroidery skills had compensated for my disfigured feet and secured the marriage offer. These details were far too intimate to share with any man, let alone him.

'Dowager Lady Fong wanted to break your spirit, but you triumphed. I am glad of it.'

'She almost succeeded,' I said, as I lifted my hand to my face, noticing the broken fingers for the first time in a long while. 'For close to two years, I kept them wrapped, first out of disgust and despair, then out of practicality, to make it easier for my thumb and little finger to meet when I sew. But after I'd retrained my hand, I no longer needed the bindings.'

Noble Siu Je reached across the narrow space that separated us and brushed the tips of my damaged fingers. My lips formed a ring of shock as a wave of longing rippled down to my belly.

'I'm glad you don't bind them,' he said. 'They are a reminder of your strength.'

His voice was warm, like the midday sun, and his startling empathy scrambled my thoughts. We exchanged a long, charged look. In his darkened eyes, I saw an intensity that matched the mounting heartbeat in my chest. Unbidden, Madam Sapphire's warning echoed: *If he fails, it will be up to you to maintain propriety at all times.* Trouble loomed unless I tethered us back to propriety. I dropped my eyes and bent over my basket to pull out three handkerchief-sized samples. My hand trembled as I laid them on my lap. Picking up the first design, I began talking quickly.

'These simplified plum blossoms could be completed even by a novice embroiderer, which will help reduce production costs.' Shifting my gaze to the second sample, I continued, 'I have placed a pair of mandarin ducks at the centre so it will catch the eye's focus when the shawl is worn. Both of these designs are easy and fast to complete.'

I dared not meet Noble Siu Je's eyes again, but I sensed his intense stare. My collar felt too tight, the air in the room seemed to thicken, and my breath grew shallow. I spoke faster and faster, all the while fixing my eyes on the samples.

'The third design features a different flower motif in the diagonally opposite corners of the shawl, a lotus in one and a vibrant peony in the other. That will give the wearer the choice of two designs, depending on the direction in which she folds the shawl.'

From my basket, I pulled out another miniature shawl, this one made of two triangles of silk. One triangle was ivory silk crêpe, the other a more durable blue silk. The border of the ivory silk crêpe was decorated with white lotus and peonies. The blue triangle featured a border of colourful blossoms and butterflies. I wrestled my face into what I hoped to be businesslike propriety and looked up. Noble Siu Je continued to regard me with a piercing intensity, like a Zoeng Kei player considering his next move. Whatever he had in mind, I would likely be a sacrificial pawn.

'Just like the third sample,' I continued, 'the contrasting designs will allow the wearer to create the illusion of two distinct shawls simply by folding it. But the unique selling point of this one is that when the lotus flowers are worn on the right side, it can be a lovely bridal accessory. This will give Western working women a touch of what their betters have. If you like, I can also show you sketches of alternative border patterns with varying degrees of intricacy to cater for different price brackets.'

I waited for him to comment. When he did not, I went on, 'The market for costly silk shawls is flooded. If you wish to stand apart from your competitors, you should present this economy line. The price of each shawl will be significantly lower, but I'm confident the volume of sales will compensate. There must be at least ten working women for every lady.

'Oh, one more thing. Perhaps these wedding shawls can be advertised as heirlooms, to be passed from mother to daughter. That will entice women to save for something they might otherwise not dream of buying.

'What do you think, sir?' I finished, straightening my shoulders to face him squarely.

A long pause followed. While we were talking, I had forgotten about the factory below us. Now, the clackety-clack of the machines drifted up and filled the room. He glanced between me and the samples on my lap. I chewed my lip and waited.

'I did not think a former *muizai* could teach me something,' he said, his voice reverent but subdued, 'yet I've learnt two business strategies from you in a week.'

'Will you present my designs in your bid?' I asked.

'They are ingenious,' he admitted. 'I have no choice but to hire you.'

Unable to contain my delight, I beamed and clapped. But his fingers trembled as he lit his pipe.

38

Linjing

Aa De had once told me I had a warrior's spirit, and though he had proved fickle, that did not change the soundness of his judgement. Like Aa Noeng, I would not surrender to my ill fate. Her letter had counselled me to accept that fate, but the revelation of her formidable scheme to safeguard her status as first wife had the opposite effect, urging me forward to reclaim my genteel life. Mother's pluck and even her death had taught me a vital lesson: lady or novice, my life and that of all women was like a two-wheeled cart – meaningless unless tethered to a strong horse. Marriage to Noble would be akin to being secured to a thoroughbred. Without a betrothal to him, I was abandoned to a lifetime of drudgery and obscurity.

With this understanding, I couldn't ignore my wrongdoing towards Little Flower. Despite my previous denials, I knew, perhaps had always known, that by insisting on her being my dowry handmaiden I had robbed her of a better life. I had been ignorant, perhaps even selfish, but *not* wicked, nothing like Peony. No, I had been terrified of Lady Li and marriage, and Little Flower was my only salvation. Surely any other desperate young lady would have made the same mistake. Well, regret was futile. Once I became Noble's wife, I'd make amends to Little Flower, bring her with me and give her the comforts she deserved. Since my aunt refused to help me, I would ignore the rules of propriety and declare my love directly to Noble, today.

I washed my hair with jasmine-scented water. I had already taken great care to sponge and scrub my skin, using a cake of lavender soap I'd procured by pawning one of my last gold rings. Once I felt certain that no trace of fishy odour lingered on my body, I dressed in my freshly laundered *saam fu*. Last, I braided my hair into two neat plaits. All the while, I resented these tasks. I had come to value Little Flower's friendship more than her services, but that didn't make it any less intolerable to live without a maid. No matter, these indignities would be abolished once I became Noble's wife.

That afternoon I would give my first lesson to Miss Pui Pui and Miss Yi Yi, and Noble had mentioned he would have a tête-à-tête with me afterwards to discuss my first impression of his sisters' aptitude for English. I couldn't have planned for a better opportunity to speak to him if I'd tried. When I'd offered my services at the Seven Sisters Festival, I'd been following Little Flower's advice, depending on this plan to charm Madam Chan into seeing me as a desirable daughter-in-law. But who knew how long that would take? Besides, every mother doted on her sons, especially the heir. If Noble implored his mother to accept our marriage, she would surely indulge him.

Throughout the two-hour lesson, I glanced at the mantel clock in the Chans' study, and even when I wasn't looking at it, I was alert to its ticking. Time dragged as I endured Miss Yi Yi and Miss Pui Pui's petty squabbles. Neither had the patience to learn the alphabet. Instead they demanded I teach them insults they could fling at their foes without the other ladies understanding them. I translated their requested put-downs into English, helping them to grapple with the slippery foreign sounds: 'Your perfume smells like cow dung'; 'Is that a mole or dried sauce on your face?' and so on. All the while, Madam Chan watched us, her shrewd eyes making me nervous. I felt her scrutiny even when I had my back to her. The young ladies burst into fits of giggles as they tripped over the words. I repressed a sigh, knowing they would soon be my sisters-in-law. Perhaps under my influence, they would become more sensible.

At last the clock struck four.

Noble strode into the room and bowed first to Madam Chan, then to me. I sensed something had unsettled him. It wasn't the expression on his face, for as usual he revealed little, but the way he plucked the leaves off a nearby *pun zoi* and crushed them between his fingers. Even so, I couldn't help but admire his broad shoulders and upright posture. I tried to catch his attention with a smile, but his gaze was distracted, unable to settle on any of us before drifting into the distance. My nerves trembled as I tried to determine if he was disinterested or trying to maintain propriety, but doubt was futile, so I cast it aside. Despite frequent sips of tea, my tongue stuck to my dry mouth as I struggled to exchange humdrum courtesies with the ladies until they took leave of us.

Once the door had safely closed behind them, I wiped my clammy hands on my skirt and rose. I stepped towards Noble and touched his arm. He jolted, but I touched him again, this time allowing my hand to linger. Brows drawn, he lifted my hand gently and moved it away, clearly concerned about decorum even in this moment. Until now we had never spent time alone, but my feelings for him had soared every time we had met since the Seven Sisters Festival, when he'd gallantly defended me against his family. I believed the god of marriages had surely tied our souls together with a strand of his enchanted red thread.

'Miss Linjing,' he began. 'I—'

'Noble Siu Je,' I burst forth, 'let us be honest and cast away all the loathsome rules of propriety. I believe you love me, and I want to assure you that I feel the same.'

He skirted around the *pun zoi*, putting it between us.

Hurt and confused, my belly churned with dread as I stammered, 'I . . . I thought you were fond of me.'

'Fond of you?' Incredulity marred his voice. The composed, dignified face that I loved shattered: his eyebrows leapt as bewilderment twisted his features.

My cheeks burnt with shame, incomprehension and fury – but it was now or never, so I pressed ahead with my questions.

'Why did you hoodwink me into falling in love with you?'

'I have done no such thing.'

'Noble Siu Je, you have acted as my champion from our first meeting. Have you forgotten how you saved me from a nasty fall?'

'It was a common act of kindness. Anyone would have helped, be it man or woman.'

'But you looked at me with such compassion. You commiserated with my reduced circumstances and offered tea. No one has treated me with such respect and kindness since my misfortune. I have liked you since that moment.'

'I am deeply sorry for the misunderstanding, but please know I enquired after you only out of respect for your aunt, whom I esteem.'

'Why did you convince your mother to give me the tutoring job?' I demanded.

'Madam Sapphire saw that you were ill-suited to silk reeling. She asked me to help if I could. I agreed to offer assistance, and I honoured that promise when the tutoring job presented itself. Nothing more.'

'Why hasn't my aunt mentioned asking you to help?'

'Perhaps she wants you to feel you've achieved something on your own.' His voice was kindly and he gave me a pitying smile, but I needed his love not his charity.

None of this made sense. Among my siblings, I had always been the clever one favoured by Aa De. How could my perceptions have been so wrong?

'But ... you defended Little Flower and gave her a chance for my sake, didn't you?'

He turned away from me to study a landscape painting on the wall as though he had never seen anything more intriguing. I dashed in front of him, blocking his view, then wished I hadn't, for the look of embarrassment and pity on his face made me feel small and stupid. But why should I blame myself when he had been the scoundrel? He continued to avoid my gaze as he wedged his thumb between his belt and his robe, drawing my attention to the ends of a tassel poking out of the wide sash. I forgot myself and snatched the object from its hiding place: it was a love knot carved from jade.

'Who has stolen your heart?' I demanded, holding it up.

He took it, his face grim, and shoved it back into his sash belt.

'Tell me!'

'Miss Linjing, for your own self-respect, I beg you to stop asking these fruitless questions. You have my pity, but that is all.'

His admonishment filled me with more shame: I was behaving like a frantic woman whom no gentleman could find attractive. Still I blurted, 'I don't want your pity! I want you to marry me, save me from—'

He cut me off with a dry, exasperated laugh. 'Marriage to a big-footed woman is impossible. In my circle, the one brave soul who acted against decorum to take a *cip si* with natural feet has lost friends and business opportunities. For his sake, it's a blessing that his parents long ago entered the afterworld, or he'd surely have been disinherited.'

'But I'm a *lady* and your equal. If not me, then who has bewitched you?'

'If you must know, I'll tell you,' he said, his eyes warning me that I wouldn't like the answer.

Ignoring a small voice of protest from my heart, I said, 'I want to know.'

In a completely different tone, he admitted, 'I'm entranced by a woman I can never be with. My family would think she is unworthy, even as a *cip si*, no matter her intelligence and grace.'

'Who is this vixen?'

Instead of replying, he flung open the doors and summoned a manservant to escort me out of their estate.

39

Little Flower

Noble Siu Je told me that the American merchant had approved the economy line; he had awarded the contract to us and ordered a thousand shawls in an assortment of my designs, to be completed in twelve weeks. To meet this tight schedule, we needed to interview and hire more sewing amahs from the neighbouring villages. Propriety forbade me to travel with only Noble Siu Je for company. Besides, since that moment of intimacy in his office, being alone with him unsettled me, so I welcomed Ming's and Joy's company.

The first small settlement we visited was along White Tail channel, one of the waterways that branched off the Dunggaa tributary, about ten miles north-east of Chan Village. The settlement, really just a cluster of houses in a horseshoe formation around a communal well, had seen better days, especially the first house we walked past: the pair of door gods guarding that family were so weathered they must have been several years old, even though the paintings are meant to be replaced at every lunar new year. The villages scattered nearby were equally impoverished, each with far too many young women eager to be hired. If I could, I would have given them all a chance, but the few apprentice positions were earmarked by Madam Sapphire for the sisters from our sanctuary. Of all the eager applicants from today, only five possessed the deftness we needed.

After the long day of interviews, we finally boarded the boat and sailed back to Chan Village. The late-eighth-month sky, smooth and cloudless, stretched overhead, like an expanse of blue silk pulled tight. Over the side of the boat, sunshine bounced off the emerald water as two boatmen rowed at the helm, the bow carving through the river's flat, yielding surface. The four of us were on the viewing deck above the cabin when Noble Siu Je suggested that Ming and Joy retreat downstairs for a few rounds of card games to pass the two-hour journey. They happily agreed, and I turned from the railing to follow them. Putting his hand on my arm, Noble Siu Je said, 'Stay, Little Flower. I wish to speak to you.' Joy cast me a look of wonder and Ming glanced at his master with a knowing half-smile.

Though Noble Siu Je's tone was businesslike, unease drummed in my chest. Yet I'd seen him many times since that moment two weeks ago without further incident. Pushing aside my worry, I gazed ahead to the bend in the waterway.

'How do you like the boat ride?' he asked.

'Out here, the air is so sweet,' I said, relieved that he wished to discuss the scenery. 'Imagine all the places this river leads to, all the towns and villages it feeds and all the lives it touches. Yet it is so peaceful. All I hear is the lapping of water against the hull.'

'Yes,' he agreed. 'Right now, there is only you and me. The way I want it to be.'

Though the boat remained steady, my body swayed. Before

I could recover from my shock, he closed the distance between us, a handspan separating our faces as he cornered me with my back pressed against the railing. Again, Madam Sapphire's caution tolled. I angled my head down and studied the silver cloud pattern on his indigo lapel.

He tilted my face up. The pressure of his forefinger on the underside of my chin, though not forceful, compelled me to meet his eyes. They pinioned me with their longing, as though he'd hiked through a desert and finally unearthed a fabled fountain. He removed his hand, but I still could not move. Caution and decorum beseeched me to push past him, hasten towards the bow and head for the ladder that would take me down to the safety of the cabin. Yet another voice, small but insistent, uttered a disconcerting truth: his desire stunned and troubled me, but it did not appal me as it should have done, as the So Hei vows demanded. Despite the breeze, my skin flamed, and a web of confusion tangled my thoughts.

From beneath his sash belt, he pulled out a pendant carved from translucent jadeite and pressed it into my palm. My thoughts cleared, a dreamer startled awake by the cold stone.

'This is a love knot,' I gasped, my fingers closing around the curved edge.

'Little Flower,' he said, 'it is but a poor imitation of my heart, which you have bewitched.'

'Sir, I am a peasant, an inconsequential common woman. You have told me countless times. What can you mean by this gift?'

'I can't offer marriage but you have my love and my protection, if you will accept it. For many sleepless nights I have paced our family library, burning through candles as I searched for a precedent in our archives. But I found nothing that might persuade my parents to accept you.' He paused, eyes dropping to the deck before he looked back at me. 'I want you for my mistress.' He grimaced, as though the word tasted bitter.

'*Mistress*.' I spoke the two characters with wariness. Though I didn't know the full meaning of the word, its shadowy nature repelled me. Aside from Madam Sapphire's warnings, Miss Hart's intelligent eyes flashed in my mind. What would she make of such a proposal? I tried to haul up her counsel from long ago but could not, yet I sensed even she, with her modern values, would urge me to get away. I darted to the right, but he took my wrist. I twisted my arm and escaped his grip.

He held up his hands and moved aside, his brow furrowed with concern and apology. 'Don't be afraid, Little Flower. I will never hurt you.' He gestured to a bench in a sheltered corner of the deck. 'Please, sit down and at least listen to me.' With an outstretched arm, he signalled for me to walk ahead of him. The thirst in his eyes had retreated, and in its place I saw a man desperate to be heard. *Haven't I often wished to speak my mind too?*

I walked to the shelter, glancing over my shoulder every few paces. He kept a broomstick length between us, and when we reached the bench, he did not sit but instead stood at a distance.

'My betrothal to Prudence is fixed,' he began. 'It is a union between our two families that can't be annulled without a rift. It is my duty to strengthen that bond. Surely you must see that.'

'I have asked nothing of you,' I replied, softly but firmly. 'It is you who is demanding something from me, something my instinct warns against.'

'I am sorry. Please forgive me. I do not blame you. Only I am frustrated, tied down, bound by rules and tradition.' He spoke jerkily, his words choked with emotion. Though moved by the depth of his feelings, I couldn't pity him, for he already enjoyed more freedom than I would ever know.

'A peasant, a former *muizai* with natural feet, and a novice, one of these points alone should repel me.' He paced the deck, walked to the railing and pushed against it as he leant over the water. When he turned, his face was a haphazard Zoeng Kei board, the pieces scattered. He reached me in three strides, formed a fist with his right hand and rubbed the knuckles with the other. 'In spite of myself, I have fallen in love with you. Without you, I cannot be happy, cannot be at peace.'

Faced with my silence, he continued: 'If we lived in another world, you and only you would be enough. I want no other wife. I need no other companion. Your quiet dignity, your quick perception, and your resolve – all these qualities have captivated me. To safeguard my heart, I treated you with cold indifference, and I resisted hiring you. But nothing worked. Yet we must abide by the conventions of this world. All I can offer is my love and a home. Little Flower, accept me as your husband in spirit, if not in name.'

By the last sentence, his voice had regained a sure-footed cadence, like a rider settling into the rhythm of a canter. He stared at me, imploring me to understand. I studied his face and saw honesty but also a presumption: that I would promptly yield. My jaw tightened.

'Is your silence a timid "yes"?' he asked, with a hopeful smile.

I lifted my chin. 'Sir, I cannot accept an arrangement I do not understand.'

He laughed and sat down beside me. I shuffled to the edge of the bench, my spine rigid.

'You are wise to question me,' he said, either ignorant of my guardedness or dismissing it. 'I would expect nothing less from you.'

He told me of his plan to establish me far from the filature and away from the prying eyes of his family and associates. Only a busy metropolis like Canton City would give us anonymity and independence. Yet it would be close enough for Noble Siu Je to visit me often. There, I would live in a grand house surrounded by towering walls to offer the highest level of privacy. In the southern corner of the house, Noble Siu Je planned to build a room walled by French-style glass doors, opening up to a central courtyard filled with pots of my favourite blooms, to give me optimal light and inspiration to pursue my art. Never again would I suffer from drudgery. I would be mistress of the house, with a generous stipend. There would be an abundance of maids and menservants to perform all household duties, leaving me free to sketch designs and embroider. If I liked, I could also embrace other artistic pursuits, like painting, sculpture and music – nothing would be too costly or troublesome for his beloved.

It was a generous offer, perhaps the dream of a thousand *muizai* with nothing to lose. But I wasn't a slave any more. *If there is a scandal, you will be blamed and I will be the first to denounce you for the sake of our sanctuary's reputation.* Madam Sapphire's admonition was a scaffold that kept me tied to sense as temptation rattled my judgement. In this moment, I almost believed Noble Siu Je's declaration. Yet experience had taught me that promises from the genteel class were not to be relied upon if my safety clashed with their self-interest. He might be like Second Fong *taai taai*, a master of deception. If she could fool a prudent woman like Lady Fong into thinking she was meek, mightn't Noble Siu Je win me over with similar trickery, only to expose himself as a wolf after he'd devoured my maidenhead?

His fingers walked the length of the bench, closing the gap between us. 'Does my plan please you?'

I sprang up. Until now, I had all but forgotten the love knot in my fist. I placed it on the bench and stepped back. 'I cannot accept your proposal.'

For the first time since his confession, doubt furrowed his brow. With parted lips, he rubbed the base of his neck.

'I must join Ming and Joy,' I said, turning to go.

He seized the pendant and stood up too. 'Wait.' He stepped towards me, but I backed away and he stopped. 'Little Flower, I would never take you by force. If you agree, you will always be under my protection. No harm or hardship shall ever come to you again. Can't you trust me?'

His words sounded inviting, like a cove in a storm. A part of me wanted to surrender, but I said, 'Trust comes with time and trials.' I folded my arms across my middle. 'I scarcely know you, sir.'

'I'm too impatient,' he admitted. 'Please, take time to think about it.' He held out the love knot again. 'Keep it until you make a decision. If you return it to me, I'll know your answer is final and I won't trouble you again.'

I stared at the jade in his opened palm, its sleek polish a stark contrast to the destiny lines that crisscrossed his skin. Though I shook my head, my hand wanted to reach for it. Perhaps he sensed this, for he said, 'Leave it only if you have no feelings for me.'

Towards evening, on the way back from the pier to the Hall of Eternal Purity, Joy reached over and plucked a cluster of red azaleas from a bush beside the path. With a teasing smile, she tucked one behind my ear. 'A tribute to Noble Siu Je's future *cip si*.'

I spun around to face her, the flower tumbling onto the trampled grass path.

299

'Don't fret,' she said, still smiling. 'I won't tell a soul, but *do* promise to spirit me away too, once you're settled in Canton. I can be your companion until I—'

I clamped my hand over her mouth. She tried to loosen my fingers, but I wouldn't let go until she stopped mumbling and ceased to struggle. I looked about us, first down the southern end of the path that led to our sanctuary, then back over my shoulder towards the quayside. Fortunately, we were alone, as far as my eyes could see. Still, I spoke as softly as I could manage. 'How did you know?' Before she could answer, I added, 'Did Ming eavesdrop on us too?'

'We grew tired of *waat faa paai* and wanted to start a game of *maa diu*, so I came on the deck to fetch you and Noble Siu Je to make up four players. That's when I saw . . .' She plucked a petal and blew it off her palm, like a kiss. I grabbed the sprig of azalea from her and tossed it into the long grass.

'Joy, please do not jest,' I hissed. 'Nothing improper happened. Still, this is a serious matter that could cause scandal and risk my life. Don't you remember what Madam Sapphire said during your So Hei ceremony?'

The playful sparkle in her eyes vanished. Two pips of bitterness glared at me. 'I didn't choose to take those vows and you don't want to either, do you?' I turned my face to the water. The bright reflection of the setting sun hurt my eyes. Joy skirted in front of me. 'You are fond of Noble Siu Je, aren't you?'

'I . . . I am grateful for his help during the Seven Sisters Festival.' I tugged at one of my braids, twisting the end into a tight rope. Joy stared at me expectantly. 'We work well together. We are business partners. That is all.'

'Liar,' Joy scoffed. 'Noble Siu Je said to leave it only if you have no feelings for him.' She pointed to the centre of my tunic-blouse. 'I saw you put the love knot in the inner pocket, so you must like him.'

I rested my hand on her shoulder and looked straight at her. 'Joy, what do you want from me?'

'I want you to seize the opportunity of a lifetime, so one day you can help me escape too.' She squeezed my hand. 'I would give my right arm for such a chance – to be a concubine to a gentleman of Noble Siu Je's wealth and standing is far, far above our station. And he is handsome. Why didn't you accept his proposal immediately?'

I stepped away. 'A mistress is not the same as a *cip si*. It is much less. It isn't even an official rank.'

'We aren't scholars. Why quibble over a word?'

'The distinction isn't trivial. Wives and *cip si* are protected by law. A mistress is a . . . isn't anything that a self-respecting woman would want to be.'

'Noble Siu Je loves you and wants to keep you in comfort. Why isn't that enough?' Joy asked, exasperated.

'How do you know he is telling me the truth?'

'He is a man of honour. Everyone says so.'

'I can't risk my life based on hearsay. If I agree to his proposal, he might take liberties, and Madam Sapphire will drown me if I lose my maidenhead. Can't you see the dangers?'

'There is a difference between surviving and living. The So Hei vows sentence us to a life of toil and emptiness.' She pressed her palms together and pointed them at me. 'You have a chance to experience romance. Most women, even the ones from genteel families, are married off to strangers who are likely much older, and many are disagreeable in appearance or temperament. Yet the brides must endure, suffer and hope that a son might bring some comfort in old age. You could spend your life with a rich, handsome and generous man who adores you. Besides, he vowed to let you pursue your art, too. What else could women like us hope for?'

'Noble Siu Je did speak of a blissful life,' I admitted. 'But what will happen to me when he no longer loves me?'

'He is besotted with you. That day will never come.'

'I won't always be youthful or fascinating. His affection might wane once I'm no longer a mystery.'

'You worry too much,' she replied dismissively. 'Many people don't live long enough to see their fortieth year. Why not enjoy the present?'

'What about children?'

'Of course he would provide for them too. And he wouldn't expect you to produce a son.'

'Whose name would they bear?'

'They would be Chans.'

'But they could not enter his family's birth register,' I pointed out, 'never worship their ancestors during festivals, never fulfil their duties on Tomb Sweeping Day, never be acknowledged. We would live a life in shadows and shame.'

'Little Flower, you used to be a *muizai* and you have *big* feet!' With a grunt, she snapped a branch from a low-hanging tree, turned to the canal, and flung it into the lapping water, then whipped back to face me. 'Noble Siu Je is offering love, security and freedom from drudgery.' She punctuated each gift with a smack of one palm against the other. 'What makes you think you can demand legitimacy too?'

I picked up a twig and thrashed the knee-high grass.

'Why do you act as if you deserve more than me, more than Linjing, more than a *lady*?' Joy grabbed my arm, her eyes ablaze.

'You are right. Perhaps I ought to accept him. But I need to be convinced he loves me, to know I'm not a fleeting paramour he'll abandon in a year.'

'I think you should accept right away, before he loses interest.'

'If his feelings are true, he'll wait. If not, I have lost nothing.'

In the distance, someone was approaching us. Though still irked by my response, Joy agreed to cut our conversation short, but not before warning me, 'Lost opportunity is like spilt water. You won't get it back.'

We walked the rest of the way in silence. I couldn't deny Joy's pragmatic counsel: accepting Noble Siu Je was probably a sensible choice. After she'd reminded me of my humble status, all my objections now seemed indulgent. After all, hadn't I chased the shawl project to escape the drudgery of silk reeling? As Noble Siu Je's mistress, I would be free to pursue my art. Shouldn't that be enough?

40

Linjing

Fool, idiot, imbecile – none of those taunts captured my sense of self-loathing. An old crone with milky eyes might have had better insight to the truth than me. Choked by shock and humiliation, I had not told a soul about what had happened between Noble and me. It seemed neither had he, for Madam Chan still allowed me to tutor her daughters, and my aunt didn't summon me to a dressing-down, which no doubt she would have if he'd told her. At least I'd been spared that shame.

But if Noble expected me to be grateful for his discretion, he'd be sorely disappointed. He'd made a grave error when he told me about his beloved faux-lady lover – I might have been blind to his true sentiments, but I wasn't stupid. During our conversation, I'd been too hurt and stunned to identify the graceful and intelligent woman he alluded to, but it didn't take long for me to realize it could be none other than Little Flower. All this time, Noble had not been mooning over me. His looks of torment had been for *her*, a slave who wouldn't even recognize the characters in her own name if I hadn't been generous enough to teach her. How could he choose a *muizai* over me? And how could she steal him from me? The sly traitor had been guarding her own interest all along as she tried to discourage me.

Though weeks had passed since my humiliation, my anger had not cooled as I hid behind a tree in a courtyard facing the new workshop at the eastern wing of the sanctuary. My nails clawed the rough bark as I eyed Noble and Little Flower through a half-open window. With her back facing me, she sat with her right forearm resting on the wooden arm support that lay across the horizontal bars of the large, rectangular embroidery frame. They were in conversation, though I couldn't eavesdrop on them from this distance. He stood to her left, leaning over the frame. As she talked, he stooped, inclining his head towards her so their cheeks almost touched. Yet they were not alone! In front of Little Flower, two rows of embroidery frames lined the long room, all facing her. The two dozen sewing amahs' heads, including Joy's, were bent over their work. Their needles glided through the stretched lengths of silk, over and under, over and under, over and under, a hypnotic spell that blinded them to the illicit affair continuing before their eyes.

Unable to stomach any more, I turned away. Plucking a hair stick from my braids, the same one I had used to suggest a blood vow between Little Flower and me, I stabbed the tender underside of my forearm until the skin split and blood oozed. Somehow the pain helped my fury recede a little, enough for me to think. Since Aa Noeng's death, Little Flower's status in the world had done nothing but rise: first, she'd entranced my aunt; next, she'd lured Noble into helping her win an embroidery contest meant for ladies only; then he'd hired her for the shawl project, and now he was her lover. All the while, I had sunk further and further into privation, everything I strove for slipping through my fingers like sand.

A thought sprouted. Maybe Little Flower had used foul magic to steal all my good fortune and cursed me with what should have been her lot. After all, Madam Chan had called her goldfish a fiend. Wasn't that proof of Little Flower's cunning and spite?

A part of me – the rational side, the one educated in English, foreign etiquette and modern thinking – shrank from this far-fetched accusation. It seemed more likely that Little Flower was another Peony, hiding her resentment until she had the means to seek revenge. After all, I had forced her to cut up her bridal quilt and revoked her betrothal, giving her good reason to hurt me. But if not for witchcraft, I couldn't understand how Noble could have measured me against a *muizai* and found her more worthy of his love. When nothing made sense, all possibilities must be considered, no matter how improbable they seemed. If Little Flower was practising foul magic, I must find proof of her malice. Only then would I be vindicated.

Back at the dormitory, I began to search Little Flower's belongings. I had no experience with foul magic, but I knew enough to look for an effigy of me made with straw or rags, stuffed with my hair or clippings of my nails. With this in mind, I rummaged through her drawers, emptying the contents onto the floorboards. But I found only harmless everyday items: hand ointment, hairpins, a comb, a handheld looking-glass that used to belong to me, her old clothes, undergarments, and a pile of rags shredded in readiness for our red-aunty visits. I shook her quilt, but nothing fell out. Padding my palm against every inch of her thin straw mattress also proved fruitless; I even overturned it, but the bamboo frame beneath was bare. To search the narrow space under the cot, I dropped to my belly and pressed one cheek against the floor, swiping my outstretched hand to the furthest corner. Still no doll in sight.

I slammed my fist against the drawers.

Only Little Flower's pillow remained untouched. I had dismissed it, for the porcelain rectangle held no place to hide an effigy. Now I picked it up, more for the sake of completeness than in expectation of a discovery. Beneath its curved bottom, in a space so narrow it could scarcely fit the thickness of my forefinger, lay a slim jade love knot. It was the same one I had discovered in Noble's sash belt.

I formed a fist around it, squeezing so hard that if it had been carved from glass it would have shattered and cut my palm. I would have welcomed the pain. But the jade remained solid and unyielding, mocking me. A part of me wanted to dash to my aunt with this piece of evidence. But the other part – the side that was only beginning to rouse from the stupor that had fogged my judgement since I had arrived here – urged me to wait.

I sagged to the floor.

To me, this love knot was irrefutable proof of an affair between Noble and Little Flower. Yet Aunt Sapphire might not believe me. After all, I could not prove I had found it among Little Flower's belongings. I needed a witness, but the dormitory was empty except for me. I could slip it back into its hiding place and summon my aunt to a search. Still, it would be my word against Little Flower's. Aunt Sapphire could easily deny seeing it and, instead, point the finger at me for planting false evidence, just as Aa Noeng had sided with Little Flower when she'd switched the silk threads. In my aunt's eyes, Little

Flower could do no wrong, and Mother had seen her in the same blameless light. If only I were as skilful as Little Flower at pretence, then I, too, might appear biddable and trustworthy enough to elicit my aunt's support and belief. I wished Noble had been sentimental enough to engrave his name or hers on the jade, but there was no marking that would expose them.

Did this mean he wanted Little Flower as a concubine or a minor wife? The union was so beneath him, so preposterous, that I would have laughed if it were about someone else. But I could not laugh.

Why had Noble not sought me out?

How could he choose Little Flower over me?

I was a genteel-born lady of high breeding, exquisite under-standing, and educated in Chinese and English. I doubted one lady among ten thousand could lay claim to the same accom-plishments. Yet Noble had fallen for a slave with deformed feet. The injustice was a dagger, thrust deep into my heart. A wave of weariness washed over me; I trembled from head to toe. It would be easier to concede defeat and follow Aa Noeng's lead. Looking up at the rafters, I imagined forming a loop with a rope and slipping it over my head. In a few minutes, all my anguish would dissolve into oblivion. I could join Aa Noeng and she would take care of me.

But no.

My mother had taken her life out of shame and guilt, and to save me from exile to a nunnery. I was not in the same situ-ation. Besides, if I died, it would only make things easier for Little Flower. *She* should be ashamed, not me. She had reached far above her station at my expense. Though my search had revealed no foul magic, I was still convinced that, through sheer cunning, she had traded her fate for mine. What if she had feigned friendship and forgiveness all along? Oh, what a fool I had been! Of course she wanted vengeance: I had stolen her golden lilies, a crime she would never pardon, even though I had acted well within my rights as a mistress. But I refused to let her win. If I could not become Noble's wife, neither should Little Flower.

41

Little Flower

'Follow me, Little Flower,' Miss Prudence said. 'We have much to discuss.'

She swayed past me on her diminutive golden lilies. A goldfish swimming in a cluster of lotus buds bedecked the silk vamps of her lotus shoes, and a tassel with a bell attached perched on the curved toe-boxes. The bells tinkled with every step, a spellbinding chime to flaunt her perfect feet. In comparison, my indigo shoes were eyesores, huge and plain. Noble Siu Je might think he loved me, but one look at my naked feet and he would surely retreat in horror, especially since his betrothed had such lovely golden lilies. If I accepted his proposal, I would be banished from the sisterhood. Where would I go when he changed his mind?

The odour of medicine saturated Miss Prudence's bedchamber. The concoction of earthy herbs mixed with the sharpness of camphor and menthol was stifling. I thought Miss Prudence would lead me to the embroidery frame by an open window where dust motes whirled in a stream of sunlight. Instead she walked past the beaded curtain into the inner chamber and settled onto a couch bed, her forearm resting on a square bolster and her golden lilies perched on a footstool.

'Sit.' She gestured to the spot beside her.

'Forgive me, Miss Prudence, but I thought you had invited me here for an embroidery lesson.'

'Oh, yes. I had to use a pretext, for how else would I persuade you to come without arousing suspicion?' She pointed to the seat again. 'Do sit.'

Unease gripped my stomach as I sat down. Miss Prudence took a deep breath as though readying herself for a long speech, but a bout of coughing choked her words. She clutched her chest, crumpling her tunic-blouse as she gasped for air.

'What can I do to help?'

She pointed to a brown glass vial on the side bureau. I raced over to fetch it and unplugged the bottle for her. With jerky hands, she raised it to her lips and drank. Splutters followed the first mouthful, and a spray of brown liquid stained her handkerchief and my *ou*. The coughing only eased after she managed three gulps, the exertion leaving a sheen of sweat on her brow, nose and upper lip.

'I've weak lungs,' she explained, still breathless. 'I probably would have perished long ago if not for this concoction of *ling zi* and liquorice root.'

'I'm sorry to hear of your poor health.'

'Are you sorry enough to return Noble *go go*'s heart?' She snatched my hand in her cold, damp one, dragging me back onto the couch. I tried to move away, shocked, but she seized my other hand, detaining me with surprising strength.

Unable to meet her eyes, I rested my gaze on the tip of her ear as I lied. 'Miss Prudence, I don't know what you mean.'

'Little Flower, I beg you to release him from your enchantment.' She pulled me forward until our faces were inches apart and I could smell her earthy breath, like wet mud. 'Madam Chan says you're a *wu lei zing*. Even my sage mother is beginning to agree.' She searched my face. 'Are you?'

An incredulous laugh burst forth before I could stop it.

'Are you?' she demanded, squeezing my hands.

'Would a fox spirit allow herself to be sold into slavery?' I countered. 'If I possessed the skill of magic, would I toil in a foul-smelling factory?'

Doubt loosened her grip. I pulled away and stood up.

'Even so, you have captured Noble *go go*'s heart. I saw the way he looked at you during the festival. He is a man so bewitched that he even defied his mother, in public. And he can't stop praising your designs! Before your arrival, he treated me like a treasure, teased me, talked to me. Now he rarely visits, and he is like a shell when he is here. Noble *go go* could never marry a big-footed girl, but since the Seven Sisters Festival, he has fallen in love with you.' She stood and tottered forward, hands clasped in supplication. 'Please, Little Flower. Return his heart to me.' She reached for my hands but I hid them in my pockets as I stepped back and shook my head.

'I love him,' she pleaded, voice as vulnerable as an open wound. 'I beg you, release him, and I'll be indebted to you for ever.' She wrenched two gold rings off her fingers, one with a ruby, the other a tourmaline, and hurled them at me. 'If that's not enough, I can give more.' The skin beneath her lavender jade bangle blanched as she tried to force the bangle past her wrist bone.

'Miss Prudence, please stop before you hurt yourself.'

'I love Noble *go go* more than I care for my life.' Tears welled in her eyes, her lips trembling. 'But I'm no match for your cunning. Please, please, please return his heart to me.'

Unable to bear her anguish any longer, I ran out of the

room. As I stumbled back to the sanctuary, my head spun. If Miss Prudence's temperament had been like Linjing's, I could have dismissed her pleadings without a thought. But I pitied her. Aside from the *wu lei zing* accusation, she was right to blame me, even if she remained ignorant of the truth. By accepting Noble Siu Je, I would hurt her. Her shrill entreaties echoed, deafening me with guilt. Although I had grown up knowing most of us would share a husband with sister-wives, this practice now felt like thievery. Though we all coveted the first-wife position, even this title wouldn't protect us from suffering when we watched our husbands neglect us and love our younger rivals. Only men could be victorious in marriage.

The man's sideways gaze slithered over my face, body and feet as he addressed Noble Siu Je. I stepped away from Noble Siu Je's desk, where I had been standing beside him to review some new designs before the stranger barged in, and went to wait behind a folding screen. From the gaps between the panels, I watched them.

'What is your purpose, Yip?' Noble Siu Je asked, frowning.

'This is no way to greet a guild member, Chan.' Yip reached for the plate of lychees at the centre of the desk, but Noble Siu Je slapped away his hand. Yip plopped into the chair opposite Noble Siu Je and jerked his head in my direction. 'The guild is buzzing with tales about your big-footed designer. Now I see what all the fuss is about – she's a temptress indeed. Those . . .' I couldn't see Yip's expression or what he gesticulated, but from the pulsing muscle in Noble Siu Je's left cheek, it must have been offensive.

'I suppose by "tales" you mean the falsehood you have spread out of spite at losing the American contract to me.'

Noble Siu Je stood up and gestured to the door. 'I do not have time to idle. Unless you have official guild business, I must see you out.'

Yip rose and faced Noble Siu Je with an oily smile. 'Trying to keep the hussy to yourself, I see.' He made a show of shielding one side of his mouth as if about to share a secret with Noble Siu Je. 'Well, do send word when you've had enough – one is so used to delicacies that one can't help but be curious about a pauper's dish, especially if another gentleman has a penchant for it.'

'Keep your filthy thoughts to yourself.' Noble Siu Je seized Yip's robe, the fastenings straining against his fist. Panic darted in Yip's widened eyes as he tried to wriggle free. 'Little Flower is an artist of impeccable understanding and virtue. I will not tolerate insults, not from you, not from anyone.' My heart warmed with gratitude, and a new sensation, an awakening, bloomed in my belly as my skin flushed.

When Noble Siu Je released him, Yip staggered backwards, and his flailing arm knocked over the rack of brushes on the desk.

'Numbskull,' Yip spat, but scrabbled for the door as soon as he regained his balance. At the threshold, he sneered, 'Take care, or you'll be like Lee. Nay. At least that nincompoop's big-footed *cip si* wasn't a *muizai* too. You'll be a bigger laughing-stock than even he is.'

Noble Siu Je's eyes were two bolts of lightning as he strode towards Yip. The coward scurried out. Noble Siu Je slammed the door behind him but did not turn back into the room. Instead he pressed his arm against the door and rested his head on it. His shoulders rose and fell as he took several deep breaths. When he didn't move away, I stepped forth from the screen and approached him. I touched his sleeve and inhaled, ready to thank him for defending me. As he whirled around, his face was not warm and inviting as I'd grown accustomed to since his declaration, but rigid with reproach.

'Little Flower, shouldn't you be supervising the sewing staff?' he demanded, his voice an icicle of blame. I would not remind him that he had summoned me here.

'I will be on my way, sir.' The words struggled to squeeze past the lump in my throat and came out halting, broken. Was one insult all it took to shake his affection?

I opened the door but he pushed it shut. 'Wait, I'm sorry.'

I continued to stare at the door, fixing my attention on its cracked-ice lattice pattern. He gently turned me to face him. I shrugged him off.

'Please forgive me, Little Flower. I shouldn't have vented my anger on you.'

'There will be others like Yip. Will you treat me badly each time you hear an insult?'

'It won't be like that.' Noble Siu Je let out an uneasy laugh, rubbed his earlobe. 'Once you're settled in Canton City, no one will know of you. Our house will be a sanctuary, cut off from vulgarity and slight. I won't allow a whisper of insult to enter those gates. In there, you will be treated with all the respect due to a wife.'

'Suppose we run into Yip or another guild member on the streets of Canton. What will you do?'

'The residence will have everything you need and plenty of servants to fetch whatever you desire. There'll be no need to leave.' His fingers gently traced the curve of my neck. I dared not breathe. 'But please accept my proposal soon, for as you've heard there is already talk about us. Yip has been a thorn in my side for years, and since he lost the bid to me, I suspect he might look for ways to hurt me and spread even worse rumours. I want you away from here before the gossip threatens your reputation and safety.'

He meant well and he'd apologized, which should have been enough. But my chest tightened. The paradise he described had the veneer of liberty, concealing another kind of jail. Only if I never scratched below the surface could I be content, perhaps not even then. Yet he was right: society had begun to gossip, and soon it would not be confined to Miss Prudence and the textile guild. If Madam Sapphire turned against me, I would be condemned to silk reeling, perhaps subjected to surveillance or worse. I should accept him. I should. But he had not yet seen my feet.

42

Linjing

A loud bark, fierce and low-pitched, signalled the *dou si*'s arrival. Aunt Sapphire, Little Flower and I turned our faces to the courtyard. The shaman, a weedy man with a flimsy moustache that dangled past his chin, wrestled with his dog's leash. Behind them, Madam Chan and her daughters, their mouths pinched with fright, teetered on their golden lilies as they kept a wide berth from the canine, a killer with muscles that rippled beneath its short black fur. I struggled to keep my face neutral as they entered our refectory, for I mustn't allow my aunt to think I had instigated this impending trial. Though, to be fair, I'd scarcely had to nudge Madam Chan before she agreed to hire a *dou si* – I had merely hastened the inevitable. In the last few weeks, the Chan women and sometimes even Miss Prudence had probed me with questions about Noble and Little Flower. I did my best to fan their suspicions, while still appearing concerned for Little Flower's reputation.

'Sapphire,' Madam Chan said, 'I'm so very glad you have agreed to this trial. Please be assured that I won't hold the sisterhood accountable, for I'm sure you have been hood-winked by this *wu lei zing* as much as the rest of us.'

'I have absolute faith in Little Flower's innocence.'

'The *dou si* will be the judge of that.' Madam Chan glanced at the shaman. 'Let us begin.'

My aunt rested a hand on Little Flower's shoulder. 'Go forth and be brave. Heaven will protect the pure and the chaste.'

With a tight half-smile, Little Flower nodded, but fear darted in her eyes as she walked to the centre of the room. We shared a brief exchange: she still saw me as an ally. A pang of guilt nettled me, but I shoved it aside. The rest of us retreated behind the safety of a table as the shaman released the hound and the creature growled and barked, pulling its lips back, revealing fangs as sharp as daggers. Little Flower's ashen lips twitched as she fought to stay motionless. At the *dou si*'s signal, the dog pounced; its front paws dug into Little Flower's shoulders and its snout pressed against her chin. She trembled and panted but did not cry out.

'Fox?' the *dou si* asked. 'Attack fox.' At the sound of his master's voice, the creature turned its head. The shaman unhooked a foxtail from his belt and suspended it before the dog. It sniffed several times, growled at Little Flower but did not bite. Instead, it released her, trotted to the courtyard and curled beneath the pomelo tree. Little Flower's shoulders slackened and her breathing quietened.

'Is she human?' Miss Yi Yi asked, voice dripping with disappointment.

'The girl could still be a *wu lei zing*, albeit an ancient one. The younger ones reek of fear and cry out as soon as my dog sniffs them. But I'm not out of tactics yet.' From his satchel, he pulled out a long yellow spell paper. 'If she is not human, she will break out in a sweat and perhaps convulse.' He pasted the paper on Little Flower's forehead and began chanting in an incomprehensible language, all the while circling her and shaking a bell.

Nothing happened to Little Flower.

My aunt yawned, and disenchantment dulled Madam Chan's and her daughters' eyes. Though I suspected Little Flower of dabbling in foul magic, I did not truly believe she was a fox spirit. Still, I had hoped this shaman would sow enough doubt in my aunt's stubborn mind to change her opinion against Little Flower. But he was proving to be a woeful charlatan.

'Clearly, there is nothing unworldly about Little Flower.' My aunt's conviction boomed across the hall, silencing the shaman.

'Not so soon, madam.' The *dou si* raised a palm. 'We still haven't applied the Ta Chi test.'

Many stories about the origins of foot-binding existed, but the *dou si* had likely chosen this one to strengthen his case against Little Flower. Perhaps he wasn't useless after all.

'What is that?' Miss Pui Pui asked eagerly.

'Long ago,' he replied, 'the last Emperor of the Shang dynasty became besotted with Consort Ta Chi. She was a wicked temptress, seducing the Emperor with her golden lilies, which no other lady had at the time. Consumed by vices, he neglected his duties and eventually lost his kingdom to bandits and rebels. Many historians agree Ta Chi was a *wu lei zing* who invented foot-binding to hide her fox feet, which only the oldest, most powerful fox spirit could shift into a convincing human form.'

Madam Chan pointed to Little Flower's feet. 'Take off your shoes and socks.'

Little Flower straightened her back and tilted her chin. 'I will not do so in front of a man.'

'Nonsense. A *dou si* is virtually a monk.' Madam Chan turned to my aunt. 'If you want to convince me, then order her to obey.'

Little Flower bowed to my aunt. 'Please, ma'am, don't ask me to forgo my dignity.'

'She's scared,' Miss Yi Yi said.

Her sister chimed, 'She's guilty.'

My aunt closed her eyes for a moment. When she opened them, she said, 'Little Flower, for the sake of your reputation, you must endure the mortification. I'm sorry.'

Little Flower took a long shaky breath. The corner of her mouth sagged as she collapsed on a stool and removed her shoes, then stripped off her socks. At the sight of her twisted toes, we all gasped. Doubt and confusion narrowed my aunt's eyes, and she looked at Little Flower as though she were a changeling. I had only glimpsed Little Flower's deformed toes once before, when the matchmaker had examined them. Then, I'd quickly averted my eyes. Now, I couldn't stop staring at them: not from fixation but indecision. I knew what Little Flower would ask of me. A small voice urged me to be truthful, but I wanted to hurt her more.

'*Zung ziu!*' The *dou si* grinned and clapped. 'Beyond doubt, this is a *wu lei zing*, powerful enough to evade my first two trials but not strong enough to complete the metamorphosis of her feet.'

'Linjing.' Little Flower glanced up at me. 'Tell them the truth.'

'I don't know what you mean.'

She rose and walked up to me. 'Tell them I had to unbind my golden lilies when I was six because of you.' I turned my head and looked away. She side-stepped and confronted me. 'Linjing, you owe me the truth!' Hurt and confusion creased her brow as she searched my face for understanding. I held her gaze, keeping my features smooth and blank. Again, my conscience whispered, but a louder voice drowned it: *She stole Noble, make her pay.* I drew myself to my full height and stared down at her. 'I remember nothing of this.' From the corner of my eye, I saw my aunt shake her head. Did she believe me or trust Little Flower?

'What should we do with this *wu lei zing*?' Madam Chan asked the shaman. 'We must get rid of her before she gains full command of my son's heart.'

'Burn her – fire is the only way to destroy these fiends.'

'That's barbaric,' I objected. 'You can't do that.' I wanted him to condemn Little Flower as a temptress, not to kill her.

'Enough of these baseless accusations.' My aunt slapped the table. 'I trust Little Flower, and unless she turns into a fox before my eyes, I'll not permit anyone—' She directed her eyes, two orbs of flint, to Madam Chan. In a voice as sturdy as rock, my aunt continued, 'With all due respect, I will not permit anyone, not even you, to harm one of my flock. The sisterhood stands behind me and, if pressed, we will *strike*.'

Madam Chan's chest heaved. Without another word to us, she summoned her daughters and left. The shaman and his dog trailed behind them. Before sweeping out of the hall too, my aunt glared at me with the same disgust that Maa Maa had reserved for me, as if I were a pile of cow dung. In Little Flower's face, I saw disillusionment at my betrayal. She would never trust me again, but I did not care. I bit the inside of my cheek until I tasted blood.

43

Little Flower

'I heard about the *dou si*,' Noble Siu Je said, glancing down at my shoes.

I shuffled, wishing I could hide them.

We had not been alone since Yip's visit. I'd come to his office on the pretext of discussing new designs. Though my mind still vacillated, I was determined to either refuse or accept him today: the *wu lei zing* trial had been a dire warning; I must be decisive to safeguard my life. If I decided on the former, I would ask Madam Sapphire for permission to take the So Hei vows on the next auspicious day. That was the only way to snuff the embers of gossip and repay her unwavering trust in me. Her defence of me against the shaman was a lantern that shone through my fog of indecision. I should choose a path of light and camaraderie over an existence in the shadows – I felt almost sure of it.

Under my tunic-blouse, the love knot weighed heavily. Returning it to Noble Siu Je would be shutting the door against a life of ease, of love, and tossing the key into an abyss. Duty urged me to act, but in his presence my heart wavered. I wanted to return to the dormitory, stow the jade back beneath my pillow, buy myself more time.

'My mother has been cruel and unjust,' he said. 'It won't happen again, I've made sure of it.' He reached for my hand, and his hold was warm and firm. I should have pulled away but found I could not. Perversely, now that I was on the verge of refusing him, I couldn't resist the pull of his touch. Instead I followed him to the settee and allowed him to ease me onto it, my fingers still cradled in his. 'My mother said you claimed to have had golden lilies. What happened?'

I looked into his eyes and saw concern and gentleness, not scepticism as I had expected. At once, my eyes brimmed with tears. I hadn't realized how much I needed him to believe me, to know that my *aa noeng* had loved me enough to dream of a better life for me. In the factory below, the whistle for morning break sounded; a clatter of clogs against the wet floor followed as the workers headed for the central courtyard, then the noises faded. With the hiss of the steam engines switched off too, silence stretched across the room, taut like the skin of a drum.

He stroked my face and blotted my damp cheeks. 'What happened to you, Little Flower?'

'My mother bound my feet when I was four, like a lady,' I began. I told him about my *aa noeng*'s last words, her hopes for me, which were dashed by Linjing's spite. My story gushed out like an overflowing river. I let him know of Lady Fong's kindness, the marriage offer that Linjing stole, and I even told him about Spring Rain. But I did not reveal Lady Fong's downfall: that wasn't my secret to share. All the while, he held my hand, our fingers entwined. His eyes were two compasses, comforting and steadfast, and when I looked into them, I believed he would guide me to safety, a place I could at last call *home*. But he still had not seen my feet. When he did—

'Now you know everything,' I concluded quickly. 'Not only do I have big feet, they're also deformed, so you may retract your offer. I won't blame you.'

I foresaw he would tell me he had made a mistake, thank me for letting him go. But he knelt down and picked up one of my feet. I flinched and cried out.

'Trust me,' he said, as he reached up and squeezed my crippled hand.

I stiffened but did not pull away again as he eased off one shoe then the other. Inside my socks, my toes huddled like a herd of frightened sheep. I shut my eyes and covered my face as he unwrapped them, exposed them. Hoofs of anguish thumped in my heart: any moment now he would reel in disgust, curse me, order me to leave. Instead he returned to my side and gently lowered my arms. 'I'm sorry to distress you. But you wouldn't have believed me if I'd simply told you that your feet won't change my feelings.' He cupped my trembling jaw. 'Little Flower, I have seen them, and I admire you, love you all the more for it.' He leant in, resting his forehead against mine, his breath, sweet with a hint of cloves, caressing my cheek, like an autumn breeze.

'Sir, I love you too.' My voice was brittle glass, poised to shatter. He kissed me. At first, I froze. But as hesitation melted away, my mouth pressed against his, warm, urgent and seeking, as though my desire had been trapped beneath ice, waiting for the thaw, and he was the sun I needed, even if I had grown used to grey skies, even if I had schooled myself to endure a perpetual winter. How had I ever thought a life of celibacy could be enough? When at last I pulled away, his eyes flashed with pleasure and vitality, echoing the rush of excitement in my veins.

'Will you come away with me?' he asked.

'I will place my life in your hands. But I have three conditions.'

'Name them and they shall be done,' he replied, as he tucked a strand of hair behind my ear.

'We must help Joy escape once I'm settled. I want her as my companion. I also want to search for Spring Rain and save her if we can.'

'Done. And the other?'

'We must not keep slaves. No *muizai*. No indentured men-servants. I want to hire staff who have a free will.'

'As you like,' he said, with a teasing laugh. 'Any other woman would take the chance to demand jewels, but not you.'

'Slavery is a cruelty I wouldn't wish on my worst enemy.'

His eyes widened. I was stunned by my sharpness too.

'You are right to be vexed,' he said, chastened. 'I shouldn't jest about slavery.'

He pulled me towards him, turning me around so my back leant against his chest and his chin rested on my head as his arms wrapped around my shoulders. In this moment, I was safe and cherished – feelings I had not experienced since I had bade farewell to my mother. If only the murmur of 'mistress' had not lurked in the recesses of my mind, I would have been happier than words could describe.

44

Little Flower

Noble Siu Je's sincerity I no longer doubted. Nor could I deny my feelings. Yet, as I waited for him to finalize the preparations needed to spirit me away, a dull ache still echoed in my mind. I hoped tonight's entertainment would fill the hollowness, if only temporarily. Noble Siu Je was hosting an opera in an open-air theatre to reward our sewing amahs for completing the first hundred shawls ahead of schedule. At this speed, they would complete the project weeks ahead of time, even without my guidance.

On my right, Joy leant forward, popping a handful of boiled peanuts into her mouth before she'd finished chewing the last. Beside her, Linjing stared ahead too, a figurine posing as a captive audience, her eyes preoccupied. In recent weeks, her cheek and jaw bones had become like sharp rocks beneath her wan skin. Purple crescents encroached beneath her eyes, and she retired to bed long before the rest of us. Even before our falling-out during the *dou si*'s trial, she had stopped prattling about Noble Siu Je, and though this was an immense relief to me, it made me wonder. Could Linjing have made advances that he'd rejected? She had seemed so in love, so sure of his regard for her, she might have been emboldened to do so. Might she also know the truth about Noble Siu Je and me? If not out of jealousy, I could think of no other reason why she'd lied and injured me; yet, if she knew, why didn't she report the scandal to her aunt, or at least confront me? The impulsive mistress I knew wouldn't hesitate to expose me, punish me. These questions troubled me, but of course I couldn't ask her, and even if she volunteered answers, I wouldn't trust them. I would be sorry to leave Madam Sapphire, but I couldn't wait to be rid of Linjing.

As I shook off these thoughts, Noble Siu Je stood up from the front row, where he was sitting with his family, and walked down the narrow aisle towards me. When our eyes met, my heart quickened and wings of longing fluttered in my belly. His hand almost brushed my shoulder as he passed, and even though we didn't touch, my skin tingled. I tried to curb these wanton feelings, but my body reacted of its own volition. If my thoughts were written on my skin, I would have been executed by now.

Distracted, I had taken little notice of the show, but *The Butterfly Lovers* was a story I knew well. It took no effort to follow the plot as I tried to fix my attention back to the stage. The performance had reached a scene where the young lovers were travelling from their scholarly academy back to their hometowns. Jingtoi repeatedly hinted to Saanbaak about her true gender, saying things like, 'Saanbaak, we are like mandarin ducks,' and 'Yours is a true *yang* soul, mine is shaded with *ying qi*.' But her clues evaded Saanbaak; he couldn't see past her male disguise, triggering a tragedy that would eventually result in Saanbaak's early death and Jingtoi throwing herself into his open grave. Unable to fulfil their love as mortals, they would emerge as a pair of butterflies, never to be parted.

The opera had been a favourite with Dowager Lady Fong, who had hired various travelling troupes to perform it over the years. Back then, alongside the Fong ladies and my fellow *muizai*, I had laughed at Saanbaak's stupidity even as I bemoaned Jingtoi's reluctance to speak plainly.

But today I couldn't laugh.

I sat motionless as the crowd around me roared with hilarity at Saanbaak's expense, many throwing handfuls of watermelon seeds and peanut shells onto the stage, jeering at his blindness. Some sisters shouted for Jingtoi to abandon her flowery language; others urged her to give up. Yet, I shared none of their feelings. The comical music that accompanied this scene had not changed and neither had the actors' lines, but my response had.

Joy swung around and muttered, 'That fool doesn't deserve her!' Without waiting for my response, she turned back to watch the drama. Joy's words were like a lash in my eye, niggling, yet no matter how I tried, I couldn't reach the source of the irritation.

When at last Noble Siu Je announced we would steal away by sea the next day, I asked him to stage a quasi-wedding night on the houseboat before we set off at dawn for Canton City. I needed this shred of legitimacy, even if it was only in my mind.

By nine in the evening, exhausted by the long hours at the silk filature, the sisters slept like the dead; even those who'd switched to the shawl project were snoring. In the cot beside me, Linjing's slow, even breaths assured me of her deep sleep. Slowly, I slid out of bed and stood over her gaunt face. Though forgiveness was impossible, pity filled my heart for a moment. I couldn't begin to imagine how it must feel to be born with everything, only to end up with nothing. I bade her a silent farewell before creeping over the tiles and descending the stairs.

Downstairs, all was quiet. I hurried to the back courtyard, slid the wooden latch to open the gate and stepped out onto a narrow path alongside the waterway that would lead me to the pier. Long grass lined both sides; the swaying blades felt like hands grasping my knees and several times I jumped. The full autumn moon beamed down from a cloudless sky, allowing me to see without a lantern. Like whispers, the leaves on the swaying branches swished in the wind. On any other night, these gentle rustlings would have been soothing, but now they made me imagine spectators squatting in the dark. At the sound of a twig snapping, I turned and called, 'Who's there?'

No answer.

I took several steps back, scanning the riverbank to my right, a line of trees to my left. Memories of my ill-fated escape from the Fong residence spilt forward, dampening my conviction and tightening my muscles. But this time I had Noble Siu Je, this time I would succeed. Nothing looked amiss. I let out my breath and kept walking until the silhouette of Noble Siu Je came into view, standing on the pier and holding a red lantern. The tension in my shoulders and back loosened the instant I saw him. Behind him rose the outline of a houseboat, gauzy curtains draped in the doorway, revealing a faint glow of candles from the interior. I hastened to him.

'Did anyone see you leave the sanctuary?' he asked.

The fierce concern in his voice moved me. 'All the sisters are asleep,' I replied, as I took his hand, leading him. He dropped a kiss on my forehead as we strode together along the pier and onto the boat.

Beyond the gauze curtains, the inner room mimicked a wedding chamber. A garland of red pompoms dangled from the rafters, paper cuttings of mandarin ducks bedecked the pillars of the canopy bed, a cloth embroidered with an intertwined dragon and phoenix covered the refreshment table. Twin scarlet candles served as a centrepiece, their flames dancing in a breeze that entered from a nearby window. A china bottle of wine sat next to the candles, flanked by two thumb-sized cups. The detailed elegance was proof of Noble Siu Je's love for me, yet the hollowness I had fought to keep at bay stalked at the edge of my happiness, reminding me that this scene was as false as a stage set.

To banish these troublesome thoughts, I said, 'I will be your bride if only for one night.'

Noble Siu Je lifted my arm, pressing my palm against his chest. 'Little Flower,' he said, 'in here, you will always be my true wife.'

Not trusting myself to speak without a sob, I turned to the table and gestured for him to pour the wine.

'With this toast,' he said, presenting me with a cup, 'I pledge my devotion and respect. I'll listen to your joys and soothe your sorrows. I will love and protect you.'

'With this toast,' I quavered, 'I pledge my heart, which I give wholly to you.'

Our arms intertwined, he drank from my cup and I from his. The liquid slid down my throat, filling me with warmth and anticipation. We returned the cups to the table and turned to each other. He reached over and untied the ribbon that held my braids together. Released from its bindings, my hair unravelled, a cascade of freedom splashing across my shoulders. With it, a rush of boldness seized me. I reached up and cradled his face in my hands, bringing his lips to meet mine. Our kiss, deep and warm, stretched on and on, like the gossamer from a lotus root that seemed to have no end.

I pulled away as I lifted his hands to the toggle at the base of my throat. He released it from the loop with the reverence of someone opening a cherished gift, sliding his hand into the collar where he caressed my throat. Tenderly, he progressed to the next toggle, following the diagonal curve of fastenings that travelled over my right breast, under my arm, and ended at my hip. He eased the *ou* off my shoulders, allowing it to slide to the floor. Standing before him with nothing but a diamond-shaped *daudau* covering my breasts and belly, I quivered with excitement as he traced his forefinger under the curve of my breasts.

At last, I understood the true ache of bodily yearning. I expected him to unfasten the ribbons around my neck and waist but he left them, moving instead to untie my trousers, allowing them to fall in one motion. Only my *daudau* remained. I flushed with delight as his hands glided across my skin from my arms to chest to belly, before lingering above my secret domain. The warmth between my legs yearned for his touch. But he stood up and walked behind me, releasing the ties around my waist and neck. Once my *daudau* fell away, he scooped me into his arms and carried me to the bed.

I lay on my side, watching him disrobe until, unabashed, I called him to me. He joined me on the bed and pulled me to my knees so that we faced each other. Like an explorer traversing a foreign terrain, my hands travelled over his broad shoulders, across his firm chest and abdomen. Unable to bear the suspense any longer, I fell back onto the mattress, pulling him to me.

I lay facing Noble Siu Je as the night slipped away. He roused once, smiled drowsily and wrapped an arm around my waist, pulling me closer before he drifted back to sleep. I lay awake and stared at the ceiling. Our union felt beautiful and wholesome . . . until I recalled he would share similar nights with Miss Prudence soon. It sickened me to envisage his other life, the public one where I wouldn't exist. I would be like the chalk marks used to outline a motif: stitch by stitch these faint lines would be buried beneath embroidery threads until all traces vanished from sight. As a slave, I had lived a worthless, invisible life. I had fought that destiny to become a person of value to the sisterhood. My peers admired me, and Madam Sapphire had singled me out as her potential successor. How could I cast all this away for a life lived behind lies and shame?

Powerful as these arguments were, something else plagued me too, something Joy had said during the opera: *That fool doesn't deserve her!* Jingtoi, a bright, intrepid young lady, who was so determined to become a scholar that she dressed as a gentleman to attend school, needed an equal, not Saanbaak, who was so dense that he couldn't see the longing in her eyes or hear the tenderness in her voice.

In other words, Saanbaak was not *a deserving man*.

Those three simple words hauled me back to the conversation I'd had with Miss Hart before my ill-fated escape attempt – those sage words belonged to her. I recalled her declaration as though I'd heard it only moments ago: she would not marry unless she met a deserving man, one who would treat her as an equal, with respect, not as an object and never as property.

With the clarity of sunshine bursting through dark clouds, I found words for the hollowness that had hovered at the edge of my consciousness for weeks.

Despite his affection, honour and generosity, Noble Siu Je

was not worthy of my love. In his eyes, though he respected my talent and character, I was still inferior, shameful, a woman he could love only in secret, behind high walls, sequestered in a metropolis.

I couldn't resent Noble Siu Je. He was confined by customs and hierarchy, but the phantom discomfort that had niggled at me since he'd first proposed 'mistress' now became an open sore. As his mistress, I would be a cherished woman in charge of my own household, without a mother-in-law, yet it was still not enough for me. I had come too far on my journey of freedom to accept a lifetime in another prison. I needed dignity and respect as much as I needed love. Only a man who felt proud to be my husband could give me these things.

Noble Siu Je was not that man.

The former Little Flower, the slave in me, tried to quash these indulgent thoughts, for to her, life as a mistress was the only route to liberty. But I was already free, at least as free as any woman could expect to be. I had shelter. The shawl project would sustain my material needs and feed my soul. In some ways, I had become like Miss Hart: a modern, independent woman with no need to exchange marriage for security.

The sky had begun to shed its night coat and dawn would soon be here. I slipped out of bed and got dressed, then gently shook Noble Siu Je's shoulders. 'Wake up. We must talk.'

He murmured groggily.

'Noble Siu Je,' I said. 'Last night is all I can give you. I can't be your mistress.'

At this, his eyes snapped open. He sat up and reached out for me but I stepped back, wrapping my arms around my waist.

'What has changed?' he croaked.

'I want a husband who isn't ashamed of me, or none at all.'

'I am not ashamed of you,' he countered. 'I admire you,

respect you. To me, no other woman is more talented and brave. You must know that.'

'Yes, you respect me. But only in private.' I pointed to the door. 'Out there, I'm an embarrassment, a shame you must keep hidden. I need you to be proud of me, not to visit me like one might sneak into an opium den.'

'I would marry you if I could. But my family would never accept a woman with natural feet, not even as a *cip si*. Besides, I must think of my father, Prudence, her family and my sisters. Our scandal would injure them in so many different ways.'

'I am not asking you to change your mind. My decision isn't an ultimatum to force your hand. I understand you have done your best. But it is not enough for me.'

'*Not enough?*' he repeated, his palm smacking the bedpost.

'Sir,' I said, 'do you think that because I have big feet and used to be a slave I should fall to my knees in gratitude for your offer?'

He said nothing, but his hard eyes were answer enough.

'In the eyes of the world that might be true,' I continued, 'but I have pride, dignity and self-respect, just like a lady. I am low of birth but I am your equal in *spirit*. If you recognized this too, you wouldn't ask me to live a life of secrecy and disgrace.'

'Little Flower, you are asking too much of me. You want a hero who can reshape the world. I am but a man, tethered to duty and expectations. I'm sorry.'

In his softened eyes, I saw sincerity and despair. The anger drained from me, leaving sorrow and longing in its wake. He held out his arms towards me. The desire to press my face to the hard muscles of his bare chest was so strong that my resolve would have crumbled if we touched. Knowing this, I hurried out of the door and ran down the pier.

45

Little Flower

My eyes stung with unshed tears, but I didn't have the luxury
to indulge my feelings. I must return to my bed before the
sisterhood roused. Heart heavy with agony, I ran the quarter
of a mile back to the sanctuary. As I rounded the final bend
of the path, my blood froze.

A figure was sitting on the steps leading to the back gate.
From this distance, I couldn't identify who it was. Should
I hide in the long grass? No. Running away would confirm
my guilt. I slowed to a walk, my breath coming in ragged
gasps. All would be well, so long as I approached her – I
could see now it was a woman – with a calm demeanour.
Going for a morning stroll wasn't a crime. When I realized it was Linjing, my pulse exploded as she stood up,
arms crossed.

'I know you spent the night with Noble Siu Je,' she said. 'I
followed you, saw him waiting on the pier, watched the two
of you disappear into the houseboat.' She spat the last words
like a cat, her upper lip curled.

An icicle of panic speared my heart. Her face was taut with

a cold rage I'd never seen before, not even when I'd told her she wasn't really a Fong.

'How long have you suspected me?' I asked, in a small voice.

'Long enough. I found the love knot too.' At this, my hands flew to my ribs where the pendant lay hidden in the pouch of my *daudau*, a keepsake I should have left behind.

'So it's in there,' Linjing said. 'All the better for me. I needed solid proof of your treachery. Now I have the love knot and your spoilt maidenhead.'

'What will it take for you to keep quiet?' I asked.

'It's too late,' she said. 'I have told my aunt. She is expecting you.'

Her betrayal plunged me into a glacial river of shock. It mightn't be too late to dash back to the boat. I looked over my shoulder to the path that would lead me back to Noble Siu Je, but devastation paralysed my limbs, and my head spun. To feel something solid, I pressed one palm against the cold brick wall. My thoughts whirled as I tried to make sense of Linjing. I had known her to be surly, selfish, but even after her lie to the shaman, I'd still thought her only capable of being casually cruel, not malicious. Yet she had betrayed me just as Second Fong *taai taai* had ensnared Lady Fong. Had Linjing been clever or had I been too stupid to see her true character?

She seized my wrist, yanking so hard that I stumbled, but she hauled me up before my knees hit the ground.

'Don't even think about running away,' she snarled.

'Linjing, you have condemned me to death. Why?'

'Don't be melodramatic,' she mocked, eyes rolling. 'My aunt adores you, just like Aa Noeng did. You heard her defend you against the *wu lei zing* charges. You'll never set foot outside the sanctuary again, but she won't execute you.'

336

'Madam Sapphire won't forgive this transgression. Please, Linjing, let me go unless you want to see me drown.'

'It's time you faced your reckoning.'

She dragged me forward as she marched to the gate. I twisted and turned, but she had the strength of a man. I dug my heels into the gravel, using all my weight to slow her down. She swung around and slapped me with her free hand. My head jerked to the side and back; the force of her blow rang in my head and my earlobe stung.

'What have I done to deserve this?' I asked.

'The question is,' she said, 'what *haven't* you done?'

'I don't understand.'

'Don't lie,' she spat. 'I don't know what foul magic you used but you've exchanged your fate for mine.'

'How can you believe such an absurd idea?'

'Since Aa Noeng died, you – a slave – have risen and risen in the world, and I, a lady, have sunk beneath contempt. No education or modern thinking can account for this reversal in our fortunes. It's perverse and wicked. If I can't blame you, then who?'

I said nothing, for I couldn't think of a response that wouldn't fan her rage.

'I did everything I could to secure Noble Siu Je,' she cried, 'but you stole him from me.'

'He never loved you.'

'You stole him with unnatural powers,' she insisted. Her lips were drawn back as her chest heaved, but I detected doubt in the quavering of her voice. Saying so wouldn't help me, though.

'If I could conjure foul magic or any sort of spell, would I have endured slavery for so many years?' I asked evenly, imitating Miss Hart's composure when she had posed new thinking that challenged Linjing's beliefs. 'Would I have allowed the mallet to smash my fingers?' When her breaths lengthened, I added, 'Afterwards, would I have permitted Dowager Lady Fong to live in peace and abundance?' Her shoulders dropped. 'If I had recently acquired mystical powers, then I would be Noble Siu Je's first wife by now, wouldn't I? Instead, all he offered was *mistress*.'

She frowned, shaking her head. She must have assumed he planned to marry me. No wonder she hated me.

'I wouldn't even have been a concubine,' I explained. 'We were supposed to sail away to Canton City, right now. He would have set me up in a mansion with servants, but I would always have lived in shame and secrecy. I have turned my back on him for the sake of dignity. I have sided with the sisterhood over love.'

Linjing's mask of hatred slackened. Her grip loosened too, but not enough for me to break free, and even if I did, I couldn't outrun her. In the distance, a cockerel crowed. An orange sun peeked over the horizon and the grey sky had lightened to blue. Soon the sisterhood would waken. Her eyes flickered: one moment savage, the next receptive, then back to hostile. Linjing was a wild beast on the verge of becoming subdued, but if I made one wrong move, she would pounce. In a calm and steady voice, like the one she'd often used to soothe horses, I urged, 'Linjing, you are not like Second Fong *taai taai* or your *maa maa*. This isn't you. They are black-hearted and old-fashioned. You're kind and progressive. Please, I beg you to be reasonable. I am sorry for your misfortune. But deep down, you must know that your downfall has nothing to do with me. I wounded your pride when I tore up my indenture paper, and for that I am sorry. I should have given you more time to adjust to your new life.

But I have never harmed you.' I reached out and touched her shoulder. 'Please, Linjing, let me go.'

She said, with a sob, 'If I can't have him, neither can you.'

In the next moment, her strength doubled as she dragged me over the threshold into the sanctuary.

Linjing marched me into Madam Sapphire's apartment, where an elderly matron, a stranger, waited beside our mother superior.

'Lie down, Little Flower,' Madam Sapphire commanded.

'On the floor, not the rug,' the stranger added. 'Now.'

'Why?' I asked.

'You will soon find out,' Linjing said.

Having no other choice, I lowered myself onto the cold tiles.

'Knees up,' the stranger ordered, in a squeaky voice that did not match her lined face and hunched back. When I didn't move, she grabbed my ankles and shoved my knees towards my chest, spreading them wide apart. Before I had time to register her intent, the old woman had yanked off my trousers and thrust her hands between my legs. I tried to squirm away, but Linjing pressed down on my shoulders, pinning me in place.

'Take your hands off me!' I cried.

Ignoring me, the old woman's fingers continued to dig into my tender flesh. All the while, Madam Sapphire and Linjing peered down at me, faces taut with anticipation. But in Madam Sapphire's eyes, dread and hope mingled. The stranger pulled her fingers out and sniffed.

'I smell sex,' the old woman pronounced.

'Are you sure?' Madam Sapphire asked.

'Madam,' the stranger said, indignant, 'I have examined countless girls over my career. I assure you this one has recently been with a man, probably no more than three or four hours ago. Without doubt, she has lost her maidenhead. Now, if you will be kind enough to pay me, I will be on my way.'

The stranger left as soon as Madam Sapphire had dropped a string of copper coins into her open palm.

Madam Sapphire ordered me to kneel in front of her. 'Why have you betrayed us?' she asked.

'I am sorry to have pained you,' I began. 'I offer no excuses. Only I vow it will not happen again. I have fallen in love with Noble Siu Je. But I have refused his offer to make me his mistress. I have chosen to stay, and I will take the So Hei vows. Please give me a second chance.'

'Oh, Little Flower, I thought you were steadfast and wise. But you have turned out no better than you ought to be – a lustful peasant.'

'Lock her up for life,' Linjing suggested, 'or she will run off with Noble Siu Je.'

'No. Little Flower must pay for her sin with her *life*. It is the way of the sisterhood, even for a novice.'

Linjing gasped, mouth agape. 'Have mercy, Aunt! You said you wanted Little Flower to be your successor. Don't you remember?'

'Rules are rules. I make no exceptions.'

Linjing's face contorted with genuine distress. My mistress, my stupid, stupid mistress: she'd really believed her aunt would spare me. I would have laughed if my life hadn't been in peril.

'Little Flower has made a grave mistake,' Linjing pressed, 'but she doesn't deserve to die. I would never have exposed her if I had thought you would execute her.'

'I must set an example for everyone,' her aunt said. 'Society tolerates us because we have sworn a vow of celibacy. It is the price we pay for freedom and respect. Our purity keeps us safe from men who would delight in tearing down our sanctuaries. I must uphold these values or the sisterhood's integrity will be in jeopardy. It takes only one tainted soul, one act of leniency, to spoil our reputation.'

'But no one has to know. Little Flower's transgression can remain a secret between us. That woman can be bribed. I'm sure of it.'

'Keeping a secret of this magnitude is like trying to contain fire with a paper bag. It's impossible.'

'Then let me go,' I implored. 'I can leave now. You can tell the sisters I have run away.'

'I cannot risk our good name for you.'

Linjing continued to argue. 'If you punish Little Flower, you will implicate Noble Siu Je too. Would you shame our employer?'

'My dear niece,' Madam Sapphire said, her mocking tone contrary to her sweet words, 'I could have stormed onto the boat the moment you told me about them, but I examined Little Flower in private because I do not want to expose Noble Siu Je. Despite his folly, he is an honourable employer, an ally I cannot lose. If his name is smeared, business might suffer too.'

'This sisterhood is a sham,' I said, before I could stop myself. 'It claims to be a sanctuary, but it is another type of prison, no different from arranged marriages. The celibacy vow is cruel. It is unnatural to suppress our need for love. You preach against male cruelty. But isn't it equally brutal to condemn me to death for one mistake?'

My courage ebbed as soon as I had finished speaking. Madam Sapphire's eyes glinted with cold detachment.

'She doesn't mean what she says!' Linjing exclaimed. 'Little Flower, apologize.'

'She must pay for her sin,' Madam Sapphire said. 'I will not be dissuaded.' To Linjing she said, 'You are *forbidden* to help her. If you disobey me, you'll be excommunicated.'

Madam Sapphire locked me into the storeroom. I glanced around for somewhere comfortable to sit, but the room was packed to the brim. Salted fish hung from the rafters in various stages of drying. Vats of pickled vegetables filled one corner, sacks of rice another. Piles of firewood, stacked in neat pyramids, took up most of the remaining space. There was nowhere to sit, except on the dirt floor. The mingled odour of wood, salt, fish and vinegar was pungent and nauseating.

I leant my back against one of the large vats and drew my knees to my chest, wrapping my bound wrists around them. Once seated, my last shred of courage crumbled. With no hope of escape, terror sank its talons into me. Bitter tears streamed down my cheeks, my nose dripped and I howled at my own stupidity. The flood of despair soaked my *ou*. I sobbed until my swollen eyes ached and my heart felt scooped out, like a dried gourd. Hours ago, life had presented me with the promise of comfort and security, but I had carelessly tossed it away.

Why couldn't I have been happy with Noble Siu Je's love?

What maiden truly enjoyed dignity and respect? Everyone knew that only mothers-in-law had those privileges, but I had felt entitled to the same.

Was I any better than Linjing? She'd twisted reality to suit herself but hadn't I done the same?

I found myself calling for my *aa noeng*, something I hadn't done for at least a decade. Was she still alive? Where was Little Brother? Perhaps my life would have turned out differently if I had followed her mantras: 'Good girls keep quiet, follow rules and obey,' and 'Life is easier for those who can swallow bitterness and accept their lot.' From my first memory, she'd repeated these warnings to me, and she'd recited them again and again the day she'd sold me to Linjing's family.

Yet I hadn't heeded her wise counsel. Instead I'd tried to rebind my feet when Lady Fong ordered them to be let out; later, I'd fought Linjing's will and run away, foolishly putting my life into the hands of strangers, only to lose three fingers to a mallet, and for what? Worst of all, I didn't learn from that mistake. Presented with a chance for the security and freedom I craved, I'd chosen to follow Miss Hart's foreign teachings, allowing her lofty words to persuade me into thinking Noble Siu Je was not deserving of me.

Maybe I was the one who was undeserving. If I'd heeded my *aa noeng*'s advice to remember my place, I would have thanked Heaven for sending me a considerate and generous protector in Noble Siu Je. Perhaps Linjing was right: I was a *muizai* who'd reached too far beyond my station. Who had ever heard of a gentleman marrying a big-footed slave?

Knowing the answer to this question, regret filled my chest. It was dense, like smoke, like soot, choking me. Exhausted, my head lolled back and I closed my eyes, seeking oblivion. I was a pilgrim who had walked ten thousand miles, only to arrive at a false temple. Miss Hart had talked about freedom, but the bright new world she spoke of admitted only Western women. For Chinese women, there were three pathways: marriage, nunnery or Celibate Sisterhood, and the last two were almost one and the same. Noble Siu Je had given me a rare fourth option. Right now, if I could, I would gladly surrender my pride and be his obedient mistress.

How could Linjing be as malicious as Second Fong *taai taai*? For the first time, I understood how Spring Rain must have felt towards her mistress. Desperation may have driven

Linjing to betrayal, but time and again her selfishness had cost me everything. Yet she was a victim too: even though she had destroyed me, her life would be none the better for it. Our fates would have been different if Master Fong hadn't severed his ties with her without even a farewell. I had not, until now, understood that in this world only men had the freedom to act, to roam, to live. This understanding plunged me into an abysmal pit, far beyond despair.

46

Linjing

What had I done?

Truth to the gods: I'd only ever wanted to humble Little Flower, make her suffer for stealing Noble. I'd never wished for her death. How could I have known of my aunt's punitive character after seeing her defend Little Flower against the *wu lei zing* charges?

Of course Little Flower had not practised foul magic! In my heart I'd never truly believed that accusation, but I'd been angry, was still angry and desperate. Having no other explanation for my downfall, it was easy to fall prey to primitive charges. Still, I shouldn't have exposed her. But I had been almost deranged since Noble's rejection, so it wasn't all my fault, was it? No, Little Flower was to blame for breaking the cardinal rule. Besides, I had a right to rage, hadn't I? The fact remained that Little Flower had reaped Heaven's blessings, while I continued to suffer. I needed to speak to her before today's execution, make her see I wasn't another Peony, ensure she didn't enter the afterworld hating me.

The sister guarding the tiny storeroom bit into the gold ring

I offered as a bribe so that she would let me visit Little Flower. Satisfied, she warned me I had half an hour, then unlocked the door and I stepped inside. The window, a small hexagon, let in only a little light from the early-morning sun. After my eyes adjusted, I spotted Little Flower curled in a corner, her eyes closed, one cheek pressed against a ceramic vat, strands of hair hanging about her face. I picked my way over and crouched beside her, shaking her arm.

'I never meant for you to die,' I blurted. 'Please, you must forgive me.'

Her head jerked up and she twisted around to face me, her expression a mixture of blame and pity. She laughed, the bitterness making me cringe. I backed away, but she snatched my forearm, tugging me with alarming strength so that I lost my balance and staggered forward, my cheek crashing against the vat. Now our faces were inches apart.

'You're a victim of this world too,' she said, 'so I cannot hate you, but I can never forgive you.'

'But you must!' I pleaded. 'I exposed you, but you're the one who committed the crime and you were foolish to come back after you lost your maidenhead. None of this is my fault.'

With the backs of her tied hands, she swiped aside the stray hairs, lifted her chin and looked straight at me. 'All our life,' she said, 'you've taken, snatched and stolen from me.'

'That's not true,' I protested. 'It is you who stole Aa Noeng's love from me! And none of this would have happened if you hadn't coveted things that are above your station. Ever since your failed attempt to run away, I have treated you with nothing but kindness and respect, as though we were best friends rather than *muizai* and mistress. Yet you repaid my benevolence with revolt and betrayal.'

'If you were a true friend, you'd have destroyed my

346

indenture paper as soon as we joined the sisterhood,' she said. 'It's time you heard the truth about yourself.'

Unwilling to hear more of her twisted perspective, I rose to leave, but the muscles in her neck were taut ropes as she roared, 'Stay! You owe me that much.'

Stunned by her ferocity, I lowered myself back to the earthen floor.

'Until just now,' she began, 'I blamed myself too. I started to believe what you've always told me – that my dreams were too lofty for a *muizai*. But your persistent denials of responsibility remind me that your spite, envy and mulishness are the culprits.' I shook my head and opened my mouth to disagree, but she cut me off. Thrusting her bound wrists into my face, she asked, 'Would I be here if you hadn't betrayed me?' Before I could reply, she added, 'Whose fault was it that I had to join the sisterhood?'

Her questions unnerved me. But the answers in my head were worse, so I turned the focus back to my mother.

'You have always tried to steal Aa Noeng's love,' I said. 'The two of you were like mother and daughter, always embroidering together, sitting side by side, murmuring under your breath. Did you once think how it hurt me?'

'Lady Fong let you rob me of my golden lilies!' Little Flower shouted, as she kicked off her shoes, lifting one foot and then the other, shoving their mutilation into my face. I shuddered and tried to turn away, but she commanded, 'Take a long, hard look! Lady Fong was a compassionate, thoughtful mistress, but I was still expendable to her. Despite your shortcomings, she loved you. She threw me scraps of kindness, yet you punished me for it.'

'No,' I argued. 'You were the disciple she wanted. I was a misfit, failing at the one skill ladies ought to excel at. If Aa

Noeng had loved me more than you, she would have forced you to remain my dowry *muizai*. But she was prepared to set you free even though I needed you.'

'She found a replacement *muizai* for you.'

'Aa Sap was slow-witted.'

'She would have been loyal to you. That was why Lady Fong chose her.'

'Hah! So you admit you weren't loyal to me.'

'You stole from me not once, but twice! First my golden lilies, then my marriage. Would you be loyal to a mistress like you?'

'But I changed,' I protested.

She scoffed.

'I've treated you as Aa Noeng treated Cerise.'

'Does it compensate for these?' she asked. I flinched as her crooked, dead fingers thudded against my cheek. 'If you were me,' she went on, 'would a few kind words suffice? Does a nicely worded command to massage your feet, fan you from dusk till dawn, empty your chamber pot, and so on, make those duties any less unpleasant?'

'You were my *muizai*. Those requests were reasonable.'

'If you hadn't sabotaged my marriage offer, I would be first daughter-in-law to a respectable banker family, perhaps with a son by now.'

'Your mother-in-law could have been worse than Maa Maa. I saved you from all that.' As soon as these words flew out of my mouth, I knew they were a poor excuse, a falsehood dredged from a time before I had seen her as a friend. But if I admitted to this mistake, I might have to accept blame for other things too ...

'Why would a spiteful woman want a *muizai* for her son?' I didn't reply. She went on: 'You witnessed Madam Chan's

348

malice, and still you wanted to marry her son. You were prepared to be at her mercy, in exchange for a genteel life. How could you still claim to have acted with the intent of saving me?'

I didn't want to hear any more. Her questions were like hands that tore at my clothes, stripping me bare. I dreaded what lay beneath. For the second time I stood to leave, but she stuck her leg out, blocking me.

'Sit down,' she said. 'I haven't finished.'

Her wrists were bound. In three leaps I could be at the door before she could even hoist herself to her feet. But I sank beside her, my knees pressing against something sharp. I didn't shift them.

'Linjing, why did you destroy me?'

'I love Noble Siu Je and you stole him.'

'Tomorrow I'll die. I deserve the truth.'

'It is the truth.' *Isn't it?*

'Linjing, you aren't capable of love,' she said, her voice matter-of-fact.

'I love him! And without you, he would love me too.'

'You need to know a person before you can love them. Tell me three things about him that only someone who loved him would know.'

'He is ... I know that he wants to ...' I swallowed and tried again. 'He likes ...' She would know if I lied. Besides, I couldn't cross that line, not now.

'Then let me tell you three things. He glared at me, avoided me, because he didn't want to fall in love with a peasant. He defended me because my embroidery is like the impressionist art he admires. I'm the first woman who has ever taught him something about business.'

In contrast to these examples, my conversations with Noble

349

were transactional, laughable. My cheeks burnt. 'You're right,' I admitted, defeated. 'I'm attracted to him, but I don't love him, and he has no tender feelings for me. I only saw what I wanted to see because I'm desperate to escape this miserable life. I can't endure hardship. I'm a coward.'

'Why did you destroy me?' she asked again. 'Noble Siu Je is the object of our rivalry, but he is not the root cause.'

'You're a peasant. I'm a lady. We were never rivals.'

'Then why did you feel threatened by me?'

Having no rebuttal, I told her the truth. 'I envy your embroidery skills. They won my mother's approval, then my aunt's esteem and Noble Siu Je's affection. Why should you be blessed with a lady's quality that rightly belonged to me? Destiny dealt me blow after blow, but you got everything you wanted. Can you blame me for despising your easy fate?'

'Being sold into slavery is a rare privilege, I see why you would envy me,' she said, with heavy irony. I dropped my eyes. She went on, 'A growling belly, daily put-downs, loneliness, mangled feet and a crippled hand are blessings indeed. I should be grateful for all these gifts. Perhaps you would be more adaptable, hardworking, and less selfish if you'd had the same opportunities as me.'

Her sarcasm shredded the last layer of my denial, exposing what I couldn't ignore any more. Little Flower was right: I should look to my own failings. To me, she had always been a useful tool. First, I'd relied on her as a crutch to compensate for my colour infirmity. Later, in the sisterhood, I had targeted my grief and resentment at her.

But the truth was, I'd never tried to learn silk reeling, not with genuine commitment, for I'd considered it beneath me. Instead I'd expected Little Flower to compensate for my laziness so I could take more breaks, sit in the fresh air to rest my throbbing feet, pretend I was still a lady. Yet I was never a real lady: I was a bastard child. All my life I'd treated Little Flower with contempt; even when I was polite, even when I sought her friendship, I'd still thought of her as my underling. But she was my superior in character. I'd been given every advantage, but at the first sign of adversity, I'd given up, while Little Flower had fought against ill fortune, hardships, injury, heartaches, crushed dreams and impossible odds.

She would have triumphed if I had not robbed her of marriage, injured her, and now sentenced her to execution. I was worse than Peony! The horror of all I had done opened a void of disgust and despair inside me. I wanted to tumble into it. Tears of regret flooded my eyes as I lifted my head to face her.

'I am truly sorry,' I wept, 'for everything. I'm to blame for it all.'

'Words are meaningless.'

'I don't expect you to forgive me, not when I can't even forgive myself. But I want you to know I finally see the truth.'

She gave me a hard stare.

I continued, 'We could never have been friends when I was your mistress and you my maid. I see it now. But things could have changed once we arrived here if I had accepted my lot and made the best of the situation. And you're right, I should have destroyed your indenture paper, set you free. Instead I blamed you because I couldn't face the truth. But I'm not a monster! If I had known my aunt would be so brutal, I would never have exposed you. Please, believe me.'

'Linjing, I'm glad you finally see the truth, and I do believe you. But it's too much to ask for my forgiveness.'

'I know,' I sobbed.

After heaving a sigh she said, 'Leave me. I have but a few hours left. Don't rob me of them as well.'

I did as she asked, self-disgust engulfing me.

Outside the storeroom, I collapsed against the wall, shaking as I wept until my voice cracked and my eyes ached. Eventually the sister on guard ordered me to leave, so I staggered away. My feet had a mind of their own, taking me back to our dormitory where I sank onto my mattress and curled on my side, staring at the gap between my cot and Little Flower's. I stretched my arm across the divide, wishing she was there to comfort me with a squeeze of my cold hands, as she had done so often during our first few weeks here.

Stripped of all my denials, I finally saw that only Little Flower had ever shown me unearned affection, shared my woes, given me solace. When Lady Li's parcel of shoes had arrived, Little Flower had been the one to stroke my back until my panic subsided. Upon Aa Noeng's death, she had helped me prepare her body for the afterworld. And at this sisterhood, she again had cocooned me from the harshness of our new life. All she'd asked in return was equality and freedom: rights that ought to belong to everyone. But we lived in a hierarchy that favoured men. Women, be it peasant or lady, first wife or minor wives, were pitched against each other, fighting among themselves for scraps of power and security. Even a So Hei sister could not escape this fate. If we could, my aunt would not have been sacrificing Little Flower in fear of jeopardizing our sisterhood's future.

Among all of us, only Little Flower had paved a different, meaningful future for herself, one that lifted other women, like Joy, out of drudgery too. And her achievements stemmed from her intelligence and tenacity; unlike Peony, me, and even Aunt Sapphire, she had never sacrificed another's happiness or safety to further her goals.

In contrast, I had always been willing to uphold destructive practices, as long as those rules benefited me. Perhaps my downfall and my mother's death could have been avoided if I had spoken to Aa Noeng, urged her to pity Peony and allow my brother to stay with his birth mother. But I had been too happy to see Maa Maa and Aa Noeng enforce a cruel practice that favoured first wives. Even here, when I could have forged a friendship with Little Flower and lived in equality among my So Hei sisters, I had instead fixated on restoring my position as a lady. By placing me in Aunt Sapphire's care, Aa Noeng had hoped to give me the means to earn my independence, perhaps even travel abroad, but I had been too attached to privilege to stand on my own feet. All my life, I had enjoyed these advantages of class without sparing a thought for the women who had forfeited their freedom, and often their dignity, to serve ladies like me.

Even if it meant I'd be cast out of the sanctuary, it was time I sacrificed for Little Flower.

Knowing Noble was the only person who could save her, I raced to his office and charged in as soon as Ming opened the door. At his desk, Noble was picking up a calligraphy brush, his sleeve dragging across the inkwell as he did so. Without attending to his stained sleeve, he rolled the brush onto a blotting stone to remove excess ink, but his hand shook as he began to write. When I called his name, surprise and wariness leapt across his face. My cheeks reddened as the memory of our last humiliating encounter resurfaced, but I pushed on, words tumbling out like pebbles. 'Noble Siu Je, I must speak to you urgently about Little Flower. Aunt Sapphire has discovered your relationship with her. She has sentenced Little Flower to death by drowning today, in three hours.'

Noble tossed the brush to one side, sprang from his desk, strode over and gripped my shoulders. 'Tell me everything,' he ordered, 'as quickly as you can.'

I told him all that had taken place. The floorboards creaked as he shifted his weight from one foot to the other. Ming gave up all pretence of work, glaring at me from his desk. Beads of sweat pricked my back as I confessed my role in Little Flower's downfall.

'You must marry Little Flower,' I concluded. 'That is the only way to save her.'

'If it were that easy, I would have taken her as second wife.'

'Do you want her to die?'

'Of course not,' he declared. 'I love her. If I could, I would marry her. But I cannot.' He tilted his head up and squeezed his eyes shut. I thought tears might roll down his face, but when he looked back at me his eyes were only darkened with torment, and I couldn't help but admire his self-control.

'All you need to do is publicly claim her,' I told him. 'The execution by drowning and So Hei vows are not Qing laws. They are only a social custom. You are the heir to the principal family in this town. You can override it.'

'I wish it were that simple.'

'It *is* that simple.' I glared at him. 'Unless you do not love her enough.'

'I have never experienced such intense feelings for anyone else.' The catch in his voice further convinced me of his sincerity. A pang of envy tightened my chest as I listened to the rest of his strained words. 'Without her, I will never be happy. But marrying her is impossible. Surely you see that.' His question was frantic. 'You must see I have no choice.'

'You cannot marry her and remain here,' I admitted. 'My aunt will never stand for it, even if your parents approve. But you are not bound to stay in Shuntak.'

He staggered back as though I had delivered a blow.

'Take heart from Little Flower and her courage. The world is wide and you are a capable young man. If you have confidence in yourself, you will succeed too. You and Little Flower could live anywhere – if you were willing to sacrifice everything for love.'

At that, he sank to the nearest stool.

'Do you love her enough to give up your home and inheritance?'

'I cannot sacrifice my family's reputation,' he said. 'You must see that?'

I did not reply.

'I'm bound by a womb betrothal,' he continued. 'I must marry Prudence. Our fathers are like brothers. Filial duty compels me to honour their pledge. Aside from shattering their alliance, the scandal will further weaken Prudence, and taint my sisters' reputations too. If there is an honourable solution that spares everyone else, I would seize it. But there isn't.'

'It takes immense courage to do what is right to save the one you love, even if it pains others,' I told him. 'Do you have what it takes?' He buried his face in his hands. 'You could migrate to another part of China. Start afresh, build your own business empire where this scandal cannot reach you. Go abroad if you must.'

'There is Hong Kong,' he said, sitting straighter, 'a city rich in opportunities, even if we must defer to the foreigners.'

'*Seize* those opportunities,' I urged. 'Fortune favours the bold.'

For a long moment, neither of us spoke. From the factory below, the hiss of the steam engines measured the stretched seconds. Ming tapped a calligraphy brush against the inkstone.

'Acting on a whim might get us both killed and destroy many other innocent lives,' Noble said finally. 'I need time to think.'

'You don't have time! Her death will haunt you for ever. Save her and save yourself.'

His expression, though alert, was still tormented by indecision. I had one more strategy that might convince him, yet revealing it would expose my shame. Weighing up the costs, I decided Little Flower's life was worth far more than my dignity.

'Noble Siu Je, do you know why I came here?' I asked.

'This isn't the time to talk about yourself.'

'I deserve your scorn, I know. But listen to me. My story, or rather my *aa noeng*'s tragedy, is worth hearing.'

'Why?'

'My mother's death is a cautionary tale. Will you at least listen?'

He rubbed the side of his neck and nodded.

'I'm a cuckoo child,' I began. 'Neither Aa Noeng nor Aa De was barren, but they couldn't have children together. My mother could have surrendered to destiny – we both know the dire fate of a childless wife. Instead she sought to fall pregnant with a male relative.'

I continued to recount all that had transpired after Peony had discovered Aa Noeng's transgression, omitting no detail, for I needed him to see the destructive nature of societal pressure. All the while, I studied his face, hoping my confession would convince him to turn his back on tradition. But I saw only more turmoil. 'Other people may not know better,' I finished, 'but you are a well-educated man. You know there is another way to live.'

There was no dawning realization. No awakening burst across his face. He remained silent, brooding. Had I convinced him?

47

Little Flower

At the assigned hour, Madam Sapphire entered the storeroom with a tray of food. She wore her hair in the usual style with a middle parting, pulled back into a simple bun. But today the strands around her temples had been so tightly drawn that the skin looked taut enough to split. She untied the rope around my wrists and thrust a bowl and chopsticks into my hands.

'Eat,' she commanded. 'Better be a sated spirit than a hungry ghoul.'

Blood oozed from the pieces of undercooked chicken thigh, staining the rice. Stomach heaving, I shook my head and set it aside.

'Suit yourself,' she said. 'Your death will be a cautionary tale that no celibate sister will forget. Do you repent?'

'I am sorry I hurt you, but I am not ashamed. My body is my property. All I have done is share it with a man I love.'

'I trusted you, but you have made a fool of me.'

'Is it fair to kill me to console your injured pride?'

'My pride, though injured by your folly, has little to do with your sentence. I might have forgiven you if all you had done was lie to me, but your sinfulness is treachery. Do you think it was easy for the first generation of sisters to band together and reject forced marriages?'

I shook my head.

'Long ago,' she said, 'before my grandmother's time, there was no such thing as a Celibate Sisterhood. Girls married whomever their families chose, be it a drunk, a man known to beat women, or an opium sot. But over time, maidens of the Pearl River Delta banded together, threatening collective suicide, using their lives as leverage to save one of their own from a lifetime of misery. Their demand was simple and humble: "Let us live as spinsters, let us be free."'

She reached up to a bunch of dried *baak coi* that dangled from the rafter, tore a fistful of leaves, crushed them and flung the fragments to the dusty floor.

'Still their families and society did not take them seriously, not until enough of those brave souls had leapt into raging rivers together, holding hands. Only then did village heads and local magistrates gradually permit women to form the Celibate Sisterhood that you take for granted.

'In exchange for this sliver of liberty, we must be chaste. Do I think chastity for freedom is a fair bargain? No. But it is the best we can secure in a world where often an ox is considered more valuable than a woman.'

Madam Sapphire's shoulders slumped as she sank down onto an upturned crate. 'I am not bloodthirsty,' she continued. 'I take no pleasure in your execution. But I must do what is needed of a mother superior. If I act with my heart rather than my head, when the truth comes out our enemies will have the perfect excuse to attack and dismantle us.'

'Who are these men you speak of, the ones who want to tear down our sanctuaries?' I asked.

'Little Flower, you are clever, but you are still young and naive. The menfolk tolerate the Celibate Sisterhood because they must. We are protected by public endorsement. But many resent our independence: for every woman who joins the sisterhood, there is one less available to be a bride and one less daughter or wife for them to control and exploit. Our existence threatens their masculinity, but as long as we uphold our pledge of chastity, we have society's support and no one can strike us down.

'As a novice, you cannot make a decision for yourself alone. Your choice has a collective consequence. This is why I must carry out your execution.'

Though I would soon die at Madam Sapphire's hands, her speech made it harder to blame her. For the first time since I'd made up my mind to become Noble Siu Je's mistress, I felt guilt, not for myself but for the cloud of shame I had cast over the sisterhood.

Briefly, Madam Sapphire reached out and touched my cheek before summoning one of the sisters to retie my wrists and march me through the courtyard and out of the sanctuary.

As soon as I stepped out of the front gate, a foul-smelling missile landed on my face. It was a mixture of rotten vegetables and putrefying offal. I retched. The perpetrator, a middle-aged man with a jaundiced colouring, jeered, 'Whore!' The mob hurled handfuls of muck and insults. Some were young children, mimicking their parents. I tried to shield my face with my hands, but the filth came thick and fast. A clump landed on my mouth. It tasted bitter, sour and fishy all at once. I spat and coughed, only to see someone burst forth from the crowd and run to protect me, shielding me with their body and bearing the brunt of the continued assaults. For several shocked seconds I did not recognize my protector, for with blazing eyes and hair that whipped in the wind, Linjing looked like Muk Laan, the brave daughter who answered the call of conscription in place of her elderly father. The other sisters stood back and watched, not with satisfaction as I might have expected, but with grimness and foreboding. Even Joy was too afraid to step forward.

'Have you no compassion?' Linjing demanded. 'Little Flower is about to be executed. Isn't that enough?'

The mob shouted their abuse louder. Her repeated entreaties for pity and compassion might as well have been spoken in a foreign tongue.

'Don't bother,' I said. 'They won't listen. Step aside and save yourself.'

Linjing huddled closer. In that moment, I felt her sincerity and regret.

'Take heart,' she whispered. 'I have spoken to Noble Siu Je. He may still come to save you.'

'Did he tell you he would?' I snapped, and saw in Linjing's expression that he had not. Before she could speak again, I added, 'If he couldn't marry me without a public scandal, why would he do so now?'

With a pained smile, she squeezed my shoulder. Eventually, the mob exhausted their supply of foul words and rubbish. They parted, allowing us to pass, and closed in behind us. As we started down the road, others joined the crowd. The spectators swelled to more than a hundred.

The overcast sky hung low and the humidity was relentless. Sweat teemed from my every pore. The stench of rot attracted flies. They clustered around us, landing on our brows, eyelids, noses, lips. Linjing shooed them away but it was a losing battle. I licked my cracked lips. What would Noble Siu Je think if he could see me now? I should resent him, curse him, for his proposal had led to my imminent death yet he would suffer no consequences. But I couldn't hate him.

My pace must have slackened because Madam Sapphire ordered, 'Get a move on. We haven't got all day.'

Linjing fell behind me and we hurried on. The paved road gave way to a dirt track. Panic steadily rose in my chest but I pushed it down. *It will be over soon.* I flinched as my eyes landed on a dead rabbit at the side of the track. A murder of crows pecked its belly, dragging out a trail of innards. I doubled over and heaved up bitter bile. Linjing wiped my mouth with her sleeve and put an arm around my shoulders as my legs wobbled.

'Can you walk?' she asked.

'I can.'

But as soon as she let go of me, someone kicked me from behind. I collapsed, my knees smashing against the hard earth. I threw out my hands to save myself and my forehead slammed against them. Linjing rushed over and Madam Sapphire allowed her to help me to my feet. The mob shouted for me to crawl the rest of the way, but Madam Sapphire said, 'We do not condone torture. The execution is punishment enough.'

I planted one foot forward, then the other. The slurs and jeers continued, but they were the whirl of wind, a meaningless whoosh. Just like in Shanxi, my true self had vanished, leaving a husk to face the worst of it.

At the riverbank, Madam Sapphire ordered me to kneel in front of the crowd while she made a speech, reiterating my crimes and my defiance. I did not listen and instead stared blankly ahead. When she finished, a man with thick arms came forward. He pushed me down on my back and bound my ankles together, then he fastened them to my wrists. So many cuts and bruises covered my body that they merged into

362

a pool of pain. The stout man heaved my head and chest off the ground while another thrust the pig cage over me. The narrow bamboo cylinder would not go past my shoulders. Another man came to help, shoving the cage harder and harder to force it down. The jagged ends gouged my cheek as he yanked the cage off my head to start again. This time, he succeeded in jamming me inside and he sealed it shut.

48

Linjing

The men carried Little Flower on their shoulders, one at each end of the cylinder, walking past the bed of reeds until they stood waist deep. As they lowered the cage, the water lapped Little Flower's face and she arched her neck, gasping for air.

'Don't give up,' I shouted desperately. 'Once you go under, hold your breath.'

Inch by inch, the cage disappeared beneath the murky water. Heeding my aunt's orders, the men remained to stand guard, waiting for her signal to haul Little Flower's body out for immediate burial with the rituals needed to exonerate her soul. Brutal though Aunt Sapphire might be, she had insisted on this shred of dignity for Little Flower.

Panic erupted as I lost sight of the cage. *One. Two. Three. Four.* I spun around, looking this way and that, searching for Noble. To my right, Aunt Sapphire stood rigid, grasping a string of prayer beads to her chest as her lips fluttered. Was she praying for her soul, or Little Flower's? Beside her, Joy pressed her fists against her mouth. The rest of the sisters formed a soundless cluster around them, with expressions that

I could not read. The villagers spread haphazardly across the bank. Mothers clutched their children's hands, men shifted their weight from one foot to the other and a trio of youths squatted on a nearby jetty. Moments ago, this frenzied mob had chanted not only for Little Flower's death but for her to suffer. Now a silence, heavy as mud, settled over their subdued faces. Perhaps murder wasn't as easy to witness as they had imagined.

Where was Noble? *Nine, ten, eleven.* How many seconds did Little Flower have left before water filled her lungs and silenced her for ever? Tears blurred my vision as I counted. *Twelve, thirteen.* My knees crushed onto the riverbank, a sharp stone piercing my trousers. I welcomed the pain, pressing harder against its jagged edge, steeling myself to accept her death even as I pressed my palms together and lifted my face to the blazing sky. *Fourteen, fifteen.* I'd do anything, pay any price, if the gods spared her life.

Heaven answered with a gush of wind that rippled the water, and crickets chirped. Was this a good omen or a sign that Little Flower had already gone? *Twenty.*

From behind me, a clear, determined voice yelled, 'Lift the cage!' With fierce strides that carved through the water, like a knife through putty, Noble pushed towards the two men, who stared with slackened jaws, too shocked and sluggish to comprehend this sudden turn of events.

'Lift it,' Noble repeated. 'Little Flower is under my protection.'

Still dumbfounded, the men remained stock-still as they stared past him to my aunt for guidance, but she was thunderstruck too. Faster than I thought humanly possible, he shoved the men aside and heaved the cage out of the river. Water gushed through the criss-cross weaving as he cradled it in his arms and strode back to a clearing on the riverbank, moving as though it weighed no more than a feather bolster. I ran towards them. From his belt, Noble pulled out a knife and slashed the bindings that sealed the opening, eased Little Flower out and sawed through the ropes that bound her wrists to her ankles. She lay limp in his arms. Eyes closed, lips blue, she did not respond to her name. But he continued to call it, as did I. Beneath her drenched tunic-blouse, her chest was as lifeless as Aa Noeng's had been. I placed my ear next to her mouth and nose, felt no breath.

'She's gone,' I choked. 'I'm sorry.'

Ignoring me, Noble laid her head and shoulders gently onto the ground and pressed his thumb on her *jan zung* meridian point. Time slowed as I clutched fistfuls of moss and mud, waiting, hoping against hope that he would succeed where I had failed to revive Aa Noeng. When he paused and inhaled deeply, I thought he had given up. Instead, he sealed Little Flower's mouth with his lips and breathed into it. Nothing happened for two breaths. Then, on the third breath, she jerked and water gushed from her mouth. He gathered her back into the crook of his arm, lifting her head up to ease the flow of her splutter. I wept and threw my forehead and palms onto the mossy ground, giving thanks to the gods.

Again and again Little Flower coughed and heaved. When the convulsions had finally settled, he lowered her head and swept wet strands of hair from her cheek and forehead, kissing her brow over and over.

'I'm sorry I arrived almost too late,' he said. 'Can you forgive me?'

She stared blankly at him, confusion mixing with relief.

'I should never have asked you to be my mistress,' he

continued. 'It was an insult to your integrity and our love. You are my equal. I will be your husband, your friend, your champion. Nothing will ever come between us.'

She reached up and touched his cheek.

'What about your family, your reputation?' she asked, voice hoarse.

'If they can't accept you, they are not worth keeping.'

Before we had time to rejoice, Master Chan marched up behind Noble. I had not seen him follow Noble to the river, but now I recognized him from sightings at the Chan residence. His unremarkable features had given the impression of a mild-tempered man. Now, two veins bulged on his forehead as he reached down, seized the end of Noble's queue and hacked the hair with a pair of scissors.

'You are no longer my heir,' he declared, clutching the severed bundle. 'But you must still face your reckoning. Leave that whore and return with me at once.'

With his arm around Little Flower's shoulders, Noble rose to his feet, lifting her with him. He replied, 'If that is what you wish, Father, then let it be. But I won't be separated from Little Flower.'

At Master Chan's bidding, two brawny menservants set upon Noble, tearing him from Little Flower. Noble punched one in the jaw and kicked the other away, as a sedan chair arrived carrying Madam Chan. Perspiration trickled on her powdered face as she hurriedly descended.

'Stand down,' she barked. 'Do not lay a hand on my son.'

The menservants fell back but stayed alert. With one hand leaning on the arm of her handmaiden, she tottered towards her husband, the delicate toes of her lotus shoes sinking into the soft mud. 'I know you're enraged,' she said to Master Chan, 'but Noble isn't to blame. He is bewitched.' She pointed a finger to Little Flower. 'Burn the *wu lei zing* and our son will recover his senses.'

The words *wu lei zing* rang out. All traces of compassion on the villagers' faces vanished, replaced by panic and hostility, their cheeks flushed and sweaty as they echoed Madam Chan's demand. I looked to my aunt, hoping she'd defend Little Flower as she had before, but she remained mute, mouth sealed in a grim line. With Aunt Sapphire's silent consent, Madam Chan ordered the menservants to wrench Little Flower from Noble's protective embrace.

Without thinking, I lunged for Noble's knife where it lay discarded on the ground, picked it up and walked towards Master and Madam Chan, holding the blade against my throat.

'Little Flower is as human as any of us,' I said. 'I'm prepared to defend her with my life. Let them go.'

The crowd exploded.

'Burn the *wu lei zing*!'

'Fetch the *dou si*!'

'Tie up the whore!'

'Save our husbands and sons!'

The group of youths hurled fistfuls of stones at Little Flower. Emboldened by the frenzied throng, the menservants continued their approach, circling Noble and Little Flower as he tightened his hold on her with his left arm and formed a fist with his right, in anticipation of the first blow.

I addressed the mob. 'Retreat, or I will slash my throat and come back to curse this village with plague or worse.'

With a half-smile, I pressed the blade deeper into my neck, drawing a rivulet of blood. I felt no pain. Instead conviction steadied my hand: in the true spirit of sisterhood, I'd gladly exchange my life for Little Flower's safety. My head spun and my vision blurred as I searched her face for forgiveness but could not be sure if the tears flowing down her cheeks were for me. As darkness swallowed my vision, Aa Noeng's spirit appeared before me, arms outstretched, beckoning me towards her with a proud smile. At last, I had earned her respect.

Epilogue

March 1895, International Settlement, Shanghai

Linjing

Dear Little Flower,

Each morning from Monday to Saturday, I get up and dress, donning an indigo skirt and a simple white muslin blouse. A pendant of the cross sits at the centre of my chest, completing the uniform of a teacher – for that's what I have become at the Methodist Orphanage for Chinese Girls. In my mind's eye, I see you frown with curiosity as you read these sentences. I promise all will be revealed below.

Abigail – Miss Hart – teaches the adolescent girls, and I look after one of the two younger classes. Are you surprised? Well, no one is more astonished than me. To think, the woman who tried to set you free has instead helped me. But, as always, I am too impatient. It is a shortcoming that I struggle to tame. Let me tell you from the beginning.

That day at the riverbank, after they let you and Noble go, a sense of clarity fell upon me. Abigail says it is a 'calling' from God, but at the time all I knew was that my destiny did not lie in Shuntak, even though Aunt Sapphire did not carry out her threat to excommunicate me. For weeks after you left, I was restless and desperate. I wanted to escape, too.

I couldn't stop thinking about Abigail's advice that with her help I could live as a modern woman in Shanghai. I wrote to her, confessing all that had happened and imploring her to help me. Months later, when I had almost given up hope, I received a letter from her brother telling me Abigail had moved to Shanghai, but he had forwarded my missive to her. It took another five months before I heard from her, but when she did reply, she sent tickets for a steamer to Shanghai and a letter of introduction to a pastor and his wife in Canton City, who agreed to be my chaperones for the long journey north. By then, Aunt Sapphire was more than happy to see me go.

Our ship arrived on the Bund, a harbour on the Whangpoo River, at the end of summer last year. My first impression of Shanghai was one of excitement and disorientation. I had never seen so many boats clustered on the river, people crowding the waterfront, rows of rickshaws lined up for customers, and pedlars of every imaginable ware, be it watermelons, hair combs, or feather dusters, roamed the streets.

Amid the crowd, Abigail's jaunty figure spotted us from the height of a landau. I wept at the sight of her familiar face. A few fine lines marked the passing of years since we last met, but her eyes still shone with the same eager optimism.

The English section of the Bund is a clean wide avenue, lined with trees and filled with all sorts of Western-style carriages, the landau the most prevalent. Here, men and women, Western and Chinese, travel freely together, sitting side by side in open-air vehicles for all to see. This rare sight alone captivated me, but I was spellbound by the glamorous Chinese ladies, who spoke with assertive voices, their musical laughter ringing like bells up and down the avenue as they gesticulated with fans, talking to their gentlemen companions. These women bore no resemblance to the demure manners of Aa Noeng or my other mothers. They were like a new species. I wanted to be like them, and I said as much to Abigail, who burst out laughing and explained they were famous courtesans out on a promenade with their clients. Being seen with these beauties was a badge of honour for gentlemen, who paid vast amounts of silver for each outing, some even losing their entire fortune on the upkeep of their paramour. I blushed to my hairline as I realized my blunder. Yet, despite learning the truth, I still admired the confidence they exuded, even as I wondered what hardship or compromises of dignity they might endure when they were away from these dazzling carriage rides.

Our orphanage sits within the English International Settlement, but there are as many Chinese citizens as foreigners for, like me, thousands have flocked to this patch of modernity seeking a different life.

Not long after my arrival, I received a marriage proposal, as first wife, from the proprietor of a hotel, the sort that caters for foreigners. He admired my English, a skill that would complement his business. With him, I could have returned to a lady's life, a tempting offer. But I did not want to abandon the sweet girls from our orphanage. Besides, if I wed, I want it to be for love, like you.

Now, let me tell you about my students. Their ruddy faces, wide smiles and buoyant remarks are refreshing, and when I ask what they would like to become once they leave the orphanage, they do not tell me they wish only to marry. Some say they aspire to be nurses at the Shanghai Hospital for Women and Children, some want to follow in our footsteps and teach the next generation of girls, others hope to be secretaries in foreign shipping companies for the chance to travel abroad, and the ones who want marriage say they will not wed until they meet a 'deserving man'. I am sure I don't need to tell you who inspires this revolutionary yardstick.

In this cosmopolitan city, a woman has a better chance to be more than a daughter, a wife and a mother. Yet I'd be a simpleton if I did not acknowledge that we are not on an equal footing with our Western neighbours, not even at this school where I'm compelled to renounce our gods, forsake our beliefs, in exchange for refuge. Though I am baptized, my heart still hasn't truly accepted the Redeemer. This I dare not confess to anyone but you, for even Abigail, as kind and generous as she is, would surely evict me for this duplicity. I do not know whether I will dedicate my life to teaching, but for now, I am content. And if I grow restless, I will not be afraid to seek my next adventure.

Once the ink has dried, I fold up the letter and stare at myself in the looking-glass on my dresser. The scar at my throat, an inch above my collarbone, is shiny. Gingerly, I trace the raised line. The wound healed long ago, yet the lightest touch, like the friction of my collar, is often enough to cause discomfort. I could seek ointments and lotions to dampen the sensation or perhaps help it fade but I refuse all remedies. I want to keep it as a reminder of the darkness that lurked in my soul with which I wrestled and won.

I last saw Little Flower on the riverbank; six seasons have passed since that day. It is likely that this letter I've penned to her will never be sent, for I do not know her address. But I write because I must; whether she will receive this first letter and others after is of less consequence. I write to Little Flower, not in apology, not with regret, but in friendship, hoping these words will be like spells that will one day bring us together again.

October 1896, Hong Kong Island

Little Flower

I still believe women are not truly free, not in Chinese society and perhaps not in this British colony either. Living here, I've learnt that Miss Hart's promises of liberty and progress were more wishful thinking than reality: though Western ladies enjoy more independence and seem not to fear their mothers-in-law they, like us, are still their husbands' lawful property, and most must wed to keep a roof over their heads. Choosing a 'deserving man' or remaining single are luxuries few women can afford, whether they are English, American or European. But with Noble as my husband – for that is what I call him these days, not Noble Siu Je and never 'sir' – I have come close to this lofty dream of freedom. We are two kites flying side by side under a new sky; the horizon feels higher and the winds of possibility lift us far above societal constraints. On Hong Kong Island, we are equals.

But life is not easy here. Like a vulture, destitution circles us: should Noble fall ill and miss a few pay packets, we would fall prey to it. Hong Kong isn't the egalitarian metropolis I had imagined either, for the Westerners have carved up the territory, saving the best districts for themselves. While they enjoy clean, wide boulevards and harbour views, we squeeze into narrow lanes and rickety houses, and traverse thoroughfares that are often piled high with refuse. Only the wealthiest Chinese escape this fate, though even they are barred from certain neighbourhoods. We live in a narrow three-storey dwelling of six poky rooms, shared with five other families. Noble and I rent a cramped room on the upper level, and even with the bed pushed against one wall, we scarcely have space for a small table, a set of drawers and a chamber pot.

Still, we have privacy, and I have no mother-in-law. For these blessings I am grateful.

*

Today marks the third anniversary of our marriage. To celebrate, Noble has a surprise for me. During the rickshaw ride, he insists I wear a blindfold. Despite this, I hear the driver's panting and I know we are going uphill, but I can't fathom why, for this direction leads to the Mid-Levels and the base of Victoria Peak, where the Chinese rarely go.

I try to ask Noble but he won't say. Instead, he holds my hand and regales me with tales from the foreign export firm where he works as a clerk.

At last the rickshaw stops. Noble removes the cloth from my eyes to reveal the base station for the Peak Tram. I gasp. The tram is red and boxy, the size of a long hall. I eye it doubtfully, unsure how it can trundle up the steep mountain. But Noble is too excited to sense my hesitation.

'I want you to see Hong Kong from the Peak,' he says. 'We can see all the way to Victoria Harbour.'

'Are you sure this is safe?'

'It is built by first-rate engineers and has been ferrying people up and down the Peak for the past seven years. You will enjoy it, I promise.'

Noble is right. At first, my heart is in my throat as the tram's steam engine hisses, throwing us back against our slatted seats as it launches itself with a jerk up the steep incline. With my eyes shut, I squeeze Noble's hand so tightly that he complains of losing feeling in his fingers. After this, I take a deep breath and peel my eyes open. To my delight, I see the late sunlight bouncing off the varnished timber interior of the tram. From the open windows, gusts of fresh breeze brush our cheeks. The greenery rushes by as the tram gathers speed. Too soon it is over, the ride lasting no more than ten minutes.

The sun, golden as the yolk of a salted egg, lingers on the horizon. In another quarter of an hour, dusk will cover the hills.

But for now, I see the harbour glimmering in the distance, the sampans and junks like toys floating on a pond. To the left, the rooftops of the Chinese district clutter together. In contrast, the European houses of the Mid-Levels and Central are neat and orderly. At this height, the difference is stark. It seems, no matter where we go, class will prevail. Injustice will shackle people of lesser means. As though sensing my dampened mood, Noble wraps his arm around my shoulders. I lean against his chest.

'Little Flower,' he says, 'today the Chinese are barred from living in Central, the Mid-Levels and the Peak. But it will not always be so. One day we will command respect and achieve equality with the English.'

'How can you be sure?'

He turns me towards him and looks into my eyes. I want to fall into the depth of their warmth. Caressing the tip of my nose with his own, Noble replies, 'You have shown me how to achieve the impossible. If we can be together despite the odds, anything is feasible, for us and for Hong Kong, but it will take time. For now, let us celebrate my promotion' – I gasp – 'to associate comprador.' He beams at me.

Knowing this is a goal he has worked towards since our arrival, I throw my arms around his neck and kiss him.

'With my new salary,' he continues, voice brimming with excitement, 'we can move to a house of our own and you can embroider again.'

At this, I let go of him and glance at my hands. A web of lines, like cracked paint, criss-crosses my knuckles and my fingers are thickened by calluses. Three years of scrubbing, laundry and cooking have left them too coarse to handle silk threads. Noble takes my hands and squeezes them.

'We can hire a housemaid and cook now,' he says, 'and seek treatment from the best apothecary to restore your skin.'

'Can we truly afford it all?' I ask.

'Of course! And soon much more. It won't be long before I rise in the ranks to join the senior compradors, and become one of the powerful brokers between the exporters of Chinese goods and the foreign companies who buy them. I could earn spectacular commissions, enough eventually to set up my own business. And in time, these are the men who will have the power to influence politics and change the laws that currently hinder the Chinese. That is how I will help to shape a better Hong Kong and build wealth, *our* wealth.'

'Do you still plan to open China's first department store?' I ask, with a teasing smile.

'Only if you are willing to work alongside me, as partners.'

I turn and lean back into the circle of his arms. The streets in the distance are lit with electrical lamps. As I gaze at this river of stars engineered by mortals, tokens of a new age, my mind travels to Linjing – my mistress, adversary and saviour – and I wonder if, in this era of possibilities, our fates might entwine again, not as before but recast into a new alliance, a friendship between true equals.

Linjing, until we meet again, wherever you are, I hope you see a similar marvel.

Jyutping Glossary

Jyutping is a romanization system for Cantonese, developed by the Linguistic Society of Hong Kong. Jyutping to Cantonese is like pinyin to Mandarin. There are other romanization systems, such as Yale. For my glossary, I have used the jyutping system.

There are six tones for each romanization syllable, for example:

mother = $aa^3\ noeng^4$
paternal grandmother = $maa^4\ maa^4$

For simplicity, I have omitted these tones.

Word/phrase	Chinese Character (same in Cantonese and Mandarin but pronounced differently)	Meaning
Aa De / aa de	阿爹	father
Aa Noeng / aa noeng	阿娘	mother
aiya	哎吔	exclamation expressing frustration, annoyance or surprise
baak coi	白菜	type of leafy vegetable, commonly called 'bok choy' in the West
baak tung	白銅	type of material/metal used for cheap imitation of silver

caa siu bao	叉燒	sweet barbecue pork bun
cip si	妾侍	concubine – the polygyny system in China often differed between families and regions. For *The Lotus Shoes*, I have based it on the practice my grandmothers witnessed in their extended family and villages. A wealthy man might have a principal wife and several minor ones – these women usually come from respectable families who are of similar status to the groom's family. A *cip si* is lesser than a wife and usually from an impoverished family; some might be former prostitutes (sing-song girls) or courtesans. She would enter a man's household without a wedding. If she becomes the favourite, then she might be promoted to a minor wife but never to first wife.
daai fu	大夫	doctor
daudau	兜兜	diamond-shaped undergarment worn by women as light bust support and tied around the neck and waist; some might have pockets
dou si	道士	shaman
Gaa Faat	家法	*Ancestral Book of Domestic Rules*
gaai laan	芥蘭	type of leafy vegetable, often called Chinese broccoli
gan	斤	measurement of weight
go go	哥哥	term of endearment for an older brother or a sweetheart
Gun Jam (jyutping), *Guan Yin* (pinyin)	觀音 送子觀音	goddess of mercy, a popular deity worshipped by women. *Sung Zi Gun Jam* – a variation of the goddess of mercy, always depicted carrying an infant boy and worshipped by women with fertility struggles.

jan zung	人中	Cantonese pronunciation for the *renzhong* (pinyin) acupuncture point, located in the centre of the indentation between the root of the nose and the margin of the upper lip. According to traditional Chinese medicine, pressing down firmly on this point could restore consciousness or resuscitate.
Jyut Lou	月老	god of marriages, worshipped by maidens
loeng	兩	measurement of weight
ling zi	靈芝	plant used for medicinal purposes, believed to have the ability to preserve *qi / hei* (life force)
lou	老	old (back then, being called old was a sign of status)
Maa Maa / maa maa	嫲嫲	paternal grandmother
maa diu	馬吊	card game
maa-zoek	麻雀	Cantonese spelling of mah-jong
muizai	妹仔	young female slave, typically sold into slavery during childhood
ou (jyutping) or *ao* (pinyin)	襖	a long-sleeved, knee-length upper garment (**tunic-blouse**) worn by Han Chinese women: it had a loose silhouette and was fastened by toggles from the throat, curving to the right underarm and ending at the hip, though some designs had a front central opening. It can be paired with a skirt or trousers.
pun zoi	盆栽	bonsai (pruned tree)
qi (pinyin) or *hei* (jyutping)	氣	life force
kwan gwaa	裙褂	a red bridal outfit, consisting of a full skirt and matching long-sleeved tunic-blouse (*ou*), both heavily embroidered

saam *saam fu*	衫 衫褲	*saam* is a broad term for upper garments for both genders: shirt, blouse, robe, gown, jacket *fu* is trousers for both genders *saam fu* is a set of tunic-blouse (female) or tunic-shirt (male) and trousers, usually cut from the same fabric and often in cotton
saan	山	mountain or mountain range
Siu Je	少爺	Young Master, used for a young gentleman whose father is still alive. If an heir loses his father early, then he might still be called 'Siu Je' until he is middle-aged.
So Hei	梳起	Celibate Sister – the literal translation is 'combed up', meaning to dress a woman's hair as though she is married after she has taken the celibate vows.
taai taai	太太	Mrs/mistress – interchangeable with madam and typically only used for married women of status
waat faa paai	挖花牌	card game
wu lei zing	狐狸精	fox spirit, a common accusation for women whom others believe hold too much influence over a man
ying (pinyin) or *jam* (jyutping)	陰	feminine *qi* / *hei* (life force)
yang (pinyin) or *joeng* (jyutping)	陽	masculine *qi* / *hei* (life force)
ze	姐	honorary term – can be attached to the name of a middle-aged or older woman to show respect or familiarity
ze ze	姐姐	term of endearment, typically used by girls to address their older sister. Sometimes adults use it too to address an older friend who is like a real sister.
Zoeng Kei	象棋	Chinese chess
zung ziu	中招	exclamation – like 'aha!' or 'got you!'

Author's Note

Long before I could read and years before I discovered *Pride and Prejudice* (the novel that sparked my lifelong love of historical fiction), I adored my grandmothers' stories from a bygone China.

In particular, I was intrigued by Autumn Moon's extraordinary fortune: this great-great-aunt of mine was born in the 1880s, during an era when a woman's worth was still almost entirely judged by the size of her golden lilies. With natural feet, Autumn Moon had no marriage expectation beyond one to a kind but poor peasant, like her father. Though she was gifted with needlework, the most she had dared to hope for was a job as a sewing amah, thereby sparing herself a life of toil in the rice fields. Yet, against all odds, her embroidery skills secured a marriage into a genteel home. Her triumph benefited her female relations too, helping many of them to marry above their station, and the good fortune trickled down the generations to my *maa maa* – she grew up in a privileged home with the luxury to embroider all day and proved to be as talented as Autumn Moon. When I was a little girl, Maa Maa showed me one of her prized double-sided embroidery pieces, a shimmering goldfish in the centre of a creamy silk handkerchief. Sadly, this artwork was lost during our migration to Australia, but its influence had woven itself into my subconscious, and eventually it inspired *The Lotus Shoes*.

In contrast, my maternal grandmother, Po Po, did not enjoy a loving or comfortable home. As a bright and inquisitive child, Po Po was desperate to attend school, but her family felt only boys were worthy of an education. Daughters didn't even deserve a full belly; food was scarce, therefore reserved for fathers and sons. Po Po's only happy childhood memories were of her own grandmother, who often hid scraps of meat beneath mounds of rice, which my *po po* ate furtively. With this upbringing, Po Po loathed the patriarchy and she longed to take the So Hei vows, but by the time she was born in about 1930 (female births were not recorded), the Great Depression had crushed the silk-reeling industry. To survive, most celibate sisters had migrated to places like Hong Kong and Singapore, working as amahs, while their sisterhoods progressively closed down. Still, Po Po admired them fiercely, and from her, I became captivated by this movement.

When I started researching for *The Lotus Shoes*, I was worried I wouldn't find any references on this worthy but under-explored piece of Chinese feminist history. Fortunately, I found these insightful sources:

1. *The Evolution of the Sisterhood in Traditional Chinese Society: From Village Girls' Houses to Chai T'angs in Hong Kong* by Andrea Patrice Sankar, a thesis written in 1978, the University of Michigan.

2. *Daughters of the Canton Delta: Marriage Patterns and Economic Strategies in South China, 1860–1930*, Janice E. Stockard. Published by the Stanford University Press, 1989.

For Chinese embroidery, foot-binding and Qing dynasty clothing, these sources were most helpful:

3. *Chinese Embroidery: An Illustrated Stitch Guide*, Shao Xiaocheng. Published by Shanghai Press and Publishing Development Co Ltd, 2018.

4. *Every Step a Lotus: Shoes for Bound Feet*, Dorothy Ko. Published by the University of California Press, 2001.

5. *Chinese Dress: From the Qing Dynasty to the Present*, Valery Garrett. Published by Tuttle Publishing, an imprint of Periplus Editions (HK) Ltd, 2007.

Acknowledgements

Though writing is often a solitary activity, *The Lotus Shoes* is a creation by many minds. The following people have all provided insightful advice or support to help me shape this story and bring it to readers across the world.

When Dad was still with us, one of his favourite mantras was 'Remember the source when you take a sip of water', meaning 'Never forget the origins of your blessings'. My agent, Madeleine Milburn, made my publication dream come true – Madeleine, I'm for ever indebted to you.

I'm blessed to work with my UK editor, Tilda Key, whose astute but gentle suggestions make the editing process smooth and enjoyable. Thank you, Tilda. To my team of wonderful US and Canadian editors, Laura Brown, Nicole Luongo and Jennifer Lambert, I'm so thrilled by your faith in *The Lotus Shoes*.

To Charlotte Cottier, my wonderful go-to grammar and punctuation guru – your exceptional line-editing skills have helped lift my prose to the next level. Over time, you have become a friend and an invaluable beta reader, and I'm most grateful we met.

Thanks also to the team at Madeleine Milburn Agency, especially Liane-Louise Smith, Valentina Paulmichl, Georgia McVeigh, Rachel Yeoh, Amanda Carungi and Saskia Arthur. I really appreciate your help along this magical but challenging journey.

To Vincent, my steadfast brother – you're the one who convinced me that 'hope', no matter the source, is powerful.

Lucas, Emmarose and Liam, I couldn't ask for better-behaved children, especially during my evening calls with the other side of the world. I also love that you chat about Little Flower and Linjing like they're people you know!

Last but not least, to Tina, my dearest cousin: I have lost count of the number of times I texted you late at night, often with thrilling news, but sometimes with panic or doubts, and no matter the reason, you're always there for me.